GRAPHIC NOVEL

GODDESS GIRLS

+ATHENA THE BRAIN+

CREATED BY
JOAN HOLUB &
SUZANNE WILLIAMS
ADAPTED BY **DAVID CAMPITI**

＊

ILLUSTRATED BY **EDUARDO GARCIA**
AT GLASS HOUSE GRAPHICS

Aladdin
New York London Toronto Sydney New Delhi

ALADDIN
An imprint of Simon & Schuster Children's Publishing Division
1230 Avenue of the Americas, New York, New York 10020
First Aladdin edition February 2022
Text copyright © 2022 by Joan Holub and Suzanne Williams
Cover illustration by Manuel Preitano.
Illustrations copyright © 2022 by Glass House Graphics
Art by Eduardo Garcia. Additional art by João Zod, Marcos Cortez, and Noza.
Lettering by Marcos Inoue. Art services by Glass House Graphics.
All rights reserved, including the right of reproduction in whole or in part in any form. ALADDIN
and related logo are registered trademarks of Simon & Schuster, Inc. For information about
special discounts for bulk purchases, please contact Simon & Schuster Special Sales at 1-866-
506-1949 or business@simonandschuster.com. The Simon & Schuster Speakers Bureau can bring
authors to your live event. For more information or to book an event contact the Simon &
Schuster Speakers Bureau at 1-866-248-3049 or visit our website at www.simonspeakers.com.
The illustrations for this book were rendered digitally.
The text of this book was set in font Anime Ace 2.0 BB at 6 points over
7.5 point leading and SteinAntik at 7 points over 8 point leading.
Manufactured in China 1121 SCP
2 4 6 8 10 9 7 5 3 1
Library of Congress Control Number 2021937751
ISBN 978-1-5344-7387-4 (hc)
ISBN 978-1-5344-7386-7 (pbk)
ISBN 978-1-5344-7388-1 (ebook)

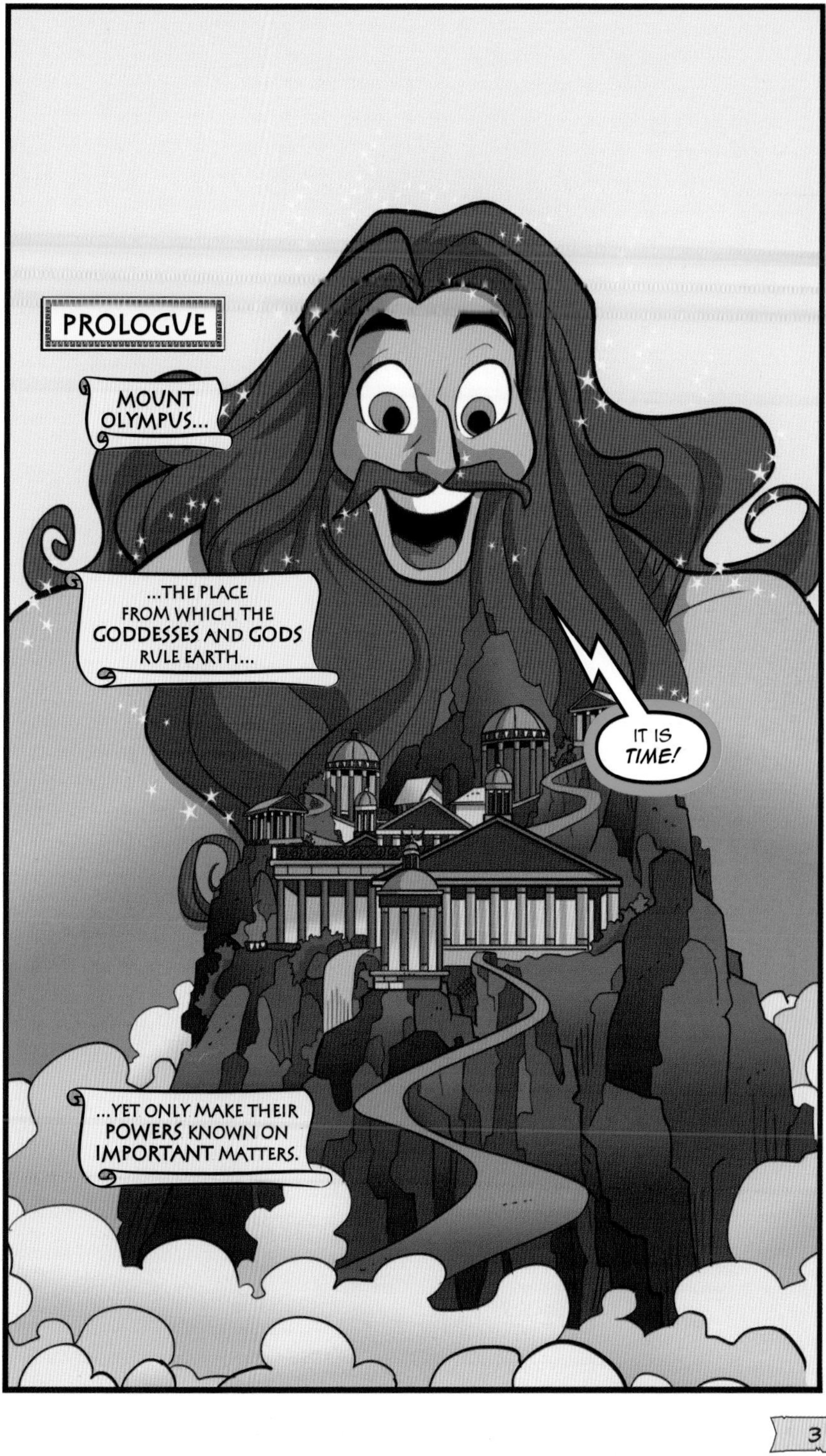
PROLOGUE
MOUNT OLYMPUS...
...THE PLACE FROM WHICH THE GODDESSES AND GODS RULE EARTH...
IT IS TIME!
...YET ONLY MAKE THEIR POWERS KNOWN ON IMPORTANT MATTERS.

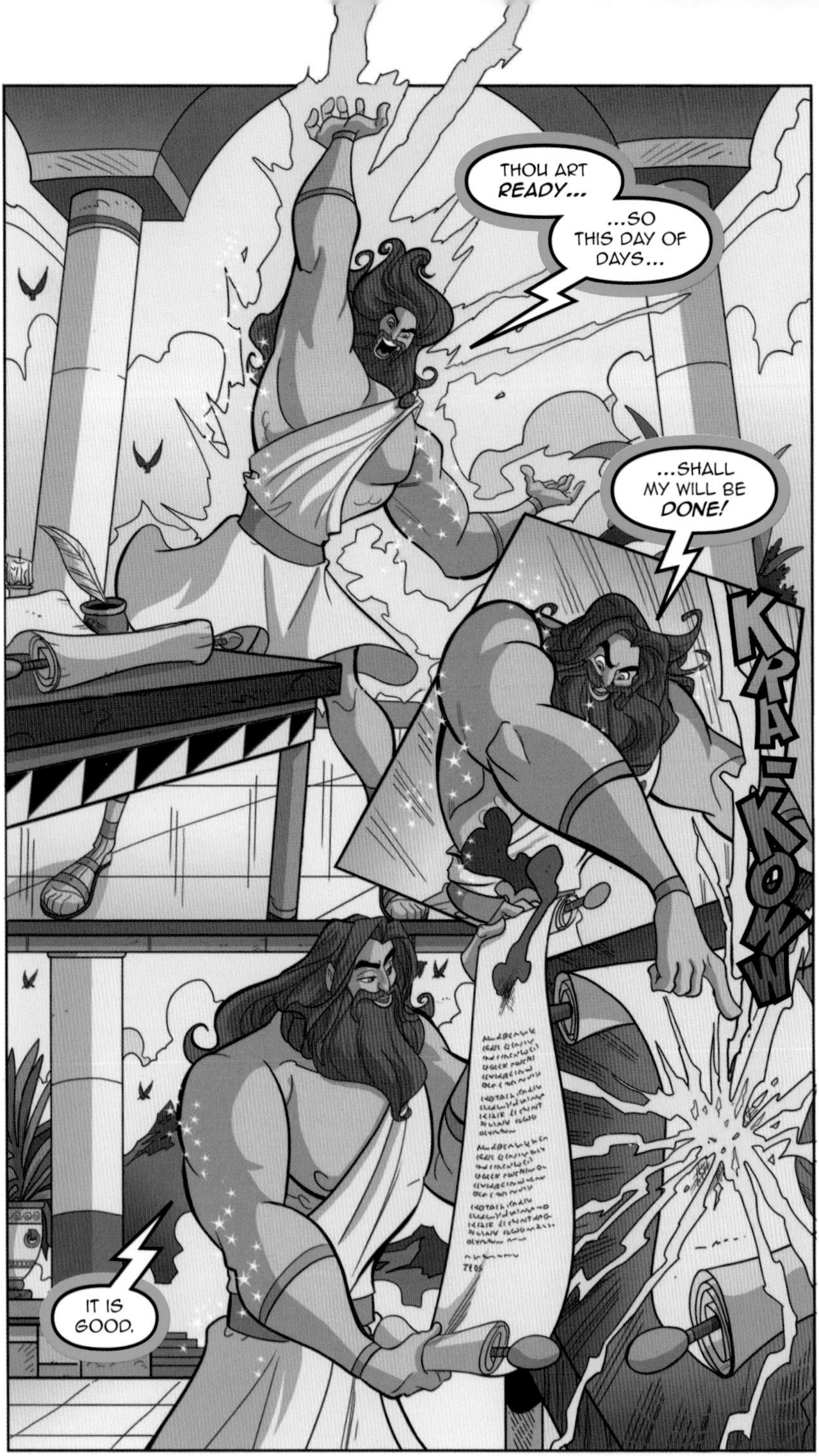
THOU ART READY...
...SO THIS DAY OF DAYS...
...SHALL MY WILL BE DONE!
KRA-KOWW
IT IS GOOD.

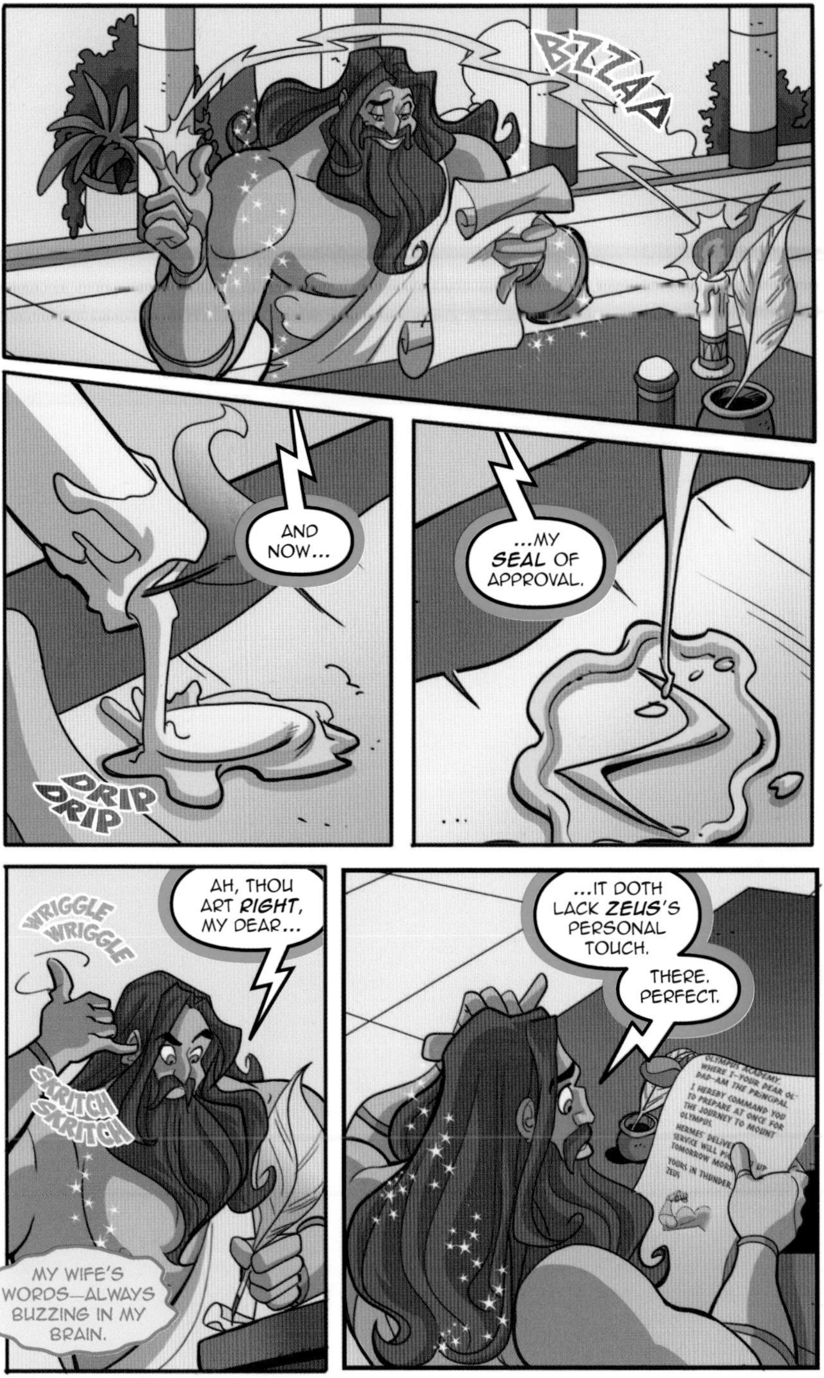
BZZAAP
AND NOW...
...MY SEAL OF APPROVAL.
DRIP DRIP
WRIGGLE WRIGGLE
AH, THOU ART RIGHT, MY DEAR...
SKRITCH SKRITCH
MY WIFE'S WORDS—ALWAYS BUZZING IN MY BRAIN.
...IT DOTH LACK ZEUS'S PERSONAL TOUCH.
THERE. PERFECT.
OLYMPUS ACADEMY,
WHERE I—YOUR DEAR OL'
DAD—AM THE PRINCIPAL.
I HEREBY COMMAND YOU
TO PREPARE AT ONCE FOR
THE JOURNEY TO MOUNT
OLYMPUS.
YOURS IN THUNDER,
ZEUS

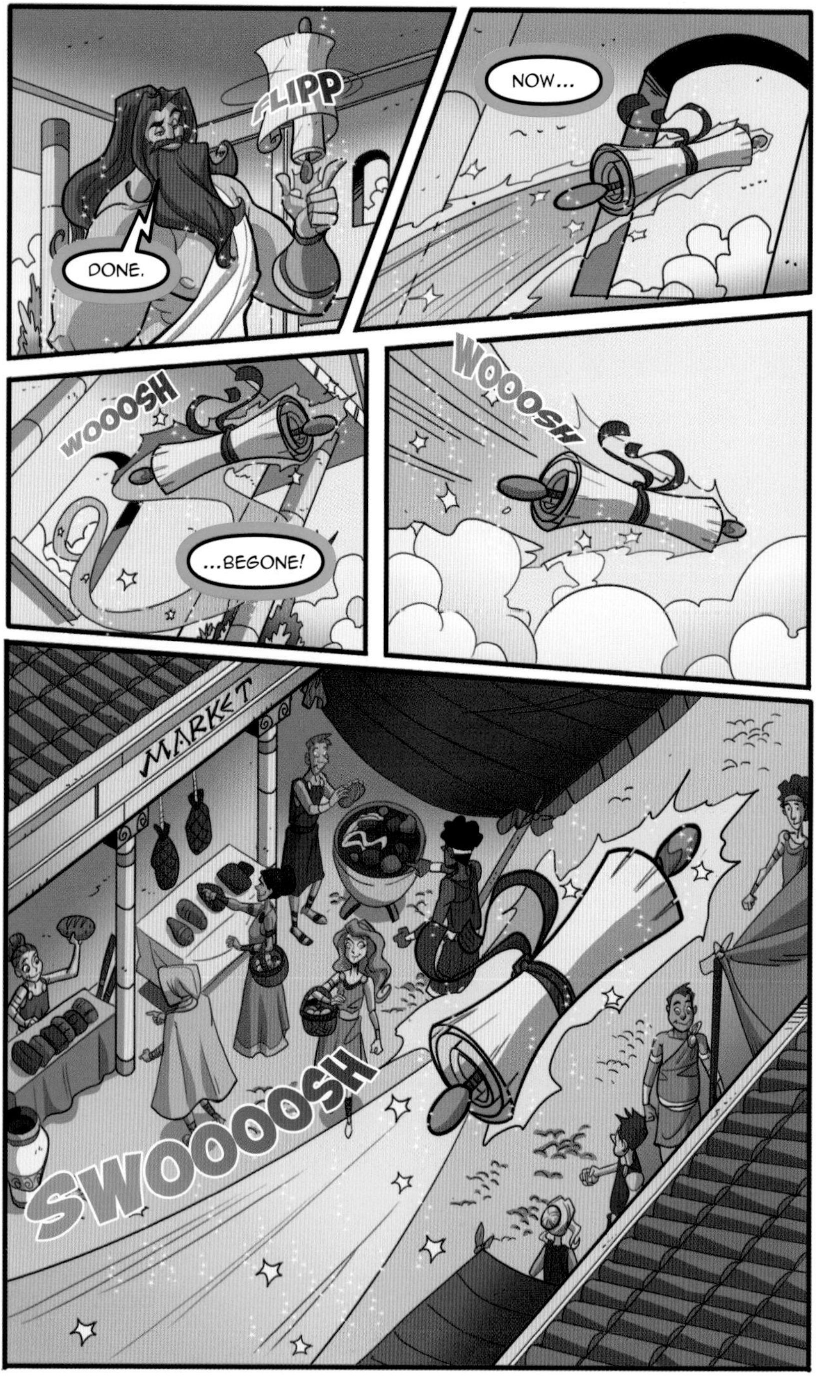
FLIPP
DONE.
NOW...
WOOOSH
...BEGONE!
WOOOSH
MARKET
SWOOOOSH

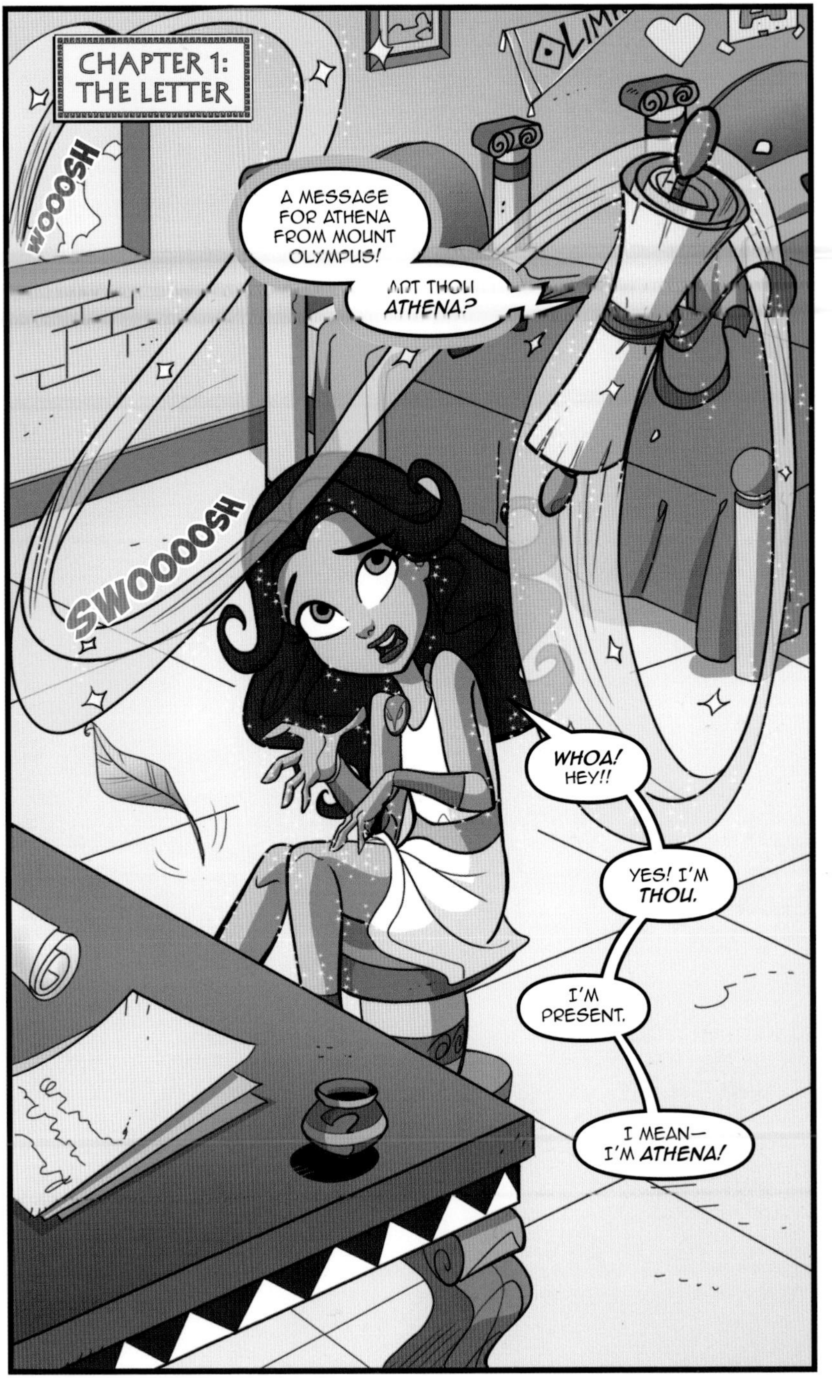
CHAPTER 1:
THE LETTER
WOOOSH
A MESSAGE FOR ATHENA FROM MOUNT OLYMPUS!
ART THOU ATHENA?
SWOOOOSH
WHOA! HEY!!
YES! I'M THOU.
I'M PRESENT.
I MEAN— I'M ATHENA!

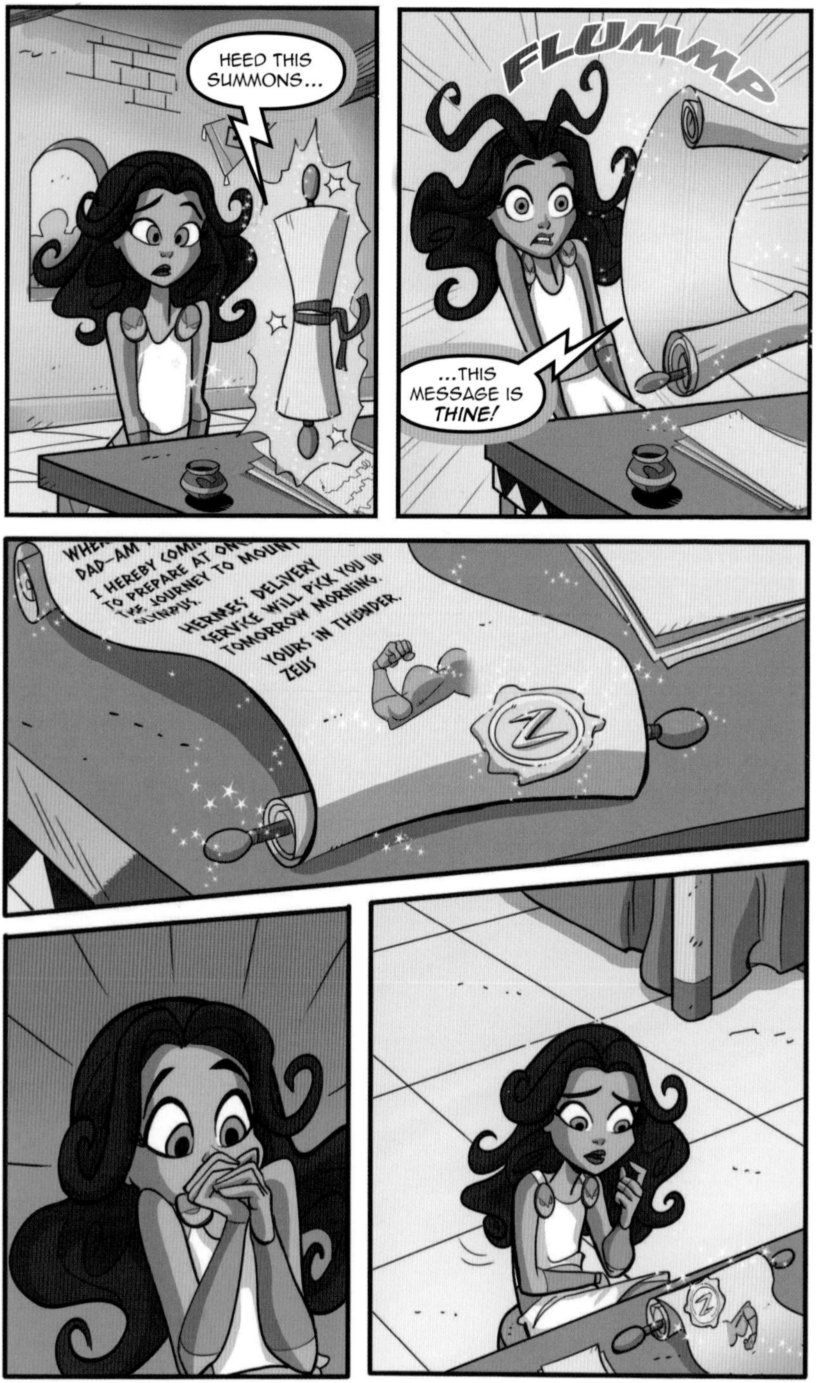
HEED THIS SUMMONS...
FLUMMP
...THIS MESSAGE IS THINE!
DAD-AM
I HEREBY
TO PREPARE AT
THE JOURNEY TO
OLYMPUS.
HERMES' DELIVERY SERVICE WILL PICK YOU UP TOMORROW MORNING.
YOURS IN THUNDER,
ZEUS

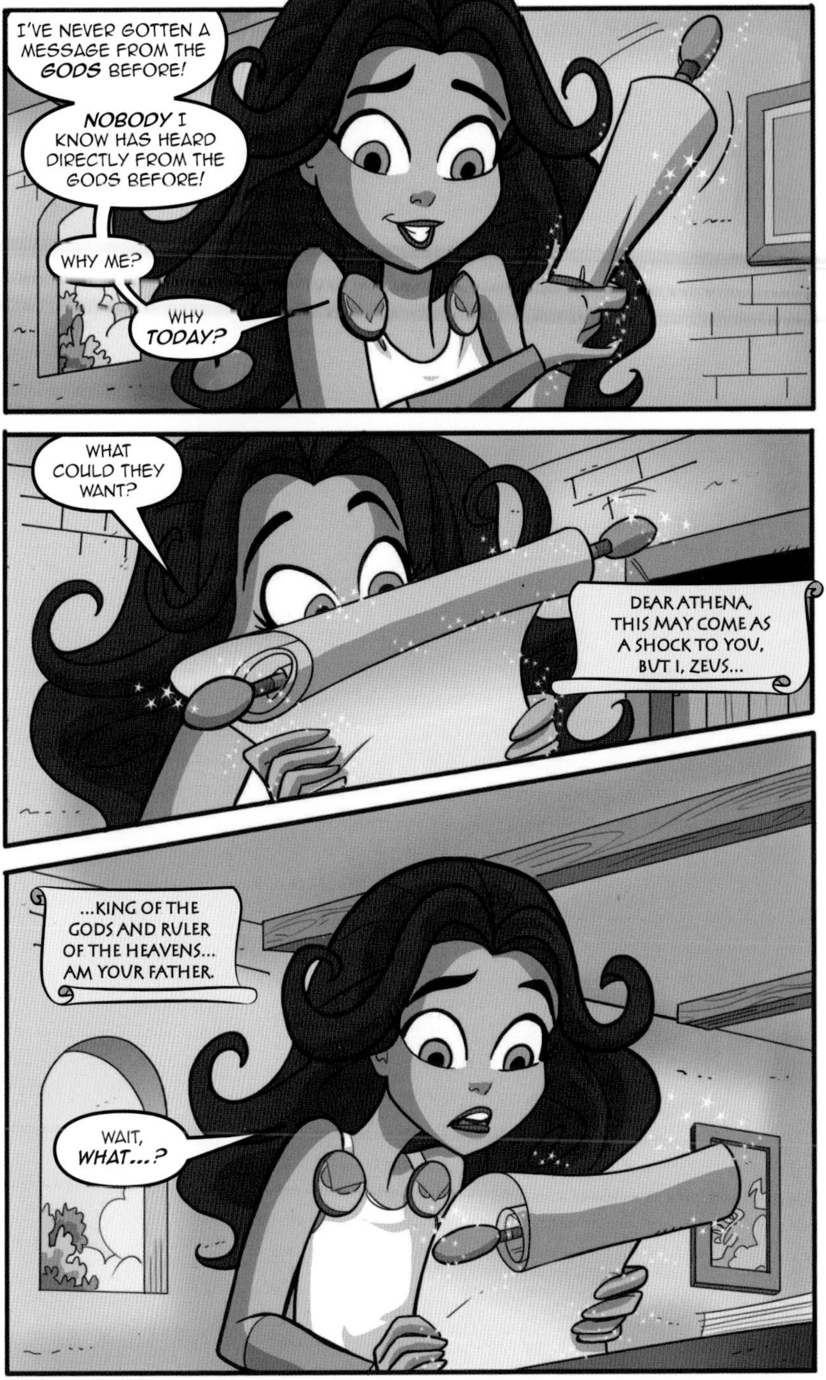
I'VE NEVER GOTTEN A MESSAGE FROM THE GODS BEFORE!
NOBODY I KNOW HAS HEARD DIRECTLY FROM THE GODS BEFORE!
WHY ME?
WHY TODAY?
WHAT COULD THEY WANT?
DEAR ATHENA, THIS MAY COME AS A SHOCK TO YOU, BUT I, ZEUS...
...KING OF THE GODS AND RULER OF THE HEAVENS... AM YOUR FATHER.
WAIT, WHAT...?

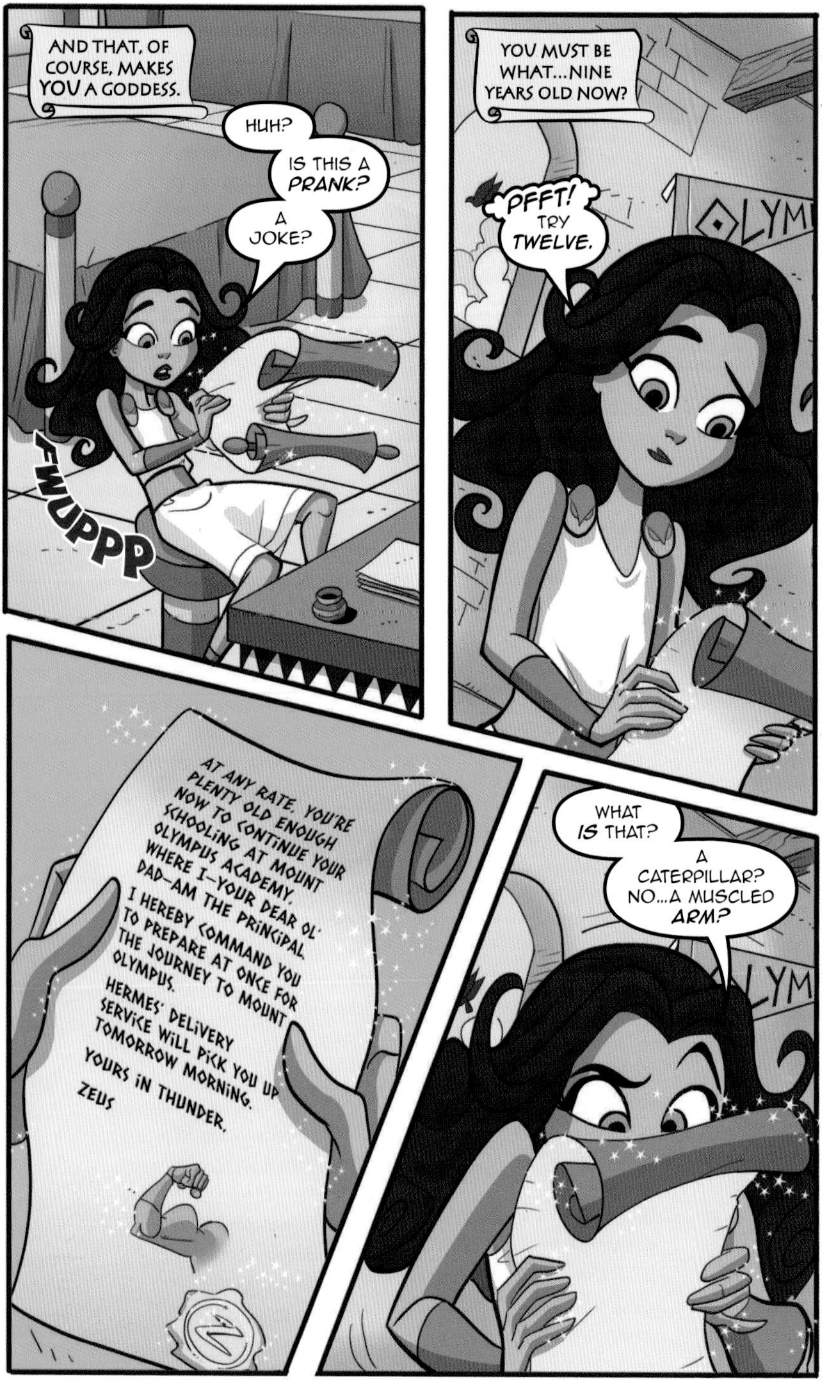
AND THAT, OF COURSE, MAKES YOU A GODDESS.
HUH?
IS THIS A PRANK?
A JOKE?
FWUPPP
YOU MUST BE WHAT...NINE YEARS OLD NOW?
PFFT! TRY TWELVE.
OLYM
AT ANY RATE, YOU'RE PLENTY OLD ENOUGH NOW TO CONTINUE YOUR SCHOOLING AT MOUNT OLYMPUS ACADEMY, WHERE I—YOUR DEAR OL' DAD—AM THE PRINCIPAL.
I HEREBY COMMAND YOU TO PREPARE AT ONCE FOR THE JOURNEY TO MOUNT OLYMPUS.
HERMES' DELIVERY SERVICE WILL PICK YOU UP TOMORROW MORNING.
YOURS IN THUNDER,
ZEUS
WHAT IS THAT?
A CATERPILLAR? NO...A MUSCLED ARM?
LYM

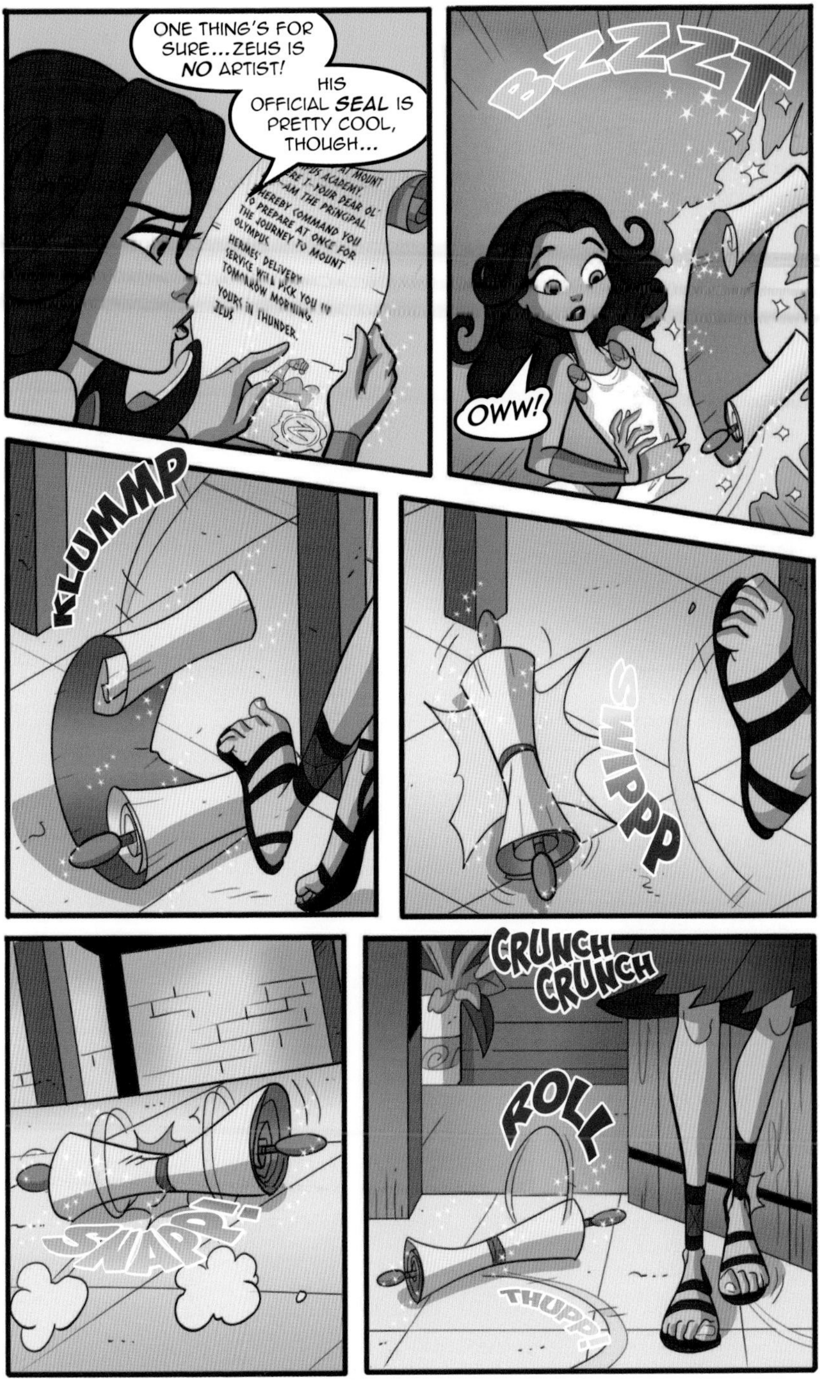
ONE THING'S FOR SURE...ZEUS IS NO ARTIST!
HIS OFFICIAL SEAL IS PRETTY COOL, THOUGH...
AM THE PRINCIPAL
HEREBY COMMAND YOU TO PREPARE AT ONCE FOR THE JOURNEY TO MOUNT OLYMPUS
HERMES' DELIVERY SERVICE WILL PICK YOU UP TOMORROW MORNING.
YOURS IN THUNDER.
ZEUS
BZZZT
OWW!
KLUMMP
SWIPPP
SNAP!
CRUNCH CRUNCH
ROLL
THUPP!

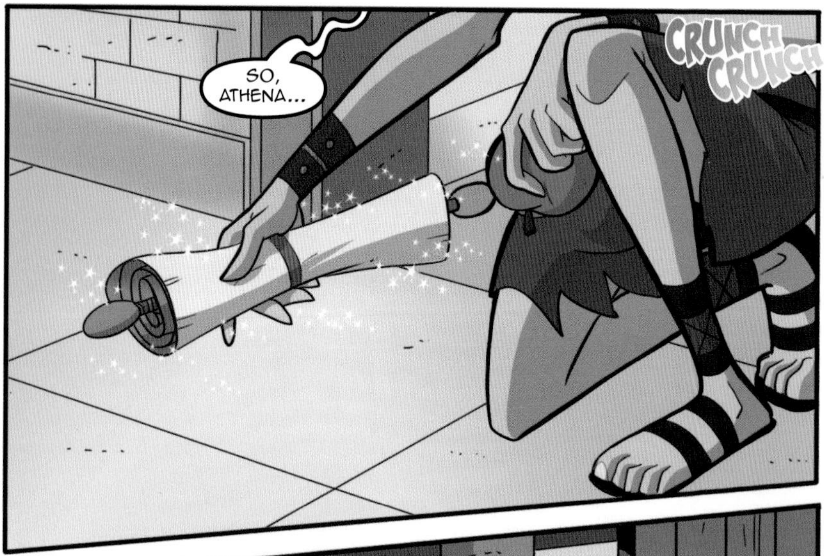
SO, ATHENA...
CRUNCH CRUNCH

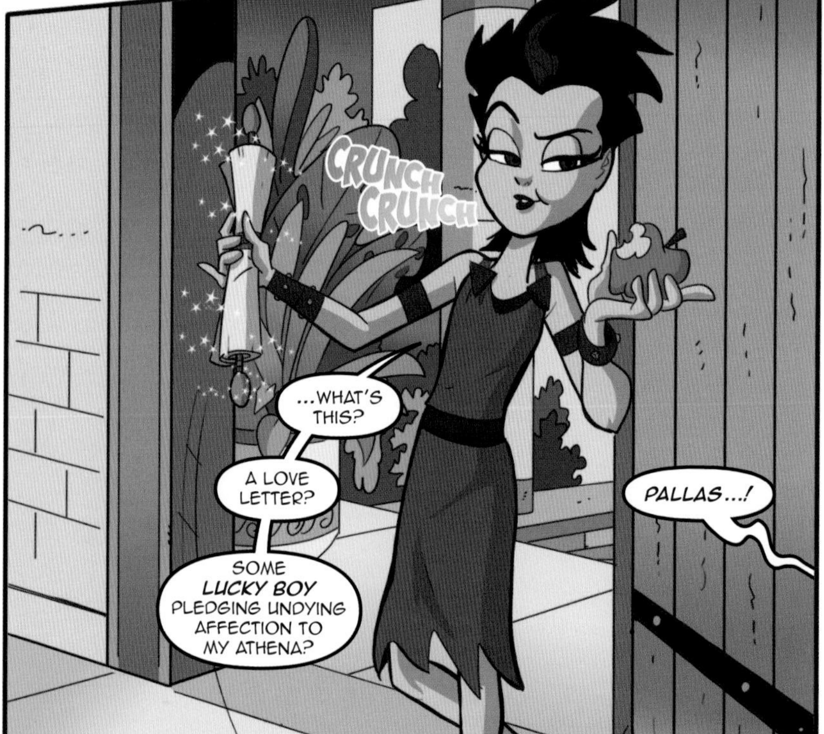
CRUNCH CRUNCH
...WHAT'S THIS?
A LOVE LETTER?
SOME *LUCKY BOY* PLEDGING UNDYING AFFECTION TO MY ATHENA?
PALLAS...!

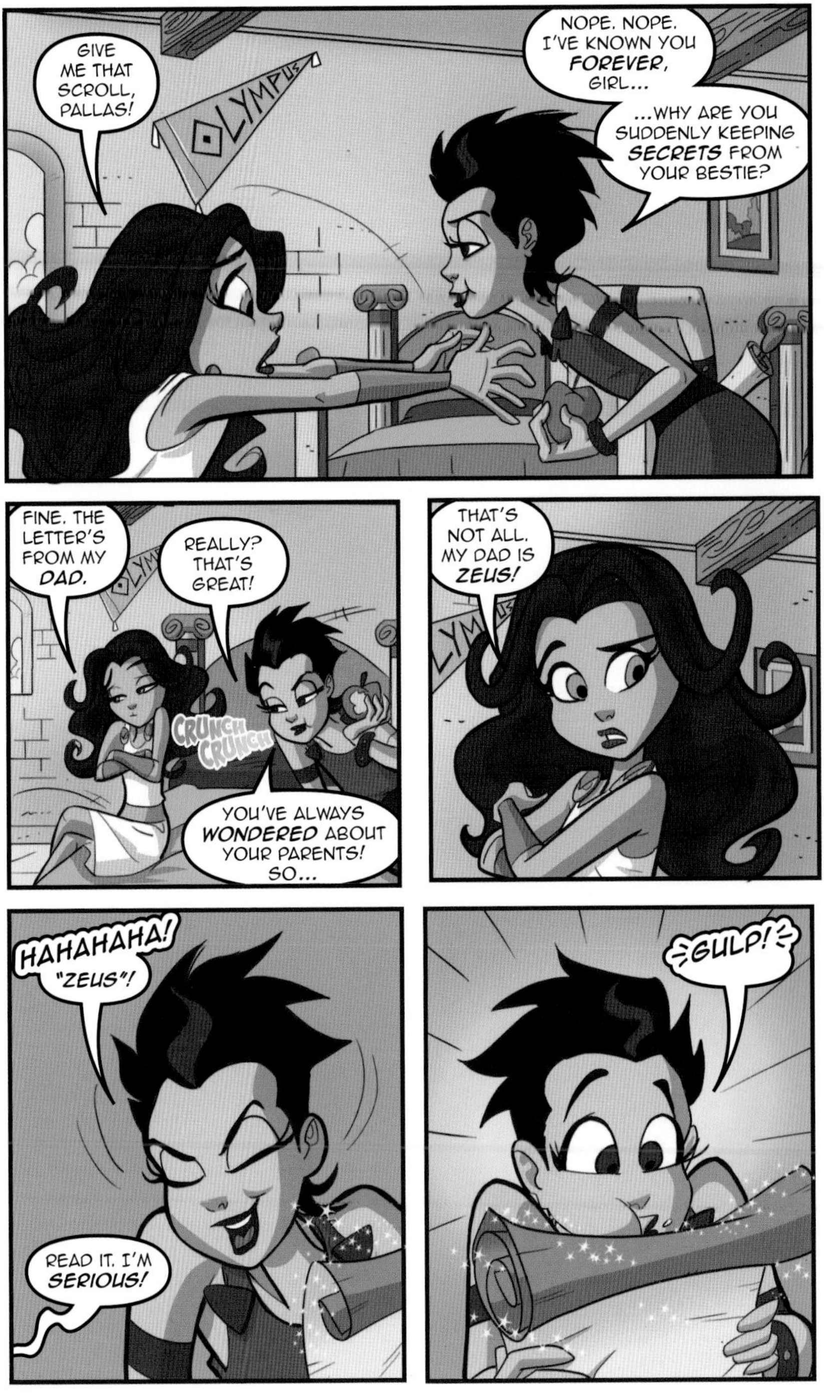

GIVE ME THAT SCROLL, PALLAS!
OLYMPUS
NOPE. NOPE. I'VE KNOWN YOU FOREVER, GIRL...
...WHY ARE YOU SUDDENLY KEEPING SECRETS FROM YOUR BESTIE?
FINE. THE LETTER'S FROM MY DAD.
REALLY? THAT'S GREAT!
CRUNCH CRUNCH
YOU'VE ALWAYS WONDERED ABOUT YOUR PARENTS! SO...
THAT'S NOT ALL. MY DAD IS ZEUS!
HAHAHAHA! "ZEUS"!
READ IT. I'M SERIOUS!
GULP!

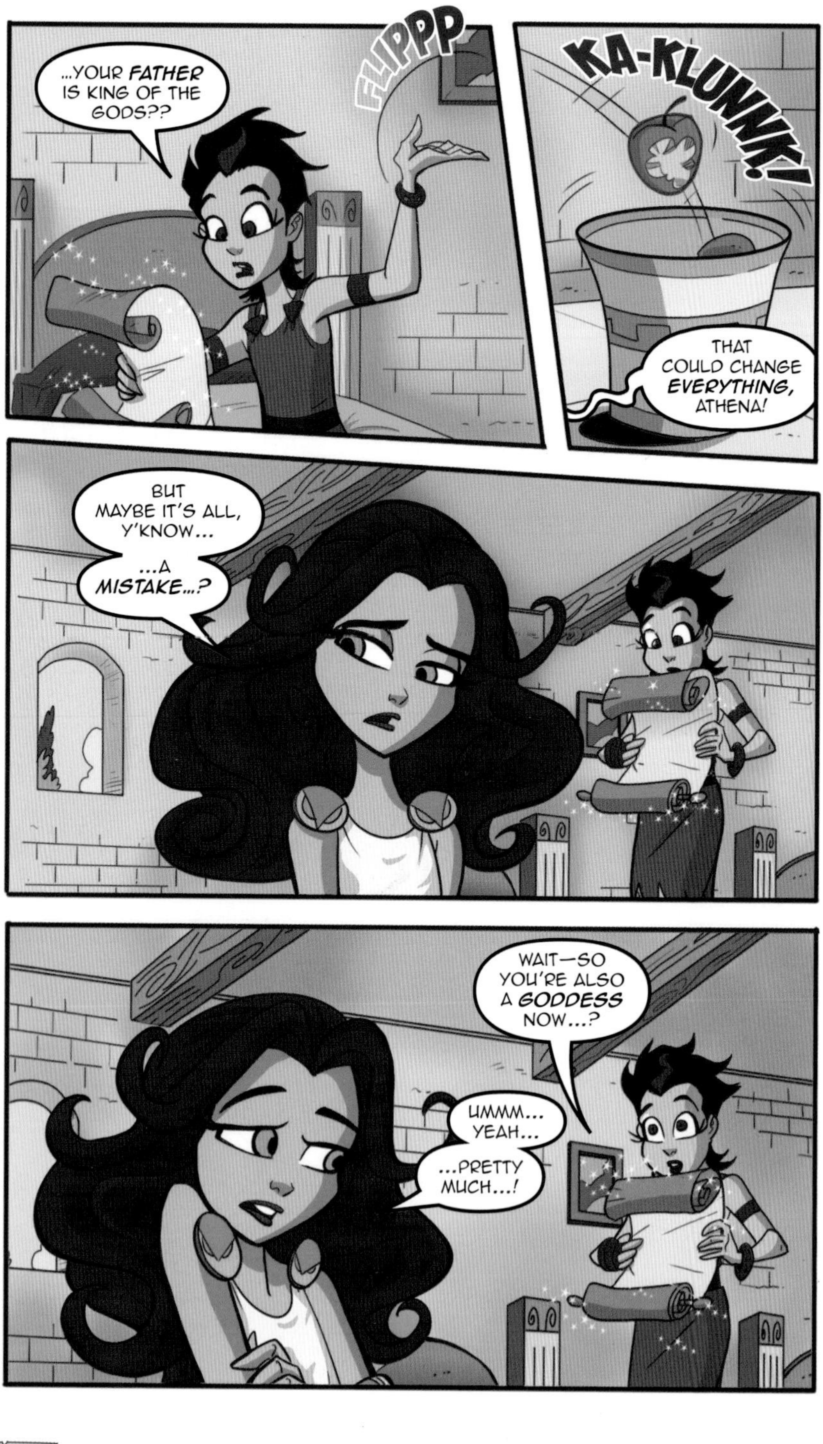

...YOUR FATHER IS KING OF THE GODS??
FLIPPP
KA-KLUNNK!
THAT COULD CHANGE EVERYTHING, ATHENA!
BUT MAYBE IT'S ALL, Y'KNOW...
...A MISTAKE...?
WAIT—SO YOU'RE ALSO A GODDESS NOW...?
UMMM... YEAH...
...PRETTY MUCH...!

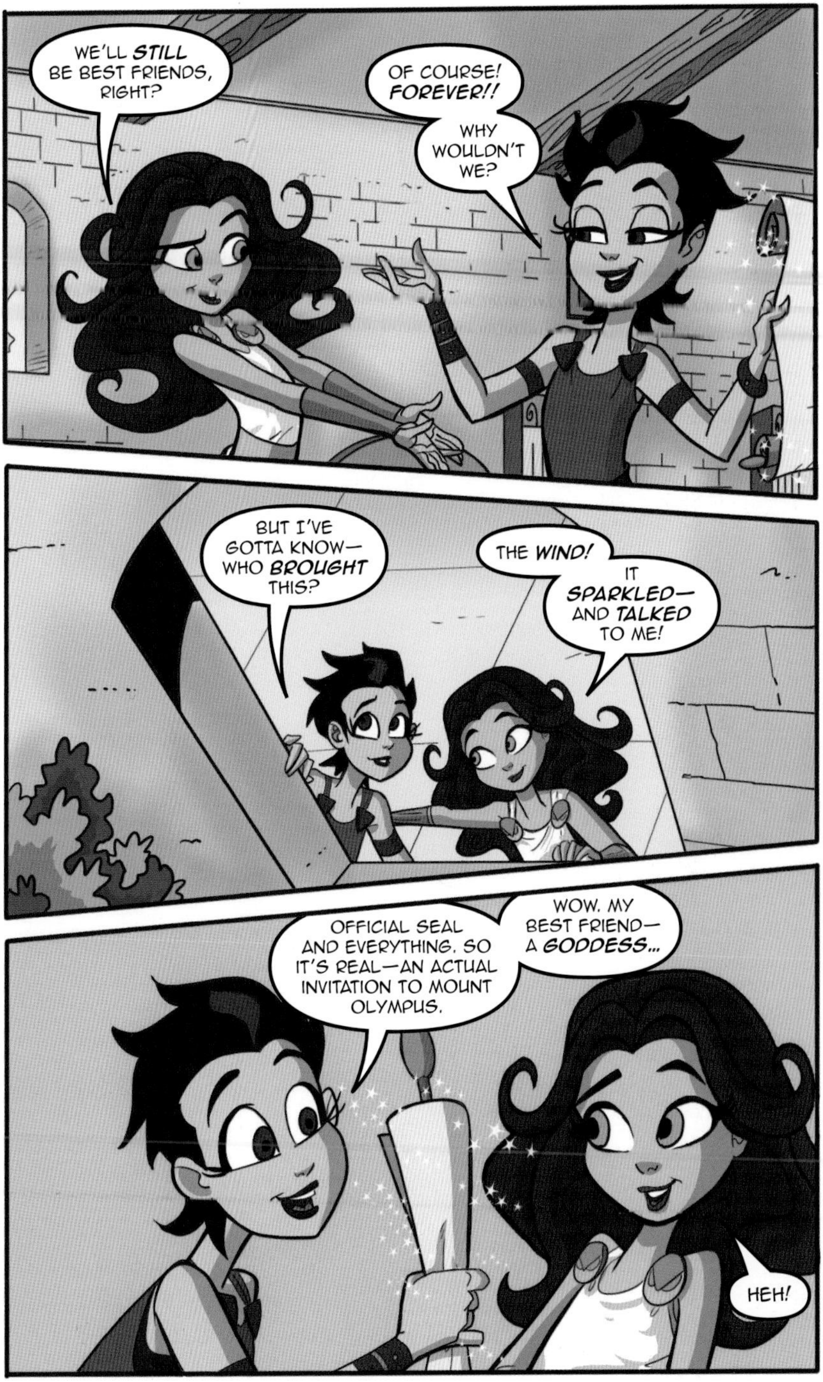
WE'LL STILL BE BEST FRIENDS, RIGHT?
OF COURSE! FOREVER!!
WHY WOULDN'T WE?
BUT I'VE GOTTA KNOW— WHO BROUGHT THIS?
THE WIND!
IT SPARKLED— AND TALKED TO ME!
OFFICIAL SEAL AND EVERYTHING. SO IT'S REAL—AN ACTUAL INVITATION TO MOUNT OLYMPUS.
WOW. MY BEST FRIEND— A GODDESS...
HEH!

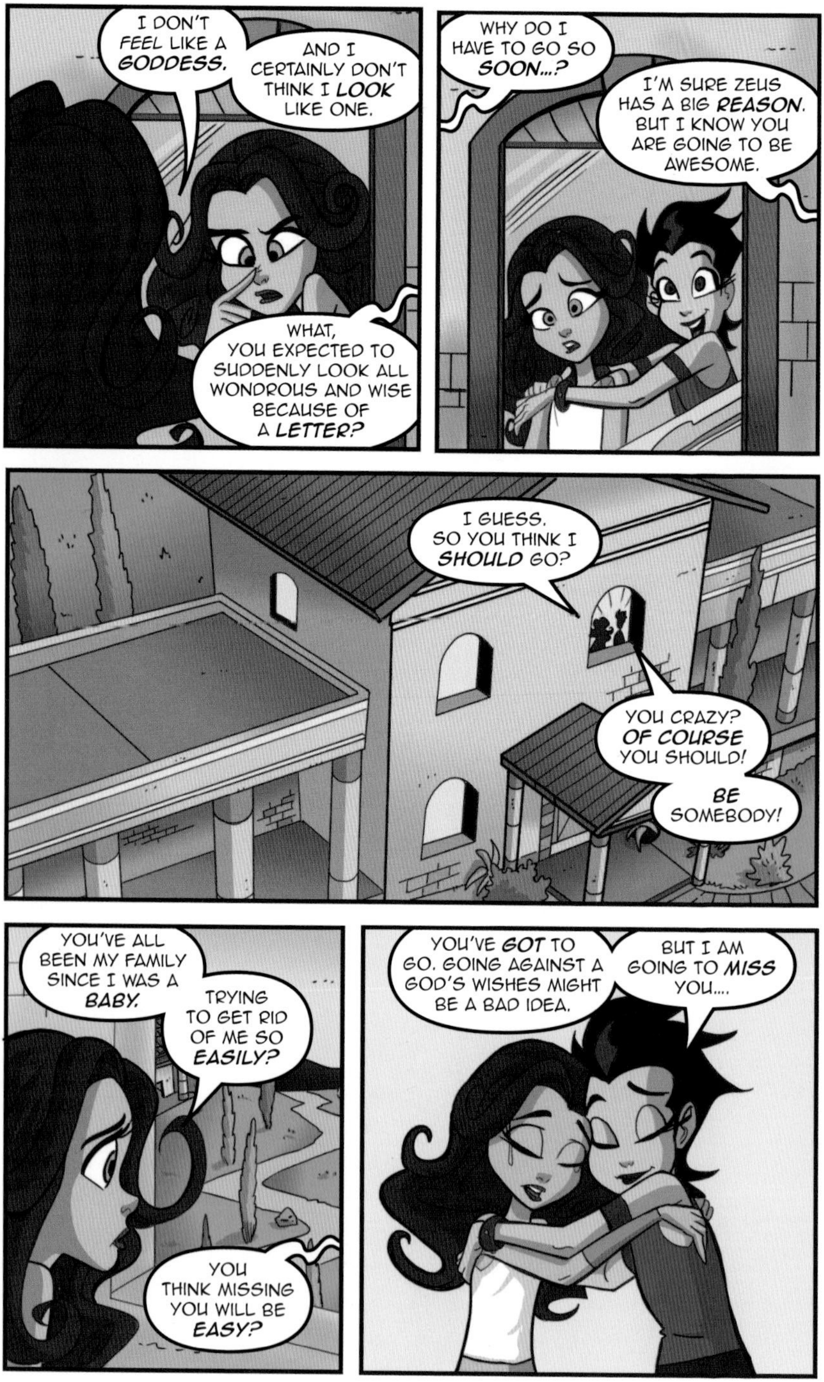
I DON'T FEEL LIKE A GODDESS.
AND I CERTAINLY DON'T THINK I LOOK LIKE ONE.
WHAT, YOU EXPECTED TO SUDDENLY LOOK ALL WONDROUS AND WISE BECAUSE OF A LETTER?
WHY DO I HAVE TO GO SO SOON...?
I'M SURE ZEUS HAS A BIG REASON. BUT I KNOW YOU ARE GOING TO BE AWESOME.
I GUESS. SO YOU THINK I SHOULD GO?
YOU CRAZY? OF COURSE YOU SHOULD!
BE SOMEBODY!
YOU'VE ALL BEEN MY FAMILY SINCE I WAS A BABY.
TRYING TO GET RID OF ME SO EASILY?
YOU THINK MISSING YOU WILL BE EASY?
YOU'VE GOT TO GO. GOING AGAINST A GOD'S WISHES MIGHT BE A BAD IDEA.
BUT I AM GOING TO MISS YOU....

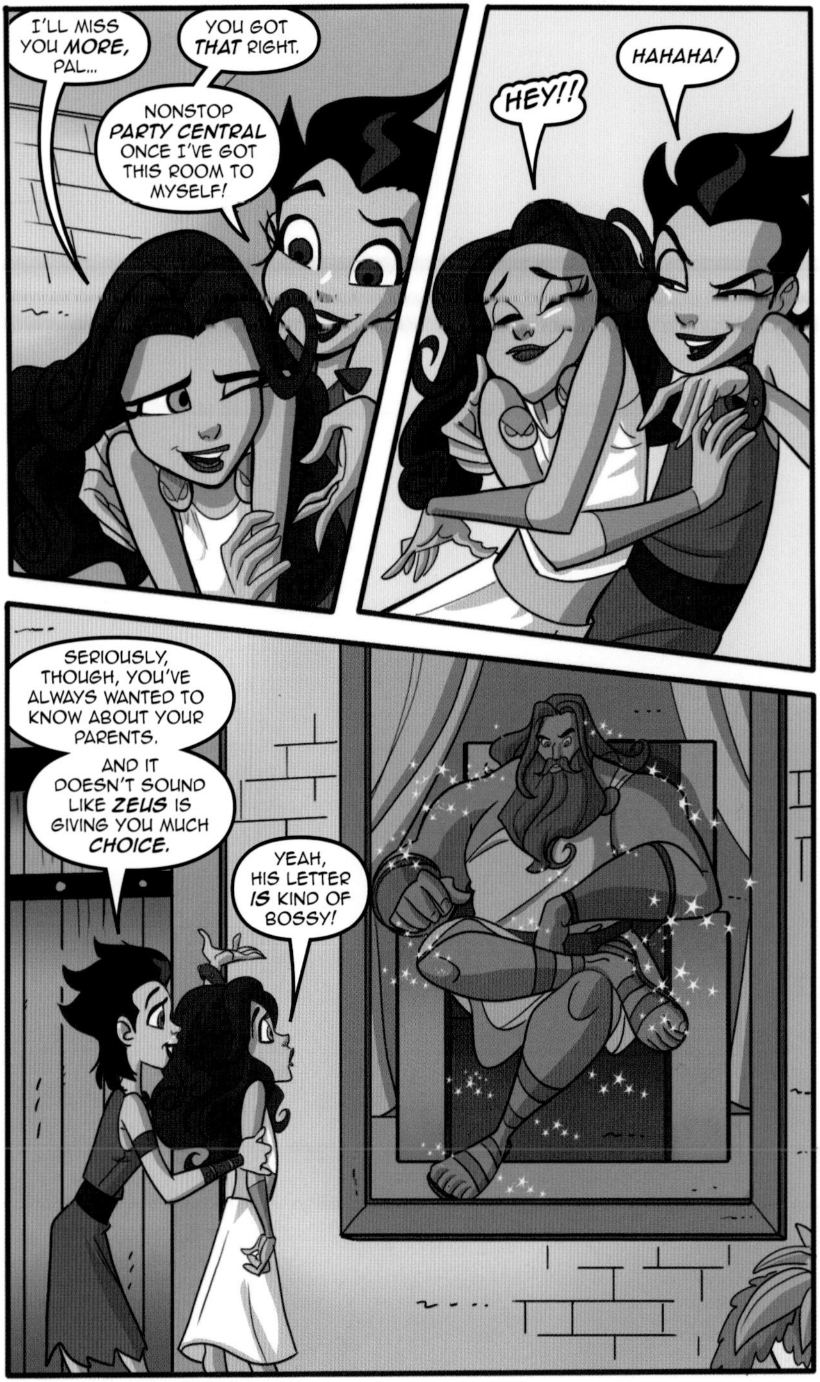
I'LL MISS YOU MORE, PAL...
YOU GOT THAT RIGHT.
NONSTOP PARTY CENTRAL ONCE I'VE GOT THIS ROOM TO MYSELF!
HEY!!
HAHAHA!
SERIOUSLY, THOUGH, YOU'VE ALWAYS WANTED TO KNOW ABOUT YOUR PARENTS.
AND IT DOESN'T SOUND LIKE ZEUS IS GIVING YOU MUCH CHOICE.
YEAH, HIS LETTER IS KIND OF BOSSY!

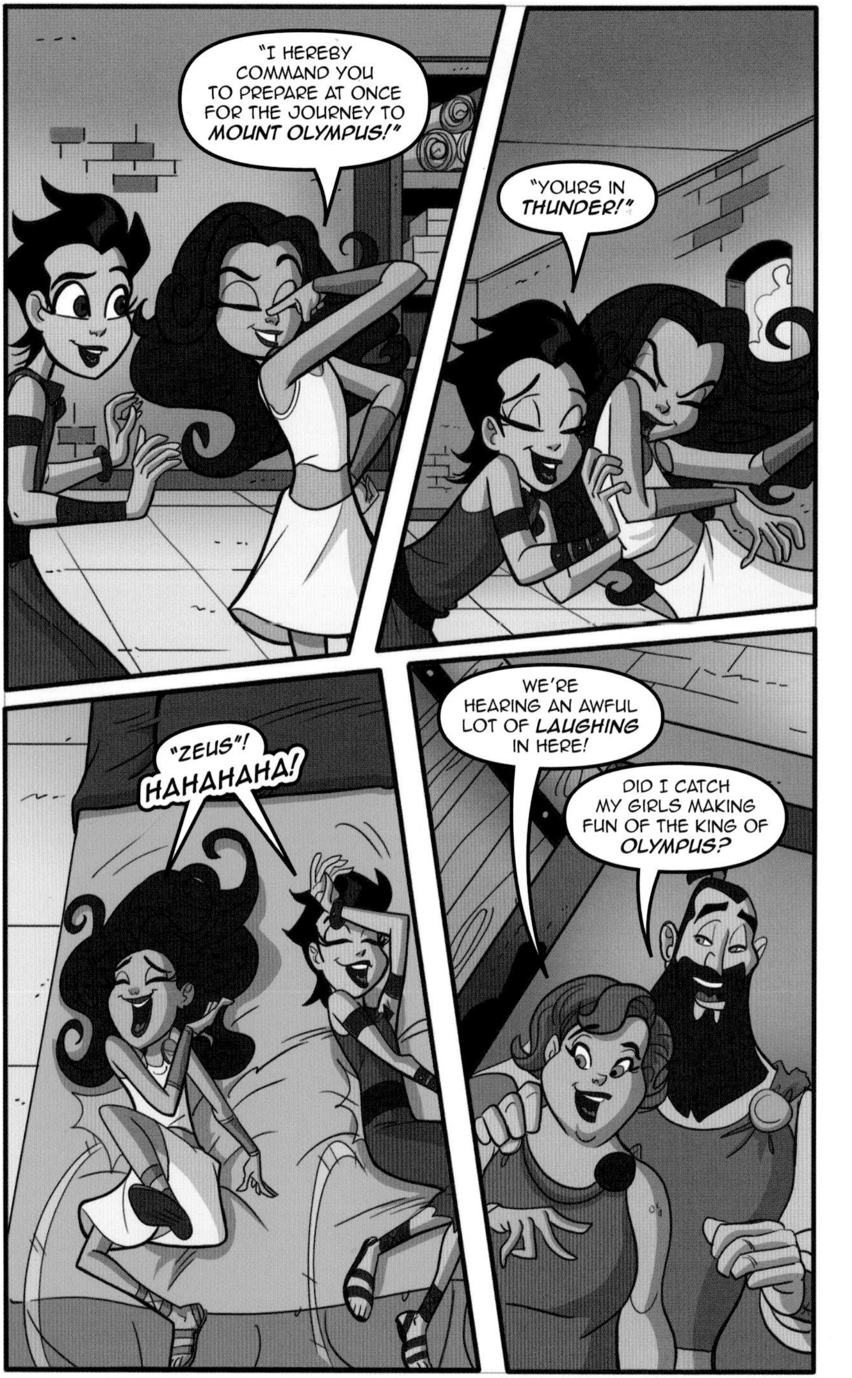
"I HEREBY COMMAND YOU TO PREPARE AT ONCE FOR THE JOURNEY TO *MOUNT OLYMPUS!*"
"YOURS IN *THUNDER!*"
"ZEUS"!
HAHAHAHA!
WE'RE HEARING AN AWFUL LOT OF *LAUGHING* IN HERE!
DID I CATCH MY GIRLS MAKING FUN OF THE KING OF *OLYMPUS?*

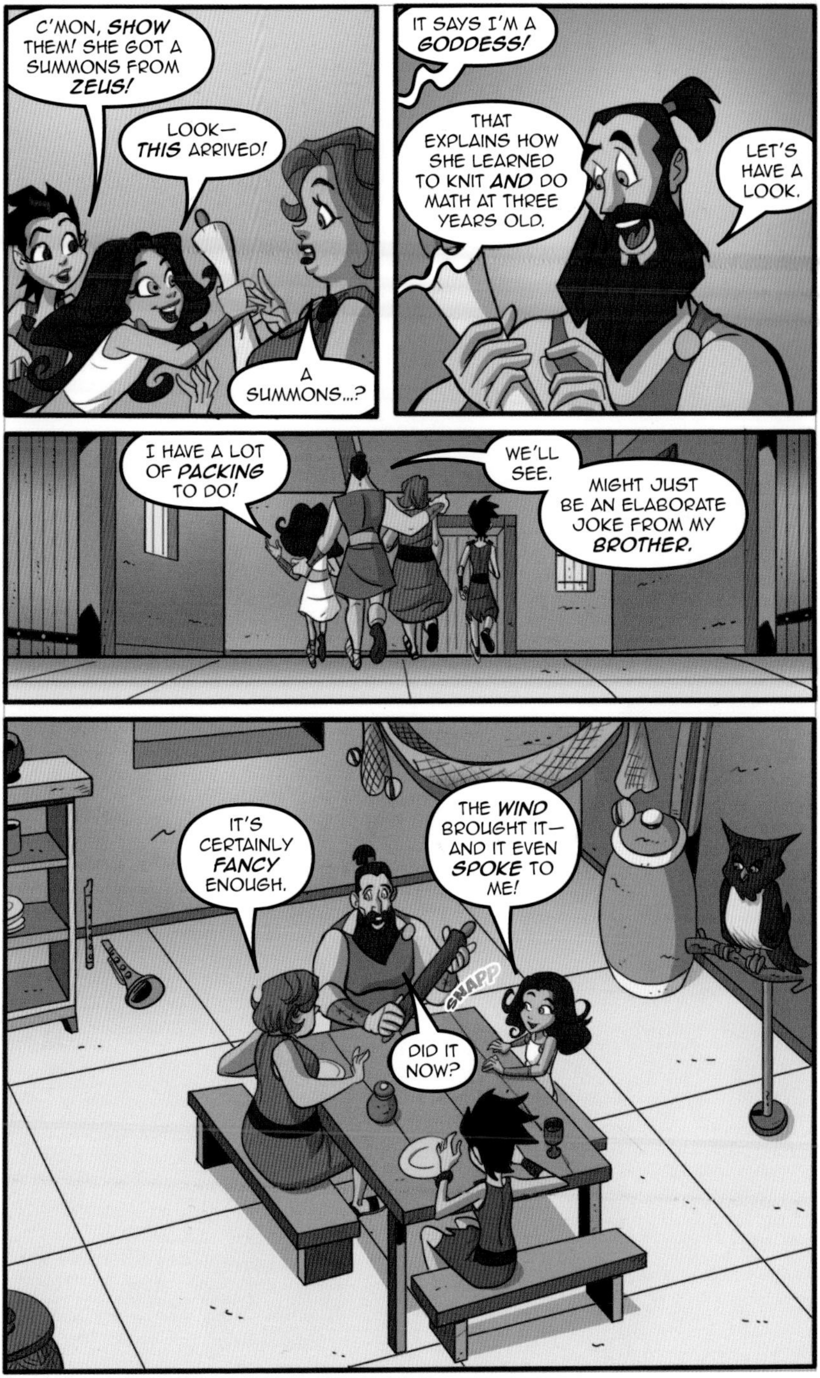
C'MON, SHOW THEM! SHE GOT A SUMMONS FROM ZEUS!
LOOK— THIS ARRIVED!
A SUMMONS...?
IT SAYS I'M A GODDESS!
THAT EXPLAINS HOW SHE LEARNED TO KNIT AND DO MATH AT THREE YEARS OLD.
LET'S HAVE A LOOK.
I HAVE A LOT OF PACKING TO DO!
WE'LL SEE.
MIGHT JUST BE AN ELABORATE JOKE FROM MY BROTHER.
IT'S CERTAINLY FANCY ENOUGH.
THE WIND BROUGHT IT— AND IT EVEN SPOKE TO ME!
SNAPP
DID IT NOW?

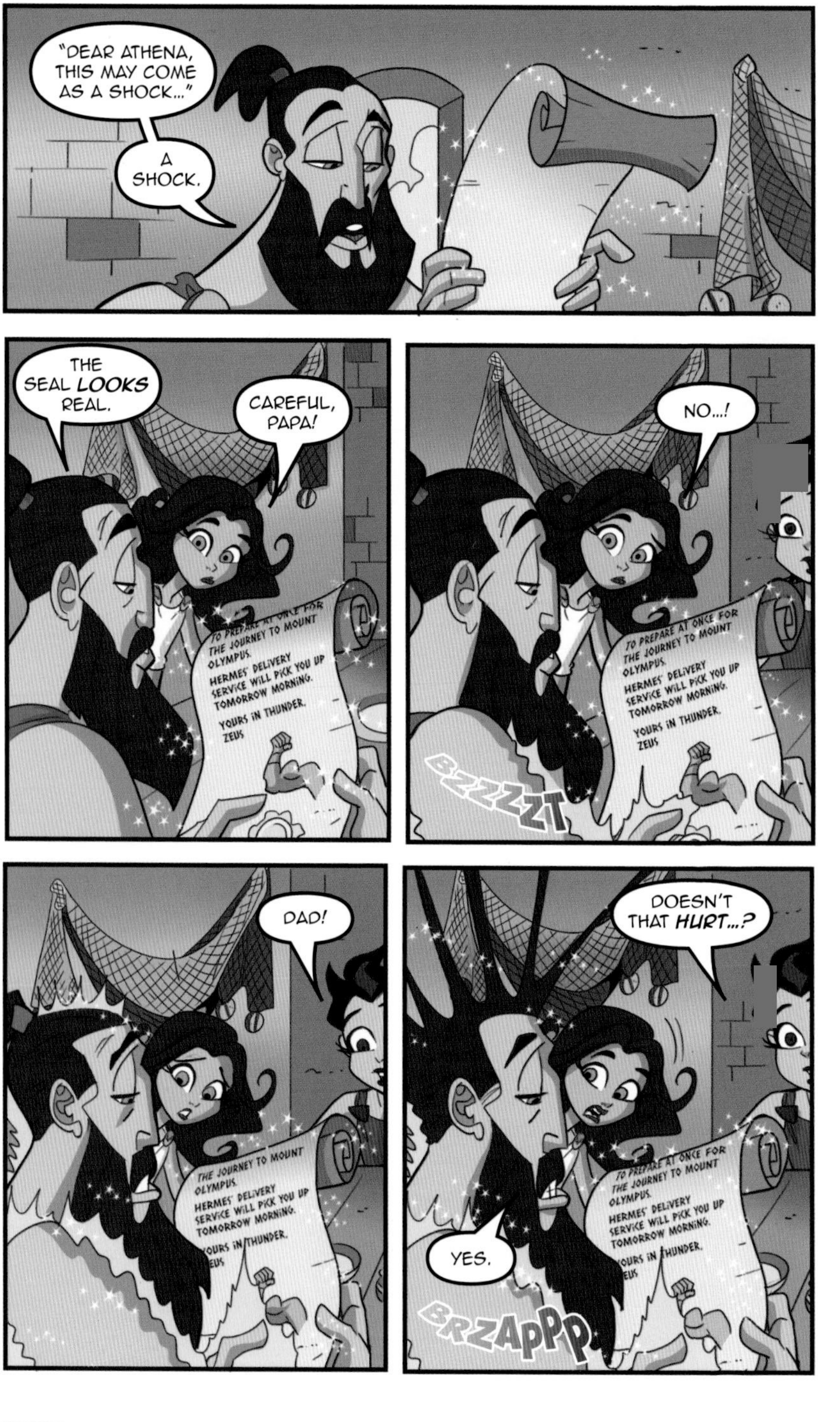
"DEAR ATHENA, THIS MAY COME AS A SHOCK..."
A SHOCK.
THE SEAL *LOOKS* REAL.
CAREFUL, PAPA!
TO PREPARE AT ONCE FOR THE JOURNEY TO MOUNT OLYMPUS.
HERMES' DELIVERY SERVICE WILL PICK YOU UP TOMORROW MORNING.
YOURS IN THUNDER,
ZEUS
NO...!
TO PREPARE AT ONCE FOR THE JOURNEY TO MOUNT OLYMPUS.
HERMES' DELIVERY SERVICE WILL PICK YOU UP TOMORROW MORNING.
YOURS IN THUNDER,
ZEUS
BZZZZT
DAD!
THE JOURNEY TO MOUNT OLYMPUS.
HERMES' DELIVERY SERVICE WILL PICK YOU UP TOMORROW MORNING.
DOESN'T THAT *HURT*...?
TO PREPARE AT ONCE FOR THE JOURNEY TO MOUNT OLYMPUS.
HERMES' DELIVERY SERVICE WILL PICK YOU UP TOMORROW MORNING.
YES.
BRZAPPP

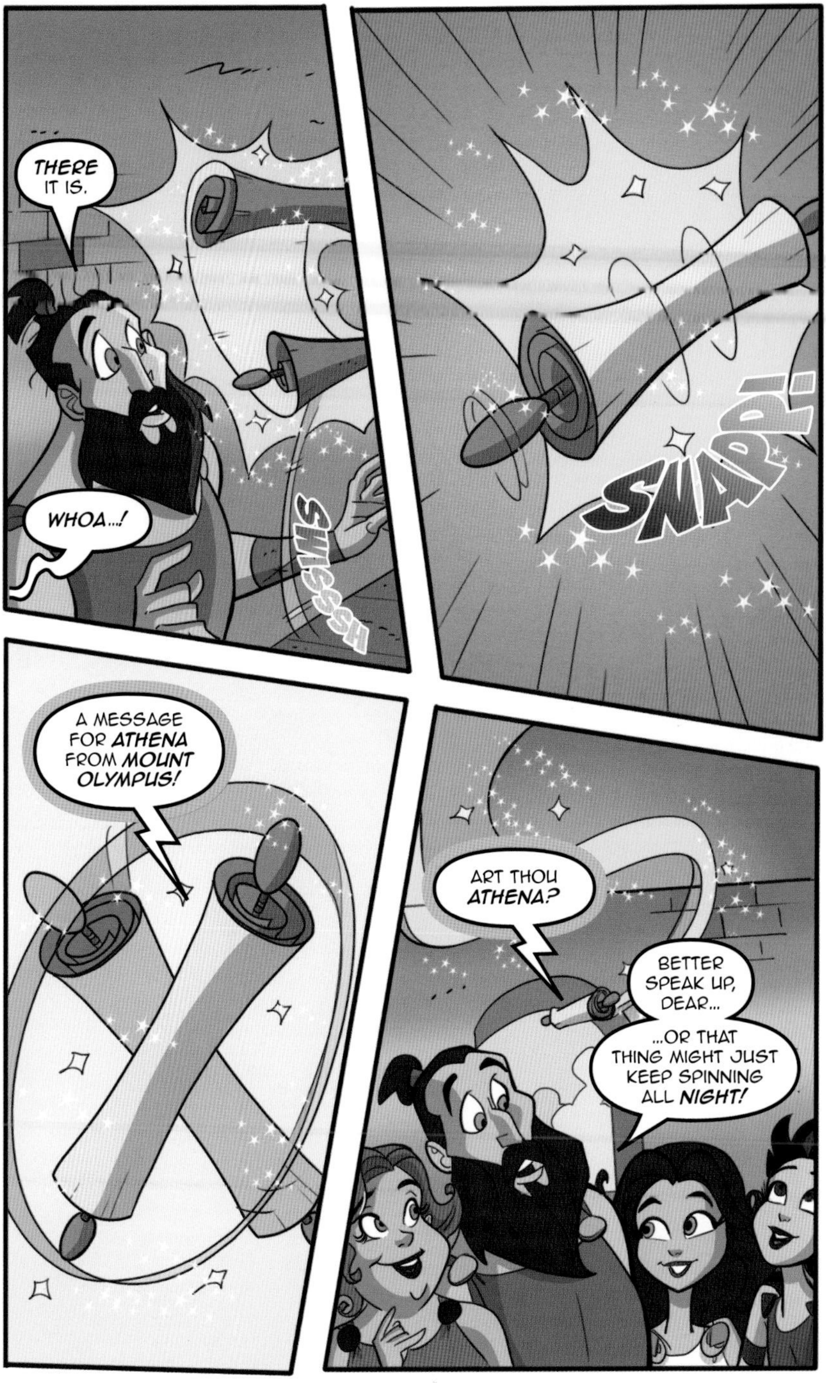
THERE IT IS.
WHOA...!
SWISSSSH
SNAP!
A MESSAGE FOR ATHENA FROM MOUNT OLYMPUS!
ART THOU ATHENA?
BETTER SPEAK UP, DEAR...
...OR THAT THING MIGHT JUST KEEP SPINNING ALL NIGHT!

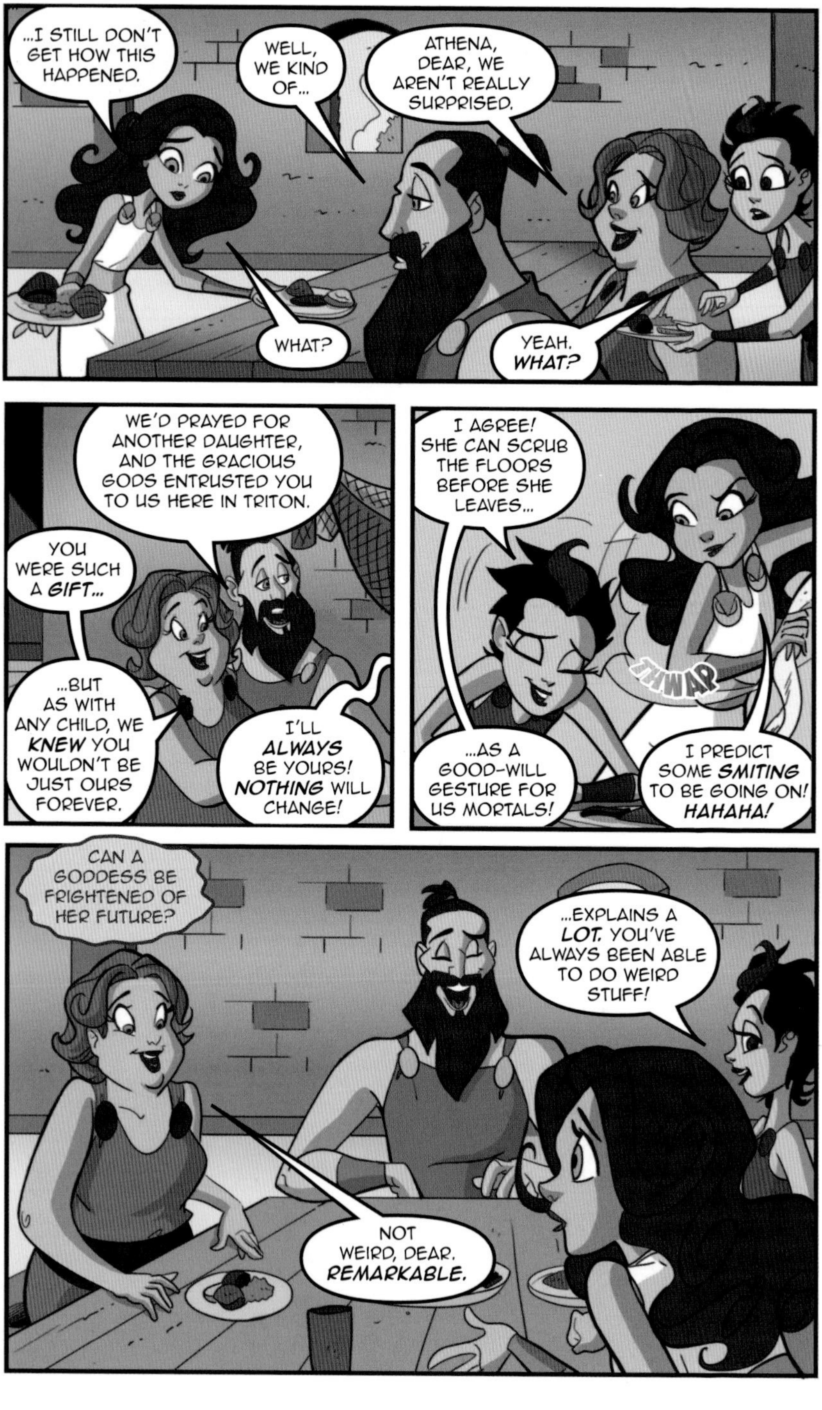
...I STILL DON'T GET HOW THIS HAPPENED.
WELL, WE KIND OF...
ATHENA, DEAR, WE AREN'T REALLY SURPRISED.
WHAT?
YEAH. WHAT?
WE'D PRAYED FOR ANOTHER DAUGHTER, AND THE GRACIOUS GODS ENTRUSTED YOU TO US HERE IN TRITON.
YOU WERE SUCH A GIFT...
...BUT AS WITH ANY CHILD, WE KNEW YOU WOULDN'T BE JUST OURS FOREVER.
I'LL ALWAYS BE YOURS! NOTHING WILL CHANGE!
I AGREE! SHE CAN SCRUB THE FLOORS BEFORE SHE LEAVES...
THWAP
...AS A GOOD-WILL GESTURE FOR US MORTALS!
I PREDICT SOME SMITING TO BE GOING ON! HAHAHA!
CAN A GODDESS BE FRIGHTENED OF HER FUTURE?
...EXPLAINS A LOT. YOU'VE ALWAYS BEEN ABLE TO DO WEIRD STUFF!
NOT WEIRD, DEAR. REMARKABLE.

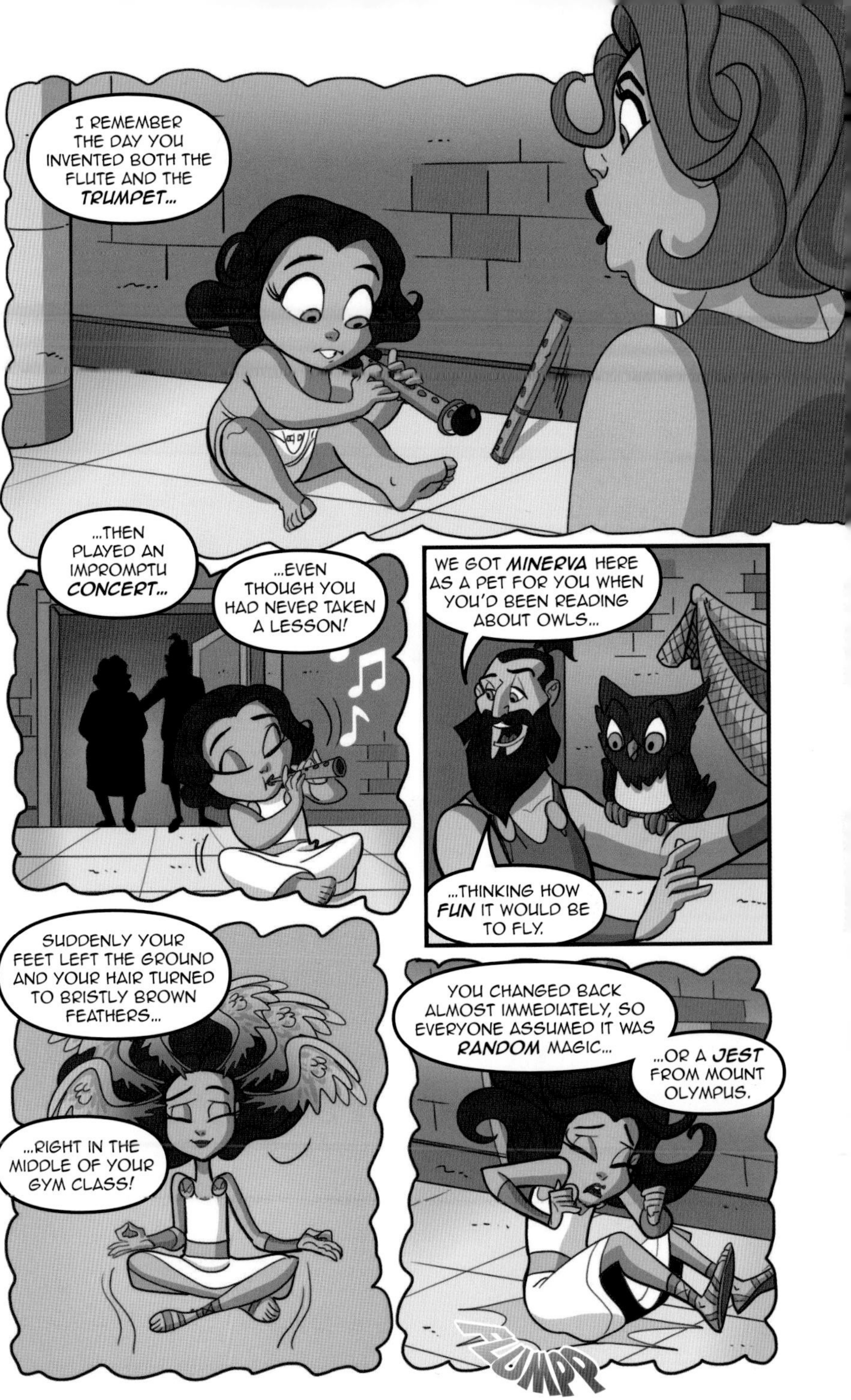
I REMEMBER THE DAY YOU INVENTED BOTH THE FLUTE AND THE *TRUMPET*...
...THEN PLAYED AN IMPROMPTU *CONCERT*...
...EVEN THOUGH YOU HAD NEVER TAKEN A LESSON!
WE GOT *MINERVA* HERE AS A PET FOR YOU WHEN YOU'D BEEN READING ABOUT OWLS...
...THINKING HOW *FUN* IT WOULD BE TO FLY.
SUDDENLY YOUR FEET LEFT THE GROUND AND YOUR HAIR TURNED TO BRISTLY BROWN FEATHERS...
...RIGHT IN THE MIDDLE OF YOUR GYM CLASS!
YOU CHANGED BACK ALMOST IMMEDIATELY, SO EVERYONE ASSUMED IT WAS *RANDOM* MAGIC...
...OR A *JEST* FROM MOUNT OLYMPUS.
FLUMPP

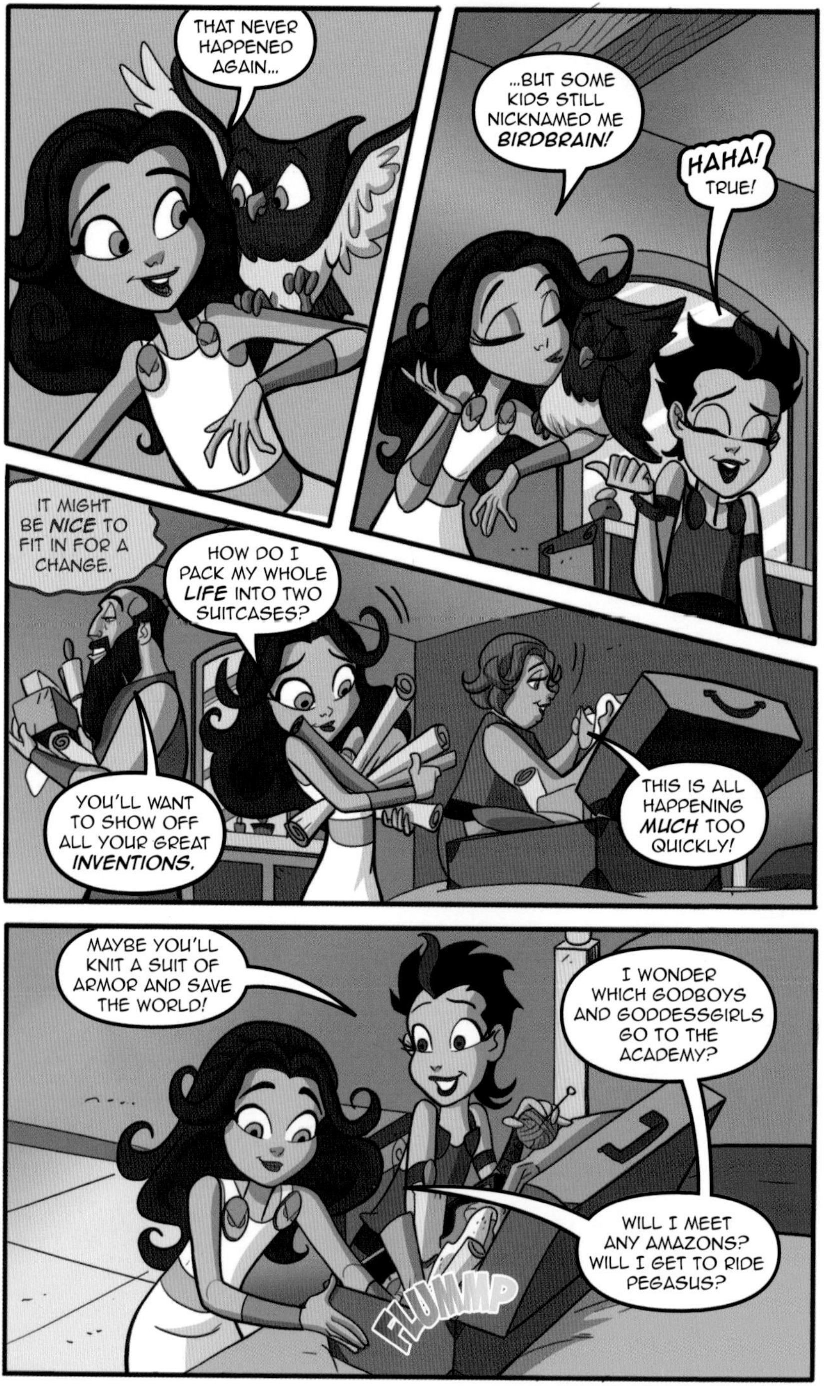
THAT NEVER HAPPENED AGAIN...
...BUT SOME KIDS STILL NICKNAMED ME BIRDBRAIN!
HAHA! TRUE!
IT MIGHT BE NICE TO FIT IN FOR A CHANGE.
HOW DO I PACK MY WHOLE LIFE INTO TWO SUITCASES?
YOU'LL WANT TO SHOW OFF ALL YOUR GREAT INVENTIONS.
THIS IS ALL HAPPENING MUCH TOO QUICKLY!
MAYBE YOU'LL KNIT A SUIT OF ARMOR AND SAVE THE WORLD!
I WONDER WHICH GODBOYS AND GODDESSGIRLS GO TO THE ACADEMY?
WILL I MEET ANY AMAZONS? WILL I GET TO RIDE PEGASUS?
FLUMMP

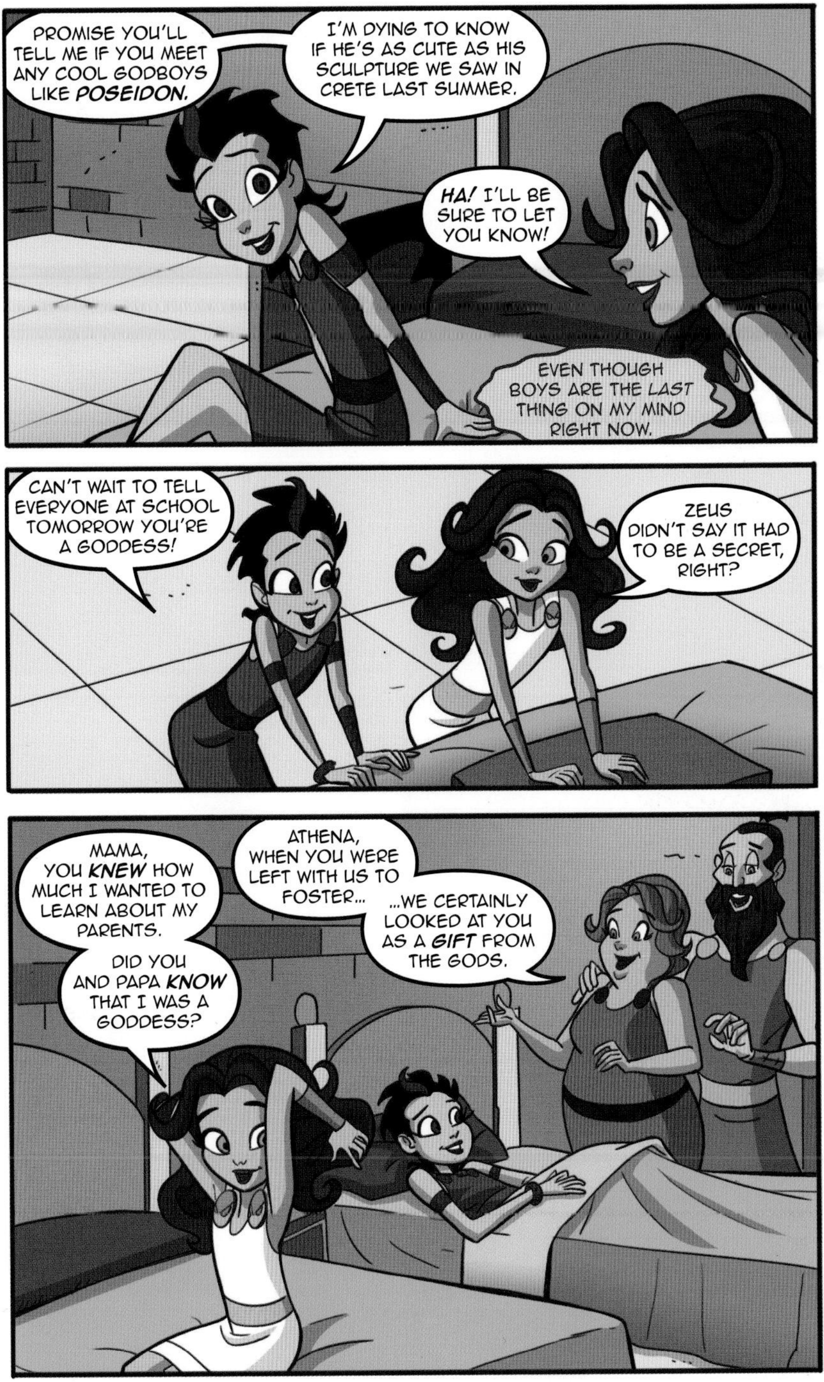
PROMISE YOU'LL TELL ME IF YOU MEET ANY COOL GODBOYS LIKE *POSEIDON.*
I'M DYING TO KNOW IF HE'S AS CUTE AS HIS SCULPTURE WE SAW IN CRETE LAST SUMMER.
HA! I'LL BE SURE TO LET YOU KNOW!
EVEN THOUGH BOYS ARE THE *LAST* THING ON MY MIND RIGHT NOW.
CAN'T WAIT TO TELL EVERYONE AT SCHOOL TOMORROW YOU'RE A GODDESS!
ZEUS DIDN'T SAY IT HAD TO BE A SECRET, RIGHT?
MAMA, YOU ***KNEW*** HOW MUCH I WANTED TO LEARN ABOUT MY PARENTS.
DID YOU AND PAPA ***KNOW*** THAT I WAS A GODDESS?
ATHENA, WHEN YOU WERE LEFT WITH US TO FOSTER...
...WE CERTAINLY LOOKED AT YOU AS A ***GIFT*** FROM THE GODS.

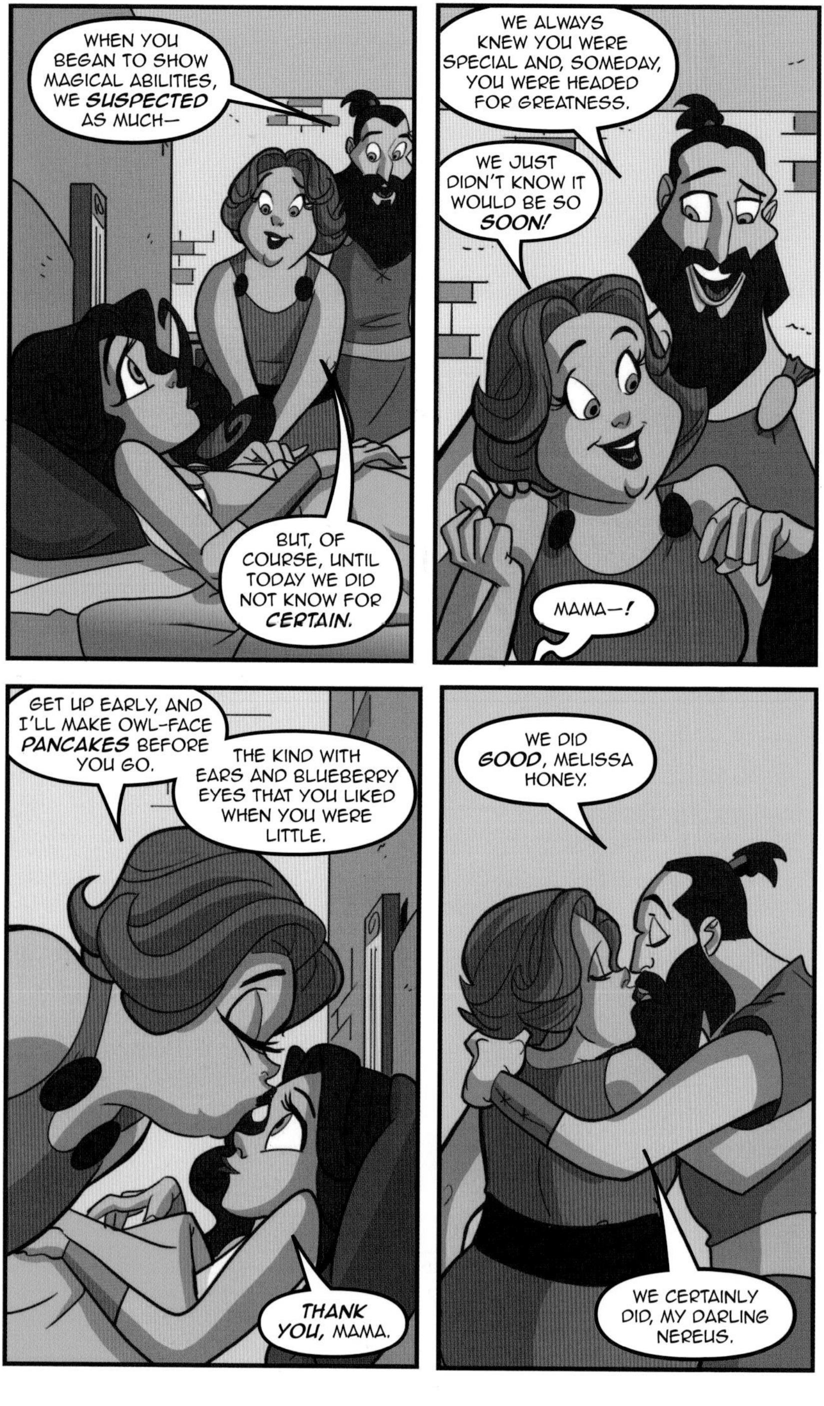
WHEN YOU BEGAN TO SHOW MAGICAL ABILITIES, WE *SUSPECTED* AS MUCH—
BUT, OF COURSE, UNTIL TODAY WE DID NOT KNOW FOR *CERTAIN.*
WE ALWAYS KNEW YOU WERE SPECIAL AND, SOMEDAY, YOU WERE HEADED FOR GREATNESS.
WE JUST DIDN'T KNOW IT WOULD BE SO *SOON!*
MAMA—!
GET UP EARLY, AND I'LL MAKE OWL-FACE *PANCAKES* BEFORE YOU GO.
THE KIND WITH EARS AND BLUEBERRY EYES THAT YOU LIKED WHEN YOU WERE LITTLE.
THANK YOU, MAMA.
WE DID *GOOD*, MELISSA HONEY.
WE CERTAINLY DID, MY DARLING NEREUS.

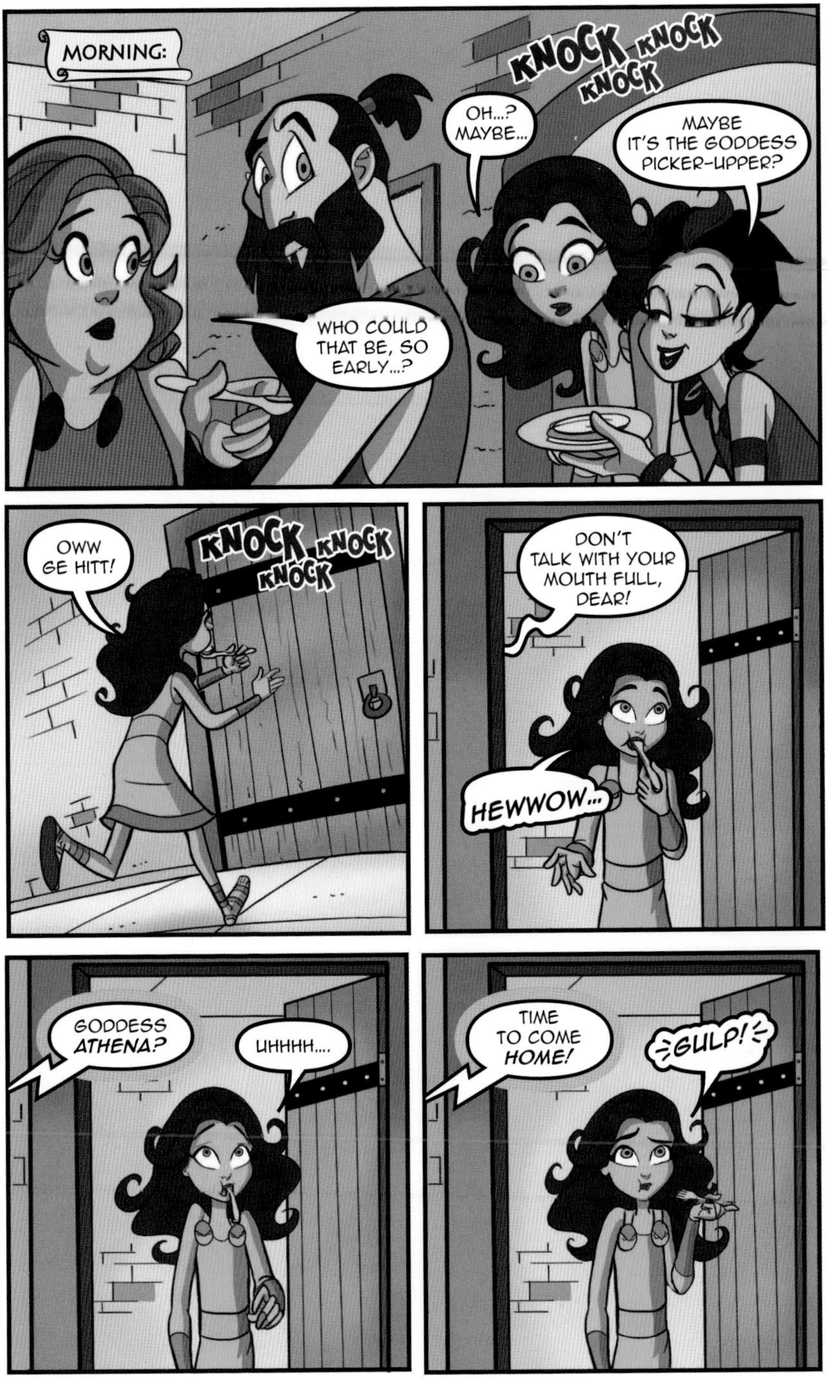
MORNING:
KNOCK KNOCK KNOCK
WHO COULD THAT BE, SO EARLY...?
OH...? MAYBE...
MAYBE IT'S THE GODDESS PICKER-UPPER?
OWW GE HITT!
KNOCK KNOCK KNOCK
DON'T TALK WITH YOUR MOUTH FULL, DEAR!
HEWWOW...
GODDESS ATHENA?
UHHHH....
TIME TO COME HOME!
GULP!

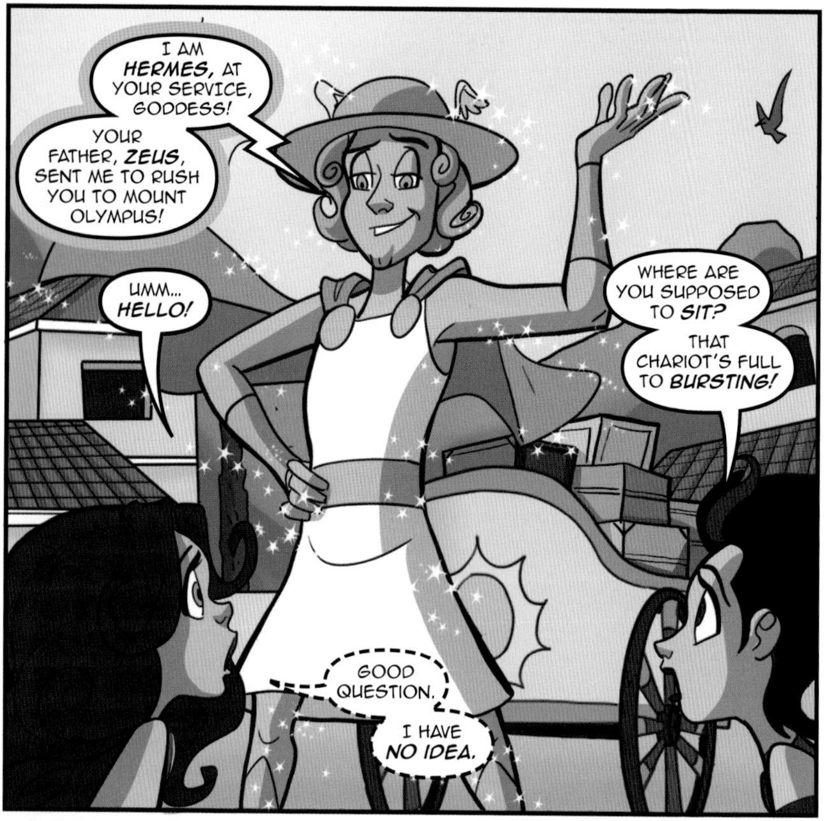

I AM HERMES, AT YOUR SERVICE, GODDESS!
YOUR FATHER, ZEUS, SENT ME TO RUSH YOU TO MOUNT OLYMPUS!
UMM... HELLO!
WHERE ARE YOU SUPPOSED TO SIT?
THAT CHARIOT'S FULL TO BURSTING!
GOOD QUESTION.
I HAVE NO IDEA.

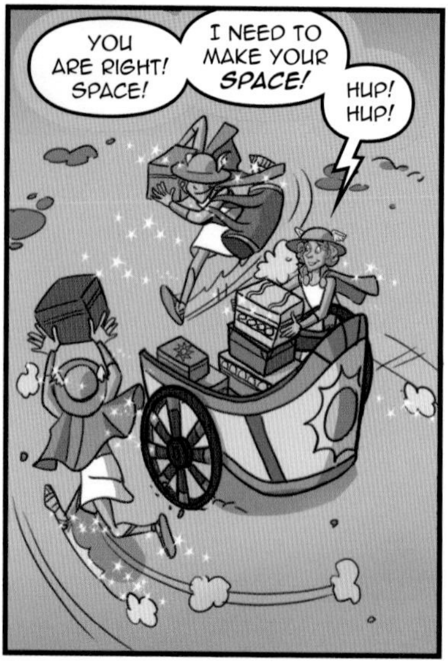

YOU ARE RIGHT! SPACE!
I NEED TO MAKE YOUR SPACE!
HUP! HUP!

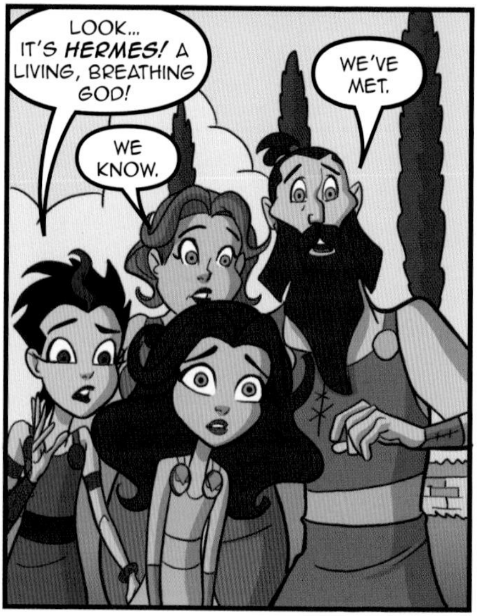

LOOK... IT'S HERMES! A LIVING, BREATHING GOD!
WE'VE MET.
WE KNOW.

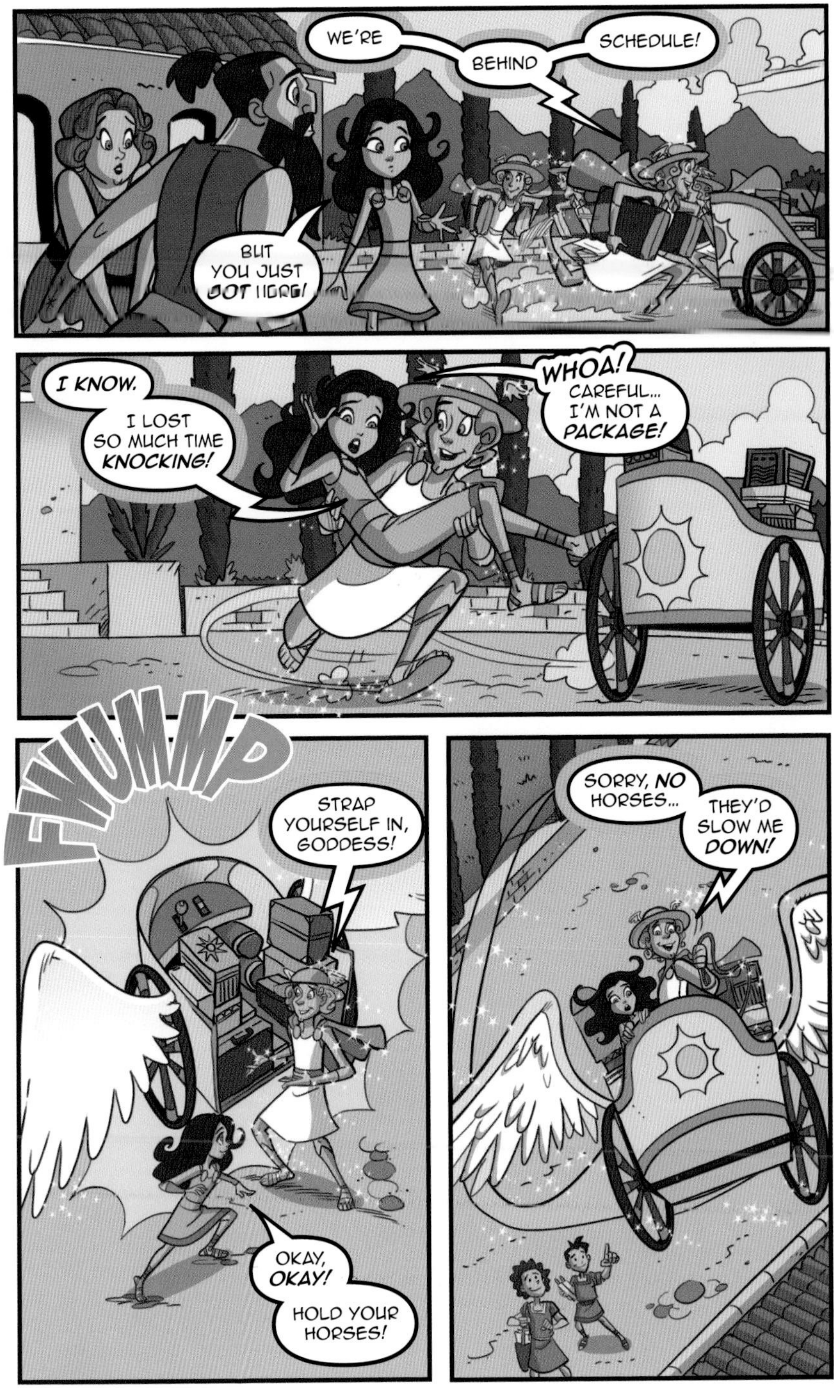
WE'RE
BEHIND
SCHEDULE!
BUT YOU JUST GOT HERE!
I KNOW.
I LOST SO MUCH TIME KNOCKING!
WHOA!
CAREFUL... I'M NOT A PACKAGE!
FWUMMP
STRAP YOURSELF IN, GODDESS!
OKAY, OKAY!
HOLD YOUR HORSES!
SORRY, NO HORSES...
THEY'D SLOW ME DOWN!

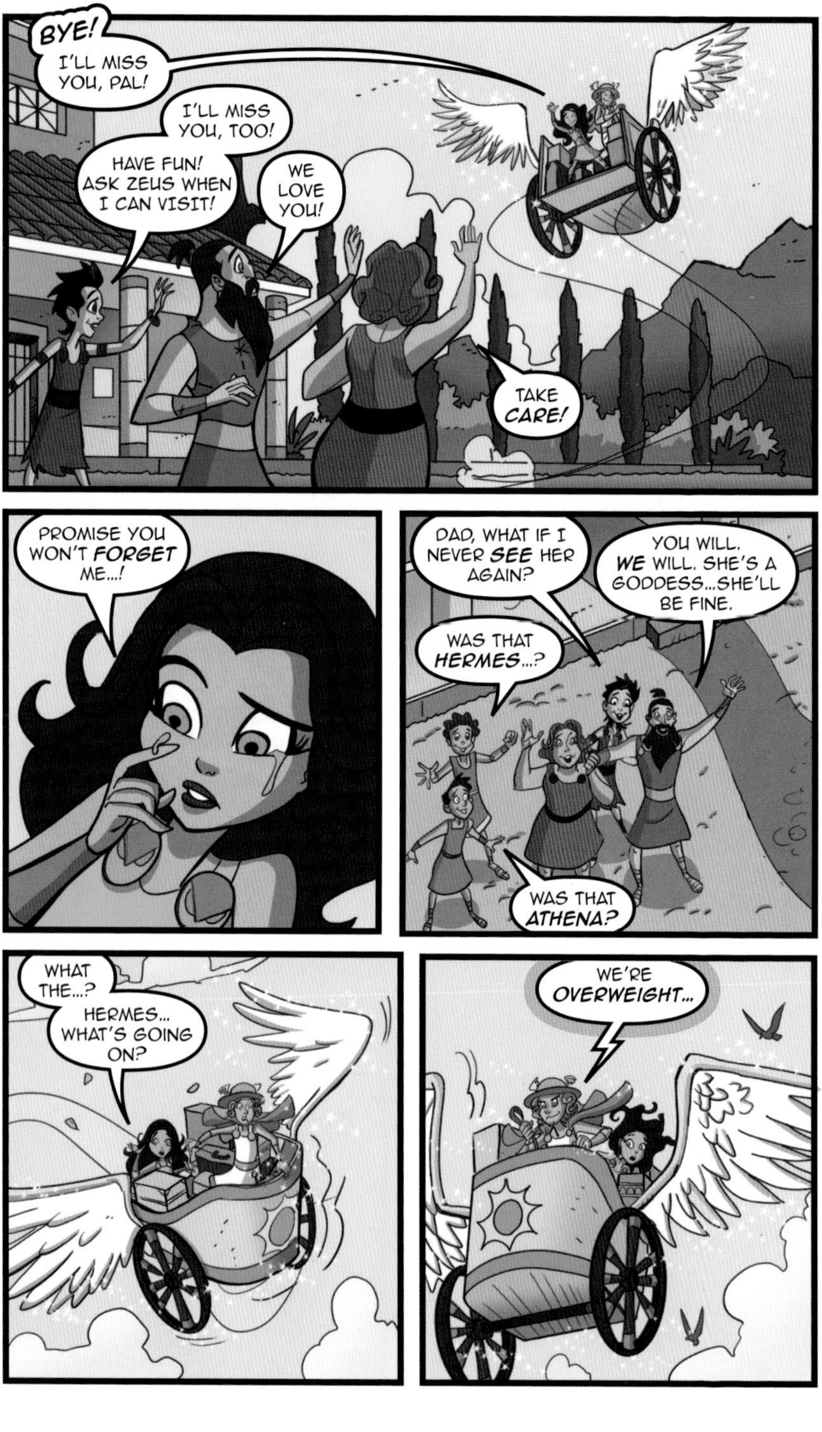
BYE!
I'LL MISS YOU, PAL!
I'LL MISS YOU, TOO!
HAVE FUN! ASK ZEUS WHEN I CAN VISIT!
WE LOVE YOU!
TAKE CARE!
PROMISE YOU WON'T FORGET ME...!
DAD, WHAT IF I NEVER SEE HER AGAIN?
YOU WILL. WE WILL. SHE'S A GODDESS...SHE'LL BE FINE.
WAS THAT HERMES...?
WAS THAT ATHENA?
WHAT THE...?
HERMES... WHAT'S GOING ON?
WE'RE OVERWEIGHT...

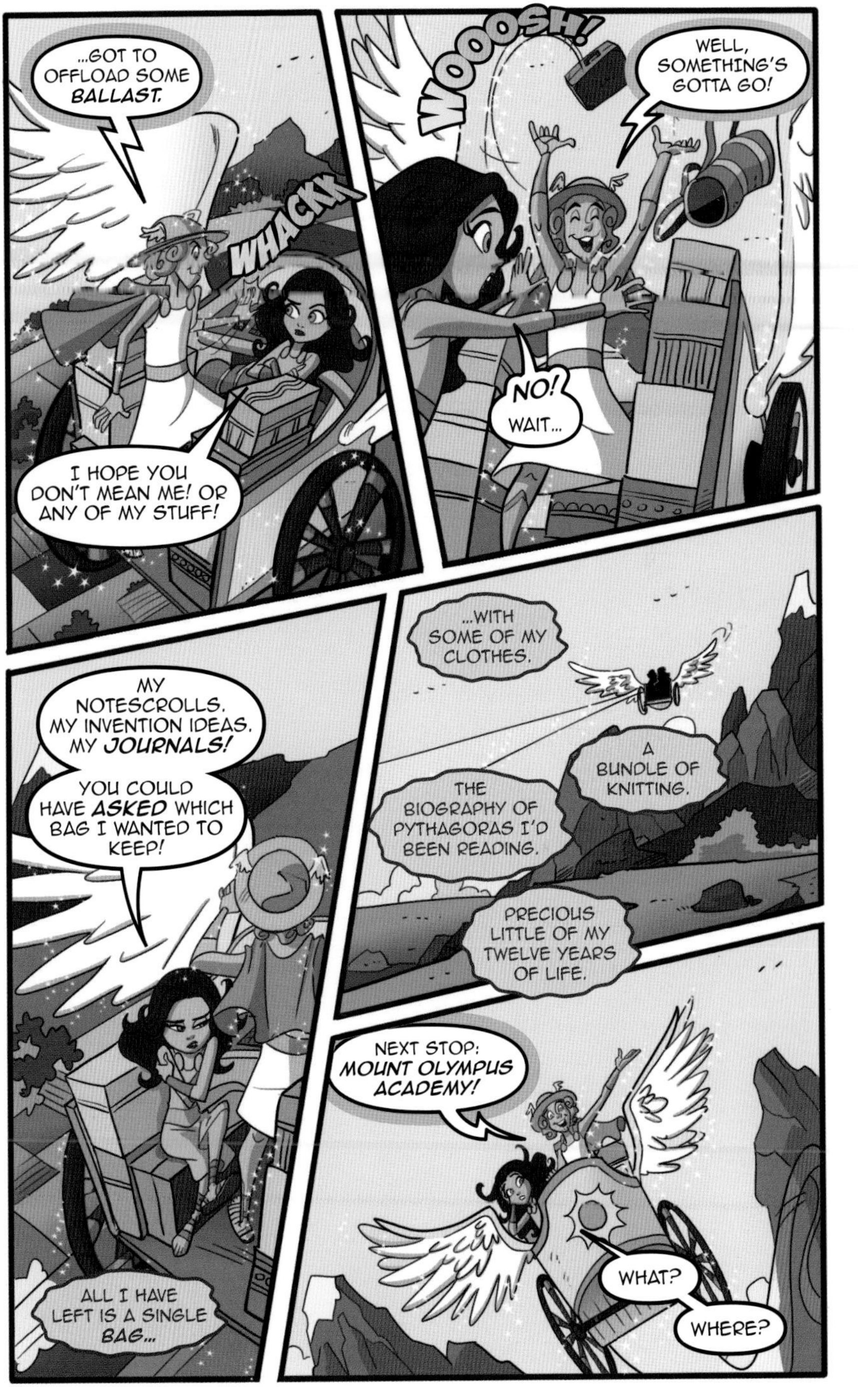
...GOT TO OFFLOAD SOME BALLAST.
WHACK!
I HOPE YOU DON'T MEAN ME! OR ANY OF MY STUFF!
WOOOSH!
WELL, SOMETHING'S GOTTA GO!
NO! WAIT...
MY NOTESCROLLS. MY INVENTION IDEAS. MY JOURNALS!
YOU COULD HAVE ASKED WHICH BAG I WANTED TO KEEP!
ALL I HAVE LEFT IS A SINGLE BAG...
...WITH SOME OF MY CLOTHES.
A BUNDLE OF KNITTING.
THE BIOGRAPHY OF PYTHAGORAS I'D BEEN READING.
PRECIOUS LITTLE OF MY TWELVE YEARS OF LIFE.
NEXT STOP: MOUNT OLYMPUS ACADEMY!
WHAT?
WHERE?

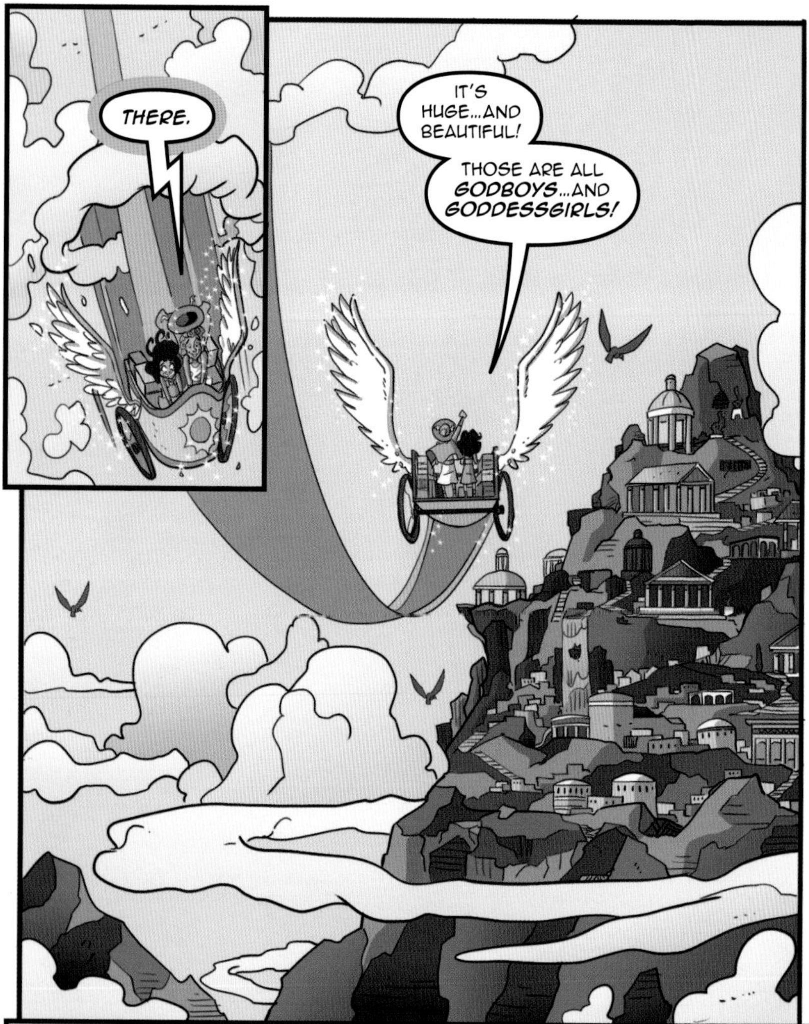
THERE.
IT'S HUGE...AND BEAUTIFUL!
THOSE ARE ALL GODBOYS...AND GODDESSGIRLS!

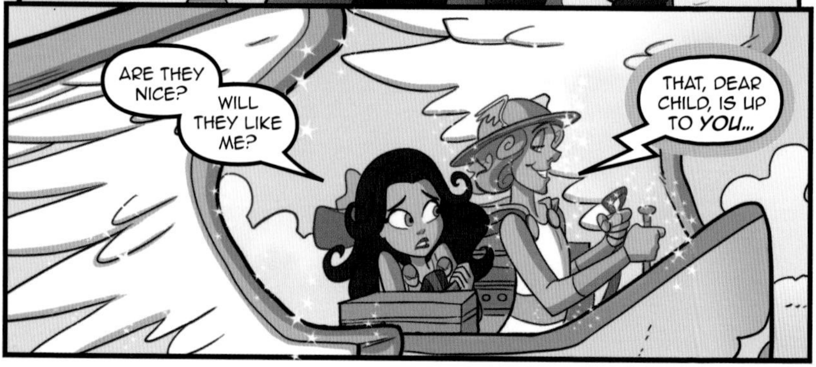
ARE THEY NICE?
WILL THEY LIKE ME?
THAT, DEAR CHILD, IS UP TO YOU...

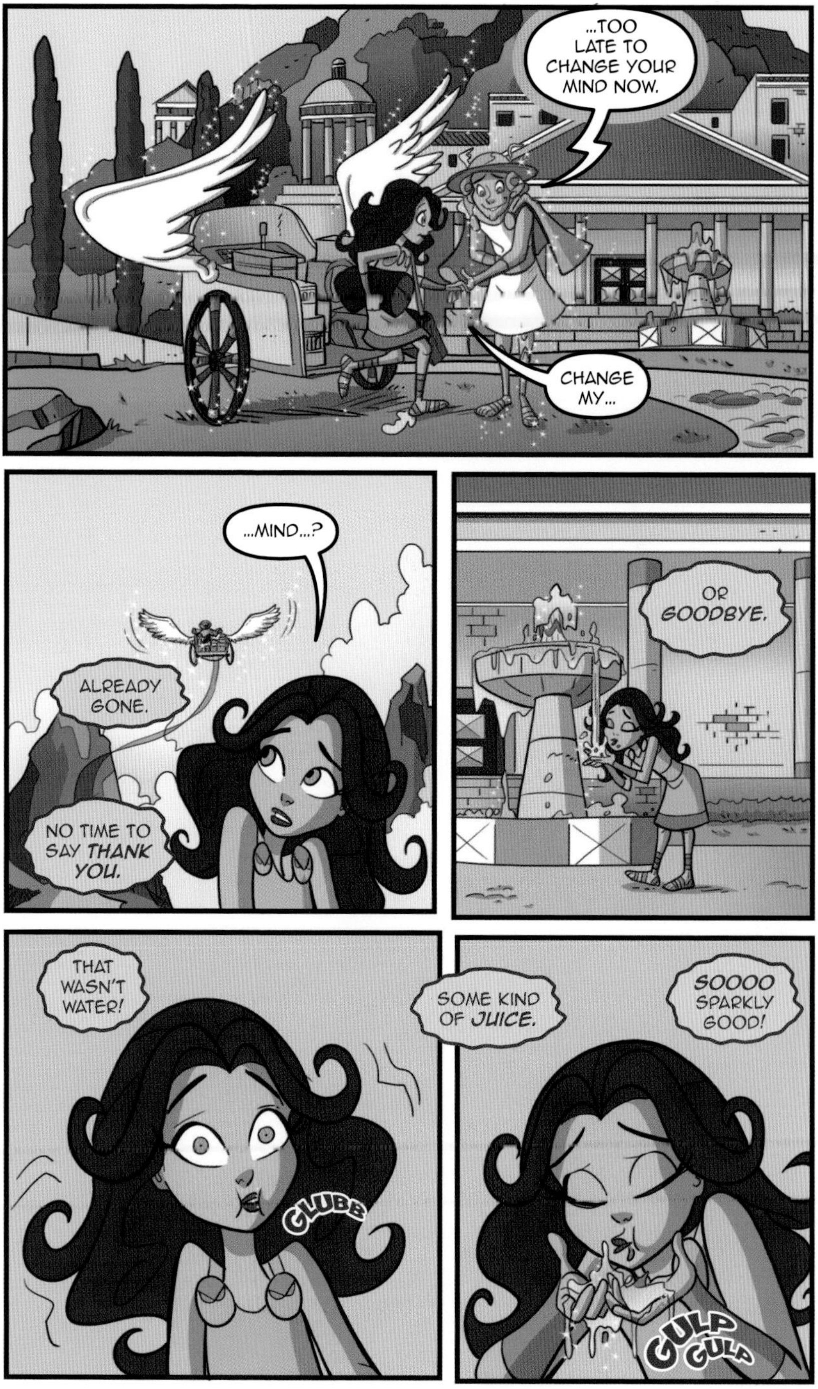
...TOO LATE TO CHANGE YOUR MIND NOW.
CHANGE MY...
...MIND...?
ALREADY GONE.
NO TIME TO SAY THANK YOU.
OR GOODBYE.
THAT WASN'T WATER!
GLUBB
SOME KIND OF JUICE.
SOOOO SPARKLY GOOD!
GULP GULP

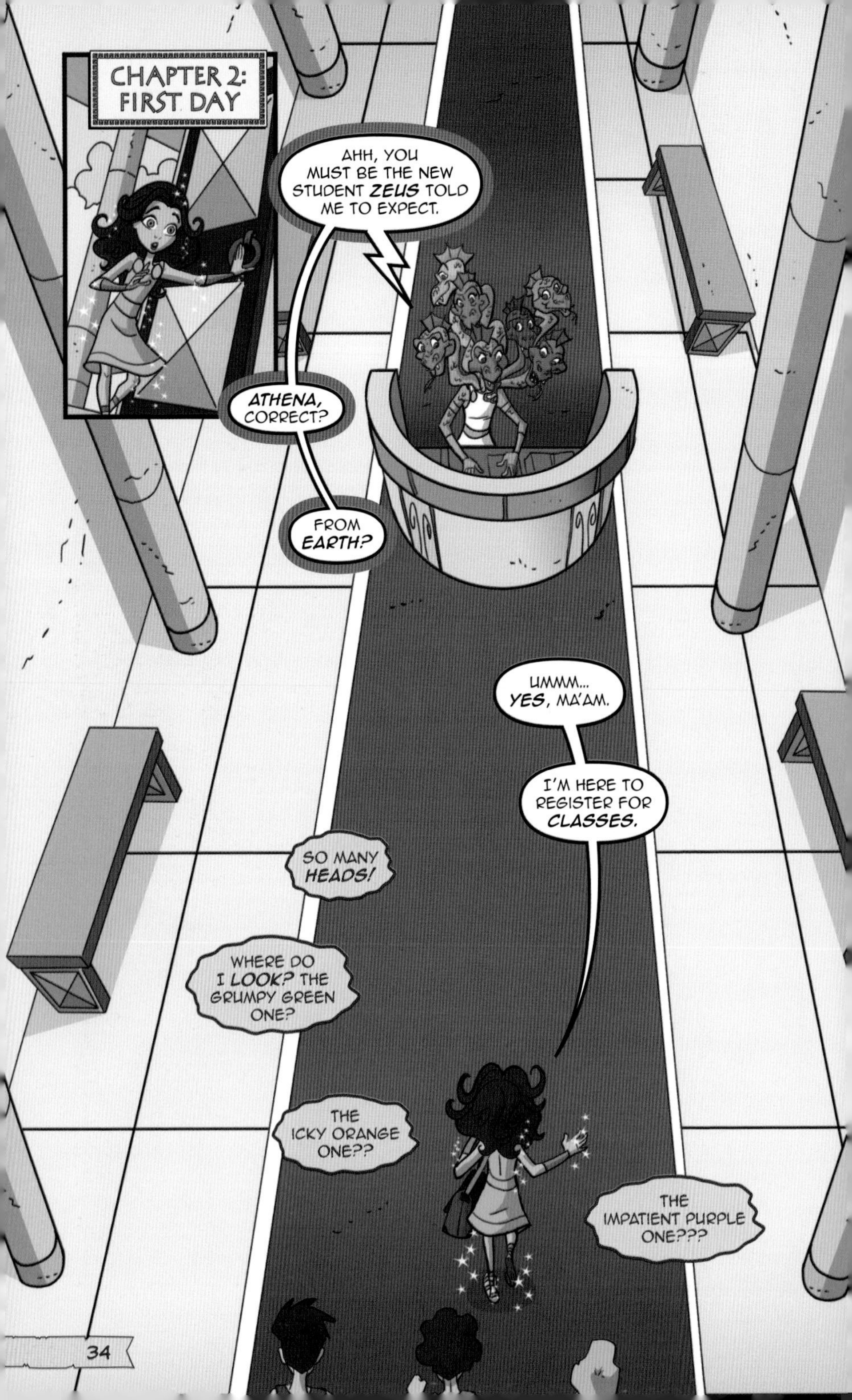
CHAPTER 2:
FIRST DAY
AHH, YOU MUST BE THE NEW STUDENT ZEUS TOLD ME TO EXPECT.
ATHENA, CORRECT?
FROM EARTH?
UMMM... YES, MA'AM.
I'M HERE TO REGISTER FOR CLASSES.
SO MANY HEADS!
WHERE DO I LOOK? THE GRUMPY GREEN ONE?
THE ICKY ORANGE ONE??
THE IMPATIENT PURPLE ONE???

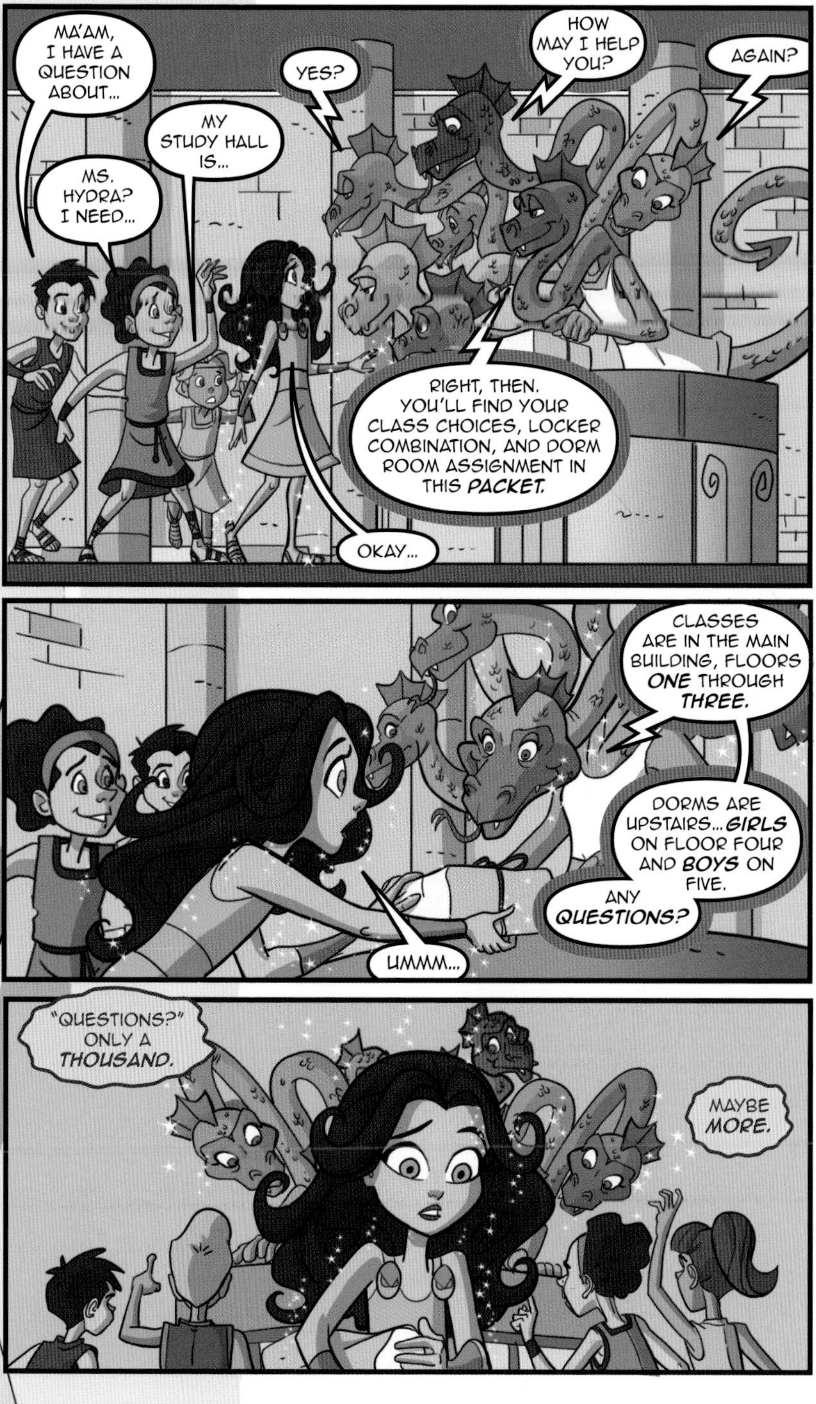
MA'AM, I HAVE A QUESTION ABOUT...
MS. HYDRA? I NEED...
MY STUDY HALL IS...
YES?
HOW MAY I HELP YOU?
AGAIN?
RIGHT, THEN. YOU'LL FIND YOUR CLASS CHOICES, LOCKER COMBINATION, AND DORM ROOM ASSIGNMENT IN THIS PACKET.
OKAY...
CLASSES ARE IN THE MAIN BUILDING, FLOORS ONE THROUGH THREE.
DORMS ARE UPSTAIRS...GIRLS ON FLOOR FOUR AND BOYS ON FIVE.
ANY QUESTIONS?
UMMM...
"QUESTIONS?" ONLY A THOUSAND.
MAYBE MORE.

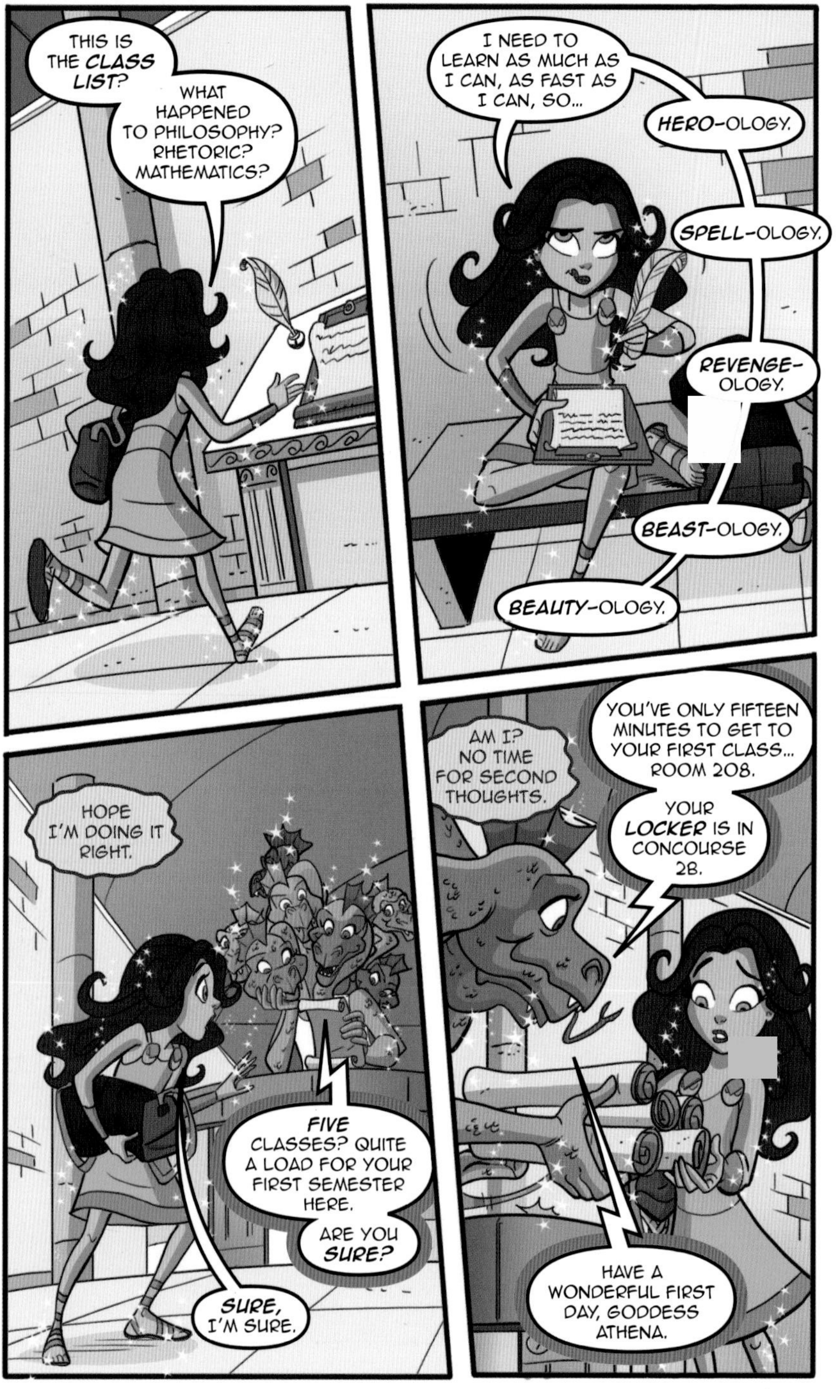
THIS IS THE CLASS LIST?
WHAT HAPPENED TO PHILOSOPHY? RHETORIC? MATHEMATICS?
I NEED TO LEARN AS MUCH AS I CAN, AS FAST AS I CAN, SO...
HERO-OLOGY.
SPELL-OLOGY.
REVENGE-OLOGY.
BEAST-OLOGY.
BEAUTY-OLOGY.
HOPE I'M DOING IT RIGHT.
FIVE CLASSES? QUITE A LOAD FOR YOUR FIRST SEMESTER HERE.
ARE YOU SURE?
SURE, I'M SURE.
AM I? NO TIME FOR SECOND THOUGHTS.
YOU'VE ONLY FIFTEEN MINUTES TO GET TO YOUR FIRST CLASS... ROOM 208.
YOUR LOCKER IS IN CONCOURSE 2B.
HAVE A WONDERFUL FIRST DAY, GODDESS ATHENA.

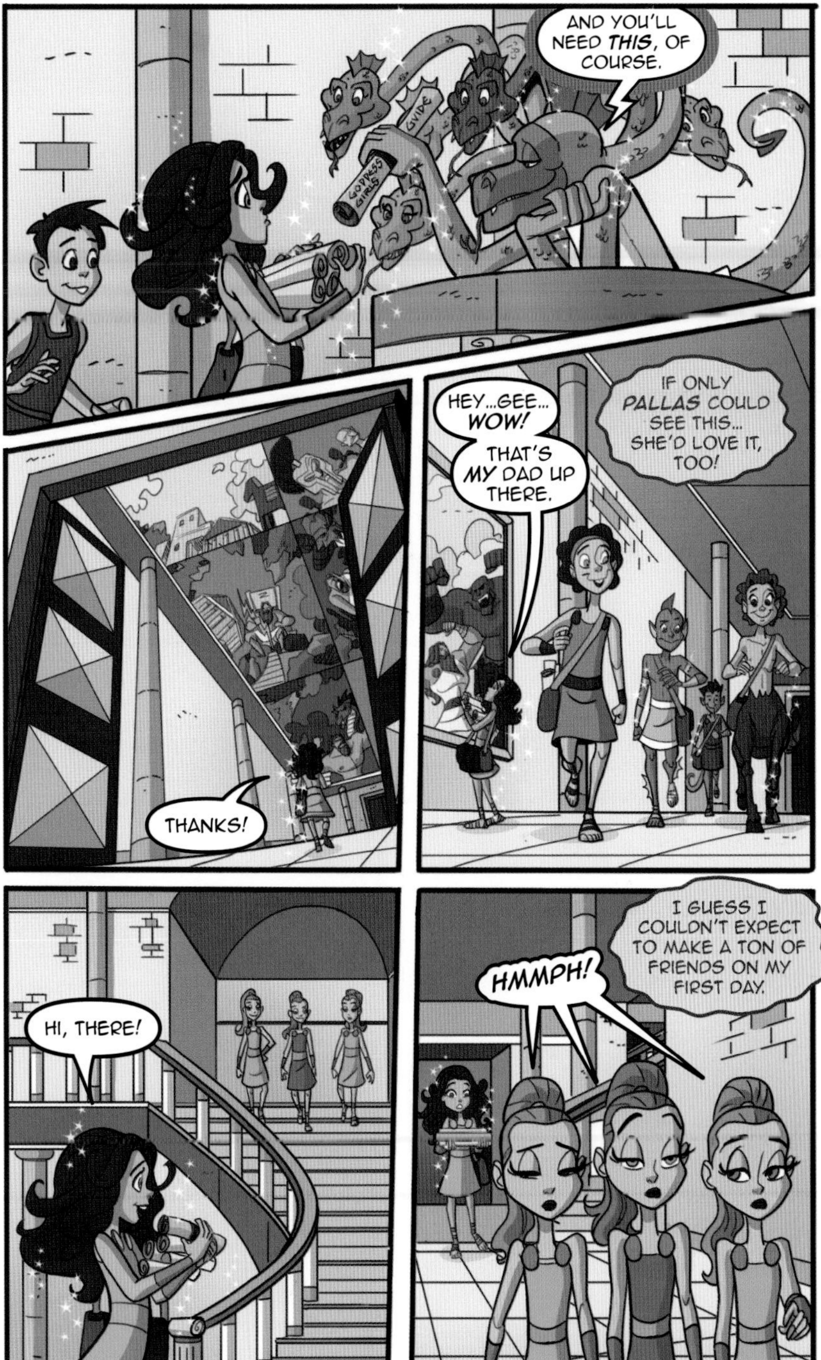
AND YOU'LL NEED THIS, OF COURSE.
GUIDE
GODDESS GIRLS
THANKS!
HEY...GEE... WOW!
THAT'S MY DAD UP THERE.
IF ONLY PALLAS COULD SEE THIS... SHE'D LOVE IT, TOO!
HI, THERE!
HMMPH!
I GUESS I COULDN'T EXPECT TO MAKE A TON OF FRIENDS ON MY FIRST DAY.

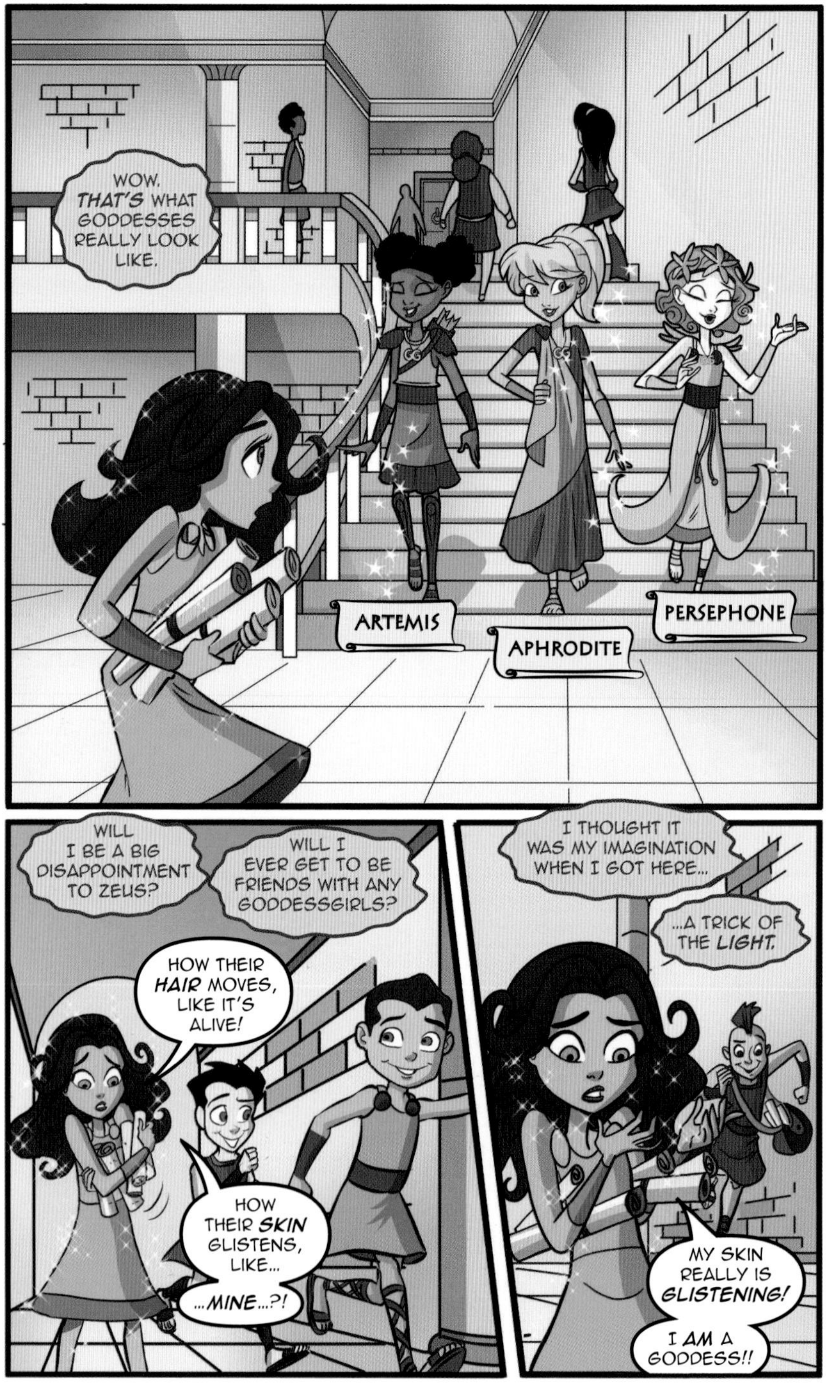
WOW. THAT'S WHAT GODDESSES REALLY LOOK LIKE.
ARTEMIS
APHRODITE
PERSEPHONE
WILL I BE A BIG DISAPPOINTMENT TO ZEUS?
WILL I EVER GET TO BE FRIENDS WITH ANY GODDESSGIRLS?
HOW THEIR HAIR MOVES, LIKE IT'S ALIVE!
HOW THEIR SKIN GLISTENS, LIKE...
...MINE...?!
I THOUGHT IT WAS MY IMAGINATION WHEN I GOT HERE...
...A TRICK OF THE LIGHT.
MY SKIN REALLY IS GLISTENING!
I AM A GODDESS!!

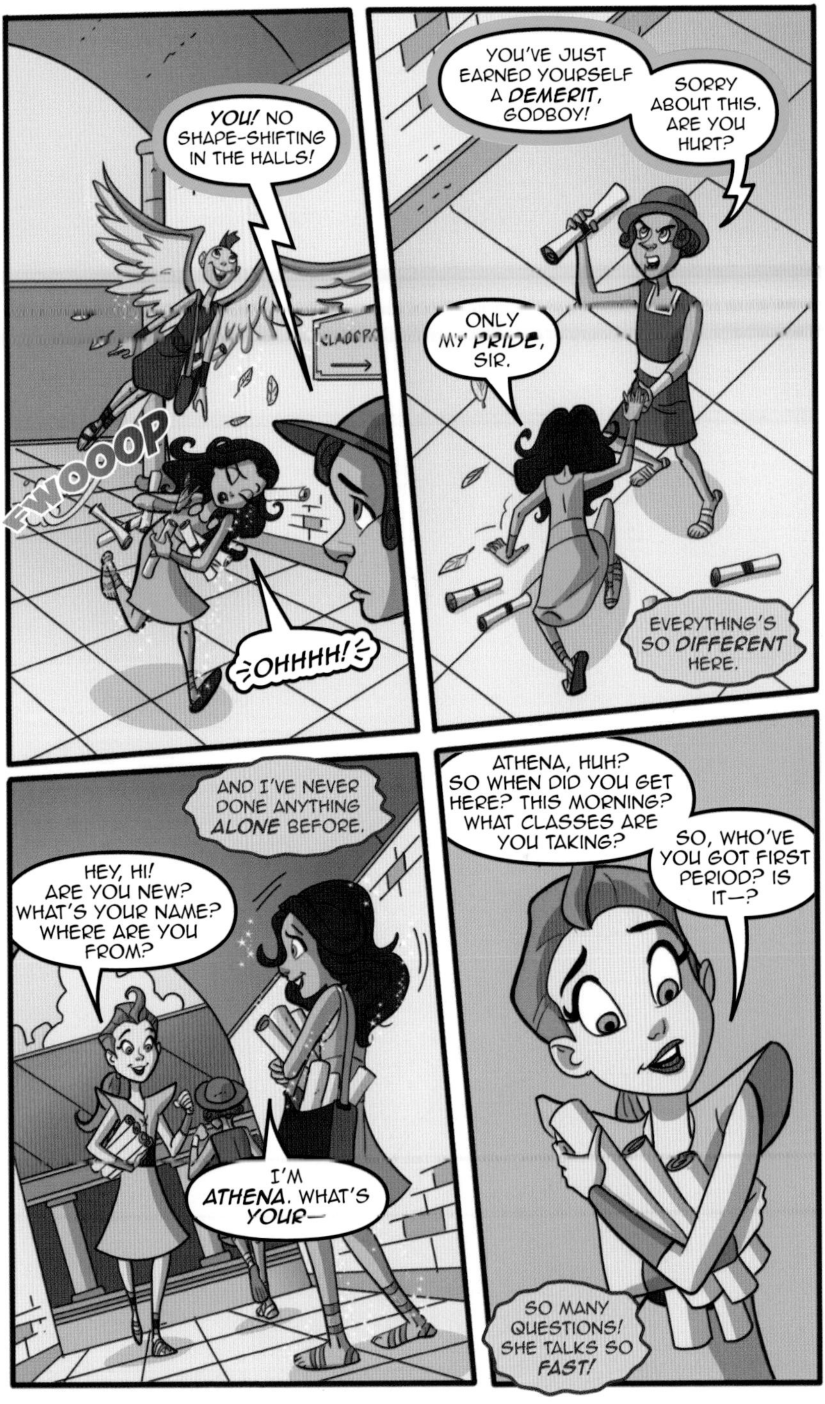
YOU! NO SHAPE-SHIFTING IN THE HALLS!
FWOOOP
OHHHH!
YOU'VE JUST EARNED YOURSELF A DEMERIT, GODBOY!
SORRY ABOUT THIS. ARE YOU HURT?
ONLY MY PRIDE, SIR.
EVERYTHING'S SO DIFFERENT HERE.
AND I'VE NEVER DONE ANYTHING ALONE BEFORE.
HEY, HI! ARE YOU NEW? WHAT'S YOUR NAME? WHERE ARE YOU FROM?
I'M ATHENA. WHAT'S YOUR—
ATHENA, HUH? SO WHEN DID YOU GET HERE? THIS MORNING? WHAT CLASSES ARE YOU TAKING?
SO, WHO'VE YOU GOT FIRST PERIOD? IS IT—?
SO MANY QUESTIONS! SHE TALKS SO FAST!

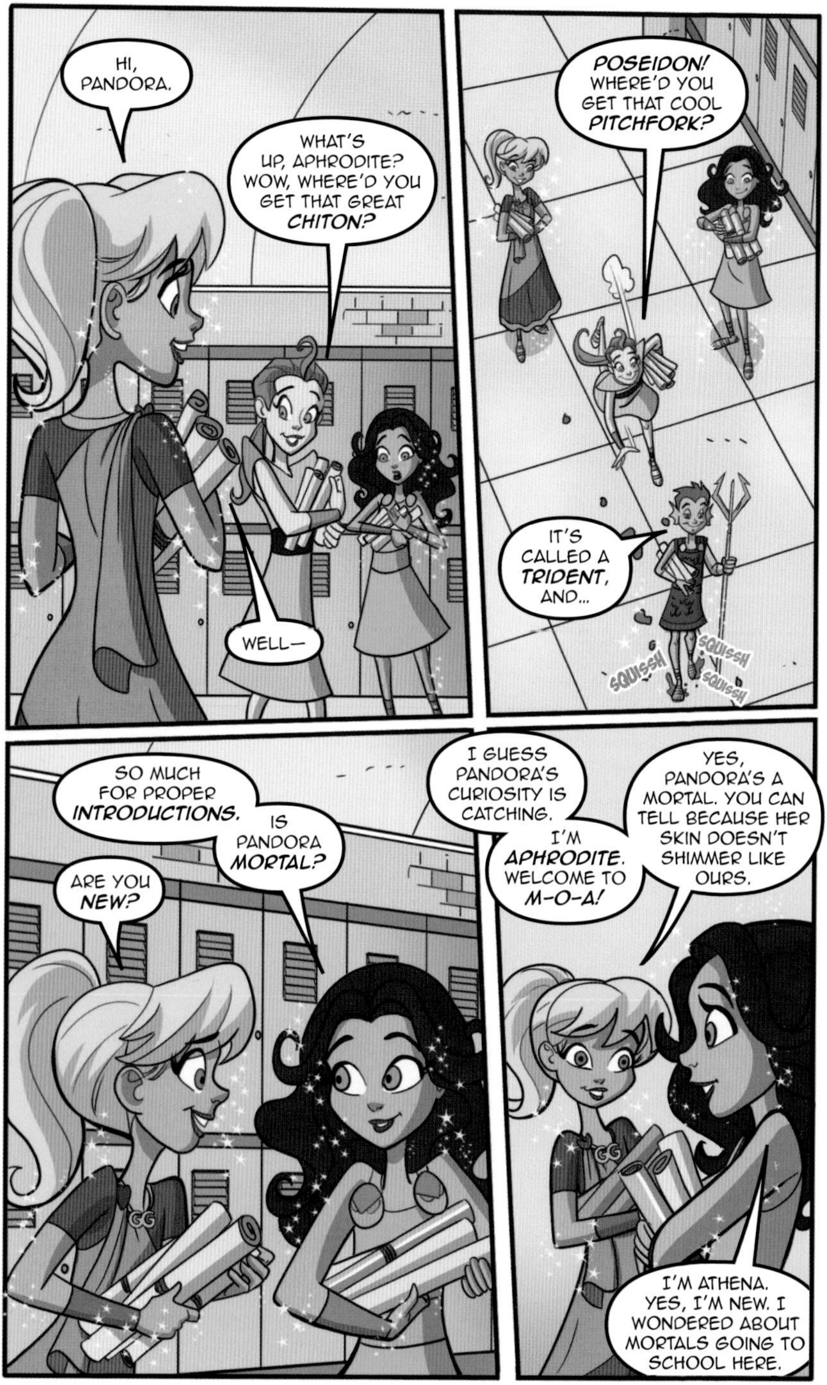
HI, PANDORA.
WHAT'S UP, APHRODITE? WOW, WHERE'D YOU GET THAT GREAT CHITON?
WELL—
POSEIDON! WHERE'D YOU GET THAT COOL PITCHFORK?
IT'S CALLED A TRIDENT, AND...
SQUISSH
SQUISSH
SQUISSH
SQUISSH
SO MUCH FOR PROPER INTRODUCTIONS.
ARE YOU NEW?
IS PANDORA MORTAL?
I GUESS PANDORA'S CURIOSITY IS CATCHING.
I'M APHRODITE. WELCOME TO M-O-A!
YES, PANDORA'S A MORTAL. YOU CAN TELL BECAUSE HER SKIN DOESN'T SHIMMER LIKE OURS.
I'M ATHENA. YES, I'M NEW. I WONDERED ABOUT MORTALS GOING TO SCHOOL HERE.

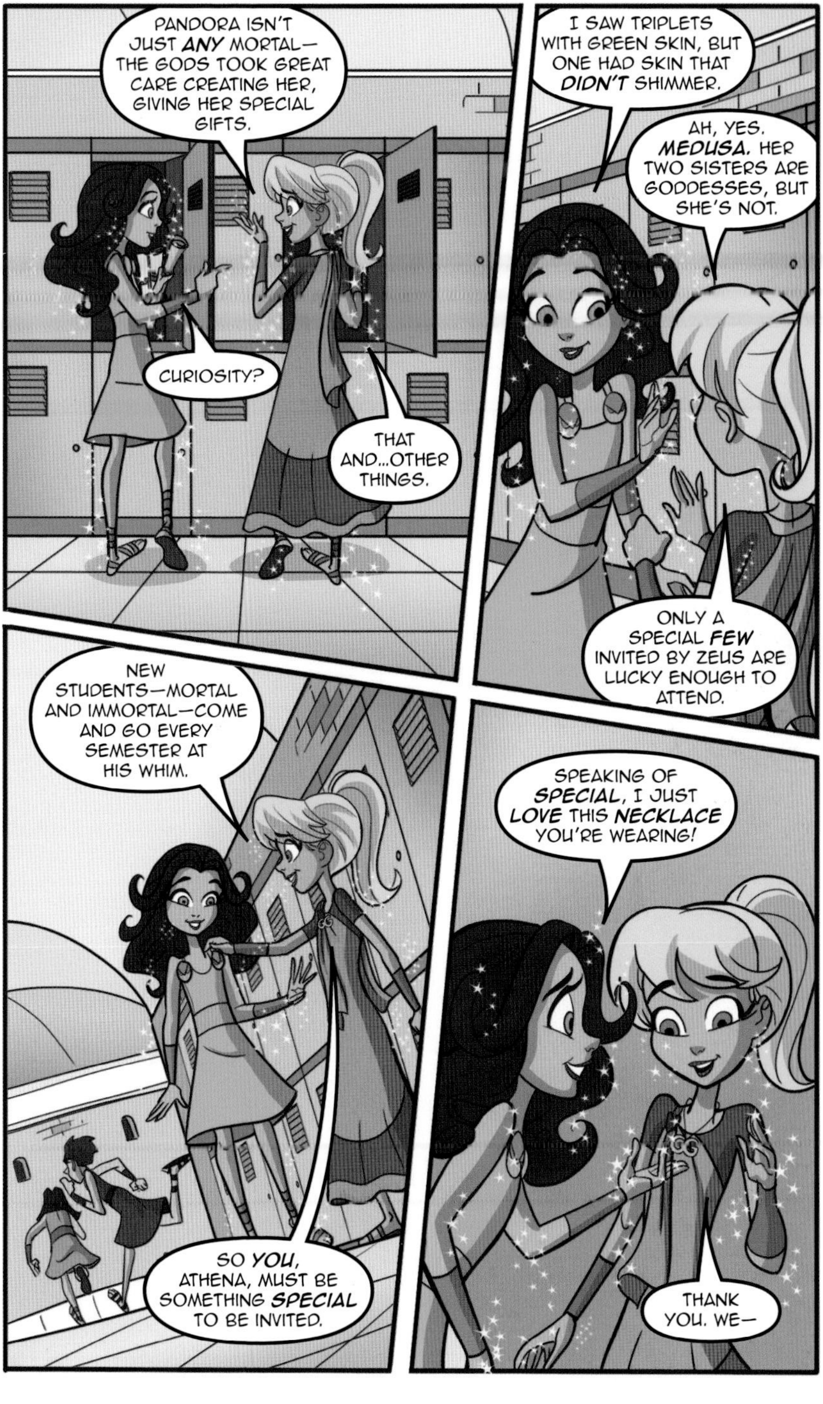
PANDORA ISN'T JUST ANY MORTAL—THE GODS TOOK GREAT CARE CREATING HER, GIVING HER SPECIAL GIFTS.
CURIOSITY?
THAT AND...OTHER THINGS.
I SAW TRIPLETS WITH GREEN SKIN, BUT ONE HAD SKIN THAT DIDN'T SHIMMER.
AH, YES. MEDUSA. HER TWO SISTERS ARE GODDESSES, BUT SHE'S NOT.
ONLY A SPECIAL FEW INVITED BY ZEUS ARE LUCKY ENOUGH TO ATTEND.
NEW STUDENTS—MORTAL AND IMMORTAL—COME AND GO EVERY SEMESTER AT HIS WHIM.
SO YOU, ATHENA, MUST BE SOMETHING SPECIAL TO BE INVITED.
SPEAKING OF SPECIAL, I JUST LOVE THIS NECKLACE YOU'RE WEARING!
THANK YOU. WE—

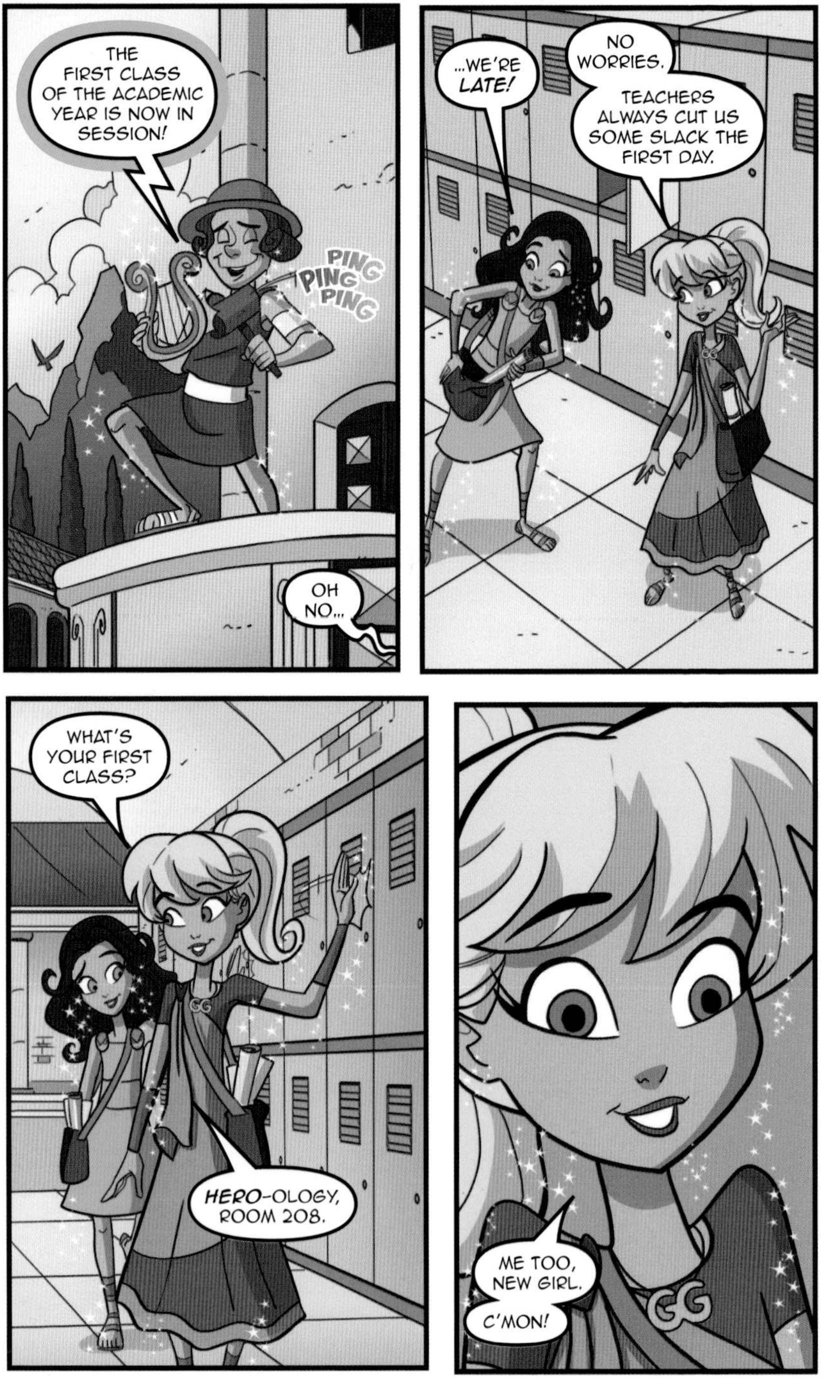
THE FIRST CLASS OF THE ACADEMIC YEAR IS NOW IN SESSION!
PING PING PING
OH NO...
...WE'RE LATE!
NO WORRIES.
TEACHERS ALWAYS CUT US SOME SLACK THE FIRST DAY.
WHAT'S YOUR FIRST CLASS?
HERO-OLOGY, ROOM 208.
ME TOO, NEW GIRL.
C'MON!

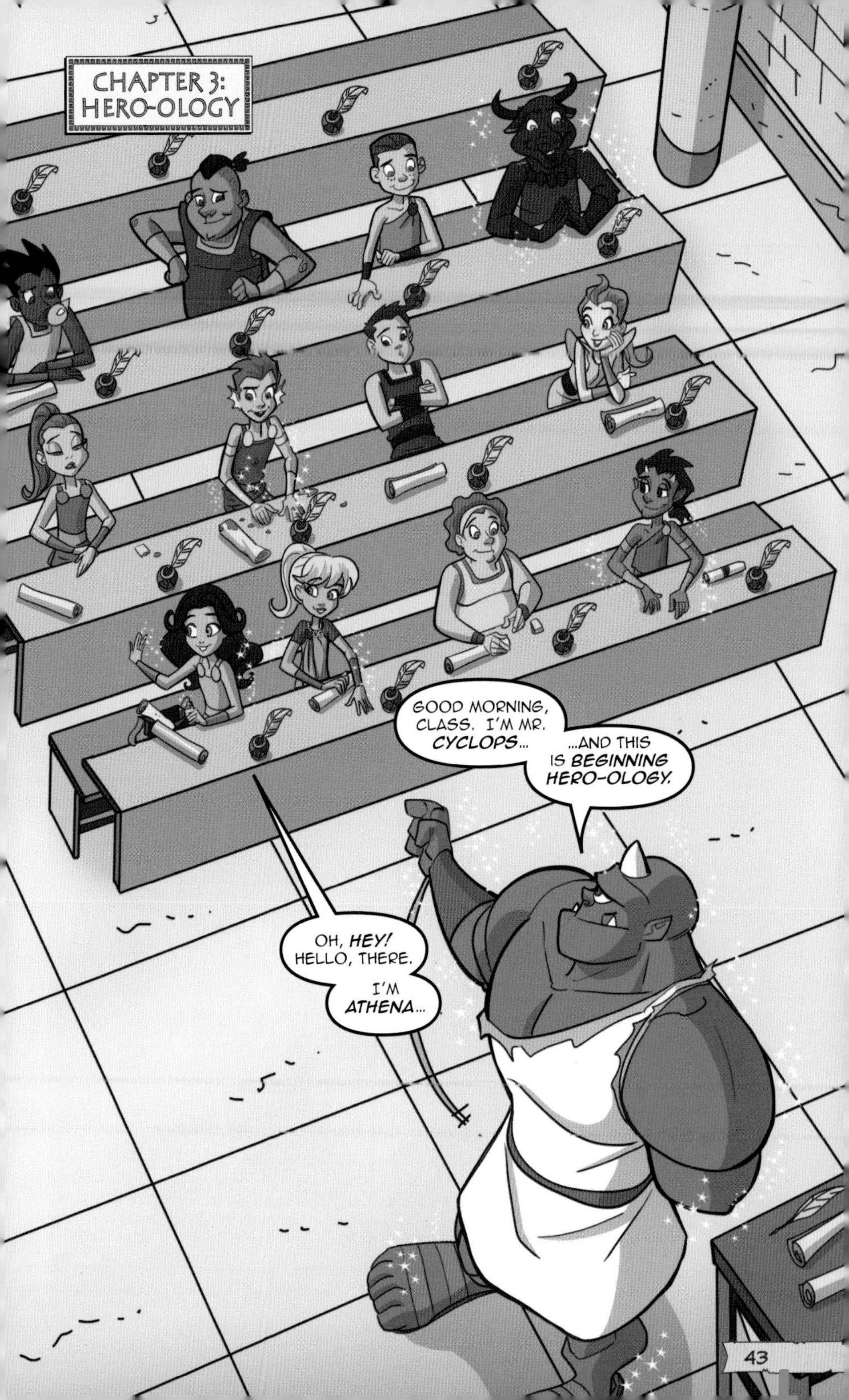
CHAPTER 3:
HERO-OLOGY
GOOD MORNING, CLASS. I'M MR. CYCLOPS...
...AND THIS IS BEGINNING HERO-OLOGY.
OH, HEY! HELLO, THERE.
I'M ATHENA...

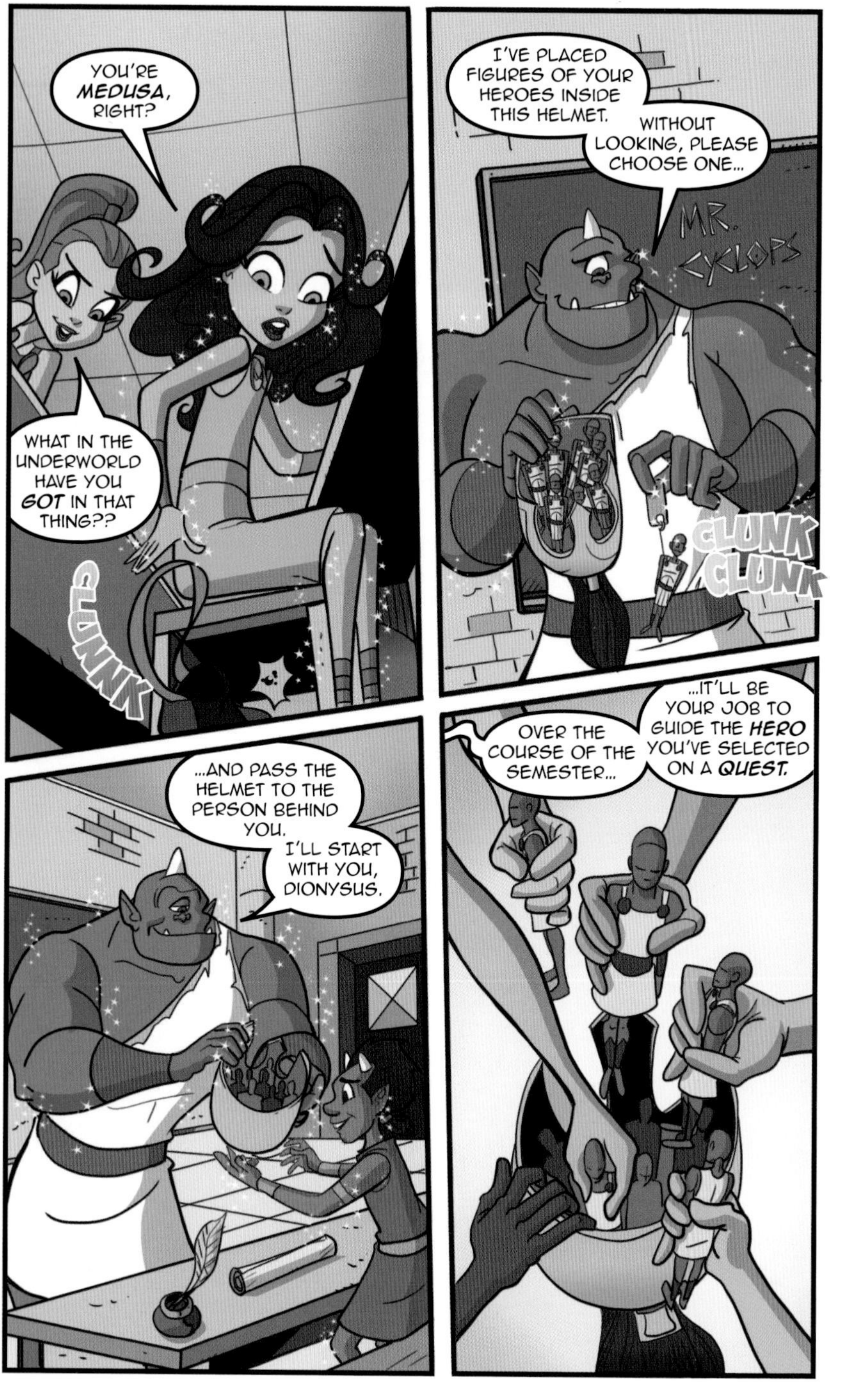
YOU'RE MEDUSA, RIGHT?
WHAT IN THE UNDERWORLD HAVE YOU GOT IN THAT THING??
CLUNNK
I'VE PLACED FIGURES OF YOUR HEROES INSIDE THIS HELMET.
WITHOUT LOOKING, PLEASE CHOOSE ONE...
MR. CYCLOPS
CLUNK CLUNK
...AND PASS THE HELMET TO THE PERSON BEHIND YOU.
I'LL START WITH YOU, DIONYSUS.
OVER THE COURSE OF THE SEMESTER...
...IT'LL BE YOUR JOB TO GUIDE THE HERO YOU'VE SELECTED ON A QUEST.

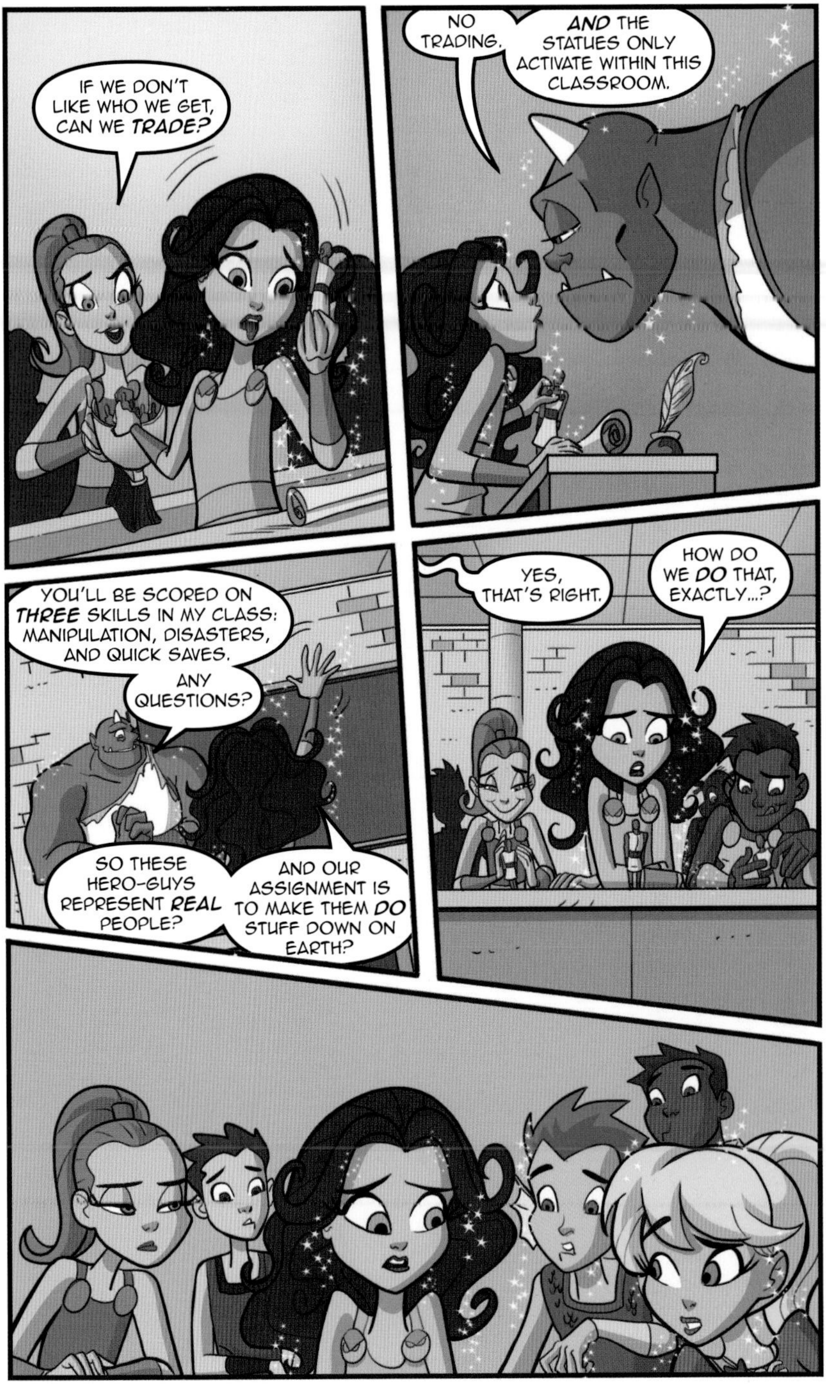
IF WE DON'T LIKE WHO WE GET, CAN WE *TRADE?*
NO TRADING.
AND THE STATUES ONLY ACTIVATE WITHIN THIS CLASSROOM.
YOU'LL BE SCORED ON *THREE* SKILLS IN MY CLASS: MANIPULATION, DISASTERS, AND QUICK SAVES.
ANY QUESTIONS?
SO THESE HERO-GUYS REPRESENT *REAL* PEOPLE?
AND OUR ASSIGNMENT IS TO MAKE THEM *DO* STUFF DOWN ON EARTH?
YES, THAT'S RIGHT.
HOW DO WE *DO* THAT, EXACTLY...?

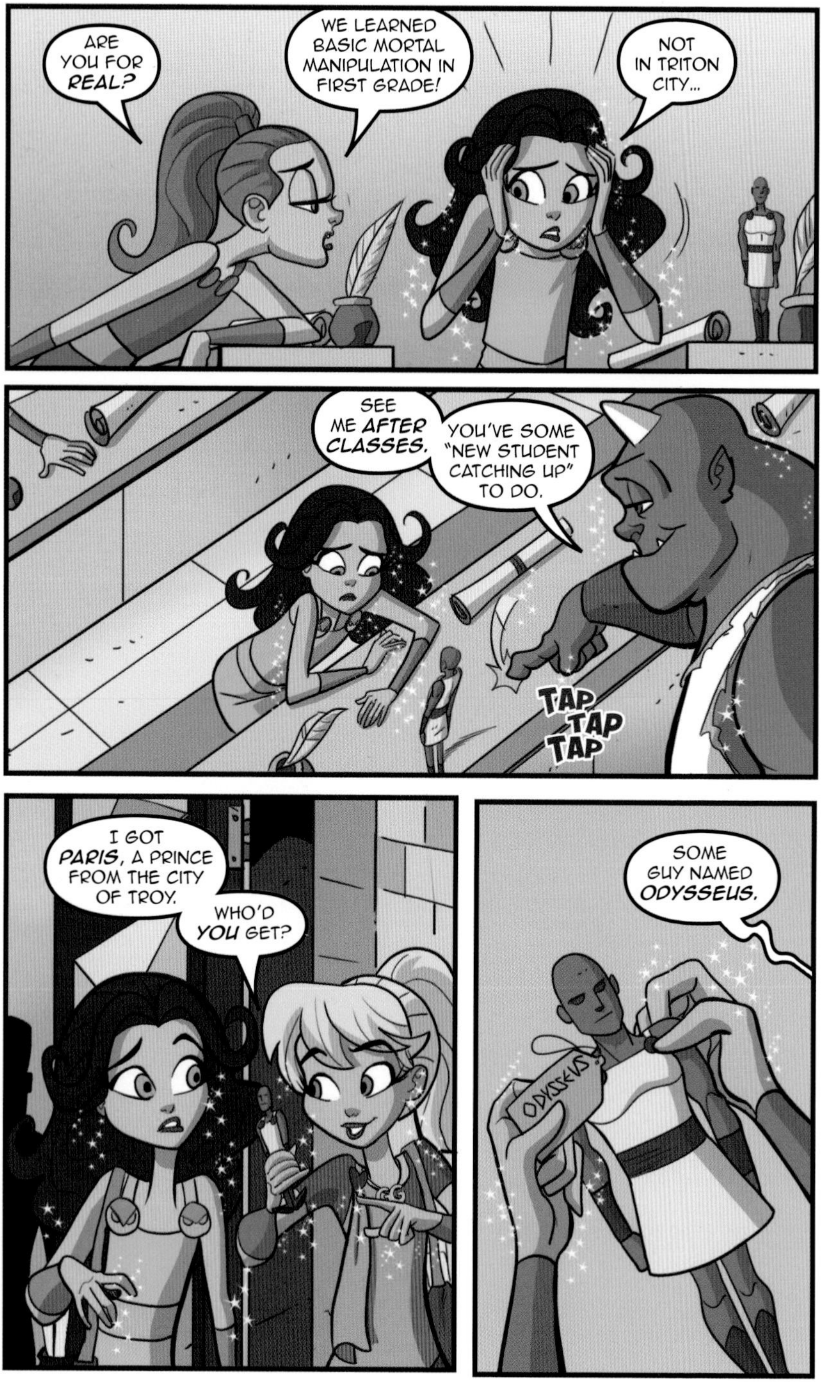
ARE YOU FOR REAL?
WE LEARNED BASIC MORTAL MANIPULATION IN FIRST GRADE!
NOT IN TRITON CITY...
SEE ME AFTER CLASSES.
YOU'VE SOME "NEW STUDENT CATCHING UP" TO DO.
TAP TAP TAP
I GOT PARIS, A PRINCE FROM THE CITY OF TROY.
WHO'D YOU GET?
SOME GUY NAMED ODYSSEUS.
ODYSSEUS

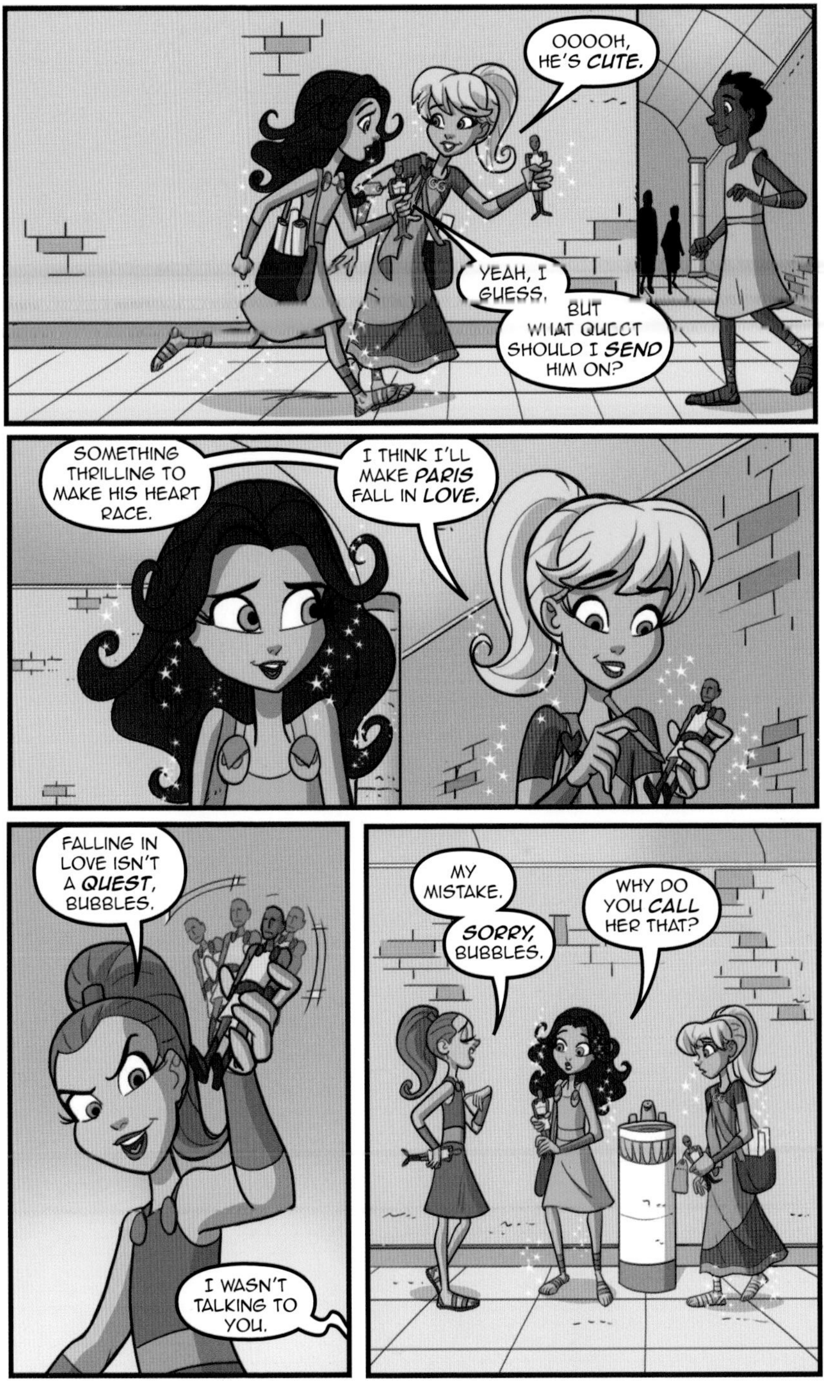
OOOOH, HE'S *CUTE.*
YEAH, I GUESS.
BUT WHAT QUEST SHOULD I *SEND* HIM ON?
SOMETHING THRILLING TO MAKE HIS HEART RACE.
I THINK I'LL MAKE *PARIS* FALL IN *LOVE.*
FALLING IN LOVE ISN'T A *QUEST,* BUBBLES.
I WASN'T TALKING TO YOU.
MY MISTAKE.
SORRY, BUBBLES.
WHY DO YOU *CALL* HER THAT?

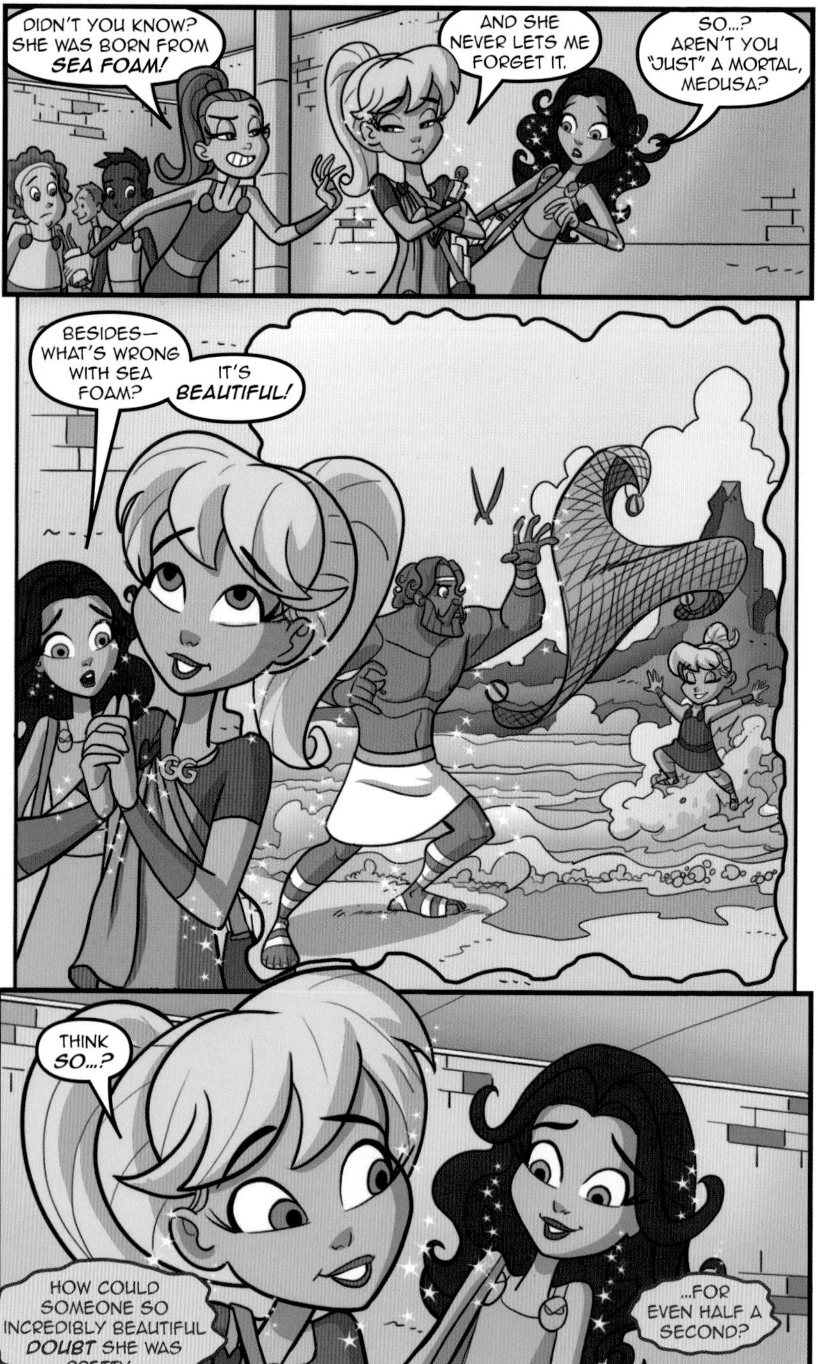
DIDN'T YOU KNOW? SHE WAS BORN FROM SEA FOAM!
AND SHE NEVER LETS ME FORGET IT.
SO...? AREN'T YOU "JUST" A MORTAL, MEDUSA?
BESIDES— WHAT'S WRONG WITH SEA FOAM?
IT'S BEAUTIFUL!
THINK SO...?
HOW COULD SOMEONE SO INCREDIBLY BEAUTIFUL DOUBT SHE WAS PRETTY...
...FOR EVEN HALF A SECOND?

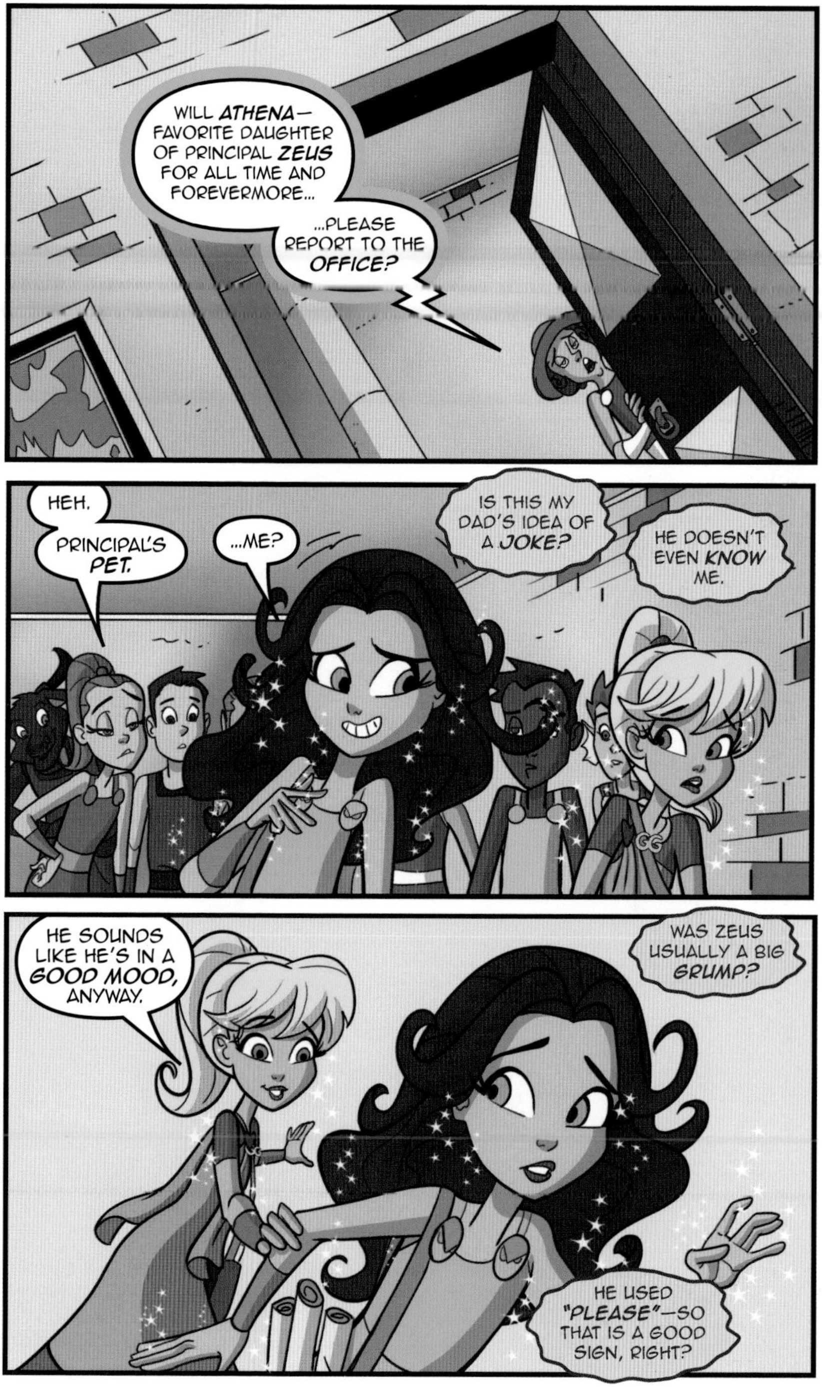
WILL ATHENA— FAVORITE DAUGHTER OF PRINCIPAL ZEUS FOR ALL TIME AND FOREVERMORE...
...PLEASE REPORT TO THE OFFICE?
HEH.
PRINCIPAL'S PET.
...ME?
IS THIS MY DAD'S IDEA OF A JOKE?
HE DOESN'T EVEN KNOW ME.
HE SOUNDS LIKE HE'S IN A GOOD MOOD, ANYWAY.
WAS ZEUS USUALLY A BIG GRUMP?
HE USED "PLEASE"—SO THAT IS A GOOD SIGN, RIGHT?

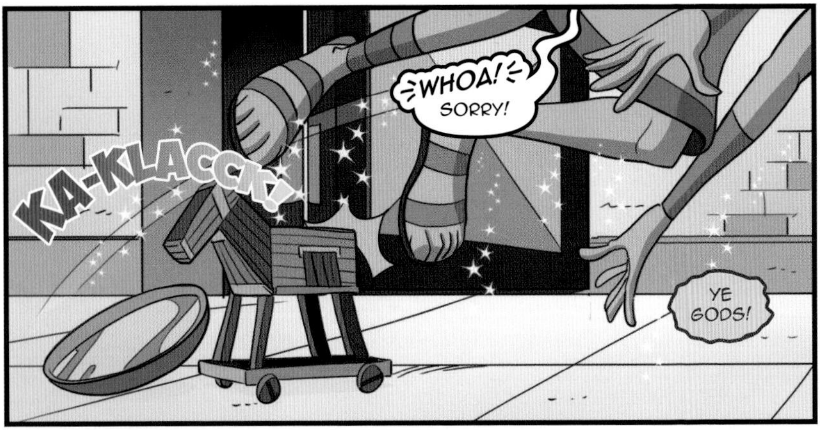
WHOA! SORRY!
KA-KLACCK!
YE GODS!

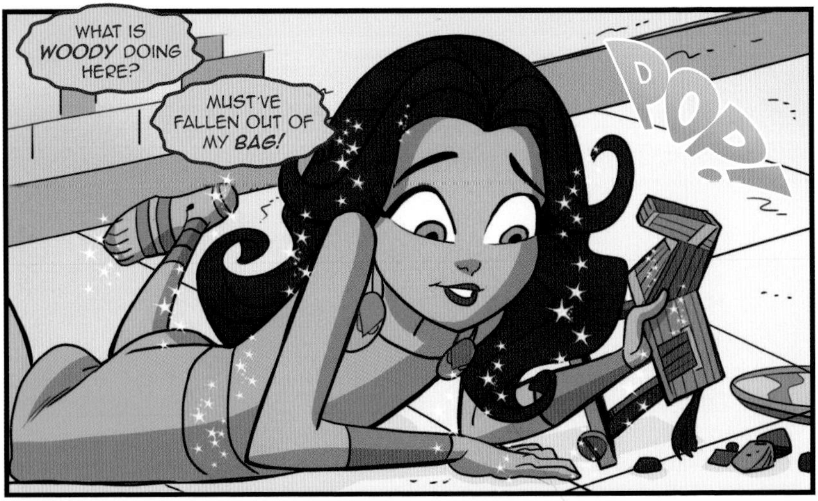
WHAT IS WOODY DOING HERE?
MUST'VE FALLEN OUT OF MY BAG!
POP!

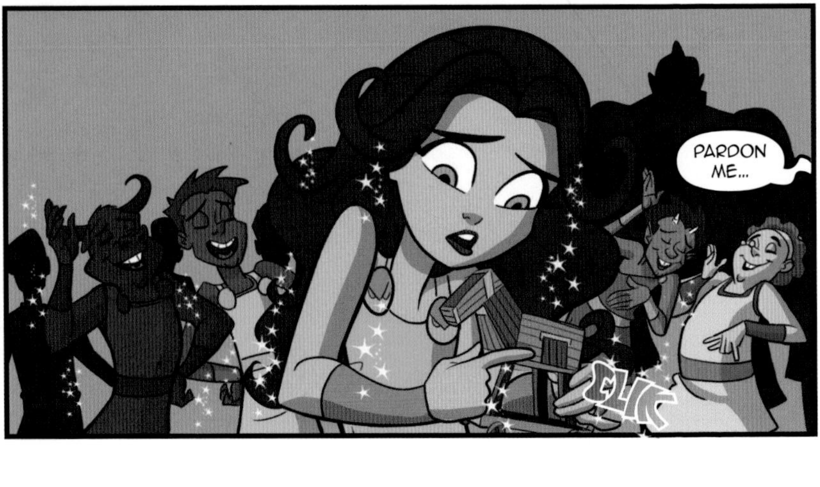
PARDON ME...

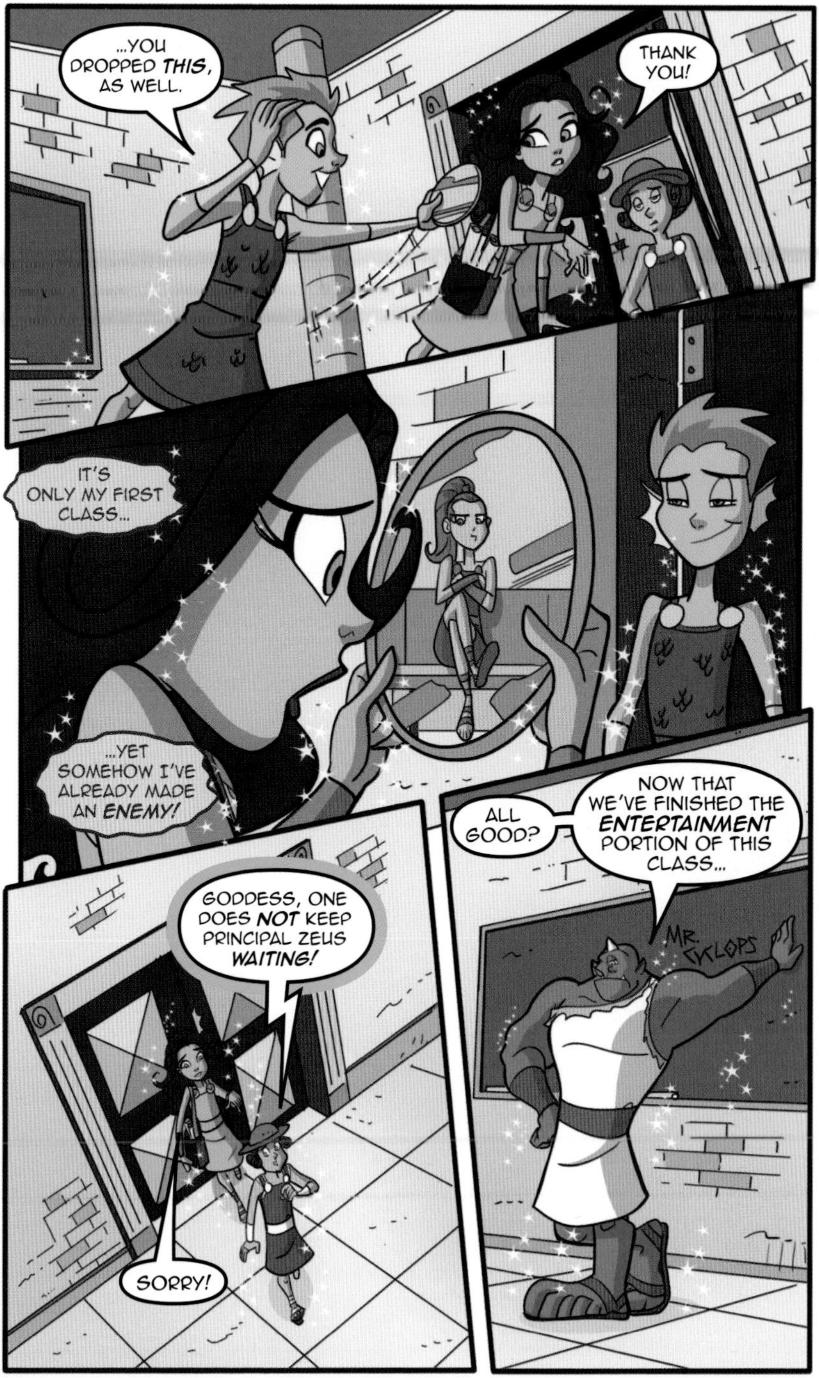
...YOU DROPPED THIS, AS WELL.
THANK YOU!
IT'S ONLY MY FIRST CLASS...
...YET SOMEHOW I'VE ALREADY MADE AN ENEMY!
GODDESS, ONE DOES NOT KEEP PRINCIPAL ZEUS WAITING!
SORRY!
ALL GOOD?
NOW THAT WE'VE FINISHED THE ENTERTAINMENT PORTION OF THIS CLASS...
MR. CYCLOPS

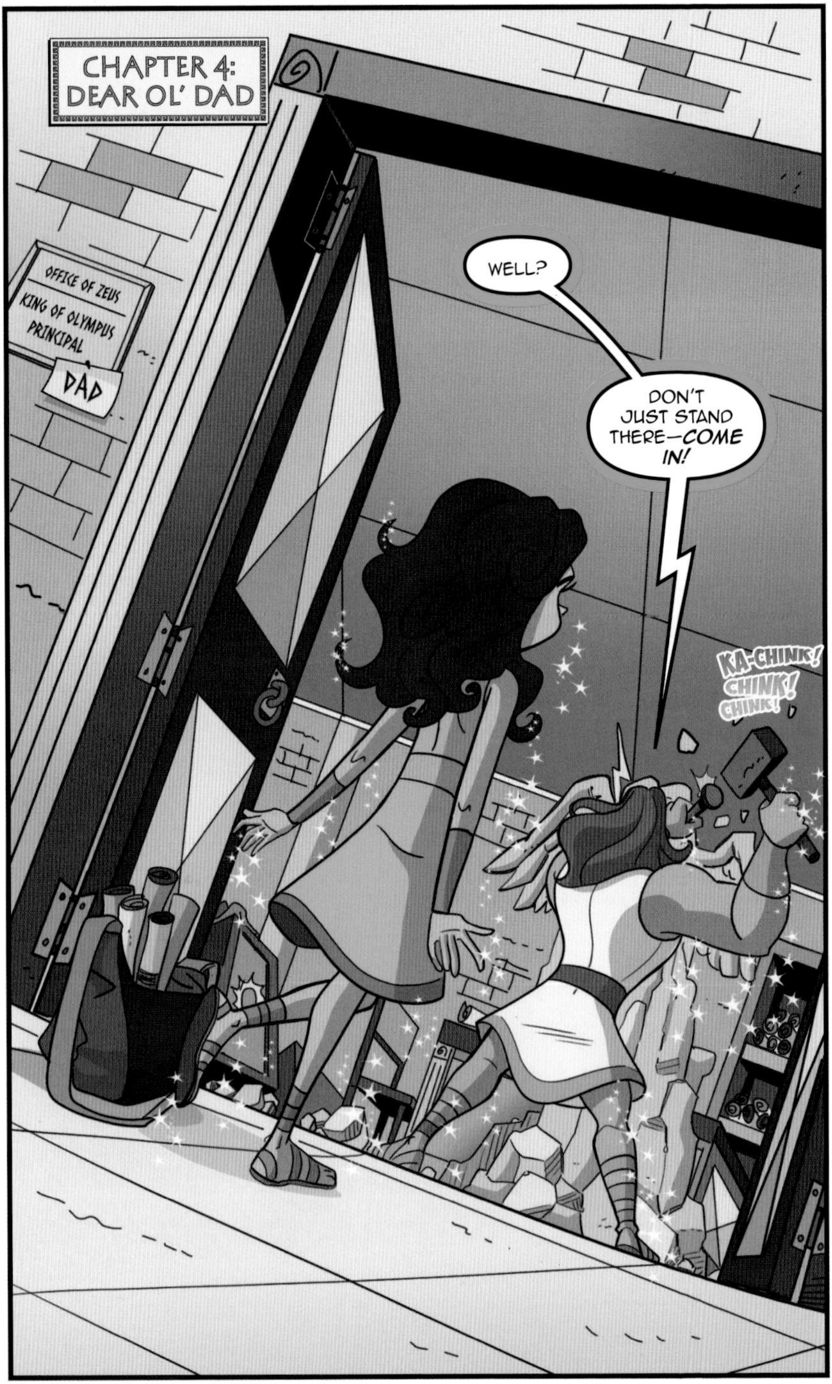
CHAPTER 4:
DEAR OL' DAD
OFFICE OF ZEUS
KING OF OLYMPUS
PRINCIPAL
DAD
WELL?
DON'T JUST STAND THERE—*COME IN!*
KA-CHINK! CHINK! CHINK!

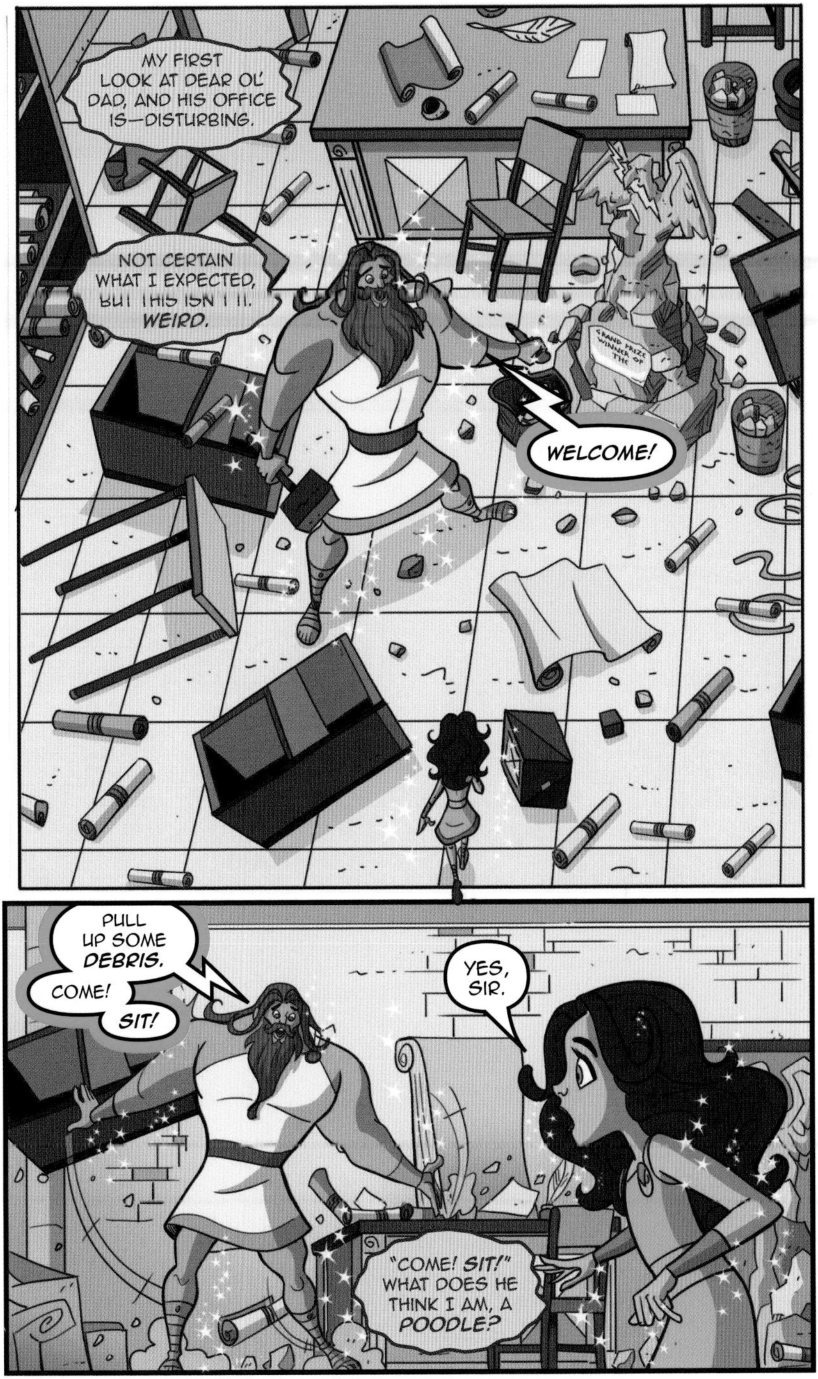
MY FIRST LOOK AT DEAR OL' DAD, AND HIS OFFICE IS—DISTURBING.
NOT CERTAIN WHAT I EXPECTED, BUT THIS ISN'T IT. WEIRD.
WELCOME!
PULL UP SOME DEBRIS.
COME!
SIT!
YES, SIR.
"COME! SIT!" WHAT DOES HE THINK I AM, A POODLE?

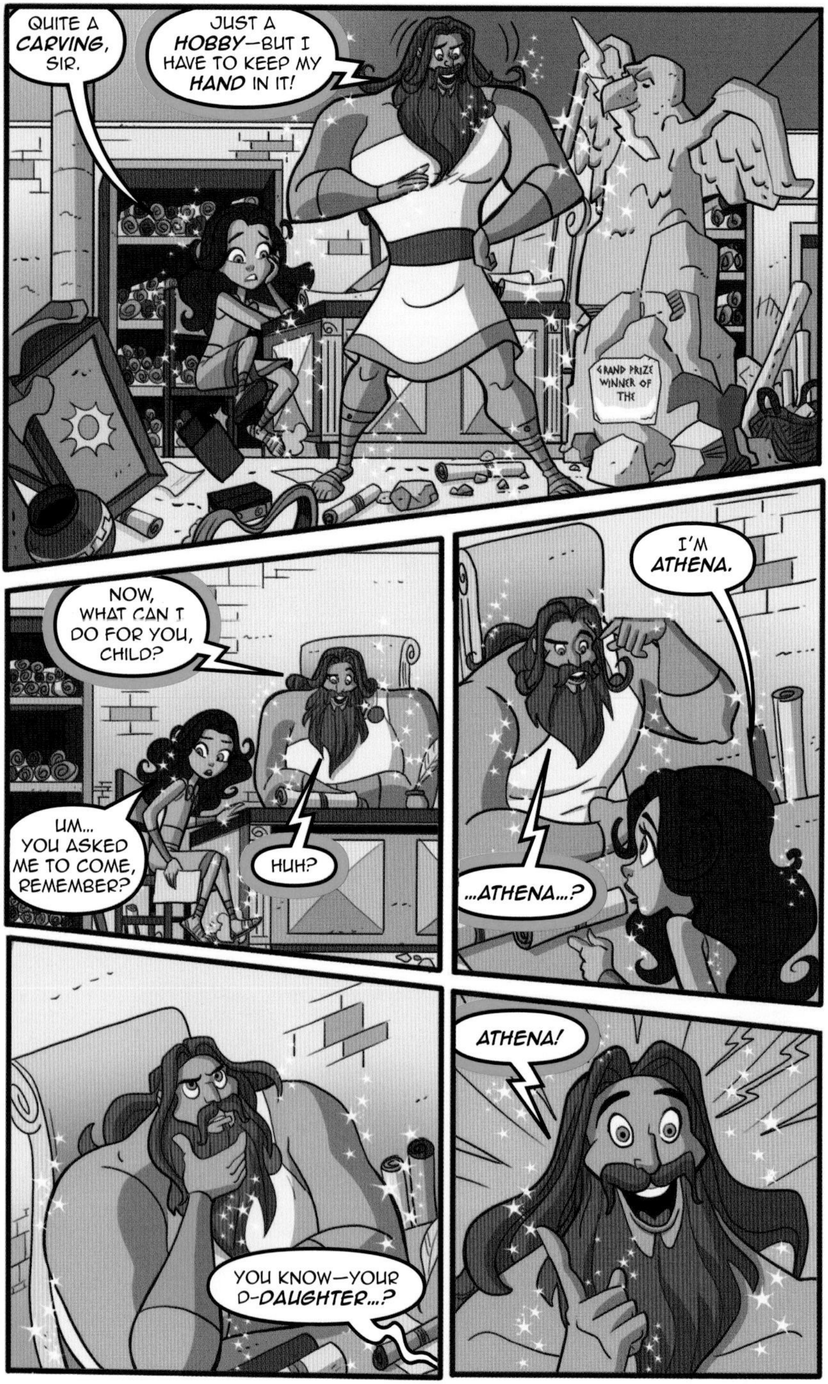
QUITE A CARVING, SIR.
JUST A HOBBY—BUT I HAVE TO KEEP MY HAND IN IT!
GRAND PRIZE WINNER OF THE
NOW, WHAT CAN I DO FOR YOU, CHILD?
UM... YOU ASKED ME TO COME, REMEMBER?
HUH?
I'M ATHENA.
...ATHENA...?
YOU KNOW—YOUR D-DAUGHTER...?
ATHENA!

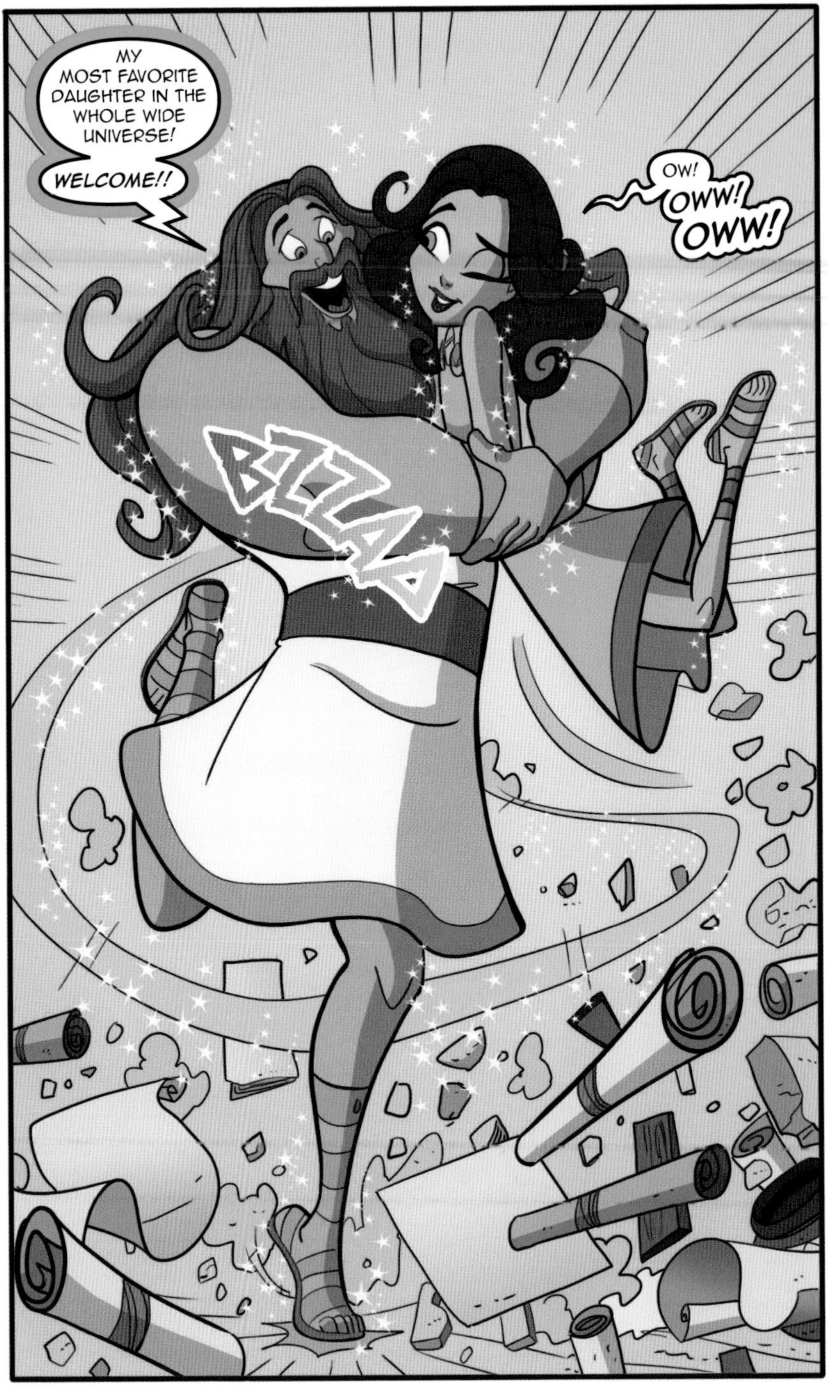
MY MOST FAVORITE DAUGHTER IN THE WHOLE WIDE UNIVERSE!
WELCOME!!
OW! OWW! OWW!
BZZZAP

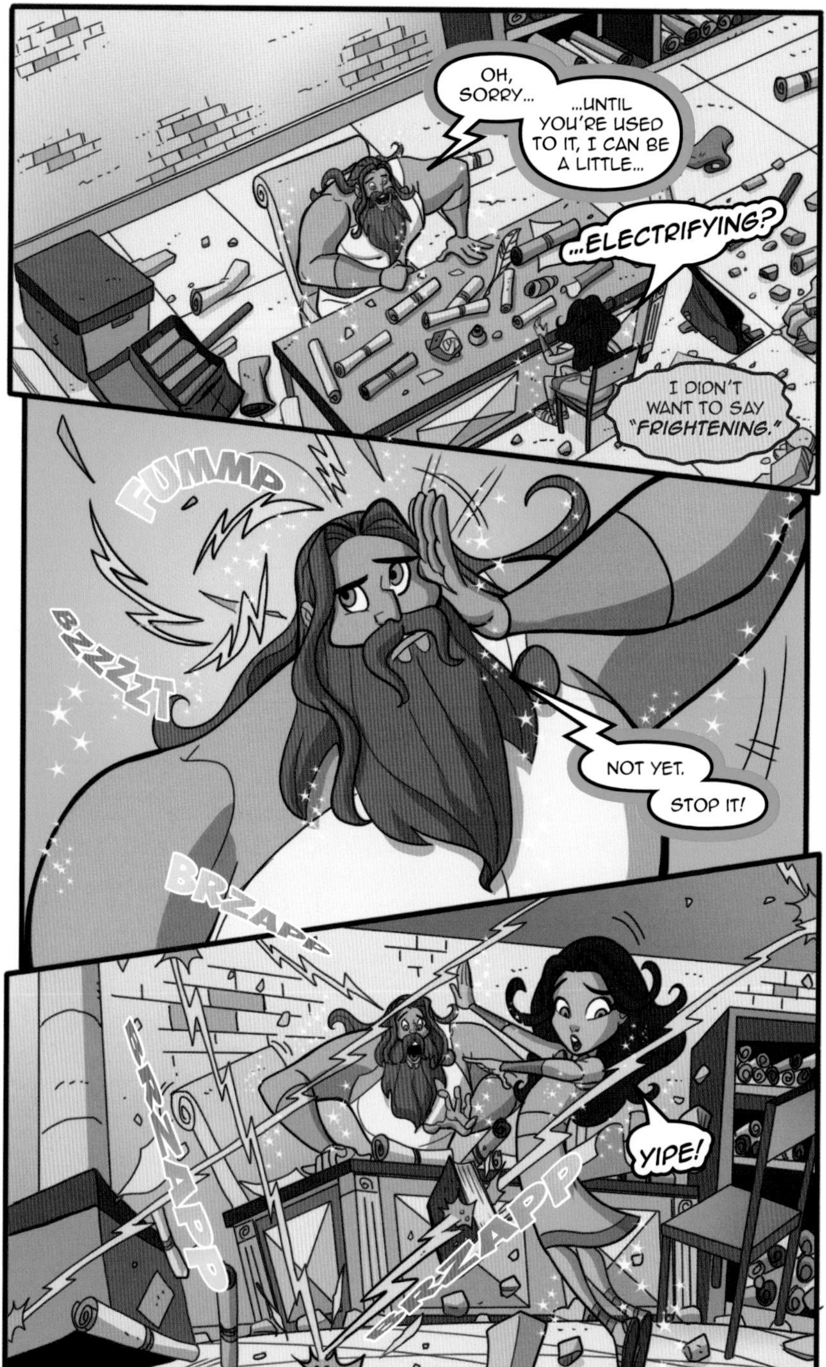
OH, SORRY...
...UNTIL YOU'RE USED TO IT, I CAN BE A LITTLE...
...ELECTRIFYING?
I DIDN'T WANT TO SAY "FRIGHTENING."
FUMMP
BZZZZT
NOT YET.
STOP IT!
BRZAPP
BRZAPP
YIPE!
BRZAPP

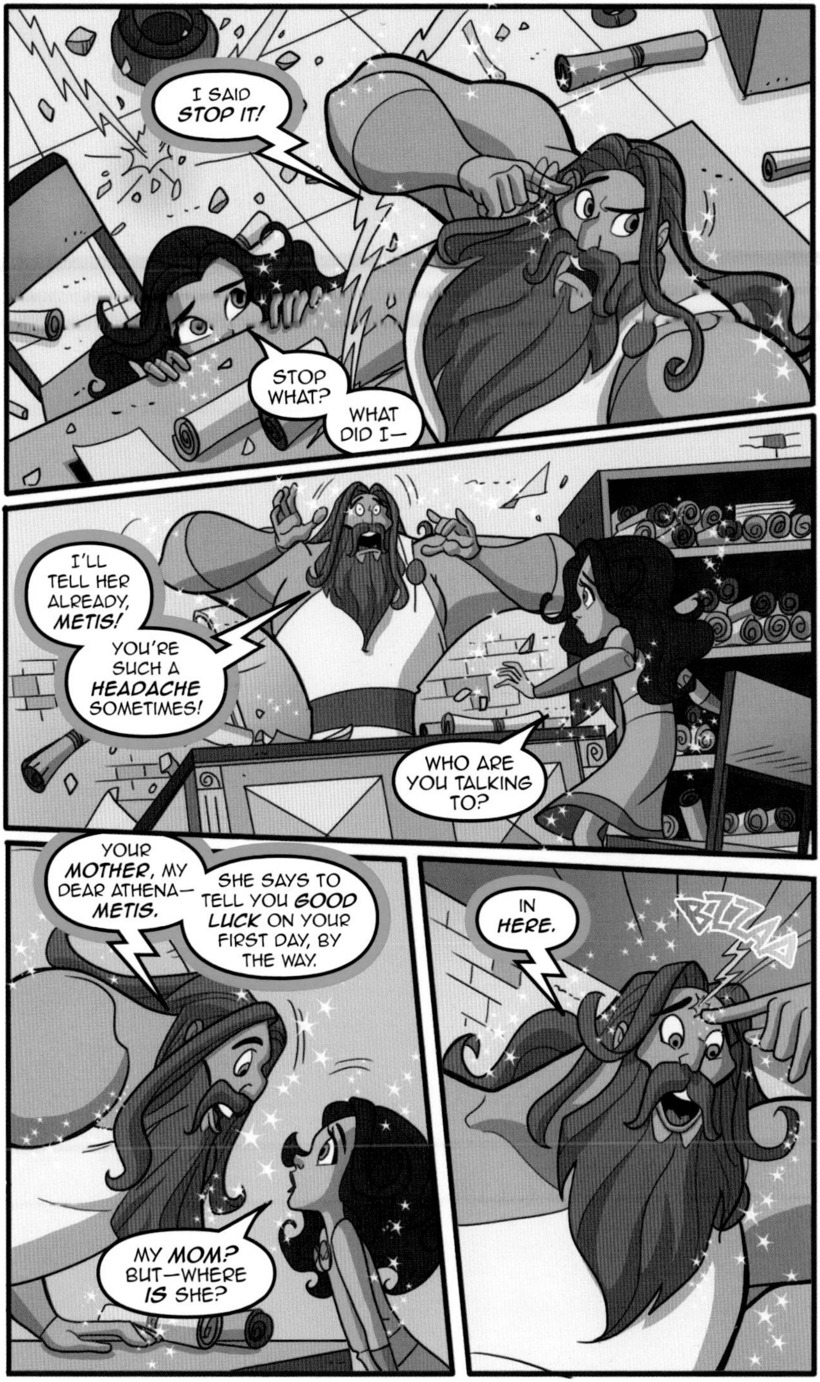
I SAID STOP IT!
STOP WHAT?
WHAT DID I—
I'LL TELL HER ALREADY, METIS!
YOU'RE SUCH A HEADACHE SOMETIMES!
WHO ARE YOU TALKING TO?
YOUR MOTHER, MY DEAR ATHENA—METIS.
SHE SAYS TO TELL YOU GOOD LUCK ON YOUR FIRST DAY, BY THE WAY.
MY MOM? BUT—WHERE IS SHE?
IN HERE.
BZZAP

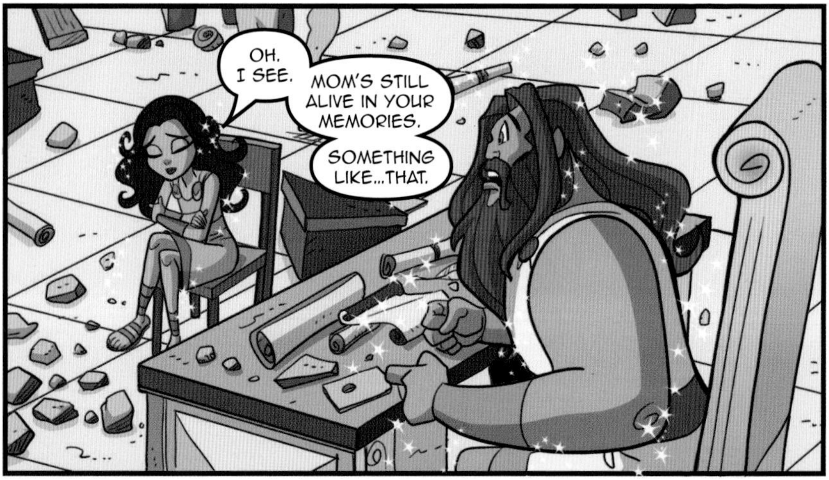
OH. I SEE.
MOM'S STILL ALIVE IN YOUR MEMORIES.
SOMETHING LIKE...THAT.

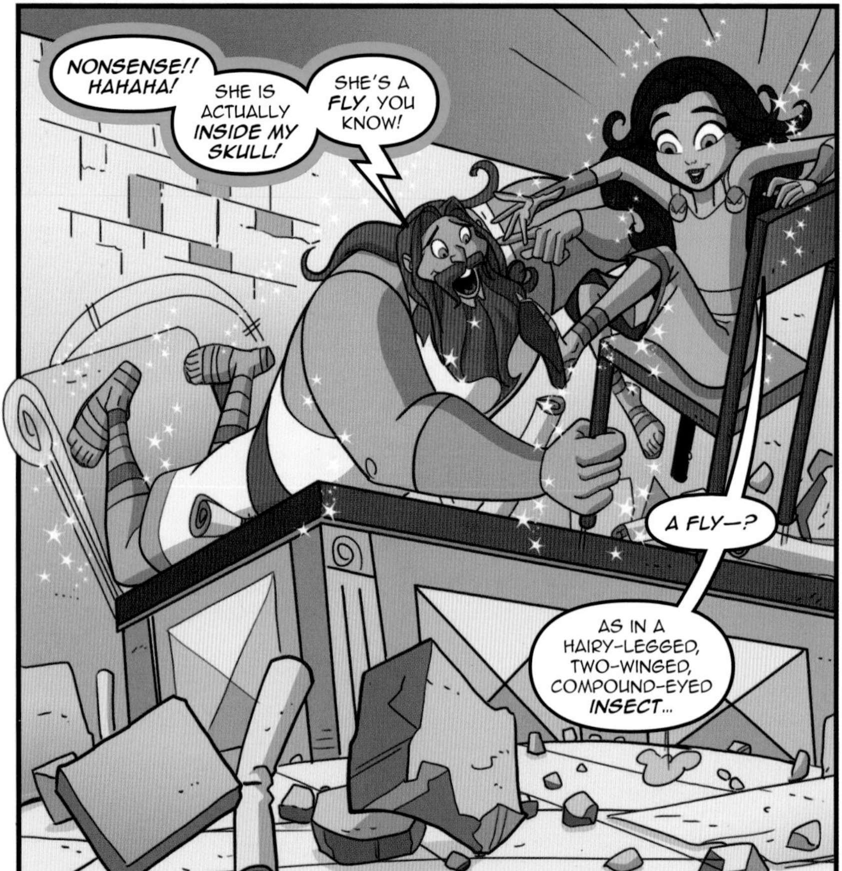
NONSENSE!! HAHAHA!
SHE IS ACTUALLY INSIDE MY SKULL!
SHE'S A FLY, YOU KNOW!
A FLY—?
AS IN A HAIRY-LEGGED, TWO-WINGED, COMPOUND-EYED INSECT...

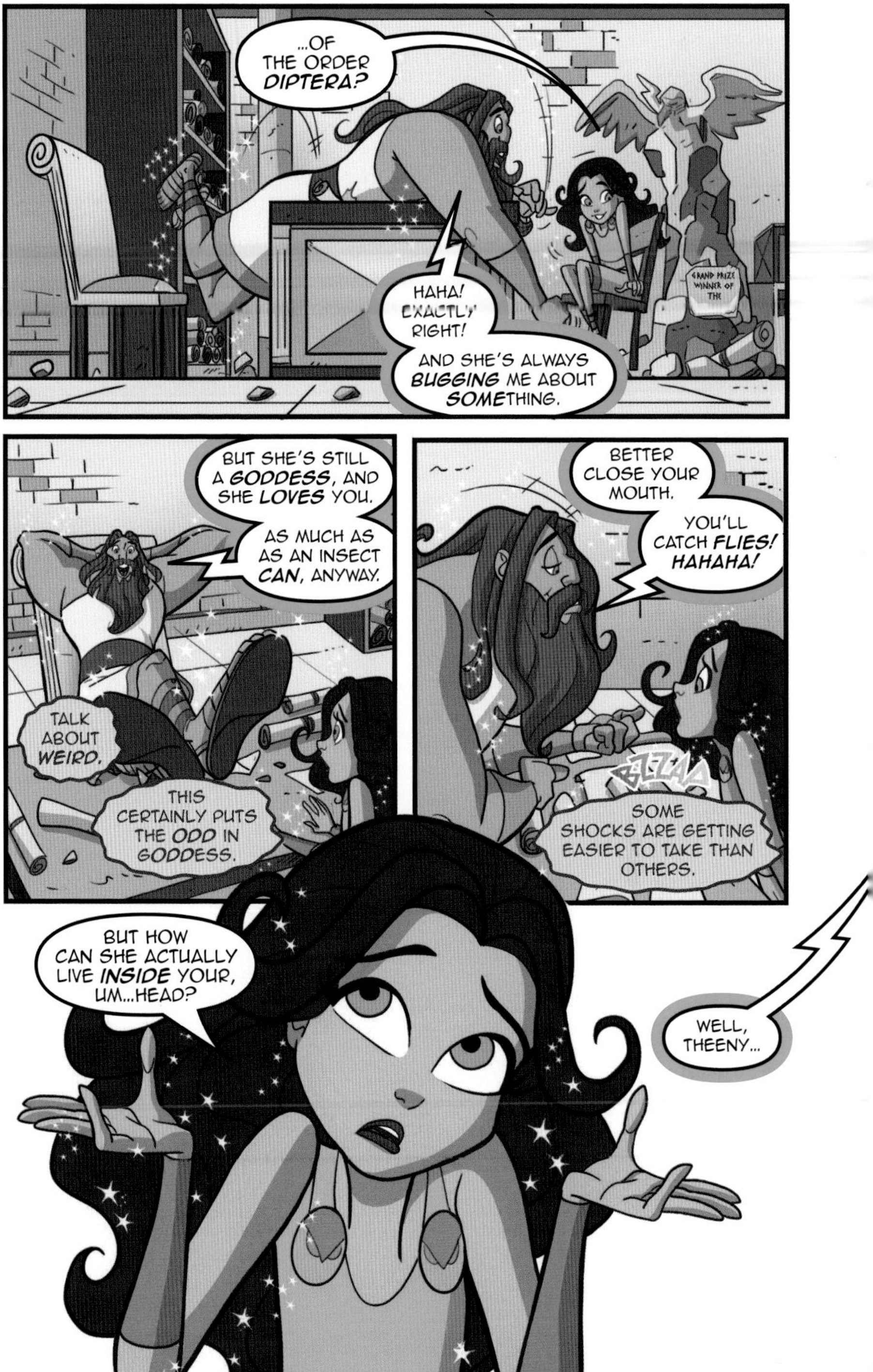
...OF THE ORDER *DIPTERA?*
HAHA! EXACTLY RIGHT!
AND SHE'S ALWAYS *BUGGING* ME ABOUT *SOME*THING.
GRAND PRIZE WINNER OF THE
BUT SHE'S STILL A *GODDESS*, AND SHE *LOVES* YOU.
AS MUCH AS AS AN INSECT *CAN*, ANYWAY.
TALK ABOUT *WEIRD*.
THIS CERTAINLY PUTS THE *ODD* IN GODDESS.
BETTER CLOSE YOUR MOUTH.
YOU'LL CATCH *FLIES! HAHAHA!*
SOME SHOCKS ARE GETTING EASIER TO TAKE THAN OTHERS.
BUT HOW CAN SHE ACTUALLY LIVE *INSIDE* YOUR, UM...HEAD?
WELL, THEENY...

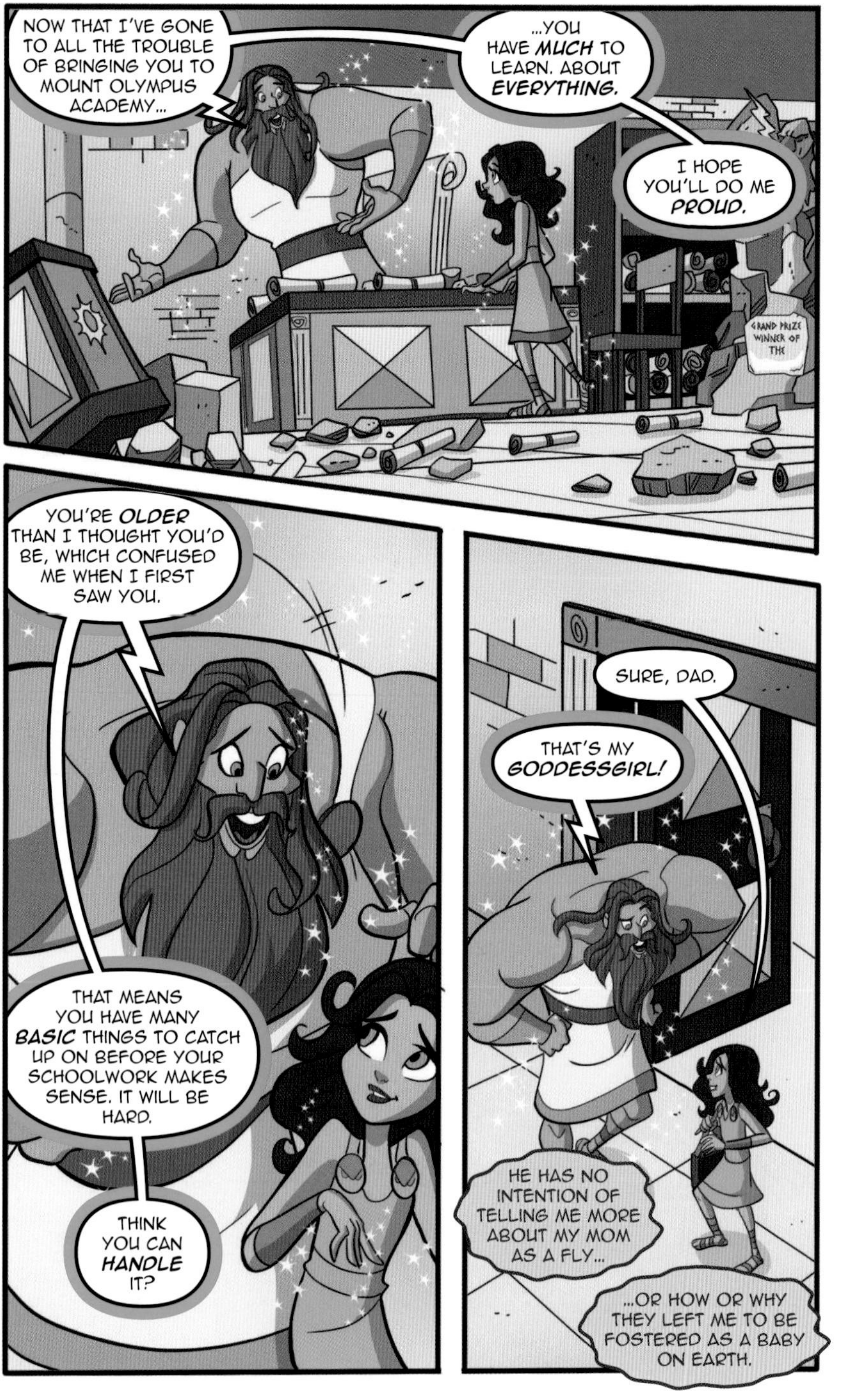
NOW THAT I'VE GONE TO ALL THE TROUBLE OF BRINGING YOU TO MOUNT OLYMPUS ACADEMY...
...YOU HAVE MUCH TO LEARN. ABOUT EVERYTHING.
I HOPE YOU'LL DO ME PROUD.
GRAND PRIZE WINNER OF THE
YOU'RE OLDER THAN I THOUGHT YOU'D BE, WHICH CONFUSED ME WHEN I FIRST SAW YOU.
THAT MEANS YOU HAVE MANY BASIC THINGS TO CATCH UP ON BEFORE YOUR SCHOOLWORK MAKES SENSE. IT WILL BE HARD.
THINK YOU CAN HANDLE IT?
SURE, DAD.
THAT'S MY GODDESSGIRL!
HE HAS NO INTENTION OF TELLING ME MORE ABOUT MY MOM AS A FLY...
...OR HOW OR WHY THEY LEFT ME TO BE FOSTERED AS A BABY ON EARTH.

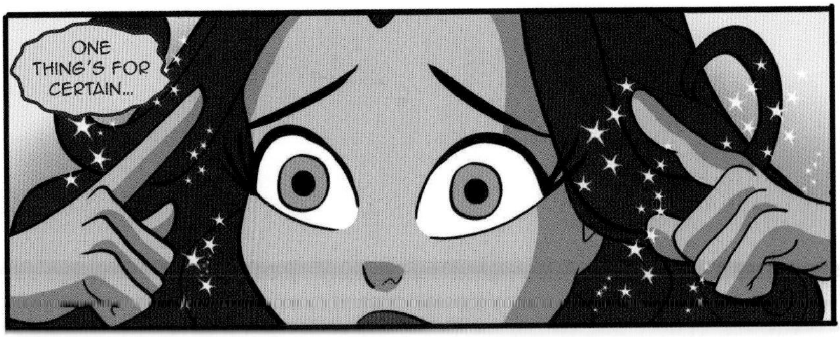
ONE THING'S FOR CERTAIN...

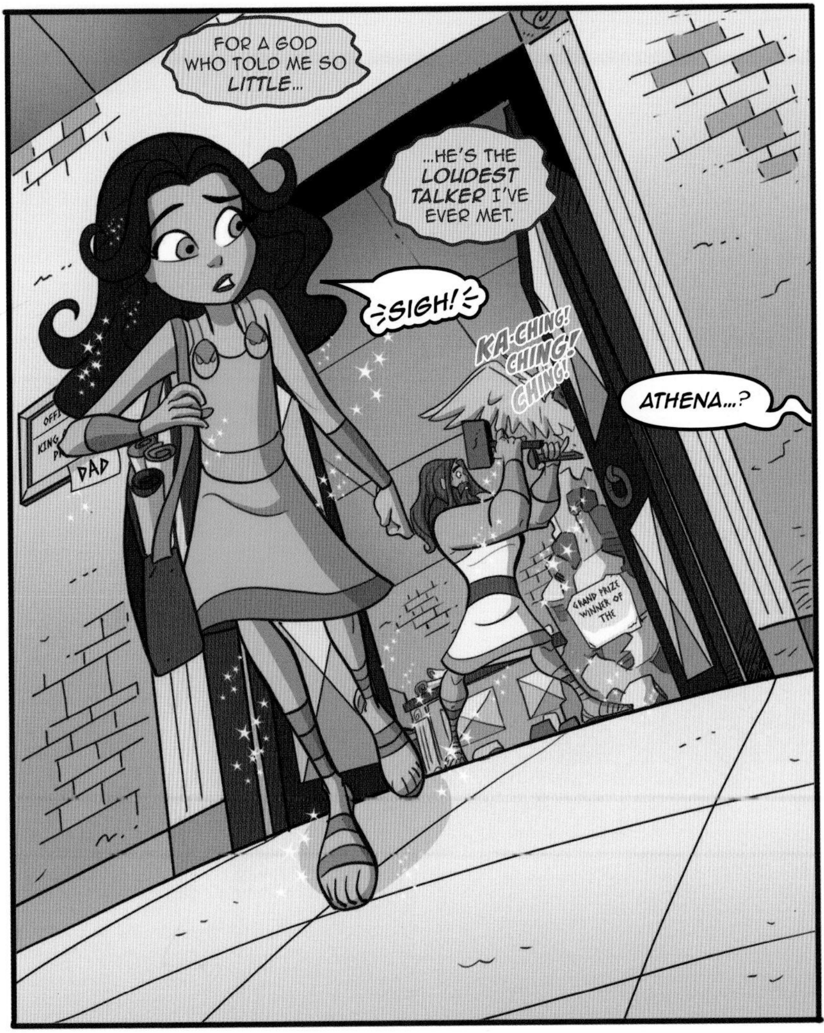
FOR A GOD WHO TOLD ME SO *LITTLE*...
...HE'S THE *LOUDEST TALKER* I'VE EVER MET.
SIGH!
KA-CHING! CHING! CHING!
ATHENA...?
DAD
GRAND PRIZE WINNER OF THE

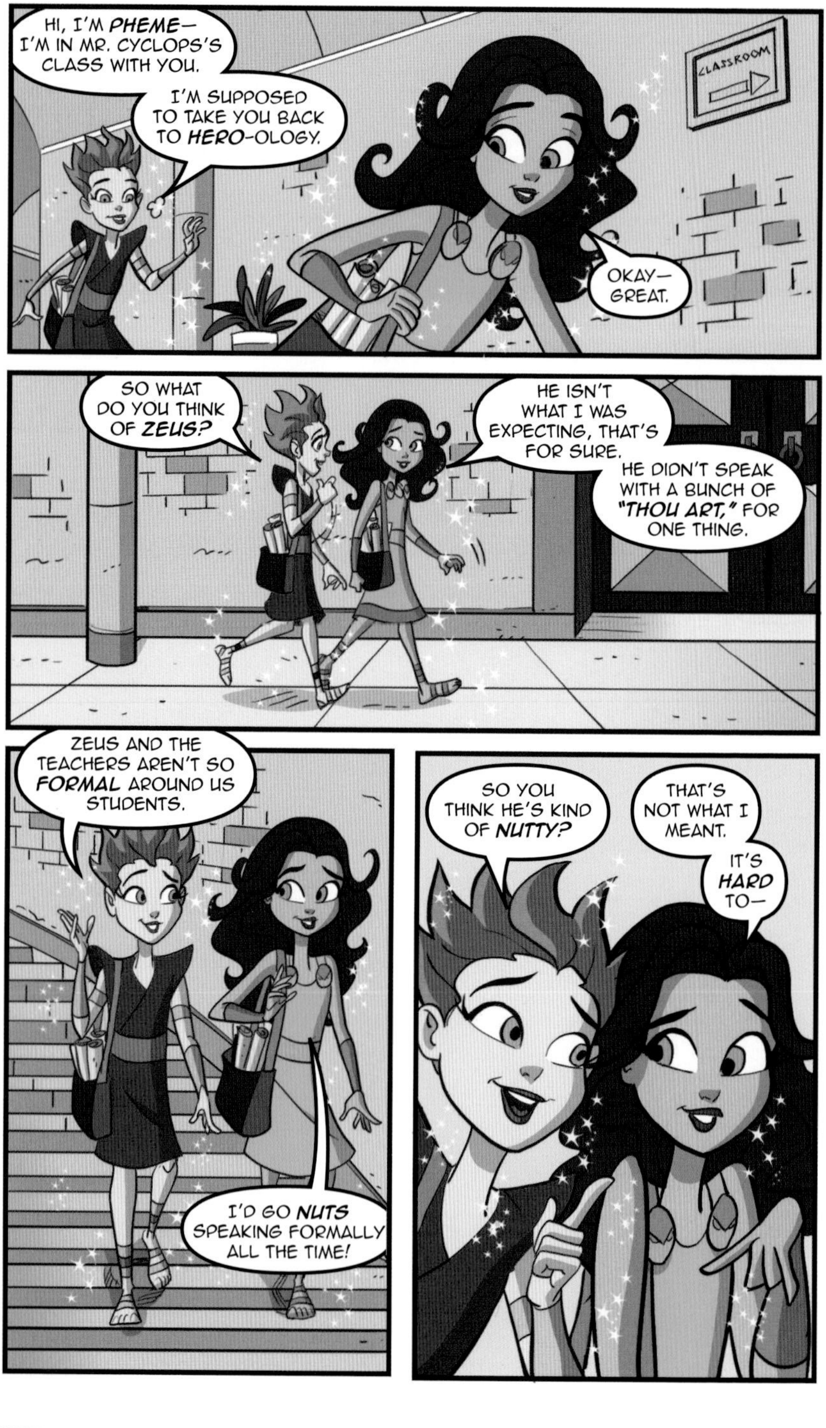
HI, I'M PHEME— I'M IN MR. CYCLOPS'S CLASS WITH YOU.
I'M SUPPOSED TO TAKE YOU BACK TO HERO-OLOGY.
CLASSROOM
OKAY— GREAT.
SO WHAT DO YOU THINK OF ZEUS?
HE ISN'T WHAT I WAS EXPECTING, THAT'S FOR SURE.
HE DIDN'T SPEAK WITH A BUNCH OF "THOU ART," FOR ONE THING.
ZEUS AND THE TEACHERS AREN'T SO FORMAL AROUND US STUDENTS.
I'D GO NUTS SPEAKING FORMALLY ALL THE TIME!
SO YOU THINK HE'S KIND OF NUTTY?
THAT'S NOT WHAT I MEANT.
IT'S HARD TO—

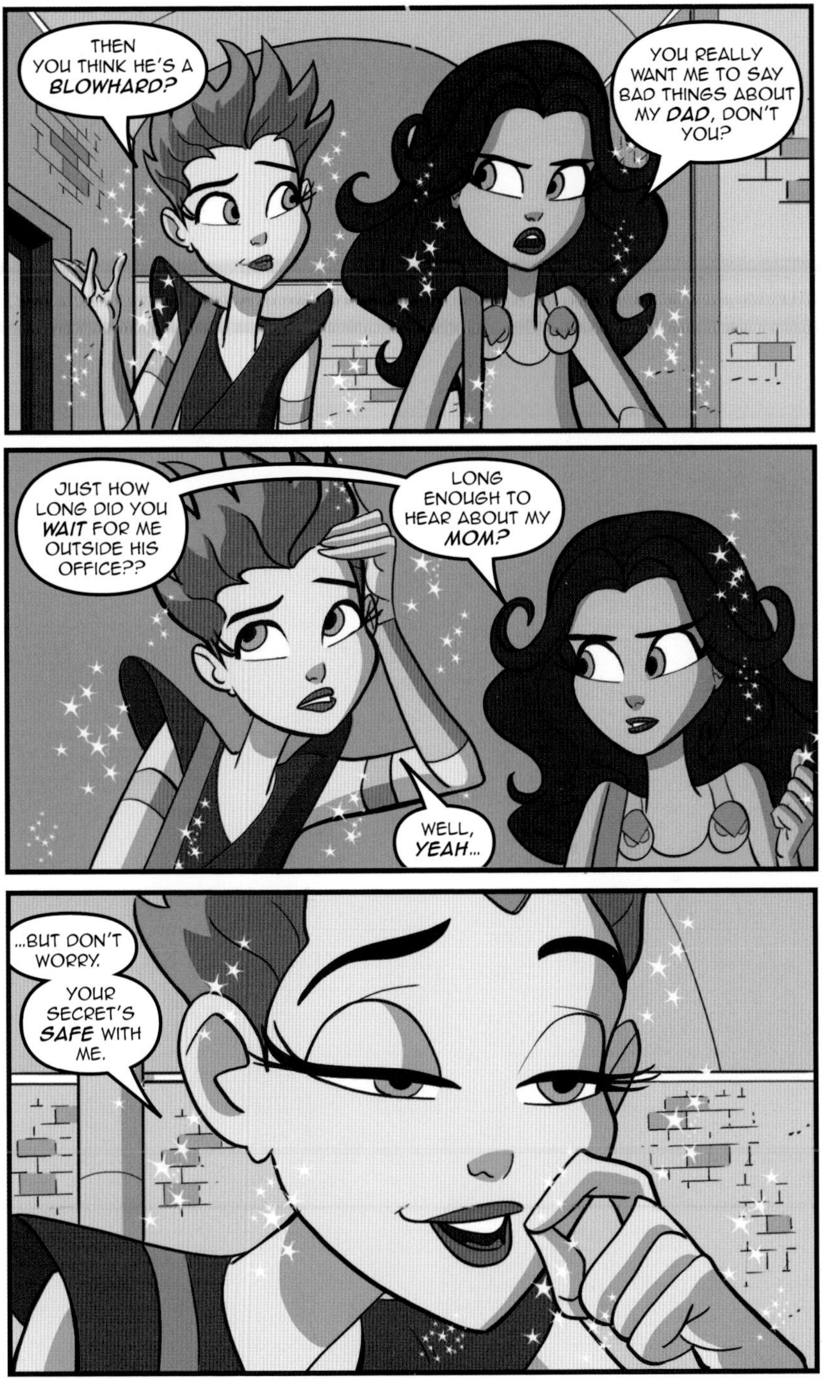
THEN YOU THINK HE'S A BLOWHARD?
YOU REALLY WANT ME TO SAY BAD THINGS ABOUT MY DAD, DON'T YOU?
JUST HOW LONG DID YOU WAIT FOR ME OUTSIDE HIS OFFICE??
LONG ENOUGH TO HEAR ABOUT MY MOM?
WELL, YEAH...
...BUT DON'T WORRY.
YOUR SECRET'S SAFE WITH ME.

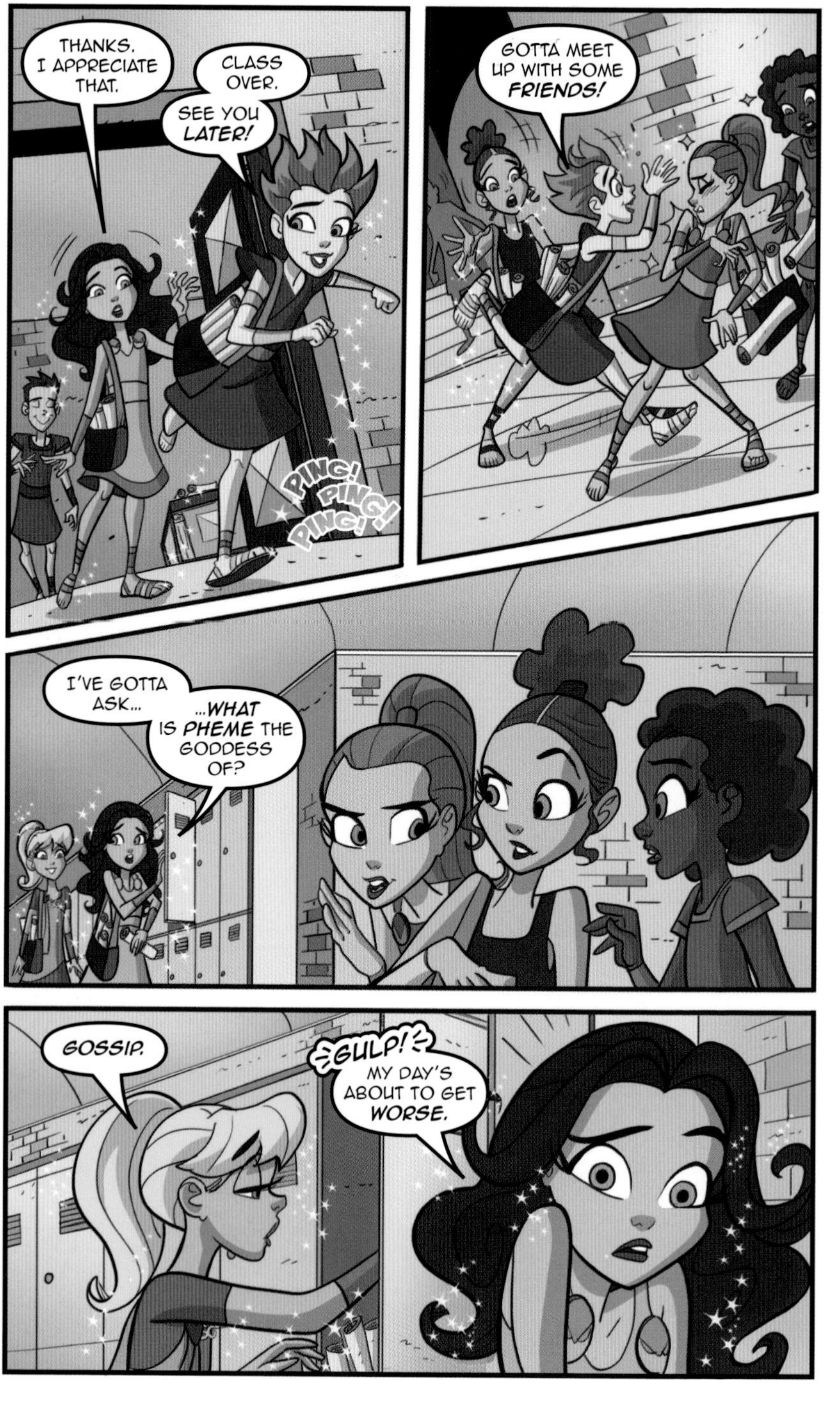
THANKS. I APPRECIATE THAT.
CLASS OVER.
SEE YOU LATER!
PING! PING! PING!
GOTTA MEET UP WITH SOME FRIENDS!
I'VE GOTTA ASK...
...WHAT IS PHEME THE GODDESS OF?
GOSSIP.
GULP!
MY DAY'S ABOUT TO GET WORSE.

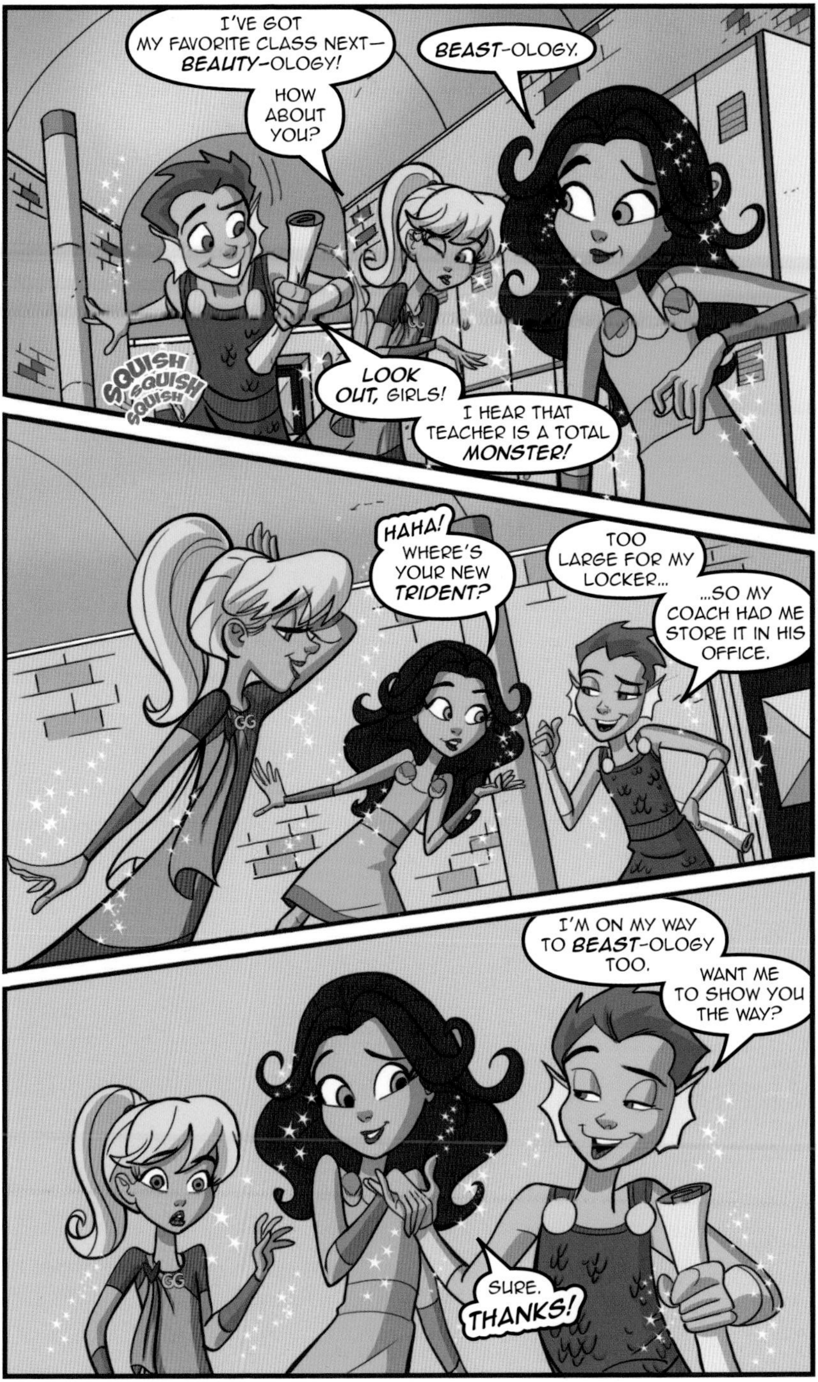
I'VE GOT MY FAVORITE CLASS NEXT— BEAUTY-OLOGY!
HOW ABOUT YOU?
BEAST-OLOGY.
SQUISH SQUISH SQUISH
LOOK OUT, GIRLS!
I HEAR THAT TEACHER IS A TOTAL MONSTER!
HAHA! WHERE'S YOUR NEW TRIDENT?
TOO LARGE FOR MY LOCKER...
...SO MY COACH HAD ME STORE IT IN HIS OFFICE.
I'M ON MY WAY TO BEAST-OLOGY TOO.
WANT ME TO SHOW YOU THE WAY?
SURE. THANKS!

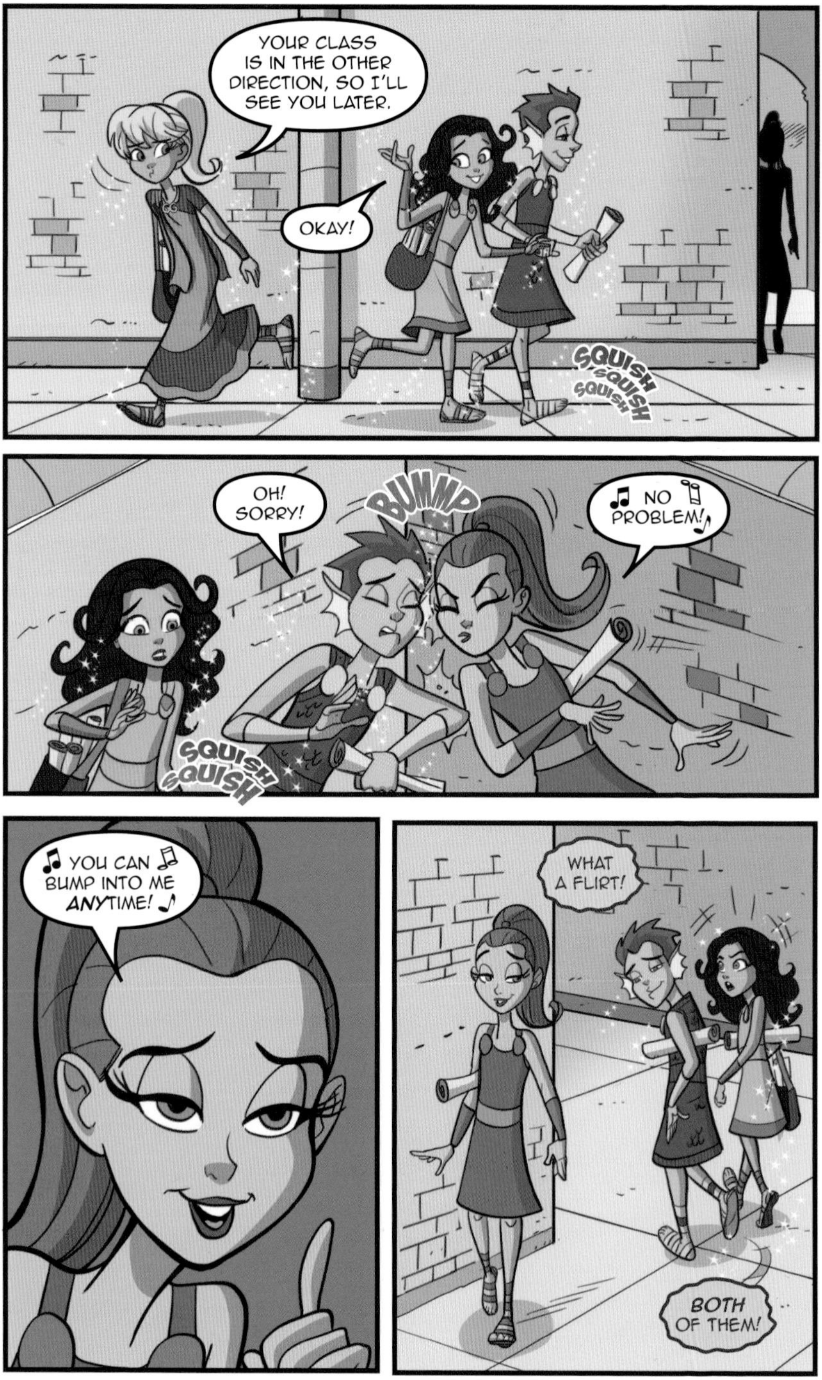
YOUR CLASS IS IN THE OTHER DIRECTION, SO I'LL SEE YOU LATER.
OKAY!
SQUISH SQUISH SQUISH
OH! SORRY!
BUMMP
♫ NO PROBLEM! ♪
SQUISH SQUISH
♫ YOU CAN BUMP INTO ME **ANY**TIME! ♪
WHAT A FLIRT!
BOTH OF THEM!

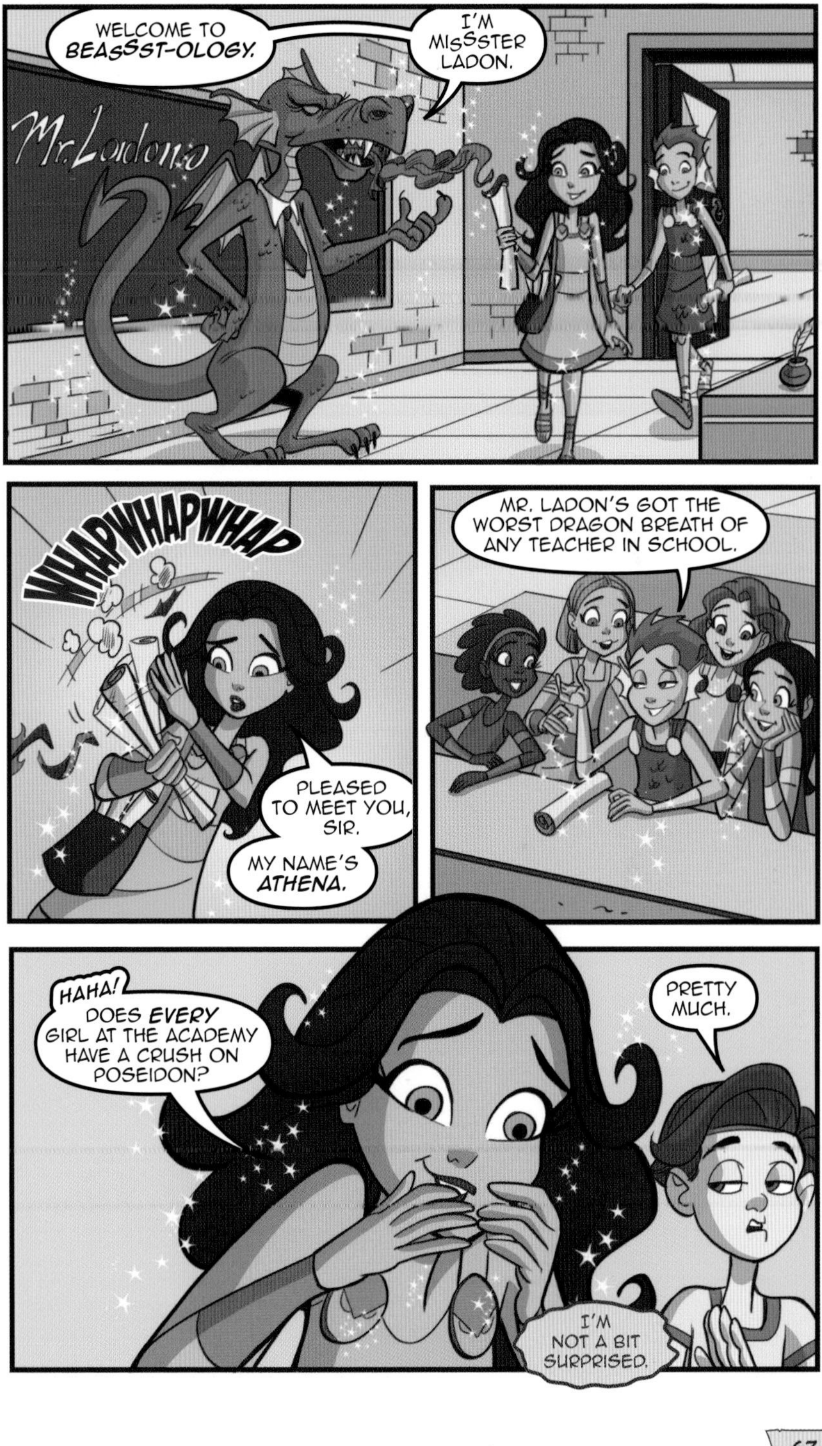
WELCOME TO BEASSST-OLOGY.
I'M MISSSTER LADON.
Mr. Ladon
WHAPWHAPWHAP
PLEASED TO MEET YOU, SIR.
MY NAME'S ATHENA.
MR. LADON'S GOT THE WORST DRAGON BREATH OF ANY TEACHER IN SCHOOL.
HAHA!
DOES EVERY GIRL AT THE ACADEMY HAVE A CRUSH ON POSEIDON?
PRETTY MUCH.
I'M NOT A BIT SURPRISED.

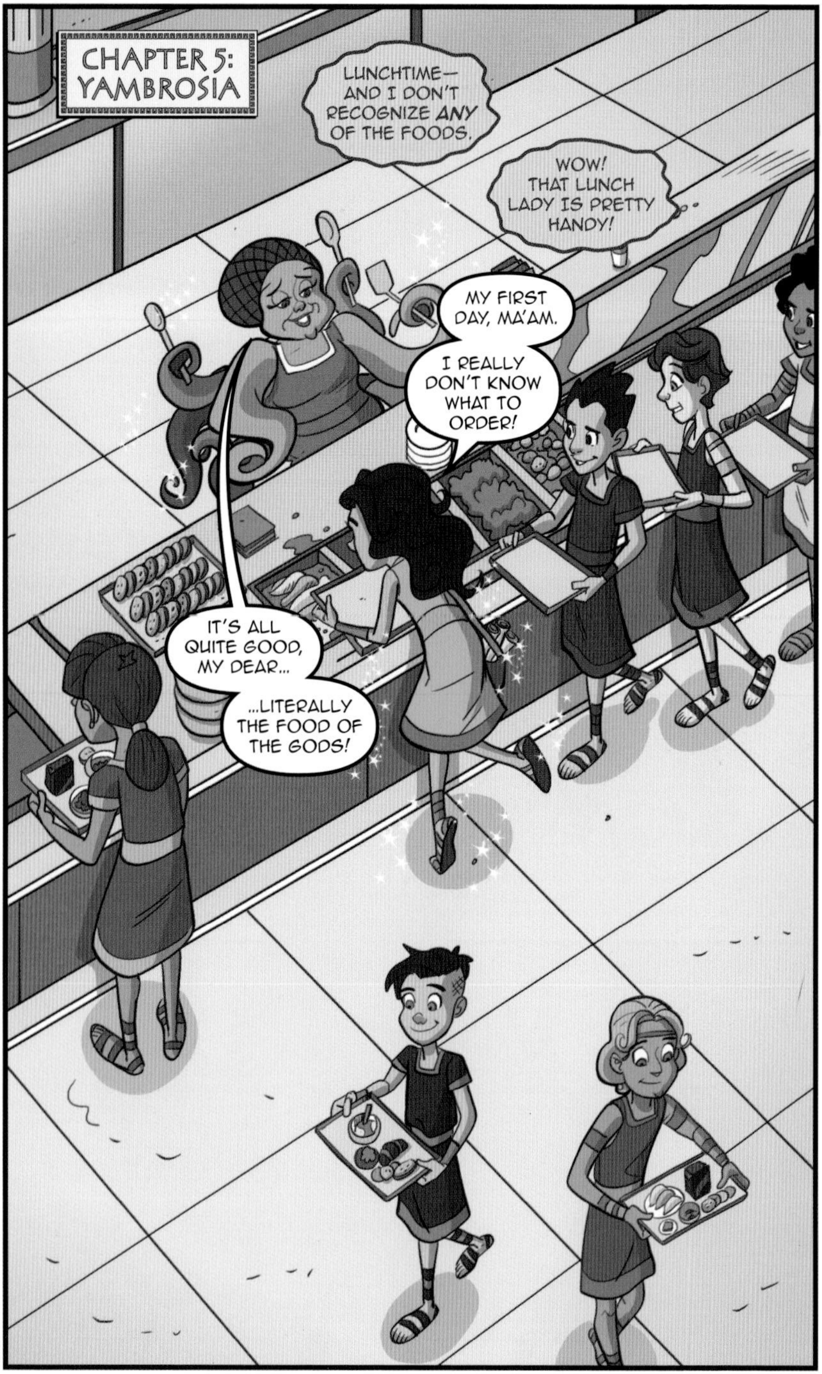
CHAPTER 5:
YAMBROSIA
LUNCHTIME—AND I DON'T RECOGNIZE ANY OF THE FOODS.
WOW! THAT LUNCH LADY IS PRETTY HANDY!
MY FIRST DAY, MA'AM.
I REALLY DON'T KNOW WHAT TO ORDER!
IT'S ALL QUITE GOOD, MY DEAR...
...LITERALLY THE FOOD OF THE GODS!

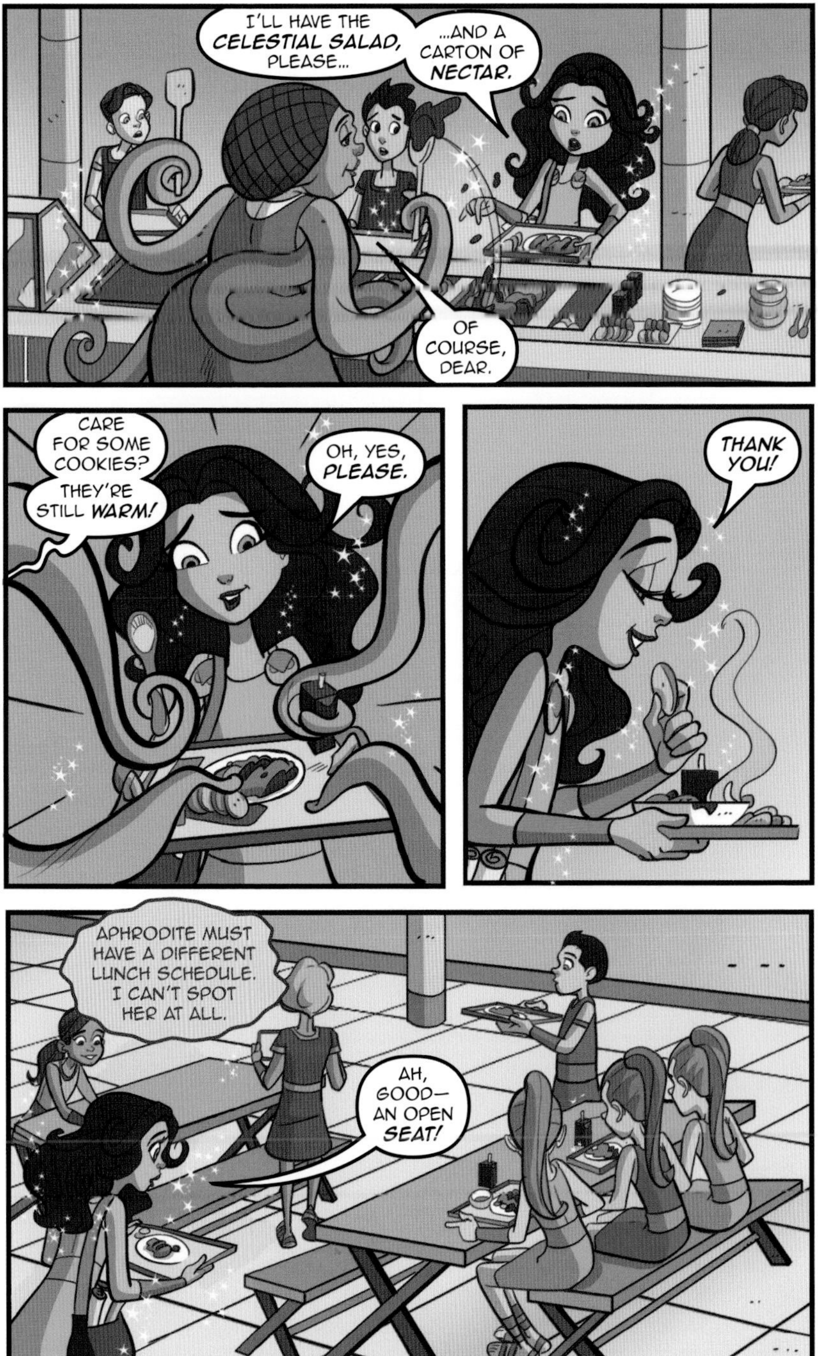
I'LL HAVE THE CELESTIAL SALAD, PLEASE...
...AND A CARTON OF NECTAR.
OF COURSE, DEAR.
CARE FOR SOME COOKIES?
THEY'RE STILL WARM!
OH, YES, PLEASE.
THANK YOU!
APHRODITE MUST HAVE A DIFFERENT LUNCH SCHEDULE. I CAN'T SPOT HER AT ALL.
AH, GOOD— AN OPEN SEAT!

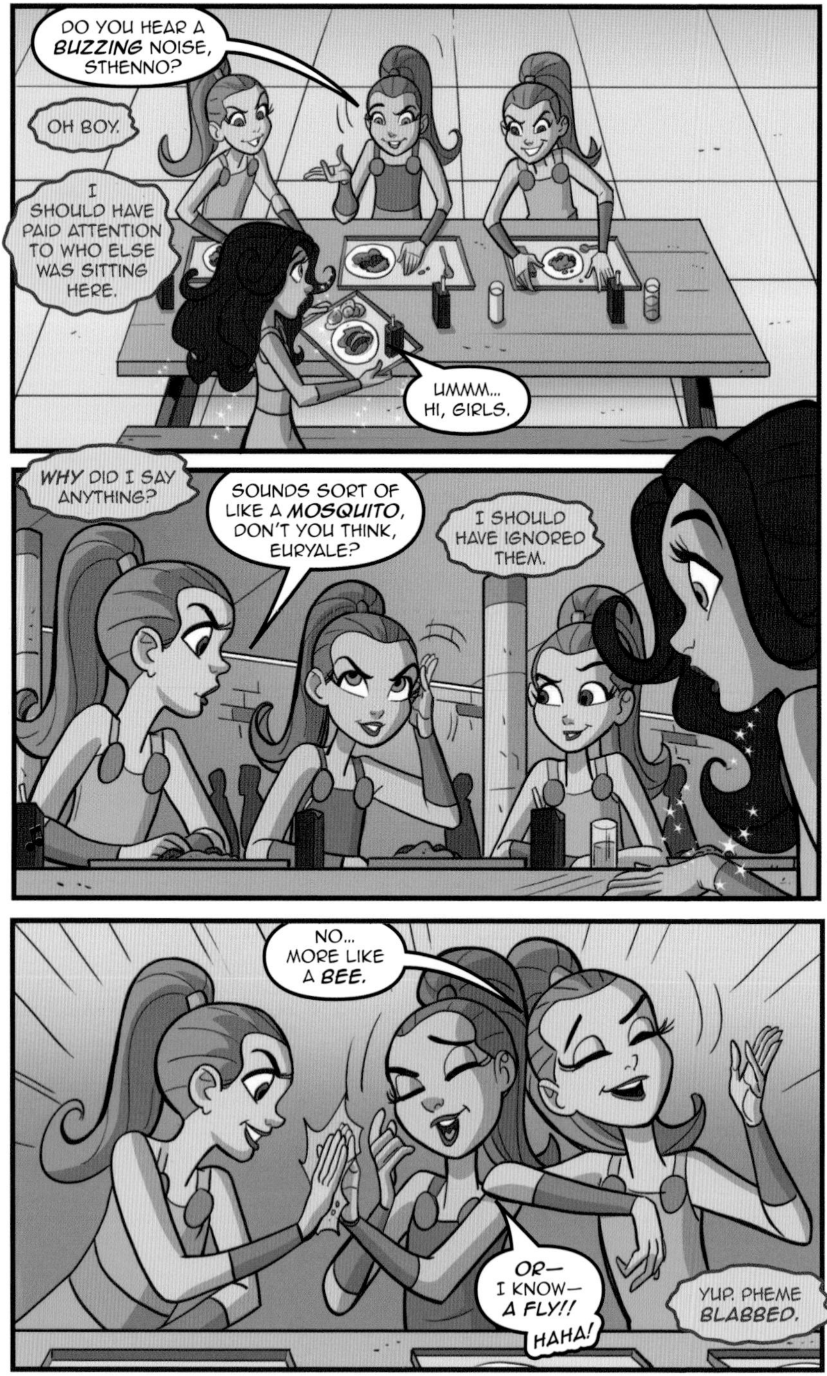
DO YOU HEAR A BUZZING NOISE, STHENNO?
OH BOY.
I SHOULD HAVE PAID ATTENTION TO WHO ELSE WAS SITTING HERE.
UMMM... HI, GIRLS.
WHY DID I SAY ANYTHING?
SOUNDS SORT OF LIKE A MOSQUITO, DON'T YOU THINK, EURYALE?
I SHOULD HAVE IGNORED THEM.
NO... MORE LIKE A BEE.
OR— I KNOW— A FLY!!
HAHA!
YUP. PHEME BLABBED.

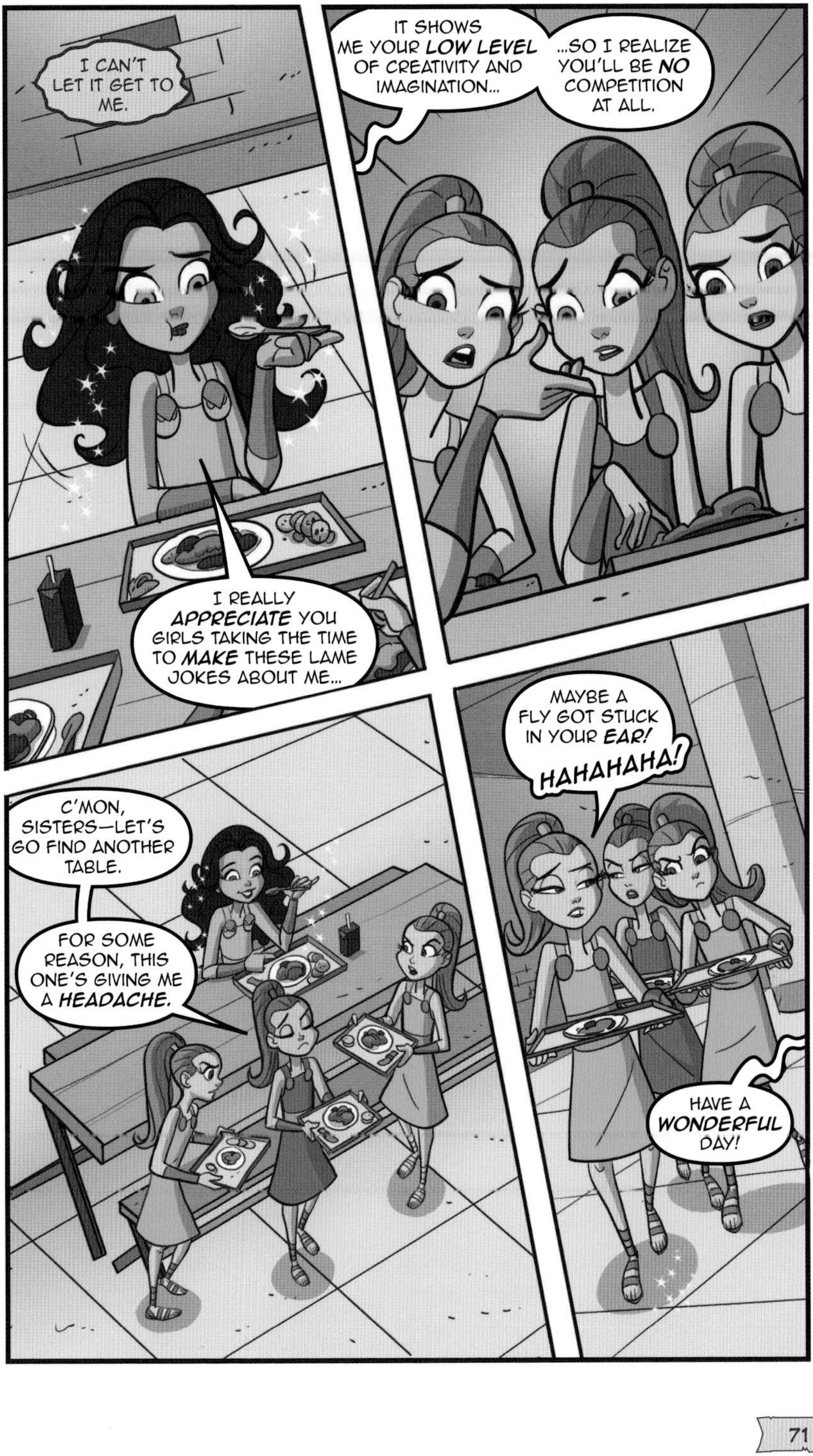
I CAN'T LET IT GET TO ME.
I REALLY APPRECIATE YOU GIRLS TAKING THE TIME TO MAKE THESE LAME JOKES ABOUT ME...
IT SHOWS ME YOUR LOW LEVEL OF CREATIVITY AND IMAGINATION...
...SO I REALIZE YOU'LL BE NO COMPETITION AT ALL.
C'MON, SISTERS—LET'S GO FIND ANOTHER TABLE.
FOR SOME REASON, THIS ONE'S GIVING ME A HEADACHE.
MAYBE A FLY GOT STUCK IN YOUR EAR!
HAHAHAHA!
HAVE A WONDERFUL DAY!

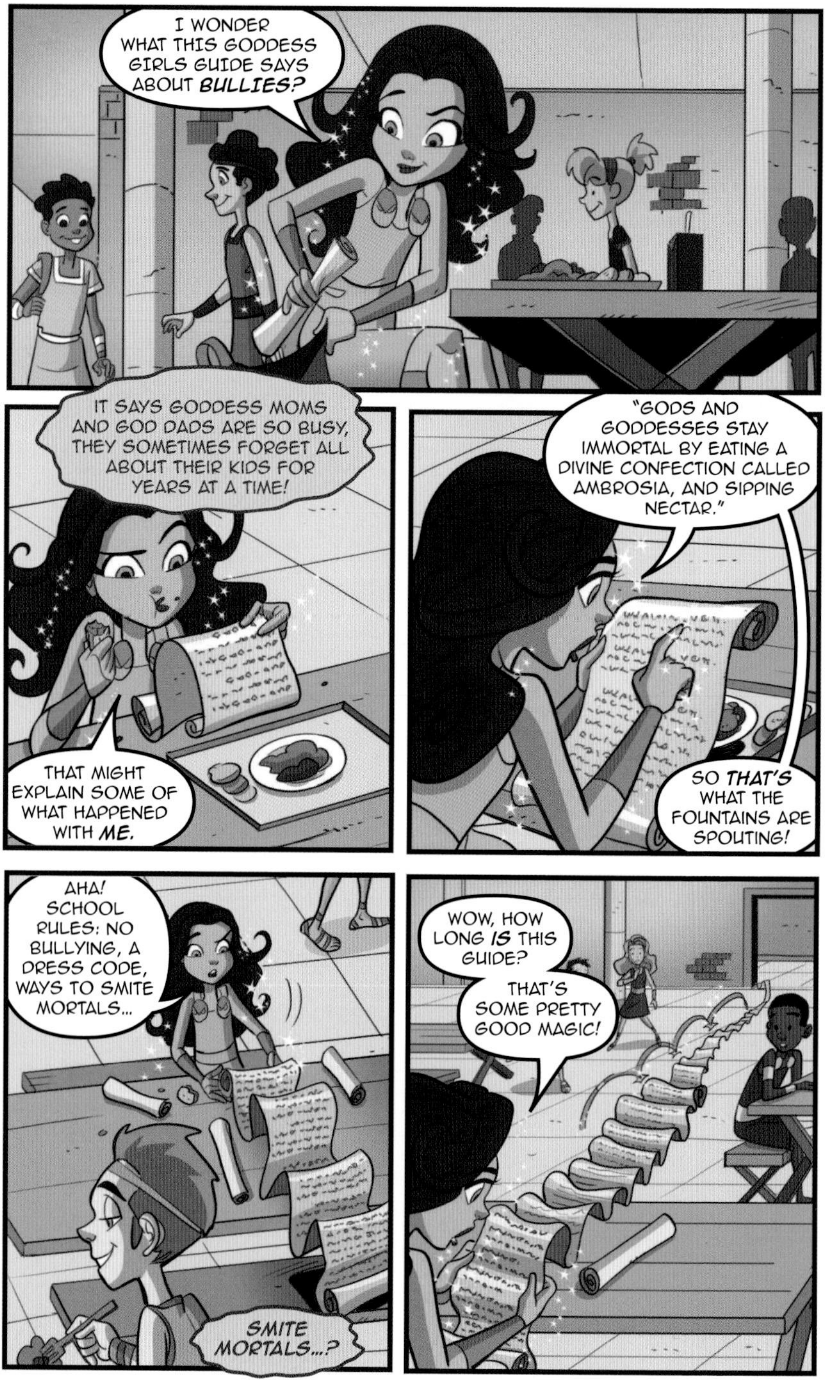
I WONDER WHAT THIS GODDESS GIRLS GUIDE SAYS ABOUT ***BULLIES?***
IT SAYS GODDESS MOMS AND GOD DADS ARE SO BUSY, THEY SOMETIMES FORGET ALL ABOUT THEIR KIDS FOR YEARS AT A TIME!
THAT MIGHT EXPLAIN SOME OF WHAT HAPPENED WITH ***ME.***
"GODS AND GODDESSES STAY IMMORTAL BY EATING A DIVINE CONFECTION CALLED AMBROSIA, AND SIPPING NECTAR."
SO ***THAT'S*** WHAT THE FOUNTAINS ARE SPOUTING!
AHA! SCHOOL RULES: NO BULLYING, A DRESS CODE, WAYS TO SMITE MORTALS...
SMITE MORTALS...?
WOW, HOW LONG ***IS*** THIS GUIDE?
THAT'S SOME PRETTY GOOD MAGIC!

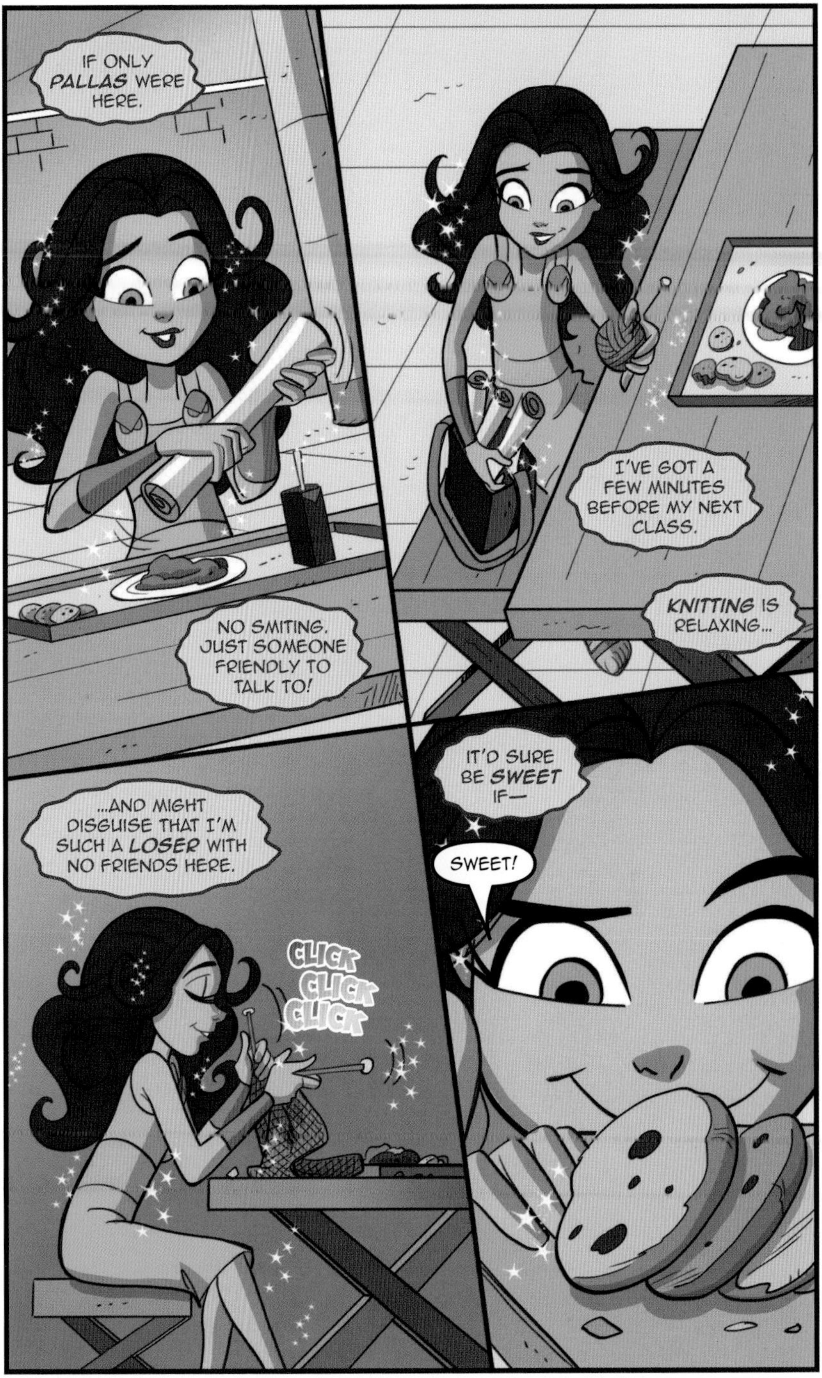
IF ONLY PALLAS WERE HERE.
NO SMITING. JUST SOMEONE FRIENDLY TO TALK TO!
I'VE GOT A FEW MINUTES BEFORE MY NEXT CLASS.
KNITTING IS RELAXING...
...AND MIGHT DISGUISE THAT I'M SUCH A LOSER WITH NO FRIENDS HERE.
CLICK CLICK CLICK
IT'D SURE BE SWEET IF—
SWEET!

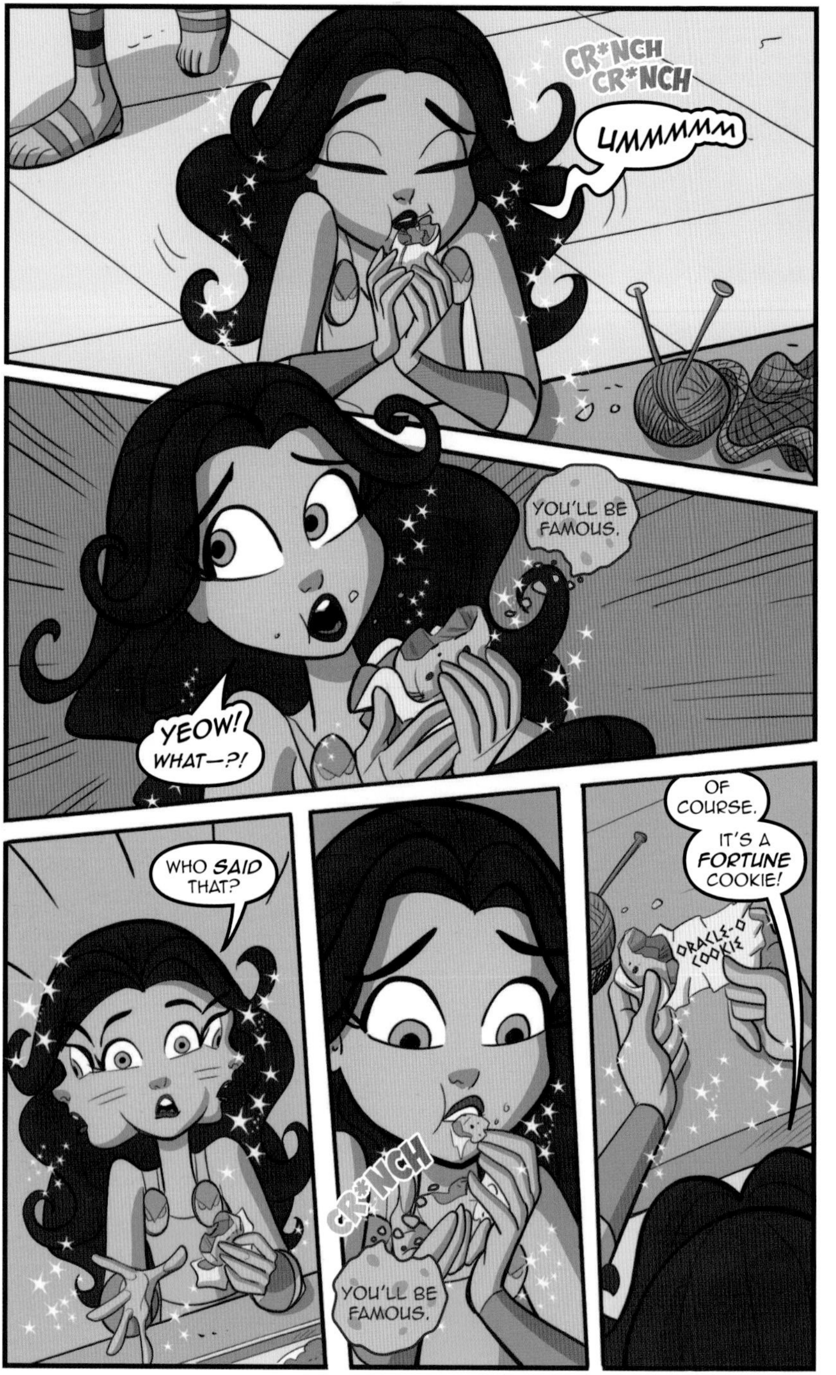
CR*NCH
CR*NCH
UMMMMM
YOU'LL BE FAMOUS.
YEOW! WHAT—?!
WHO SAID THAT?
CR*NCH
YOU'LL BE FAMOUS.
OF COURSE.
IT'S A FORTUNE COOKIE!
ORACLE-O COOKIE

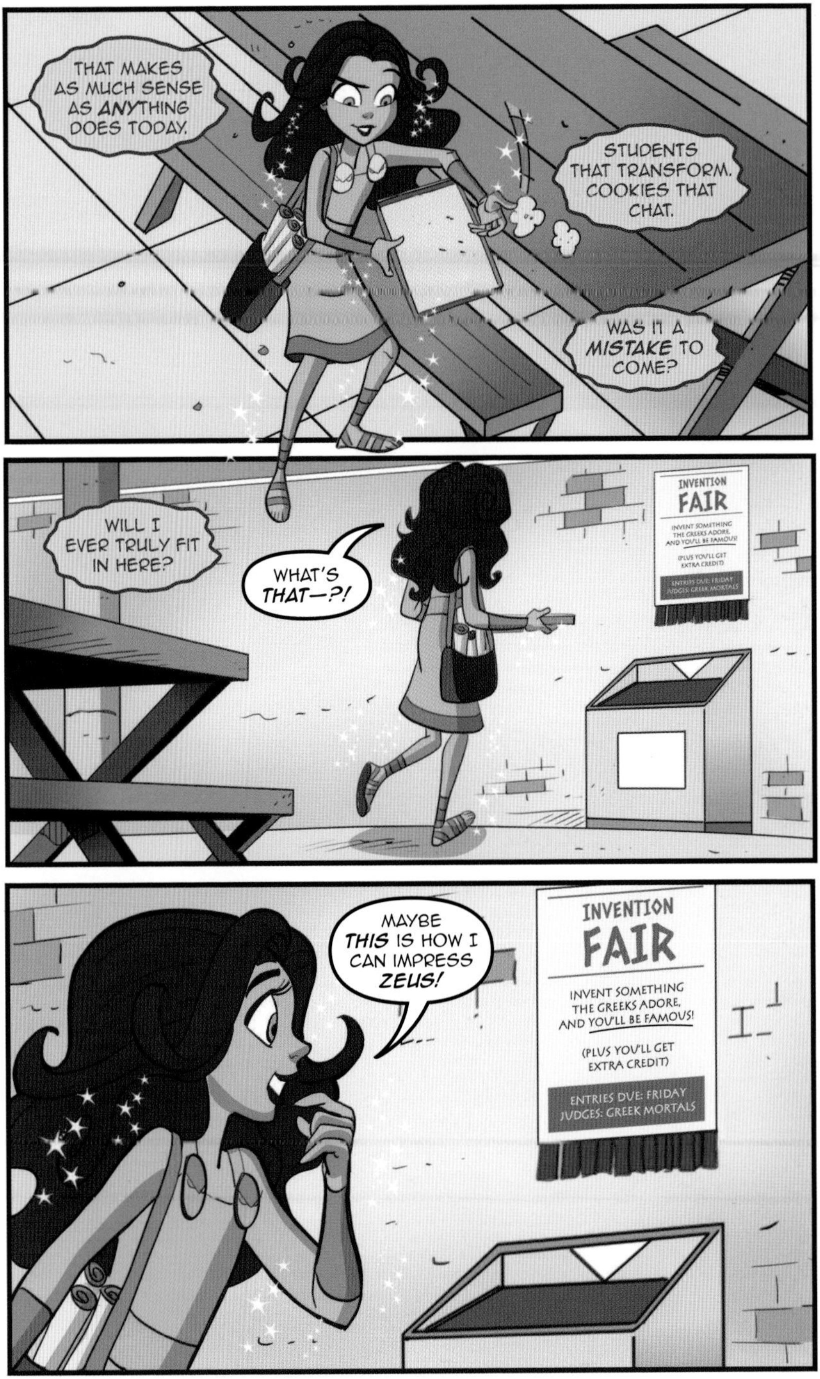
THAT MAKES AS MUCH SENSE AS ANYTHING DOES TODAY.
STUDENTS THAT TRANSFORM. COOKIES THAT CHAT.
WAS IT A MISTAKE TO COME?
WILL I EVER TRULY FIT IN HERE?
WHAT'S THAT—?!
INVENTION FAIR
INVENT SOMETHING THE GREEKS ADORE, AND YOU'LL BE FAMOUS!
(PLUS YOU'LL GET EXTRA CREDIT)
ENTRIES DUE: FRIDAY
JUDGES: GREEK MORTALS
MAYBE THIS IS HOW I CAN IMPRESS ZEUS!

"FAMOUS." THAT'S QUITE A *COINCIDENCE!*...

...OR IS IT?

THWIPP!

HEY— PLANNING TO *ENTER?*

MAYBE. YOU?

SQUISH SQUISH SQUISH

FAIR

INVENT SOMETHING GREEKS ADORE, AND YOU'LL BE FAMOUS!

...US YOU'LL GET XTRA CREDIT!

NTRIES DUE: FRIDAY JUDGES: GREEK MORTALS

SRIPPA

SURE! AND I'M IN IT TO *WIN* IT!

RUMOR HAS IT YOU'RE PRETTY *BRAINY.* I'LL LET YOU BE MY *ASSISTANT!*

DRIP DRIP

HIS *ASSISTANT??*

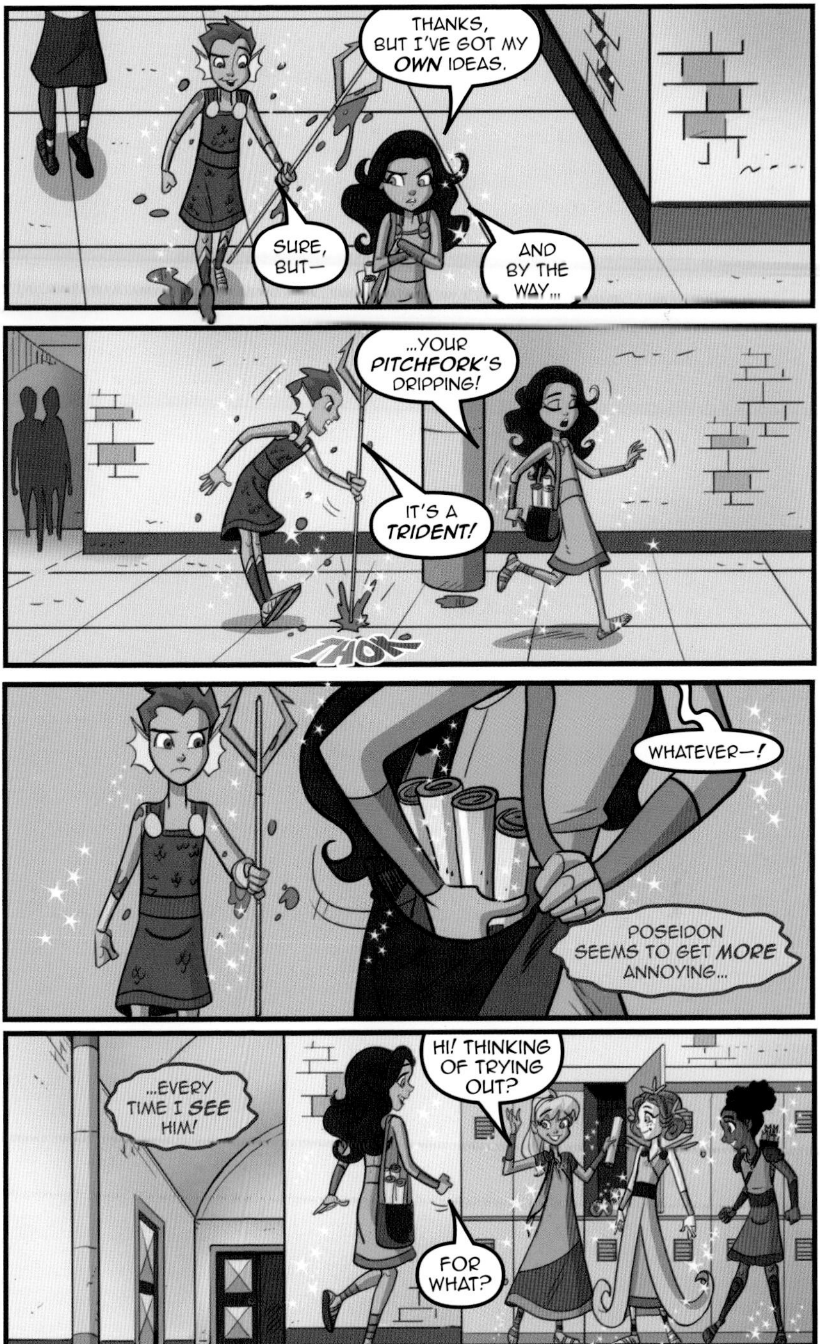

THANKS, BUT I'VE GOT MY OWN IDEAS.
SURE, BUT—
AND BY THE WAY...
...YOUR PITCHFORK'S DRIPPING!
IT'S A TRIDENT!
THOK
WHATEVER—!
POSEIDON SEEMS TO GET MORE ANNOYING...
...EVERY TIME I SEE HIM!
HI! THINKING OF TRYING OUT?
FOR WHAT?

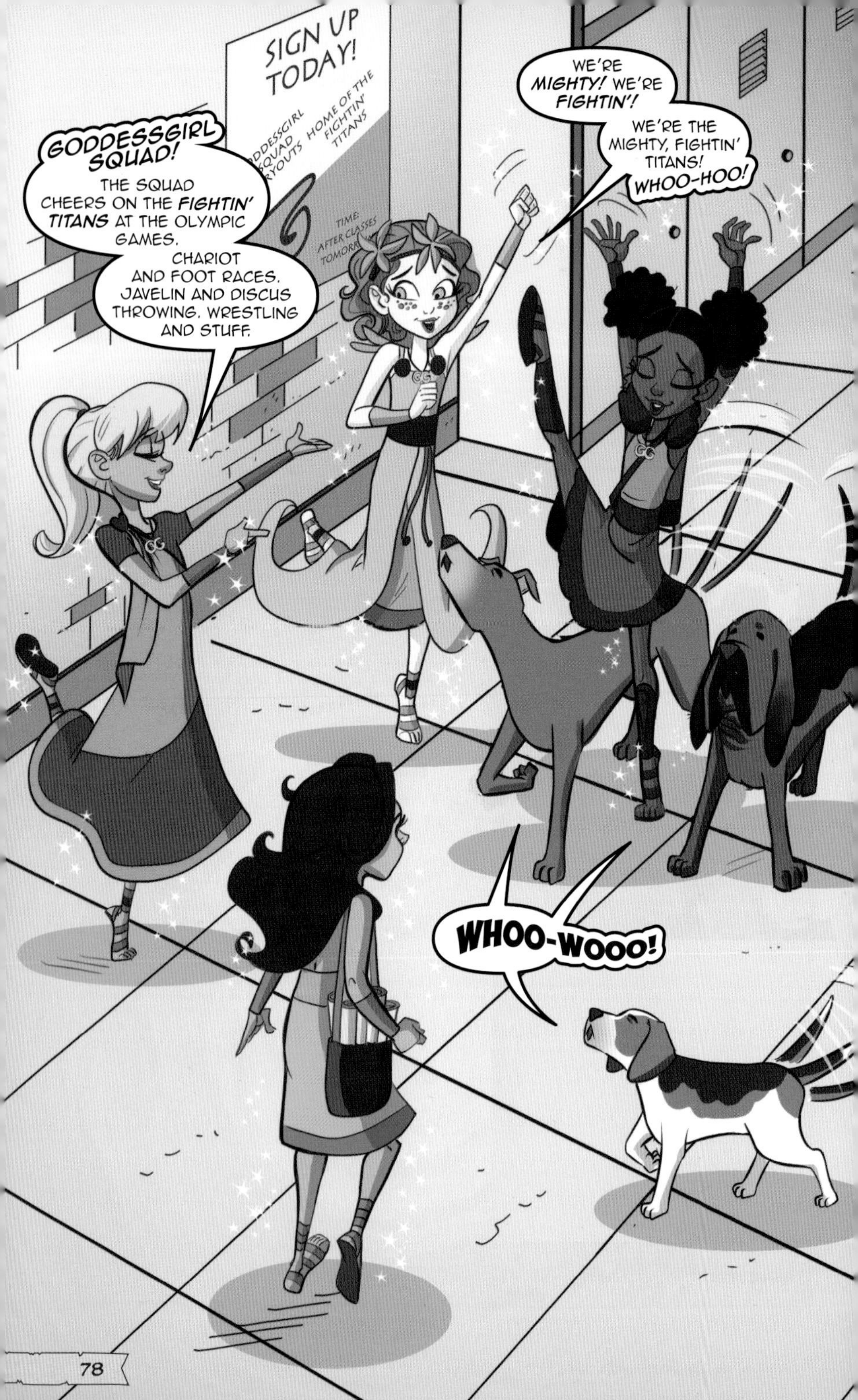

SIGN UP TODAY!
HOME OF THE FIGHTIN' TITANS
TIME: AFTER CLASSES
GODDESSGIRL SQUAD! THE SQUAD CHEERS ON THE FIGHTIN' TITANS AT THE OLYMPIC GAMES.
CHARIOT AND FOOT RACES. JAVELIN AND DISCUS THROWING. WRESTLING AND STUFF.
WE'RE MIGHTY! WE'RE FIGHTIN'!
WE'RE THE MIGHTY, FIGHTIN' TITANS! WHOO-HOO!
WHOO-WOOO!

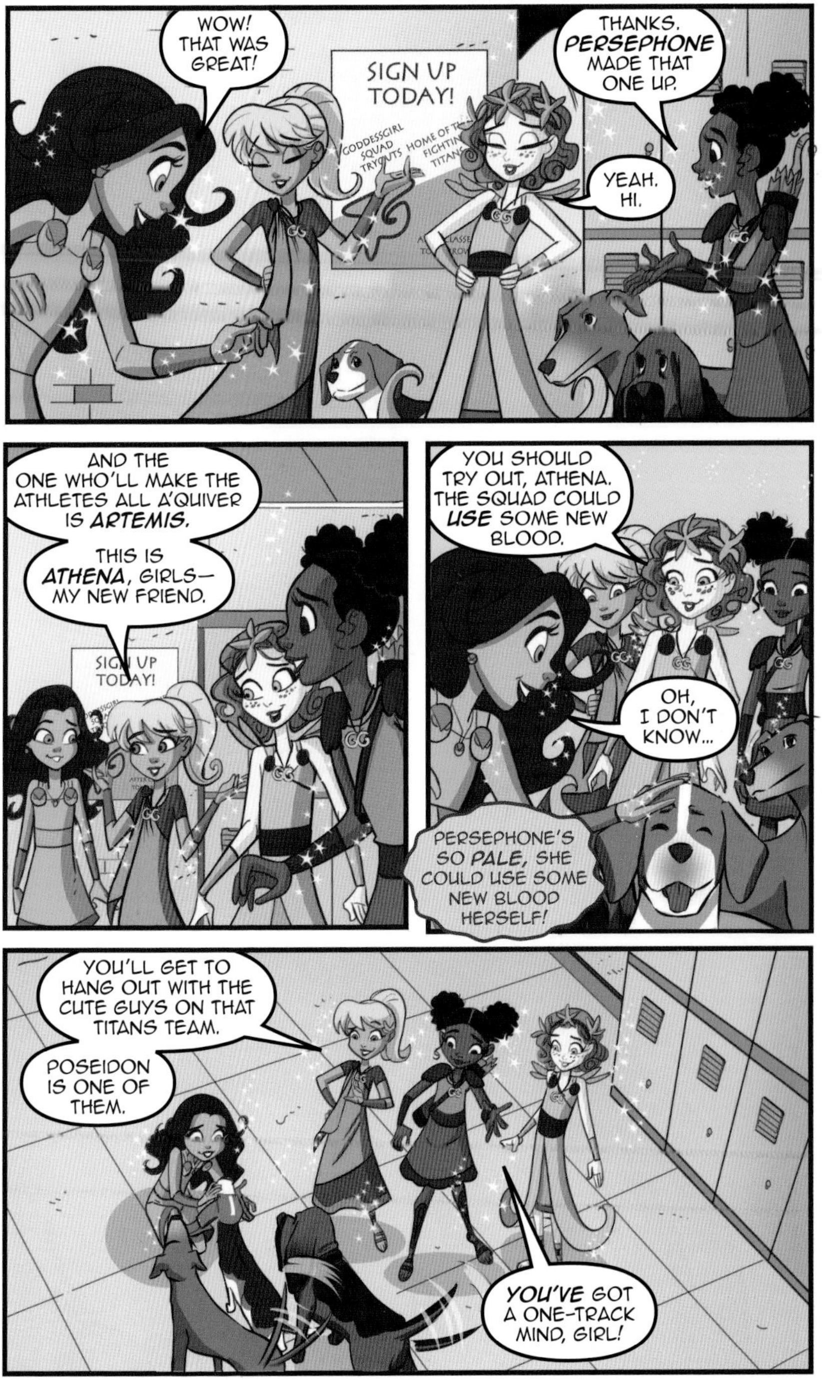
WOW! THAT WAS GREAT!
SIGN UP TODAY!
GODDESSGIRL SQUAD TRYOUTS
HOME OF THE FIGHTING TITANS
THANKS. PERSEPHONE MADE THAT ONE UP.
YEAH. HI.
AND THE ONE WHO'LL MAKE THE ATHLETES ALL A'QUIVER IS ARTEMIS.
THIS IS ATHENA, GIRLS— MY NEW FRIEND.
SIGN UP TODAY!
YOU SHOULD TRY OUT, ATHENA. THE SQUAD COULD USE SOME NEW BLOOD.
OH, I DON'T KNOW...
PERSEPHONE'S SO PALE, SHE COULD USE SOME NEW BLOOD HERSELF!
YOU'LL GET TO HANG OUT WITH THE CUTE GUYS ON THAT TITANS TEAM.
POSEIDON IS ONE OF THEM.
YOU'VE GOT A ONE-TRACK MIND, GIRL!

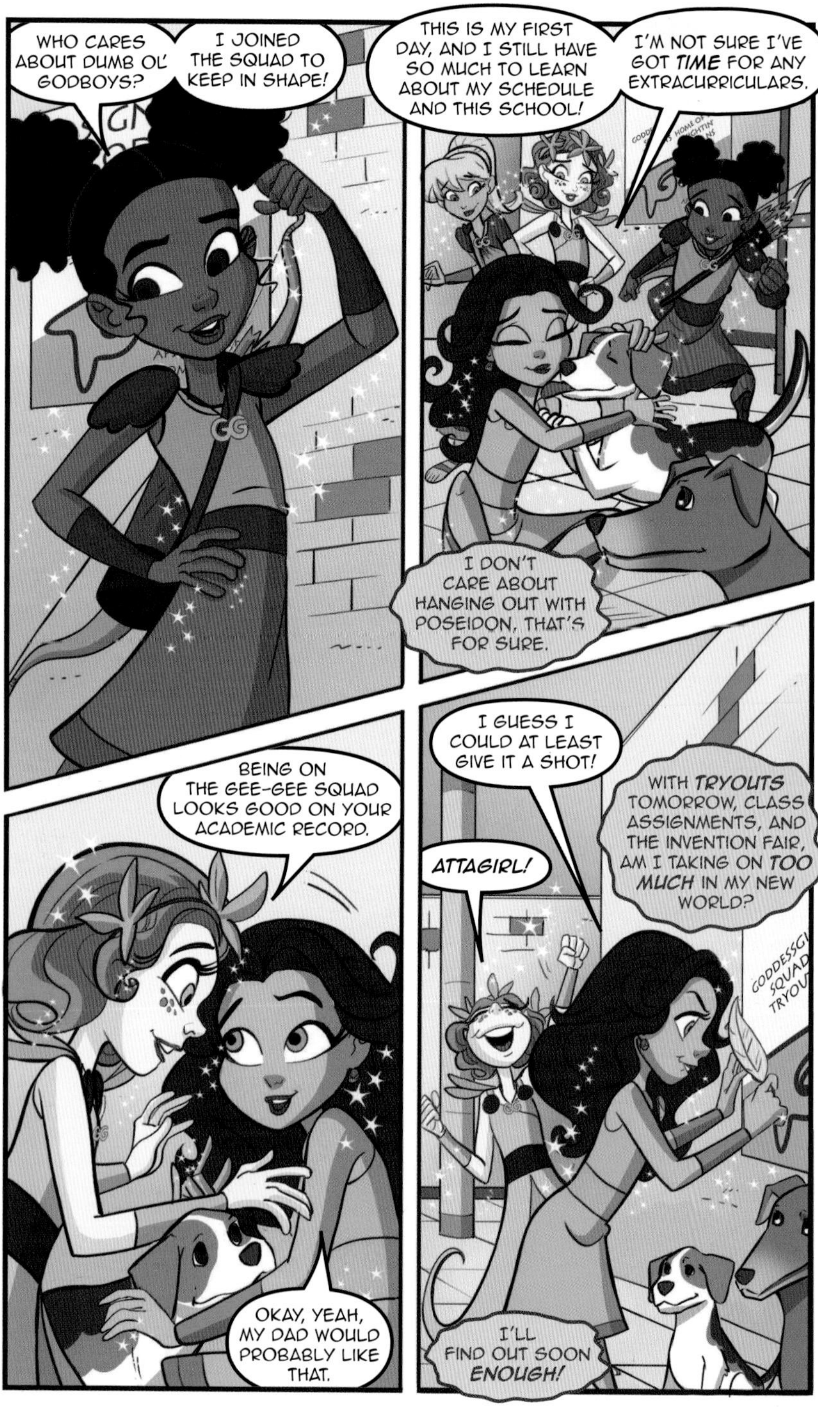
WHO CARES ABOUT DUMB OL' GODBOYS?
I JOINED THE SQUAD TO KEEP IN SHAPE!
THIS IS MY FIRST DAY, AND I STILL HAVE SO MUCH TO LEARN ABOUT MY SCHEDULE AND THIS SCHOOL!
I'M NOT SURE I'VE GOT *TIME* FOR ANY EXTRACURRICULARS.
I DON'T CARE ABOUT HANGING OUT WITH POSEIDON, THAT'S FOR SURE.
BEING ON THE GEE-GEE SQUAD LOOKS GOOD ON YOUR ACADEMIC RECORD.
OKAY, YEAH, MY DAD WOULD PROBABLY LIKE THAT.
I GUESS I COULD AT LEAST GIVE IT A SHOT!
ATTAGIRL!
WITH *TRYOUTS* TOMORROW, CLASS ASSIGNMENTS, AND THE INVENTION FAIR, AM I TAKING ON *TOO MUCH* IN MY NEW WORLD?
I'LL FIND OUT SOON *ENOUGH!*

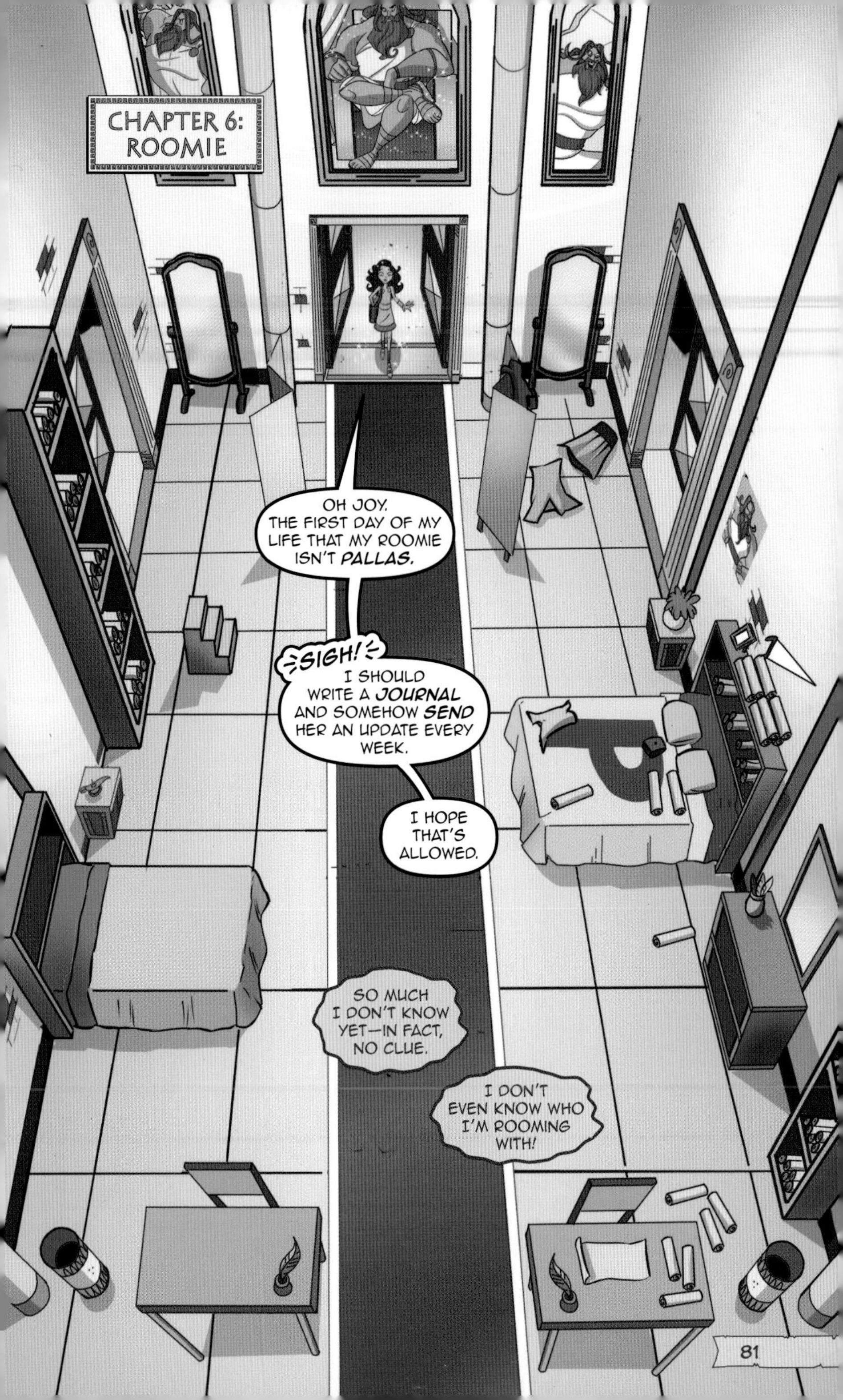
CHAPTER 6:
ROOMIE
OH JOY. THE FIRST DAY OF MY LIFE THAT MY ROOMIE ISN'T PALLAS.
SIGH!
I SHOULD WRITE A JOURNAL AND SOMEHOW SEND HER AN UPDATE EVERY WEEK.
I HOPE THAT'S ALLOWED.
SO MUCH I DON'T KNOW YET—IN FACT, NO CLUE.
I DON'T EVEN KNOW WHO I'M ROOMING WITH!

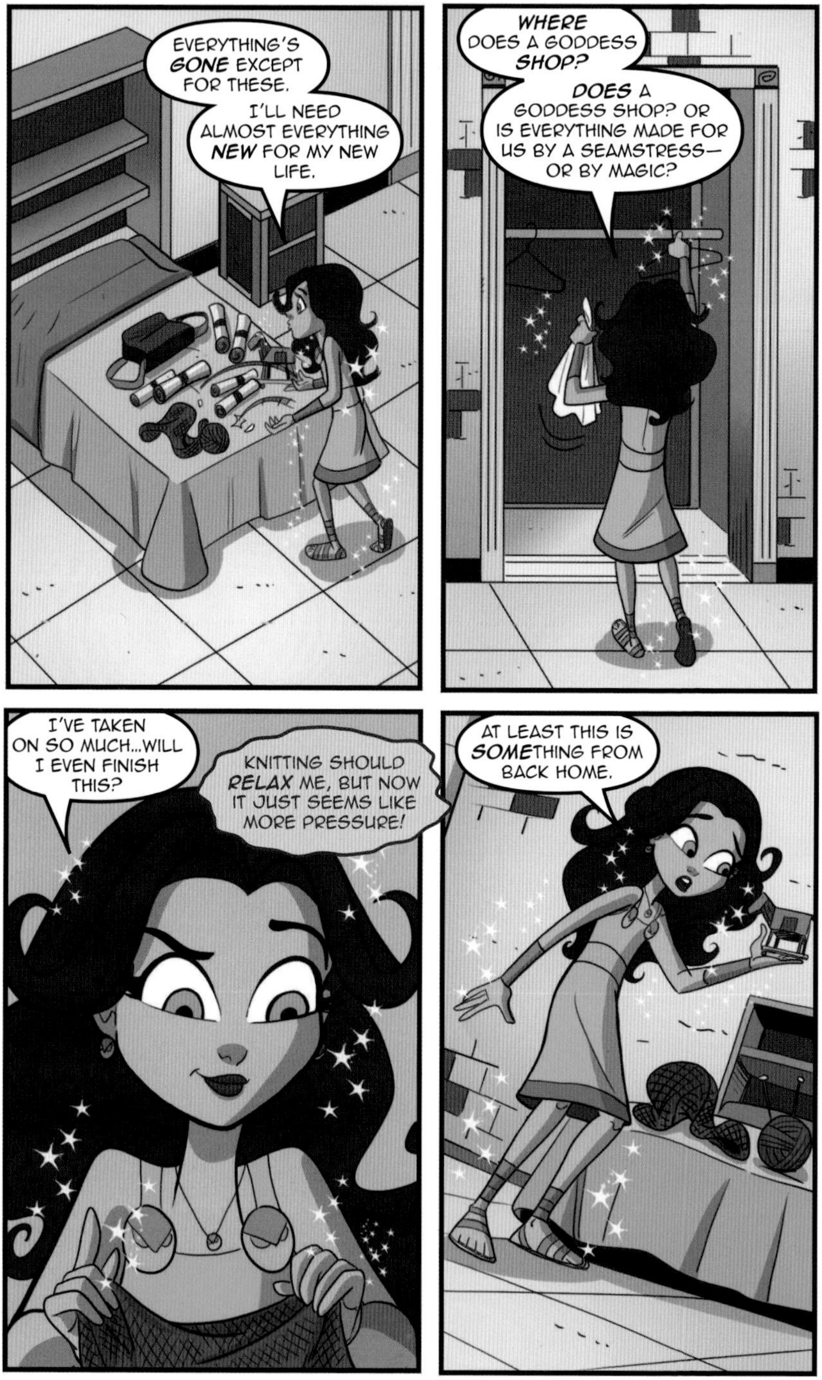
EVERYTHING'S GONE EXCEPT FOR THESE.
I'LL NEED ALMOST EVERYTHING NEW FOR MY NEW LIFE.
WHERE DOES A GODDESS SHOP?
DOES A GODDESS SHOP? OR IS EVERYTHING MADE FOR US BY A SEAMSTRESS— OR BY MAGIC?
I'VE TAKEN ON SO MUCH...WILL I EVEN FINISH THIS?
KNITTING SHOULD RELAX ME, BUT NOW IT JUST SEEMS LIKE MORE PRESSURE!
AT LEAST THIS IS SOMETHING FROM BACK HOME.

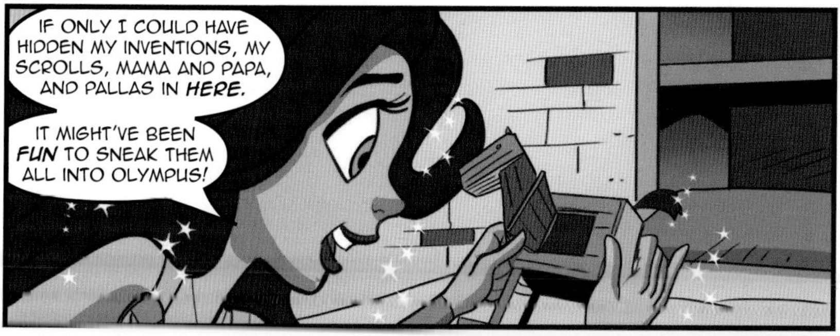
IF ONLY I COULD HAVE HIDDEN MY INVENTIONS, MY SCROLLS, MAMA AND PAPA, AND PALLAS IN HERE.
IT MIGHT'VE BEEN FUN TO SNEAK THEM ALL INTO OLYMPUS!

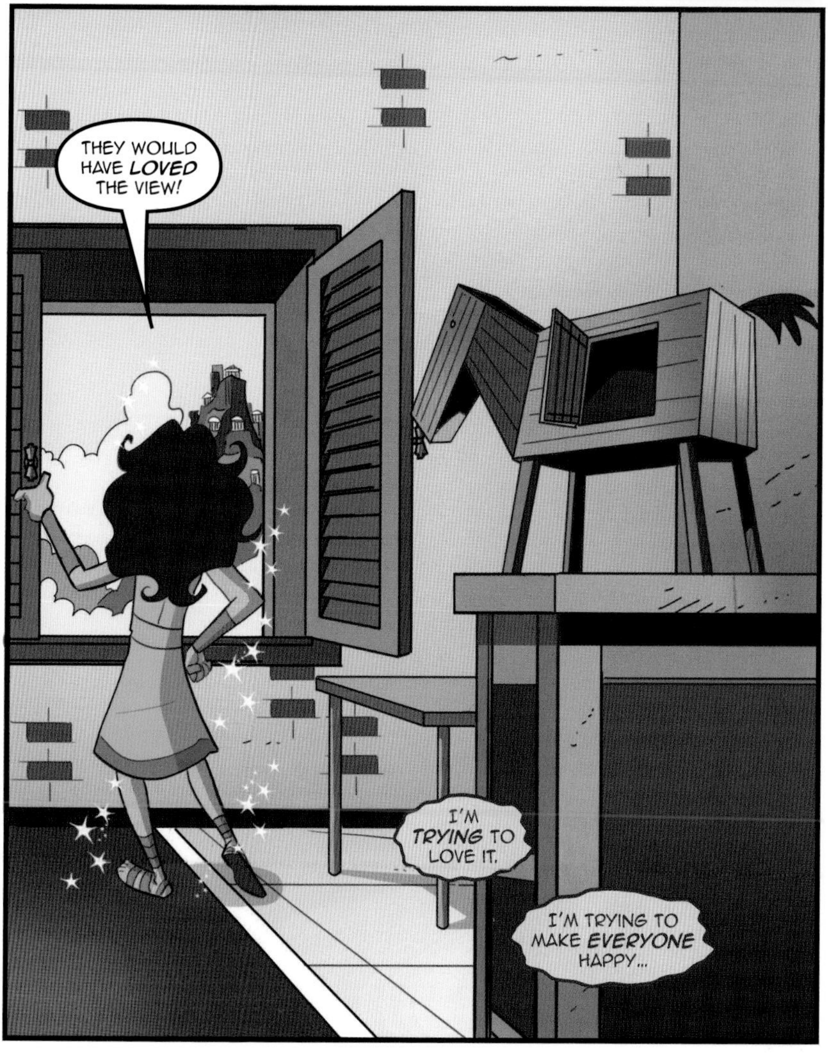
THEY WOULD HAVE LOVED THE VIEW!
I'M TRYING TO LOVE IT.
I'M TRYING TO MAKE EVERYONE HAPPY...

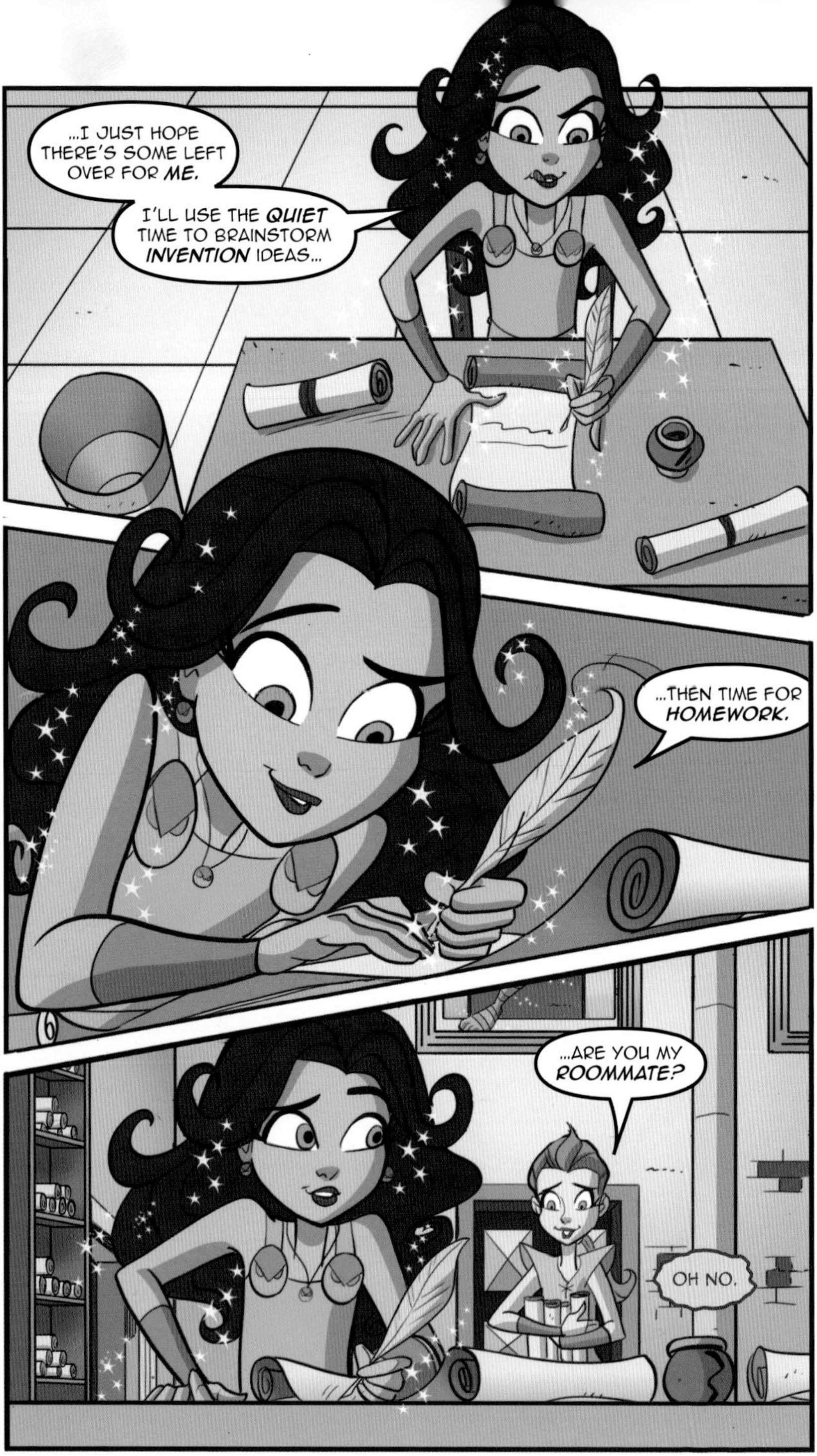
...I JUST HOPE THERE'S SOME LEFT OVER FOR *ME.*
I'LL USE THE *QUIET* TIME TO BRAINSTORM *INVENTION* IDEAS...
...THEN TIME FOR *HOMEWORK.*
...ARE YOU MY *ROOMMATE?*
OH NO.

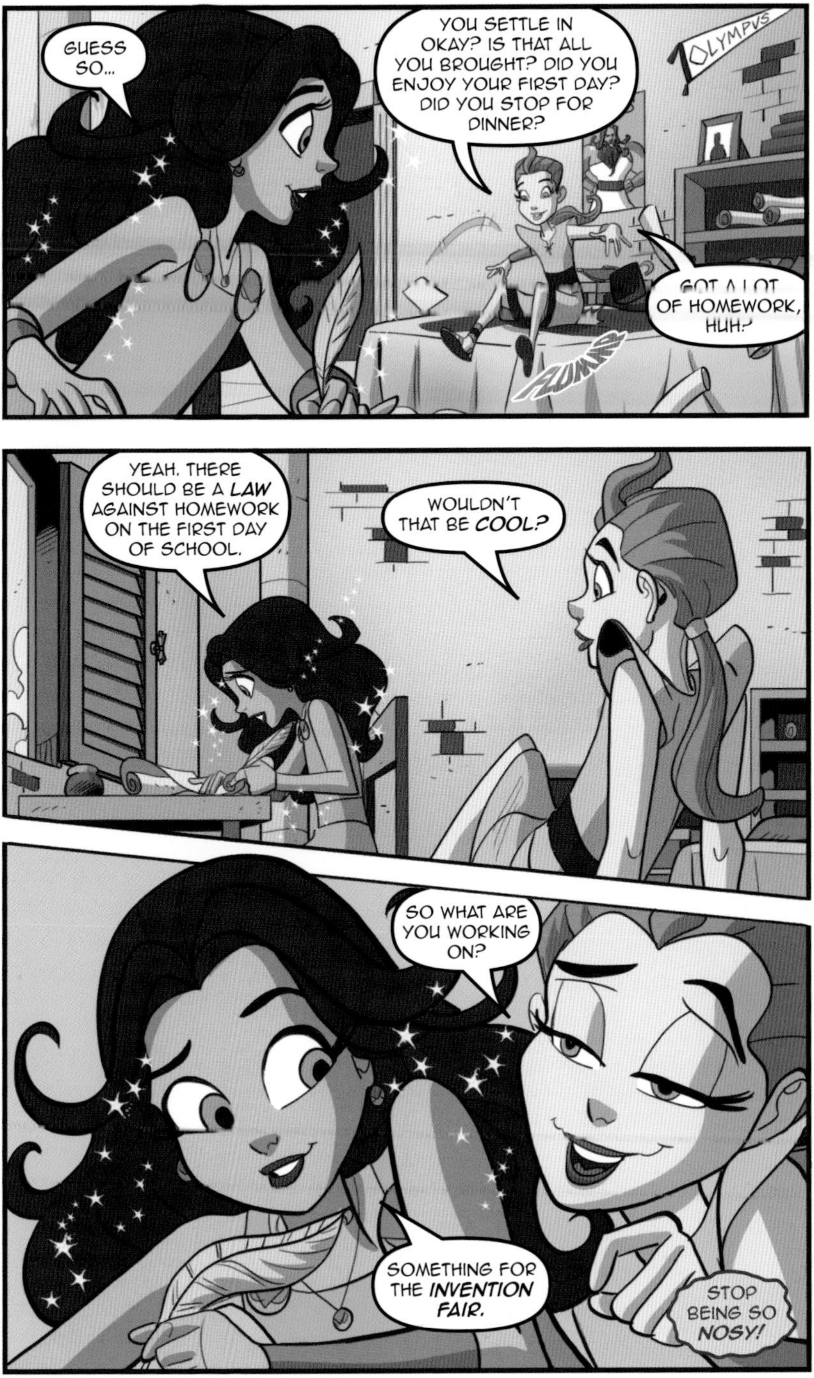
GUESS SO...
YOU SETTLE IN OKAY? IS THAT ALL YOU BROUGHT? DID YOU ENJOY YOUR FIRST DAY? DID YOU STOP FOR DINNER?
OLYMPVS
GOT A LOT OF HOMEWORK, HUH?
YEAH. THERE SHOULD BE A *LAW* AGAINST HOMEWORK ON THE FIRST DAY OF SCHOOL.
WOULDN'T THAT BE *COOL?*
SO WHAT ARE YOU WORKING ON?
SOMETHING FOR THE *INVENTION FAIR.*
STOP BEING SO *NOSY!*

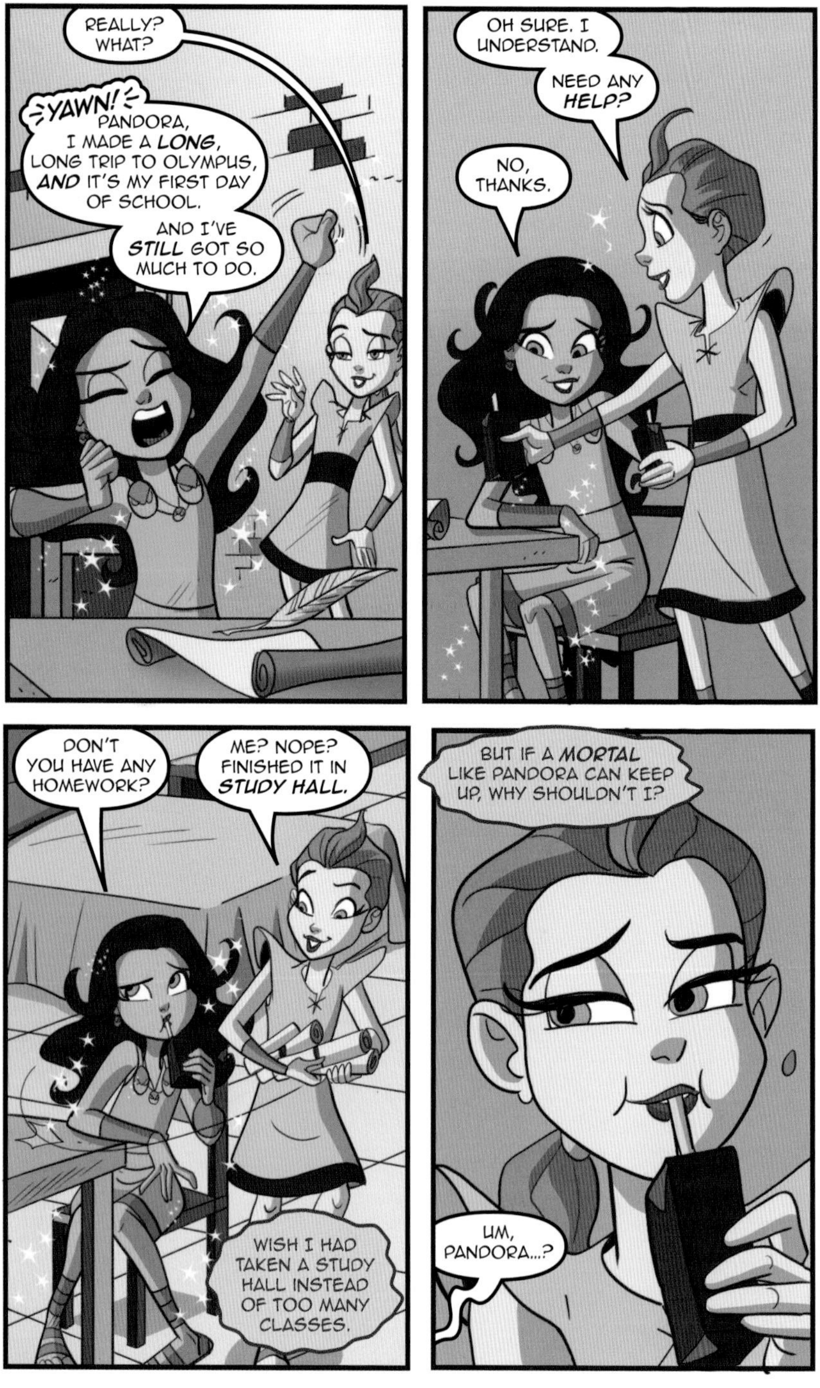

REALLY? WHAT?
YAWN!
PANDORA, I MADE A LONG, LONG TRIP TO OLYMPUS, AND IT'S MY FIRST DAY OF SCHOOL.
AND I'VE STILL GOT SO MUCH TO DO.
OH SURE. I UNDERSTAND.
NEED ANY HELP?
NO, THANKS.
DON'T YOU HAVE ANY HOMEWORK?
ME? NOPE? FINISHED IT IN STUDY HALL.
WISH I HAD TAKEN A STUDY HALL INSTEAD OF TOO MANY CLASSES.
BUT IF A MORTAL LIKE PANDORA CAN KEEP UP, WHY SHOULDN'T I?
UM, PANDORA...?

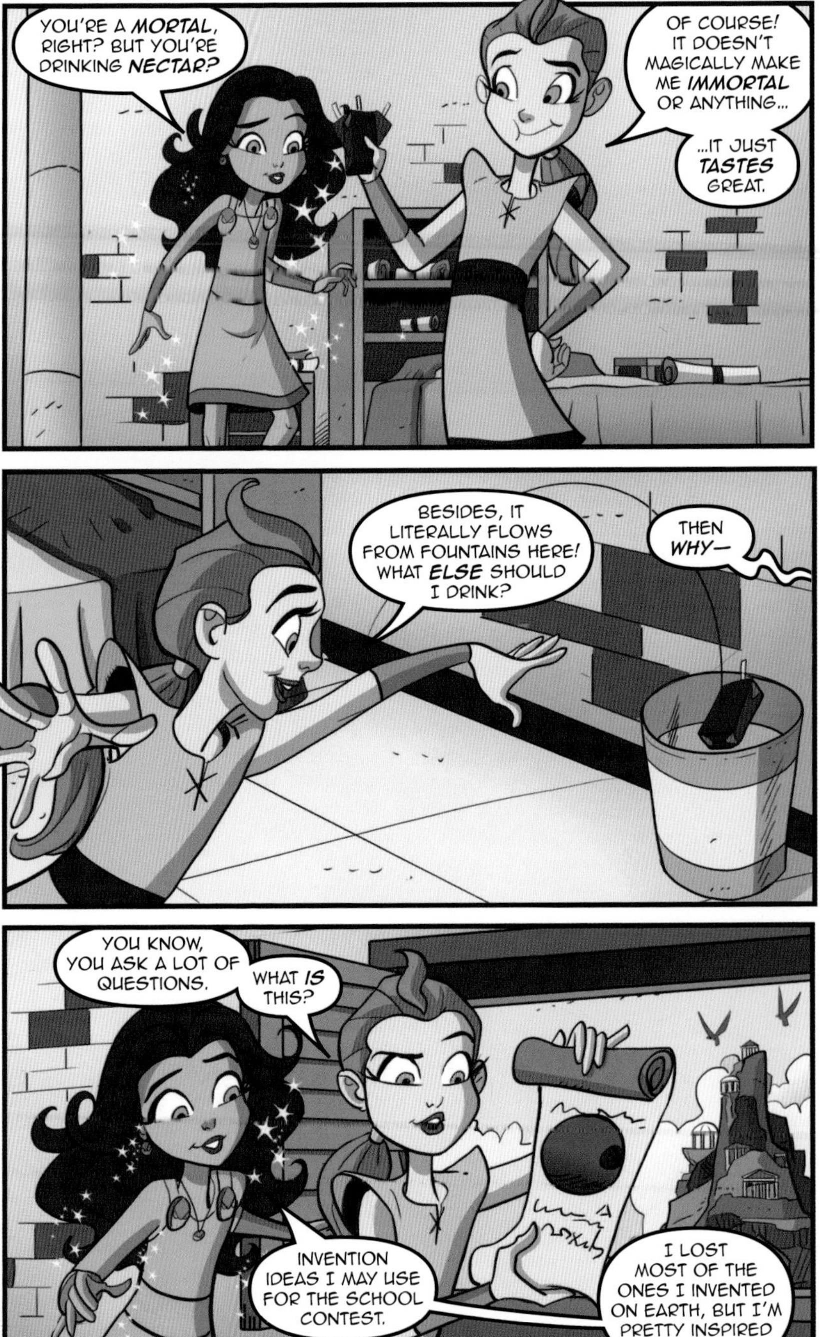
YOU'RE A MORTAL, RIGHT? BUT YOU'RE DRINKING NECTAR?
OF COURSE! IT DOESN'T MAGICALLY MAKE ME IMMORTAL OR ANYTHING...
...IT JUST TASTES GREAT.
BESIDES, IT LITERALLY FLOWS FROM FOUNTAINS HERE! WHAT ELSE SHOULD I DRINK?
THEN WHY—
YOU KNOW, YOU ASK A LOT OF QUESTIONS.
WHAT IS THIS?
INVENTION IDEAS I MAY USE FOR THE SCHOOL CONTEST.
I LOST MOST OF THE ONES I INVENTED ON EARTH, BUT I'M PRETTY INSPIRED HERE.

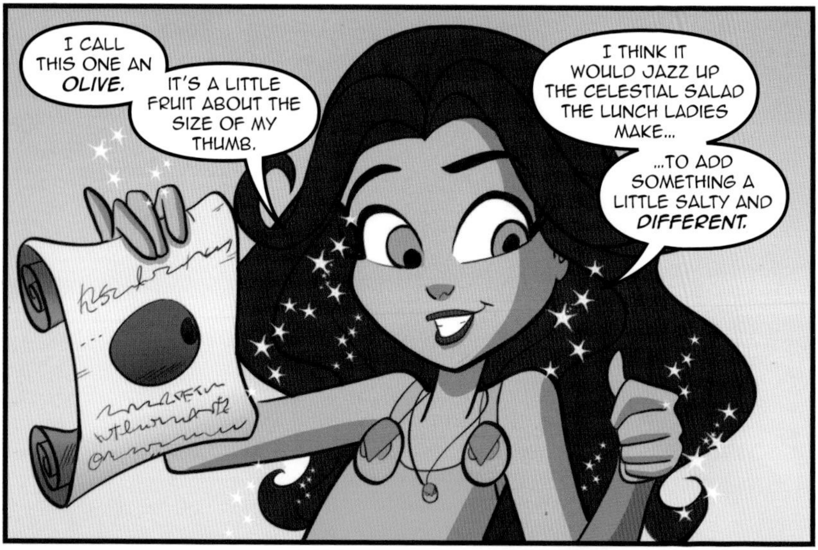
I CALL THIS ONE AN *OLIVE.*
IT'S A LITTLE FRUIT ABOUT THE SIZE OF MY THUMB.
I THINK IT WOULD JAZZ UP THE CELESTIAL SALAD THE LUNCH LADIES MAKE...
...TO ADD SOMETHING A LITTLE SALTY AND *DIFFERENT.*

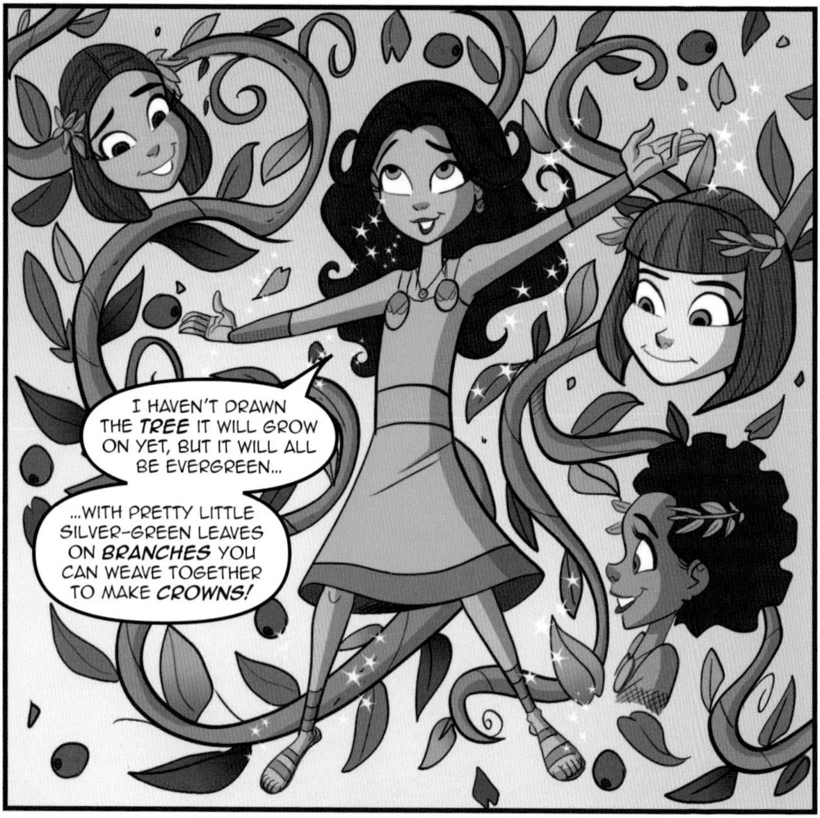
I HAVEN'T DRAWN THE *TREE* IT WILL GROW ON YET, BUT IT WILL ALL BE EVERGREEN...
...WITH PRETTY LITTLE SILVER-GREEN LEAVES ON *BRANCHES* YOU CAN WEAVE TOGETHER TO MAKE *CROWNS!*

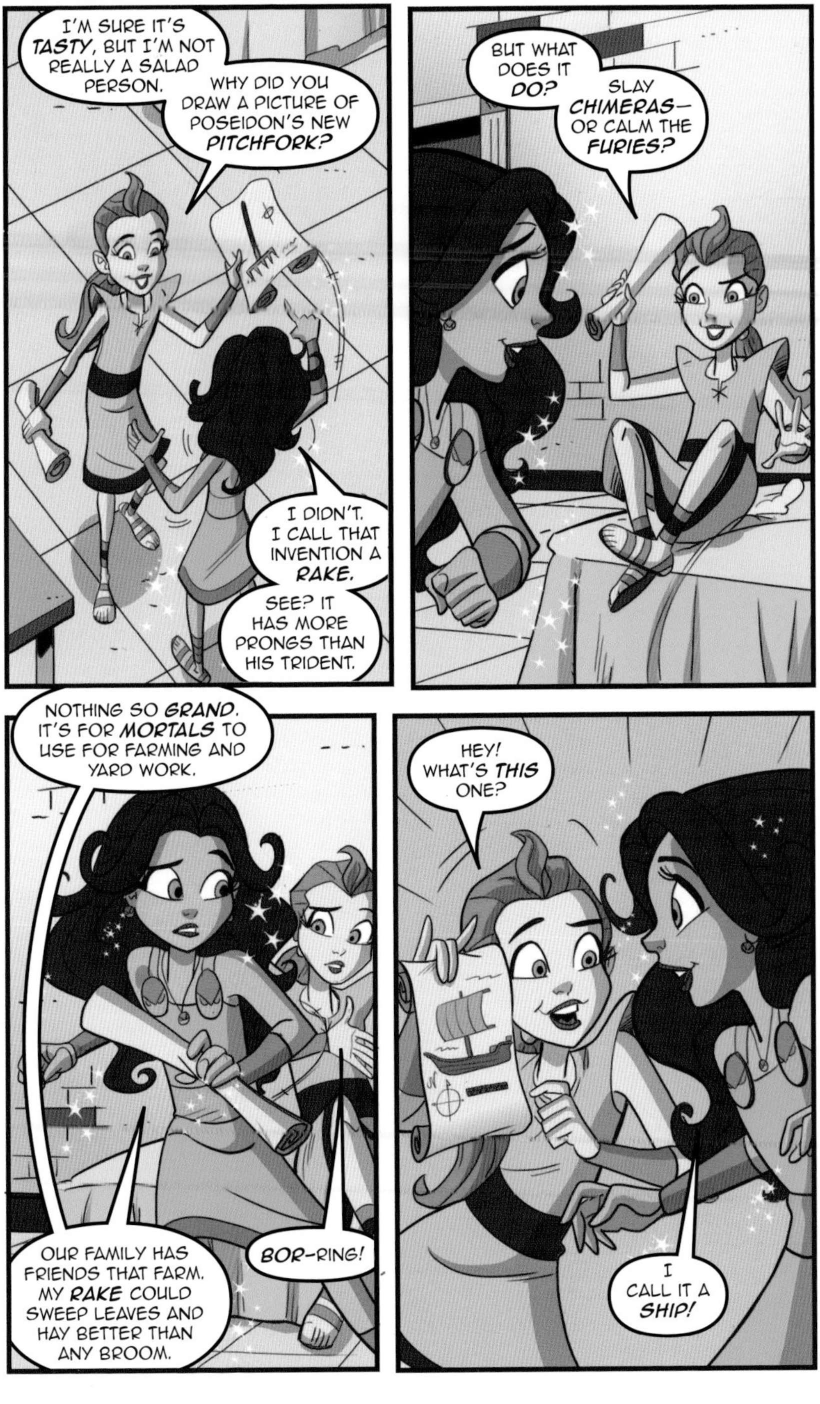
I'M SURE IT'S *TASTY*, BUT I'M NOT REALLY A SALAD PERSON.
WHY DID YOU DRAW A PICTURE OF POSEIDON'S NEW *PITCHFORK?*
I DIDN'T. I CALL THAT INVENTION A *RAKE.*
SEE? IT HAS MORE PRONGS THAN HIS TRIDENT.
BUT WHAT DOES IT *DO?*
SLAY *CHIMERAS*— OR CALM THE *FURIES?*
NOTHING SO *GRAND*. IT'S FOR *MORTALS* TO USE FOR FARMING AND YARD WORK.
OUR FAMILY HAS FRIENDS THAT FARM. MY *RAKE* COULD SWEEP LEAVES AND HAY BETTER THAN ANY BROOM.
BOR-RING!
HEY! WHAT'S *THIS* ONE?
I CALL IT A *SHIP!*

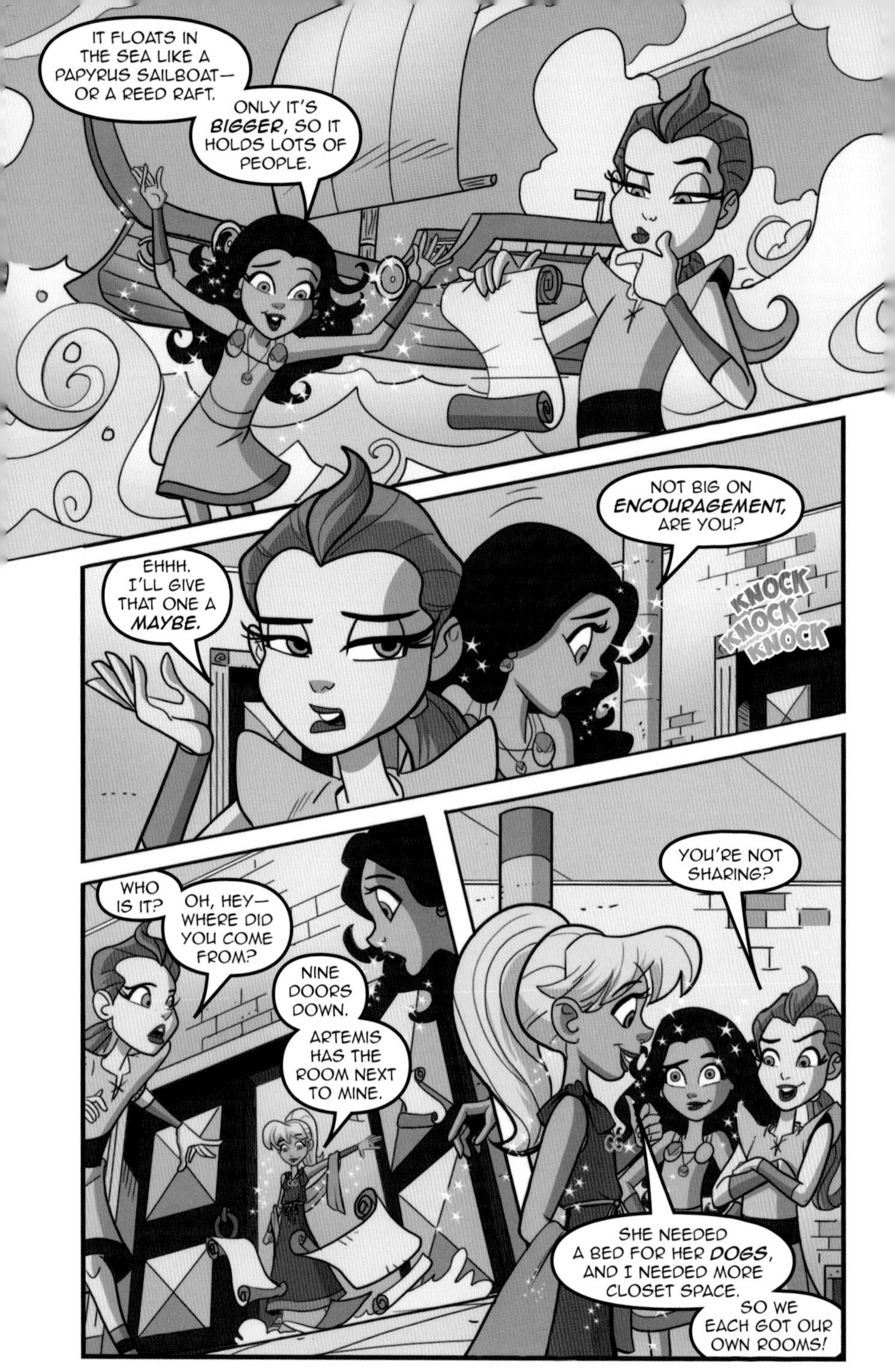
IT FLOATS IN THE SEA LIKE A PAPYRUS SAILBOAT— OR A REED RAFT.
ONLY IT'S *BIGGER*, SO IT HOLDS LOTS OF PEOPLE.
NOT BIG ON *ENCOURAGEMENT,* ARE YOU?
EHHH. I'LL GIVE THAT ONE A *MAYBE.*
KNOCK KNOCK KNOCK
WHO IS IT?
OH, HEY— WHERE DID YOU COME FROM?
NINE DOORS DOWN.
ARTEMIS HAS THE ROOM NEXT TO MINE.
YOU'RE NOT SHARING?
SHE NEEDED A BED FOR HER *DOGS*, AND I NEEDED MORE CLOSET SPACE.
SO WE EACH GOT OUR OWN ROOMS!

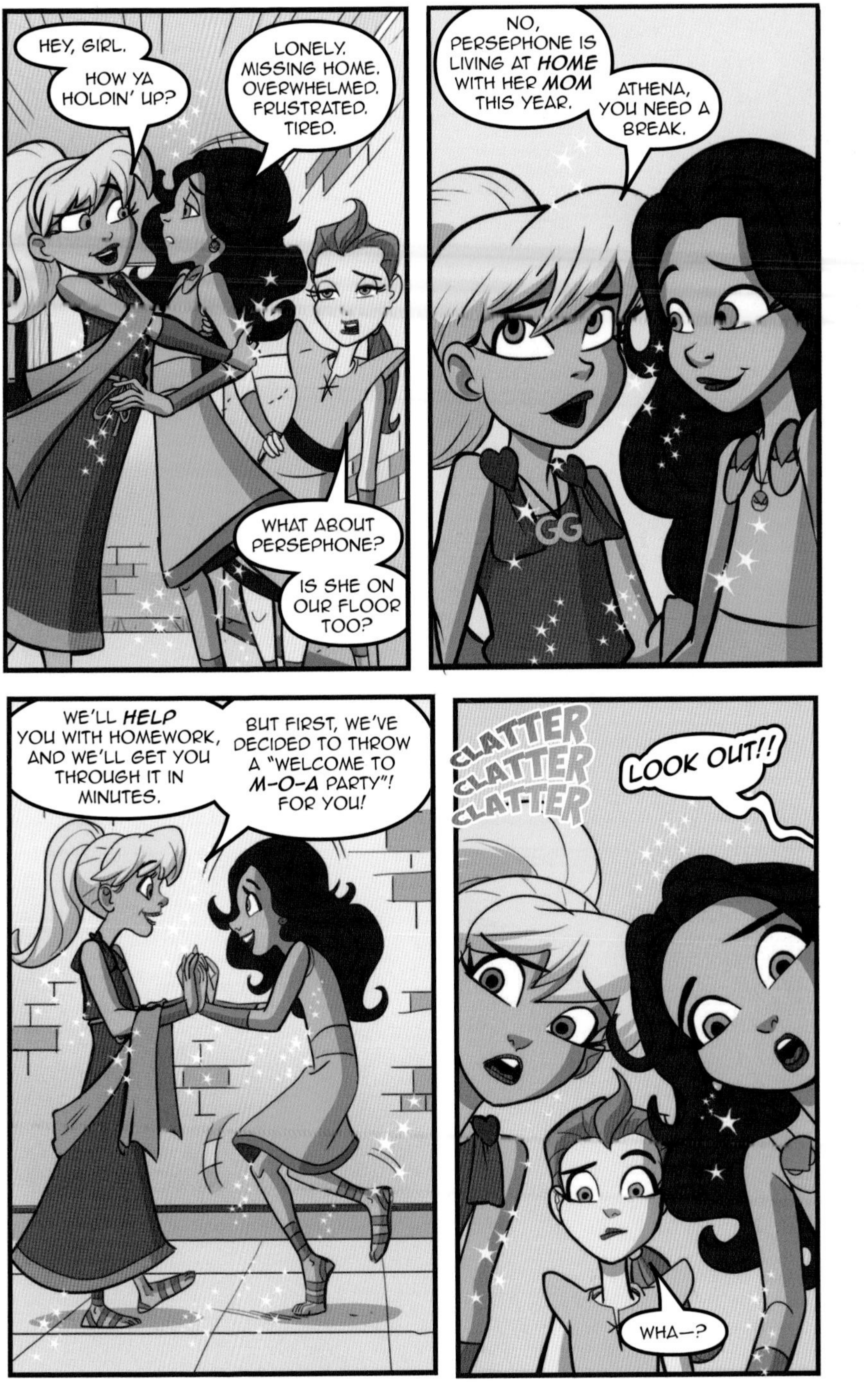
HEY, GIRL.
HOW YA HOLDIN' UP?
LONELY. MISSING HOME. OVERWHELMED. FRUSTRATED. TIRED.
WHAT ABOUT PERSEPHONE?
IS SHE ON OUR FLOOR TOO?
NO, PERSEPHONE IS LIVING AT HOME WITH HER MOM THIS YEAR.
ATHENA, YOU NEED A BREAK.
WE'LL HELP YOU WITH HOMEWORK, AND WE'LL GET YOU THROUGH IT IN MINUTES.
BUT FIRST, WE'VE DECIDED TO THROW A "WELCOME TO M-O-A PARTY"! FOR YOU!
CLATTER CLATTER CLATTER
LOOK OUT!!
WHA—?

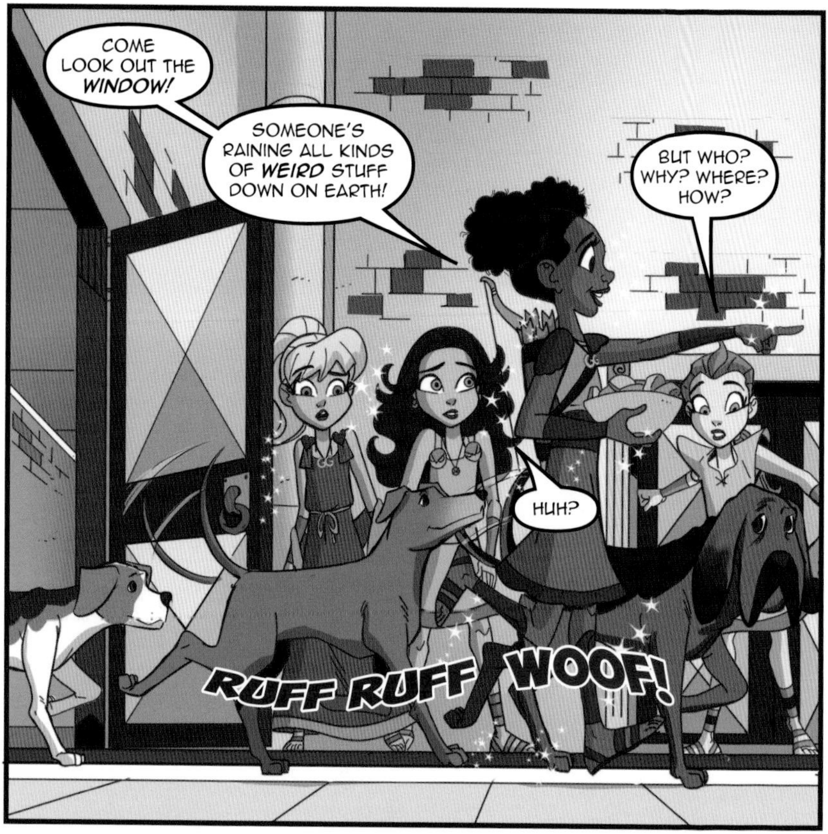
COME LOOK OUT THE *WINDOW!*
SOMEONE'S RAINING ALL KINDS OF *WEIRD* STUFF DOWN ON EARTH!
BUT WHO? WHY? WHERE? HOW?
HUH?
RUFF RUFF WOOF!

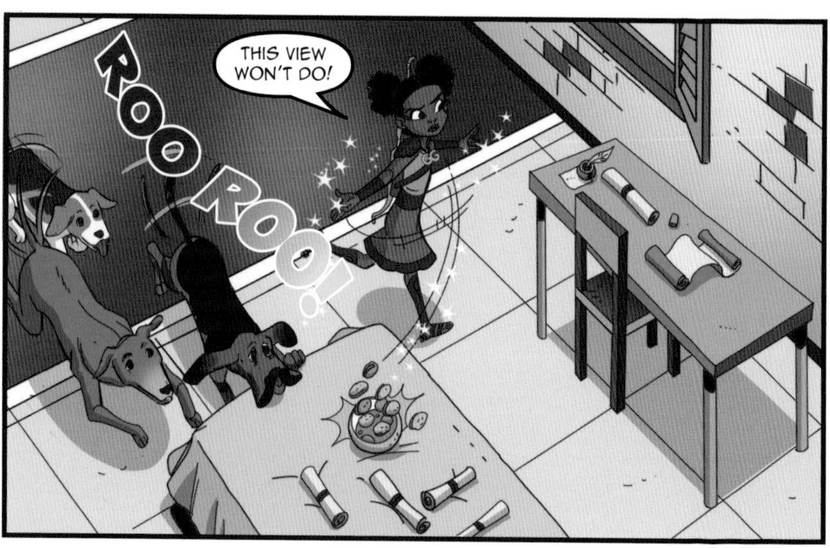
THIS VIEW WON'T DO!
ROO ROO!

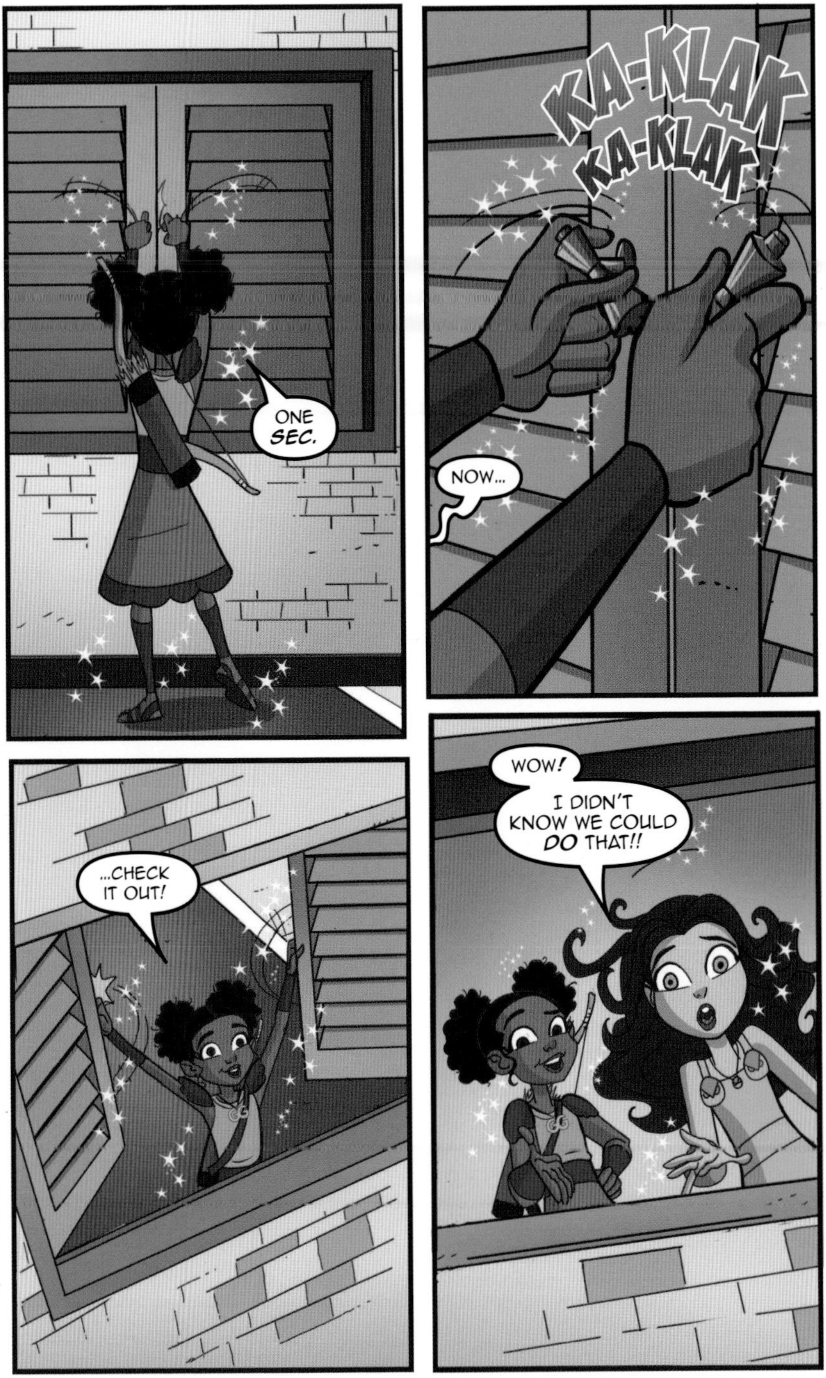
ONE SEC.
KA-KLAK KA-KLAK
NOW...
...CHECK IT OUT!
WOW!
I DIDN'T KNOW WE COULD DO THAT!!

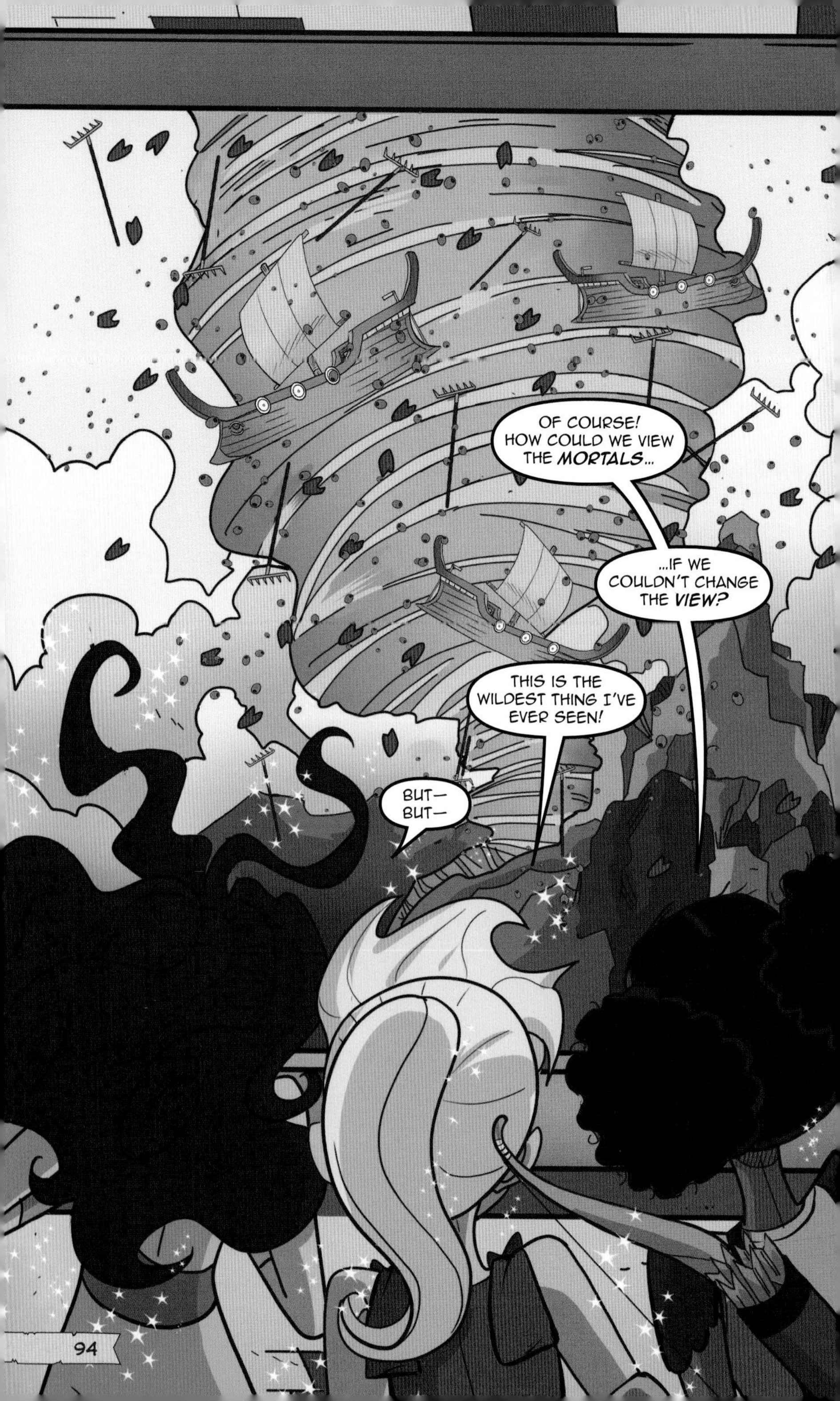
OF COURSE! HOW COULD WE VIEW THE MORTALS...
...IF WE COULDN'T CHANGE THE VIEW?
THIS IS THE WILDEST THING I'VE EVER SEEN!
BUT— BUT—

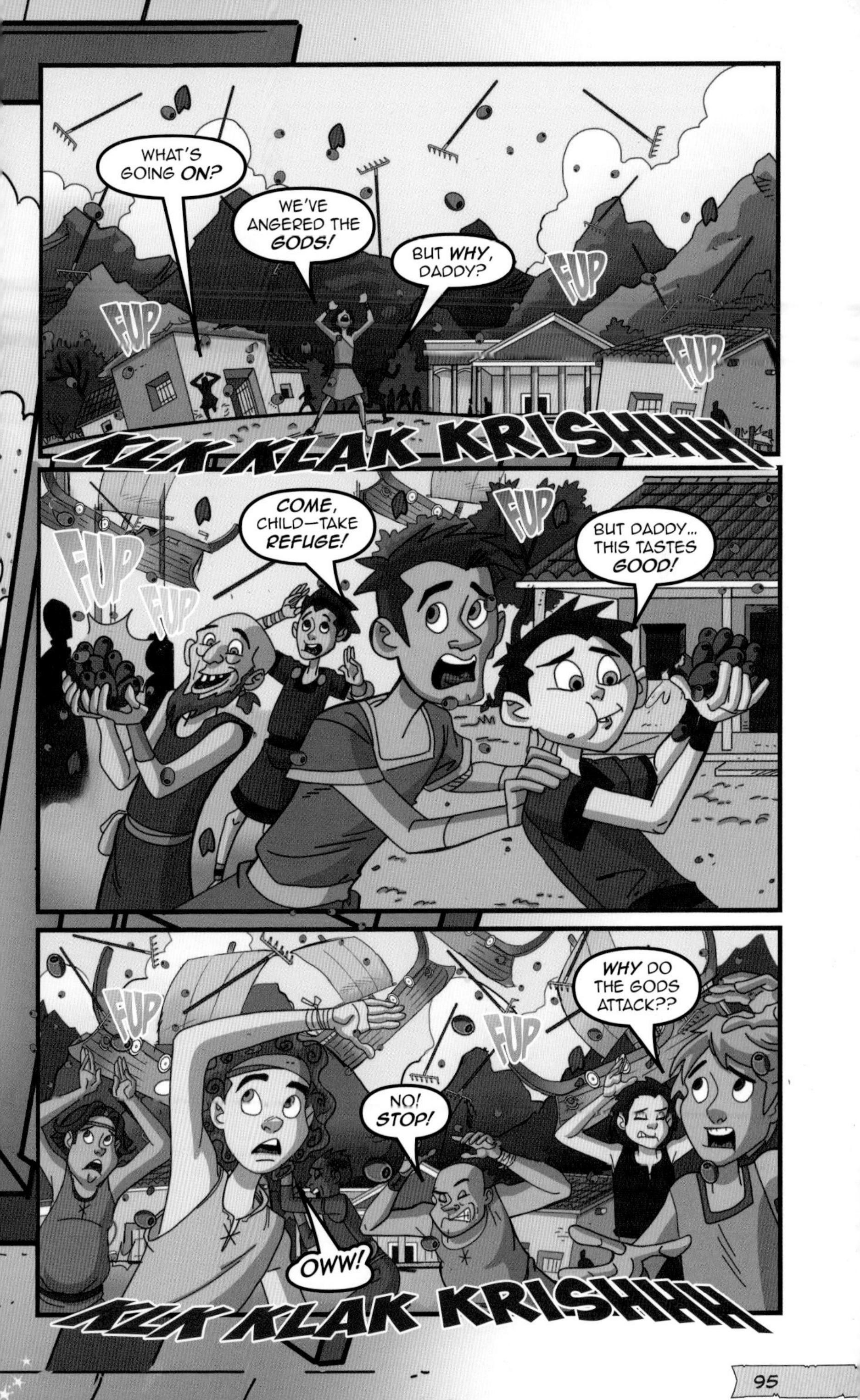
WHAT'S GOING ON?
WE'VE ANGERED THE GODS!
BUT WHY, DADDY?
FUP
FUP
FUP
KLK KLAK KRISHHH
FUP
FUP
FUP
COME, CHILD—TAKE REFUGE!
BUT DADDY... THIS TASTES GOOD!
FUP
FUP
WHY DO THE GODS ATTACK??
NO! STOP!
OWW!
KLK KLAK KRISHHH

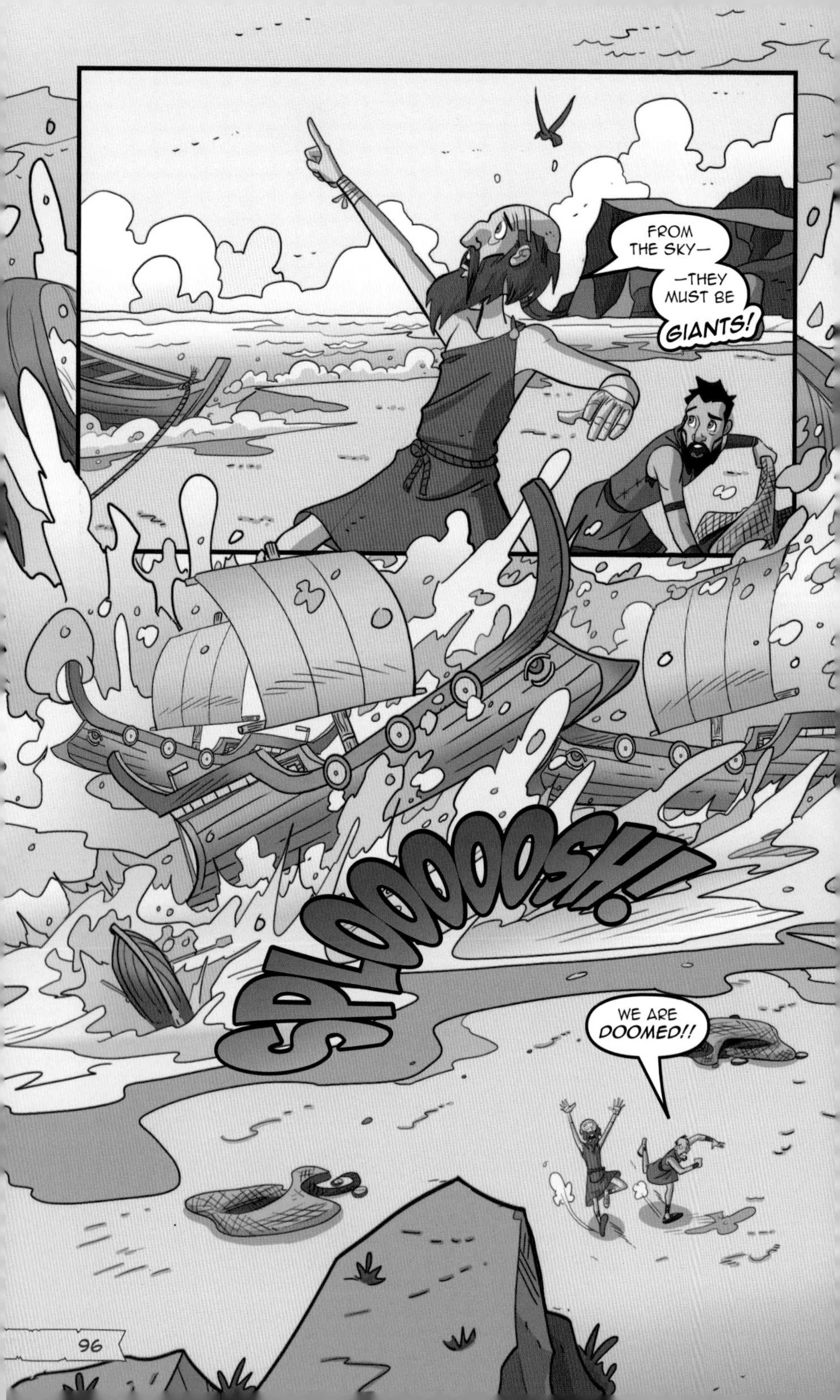
FROM THE SKY—
—THEY MUST BE GIANTS!
SPLOOOOOSH!!
WE ARE DOOMED!!

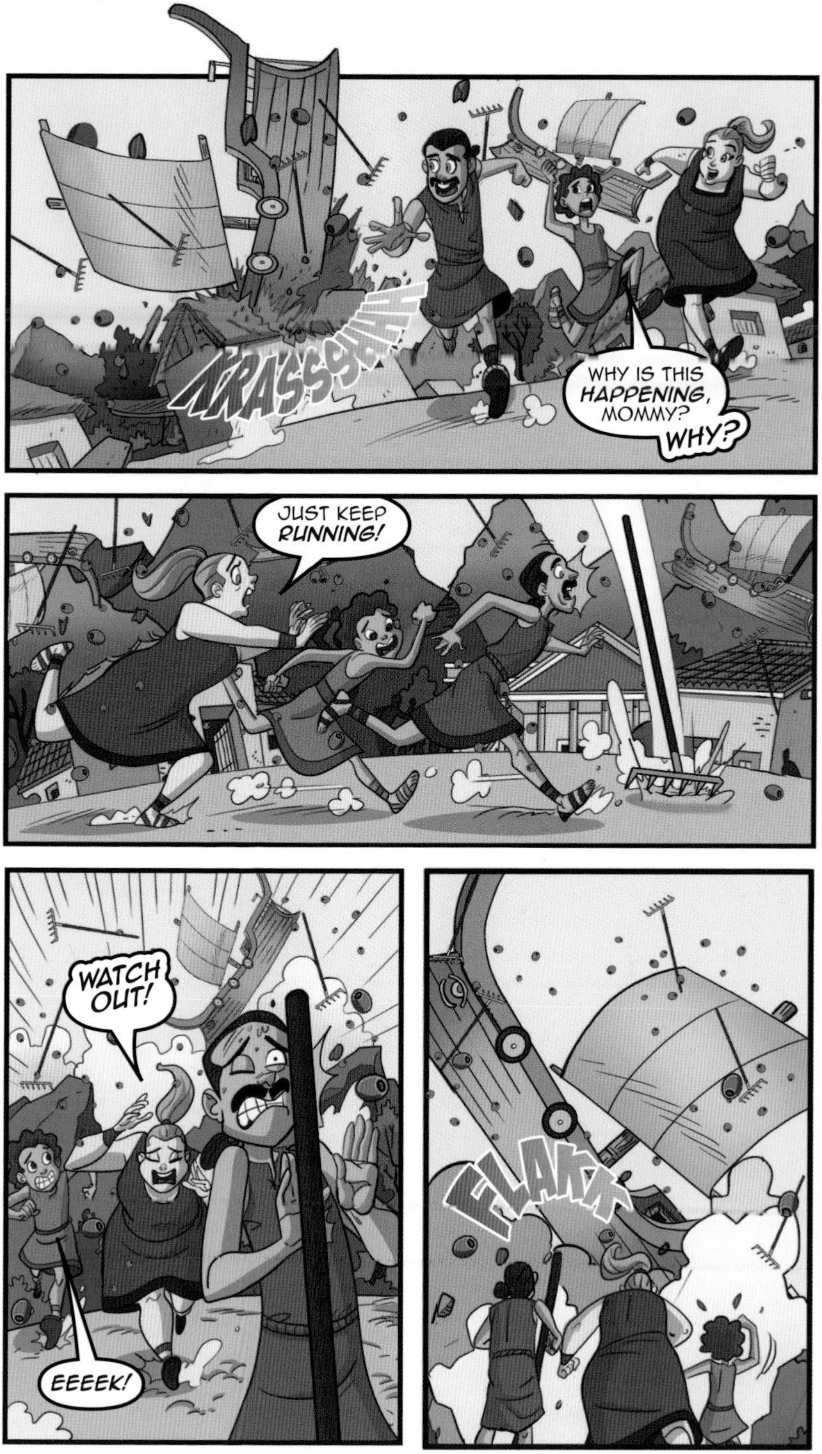
KRASSSHHH
WHY IS THIS HAPPENING, MOMMY? WHY?
JUST KEEP RUNNING!
WATCH OUT!
EEEEK!
FLAKK

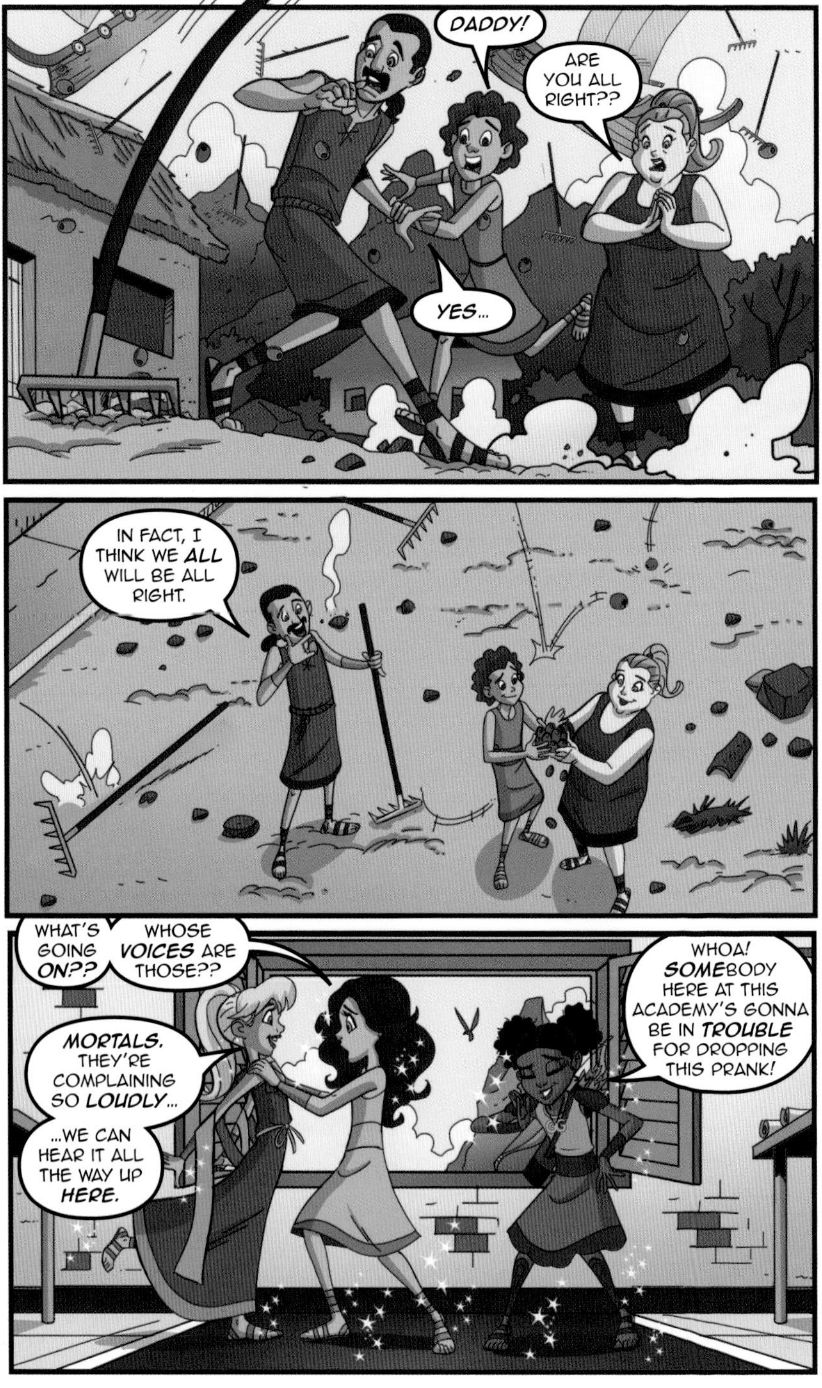
DADDY!
ARE YOU ALL RIGHT??
YES...
IN FACT, I THINK WE ALL WILL BE ALL RIGHT.
WHAT'S GOING ON??
WHOSE VOICES ARE THOSE??
MORTALS. THEY'RE COMPLAINING SO LOUDLY...
...WE CAN HEAR IT ALL THE WAY UP HERE.
WHOA! SOMEBODY HERE AT THIS ACADEMY'S GONNA BE IN TROUBLE FOR DROPPING THIS PRANK!

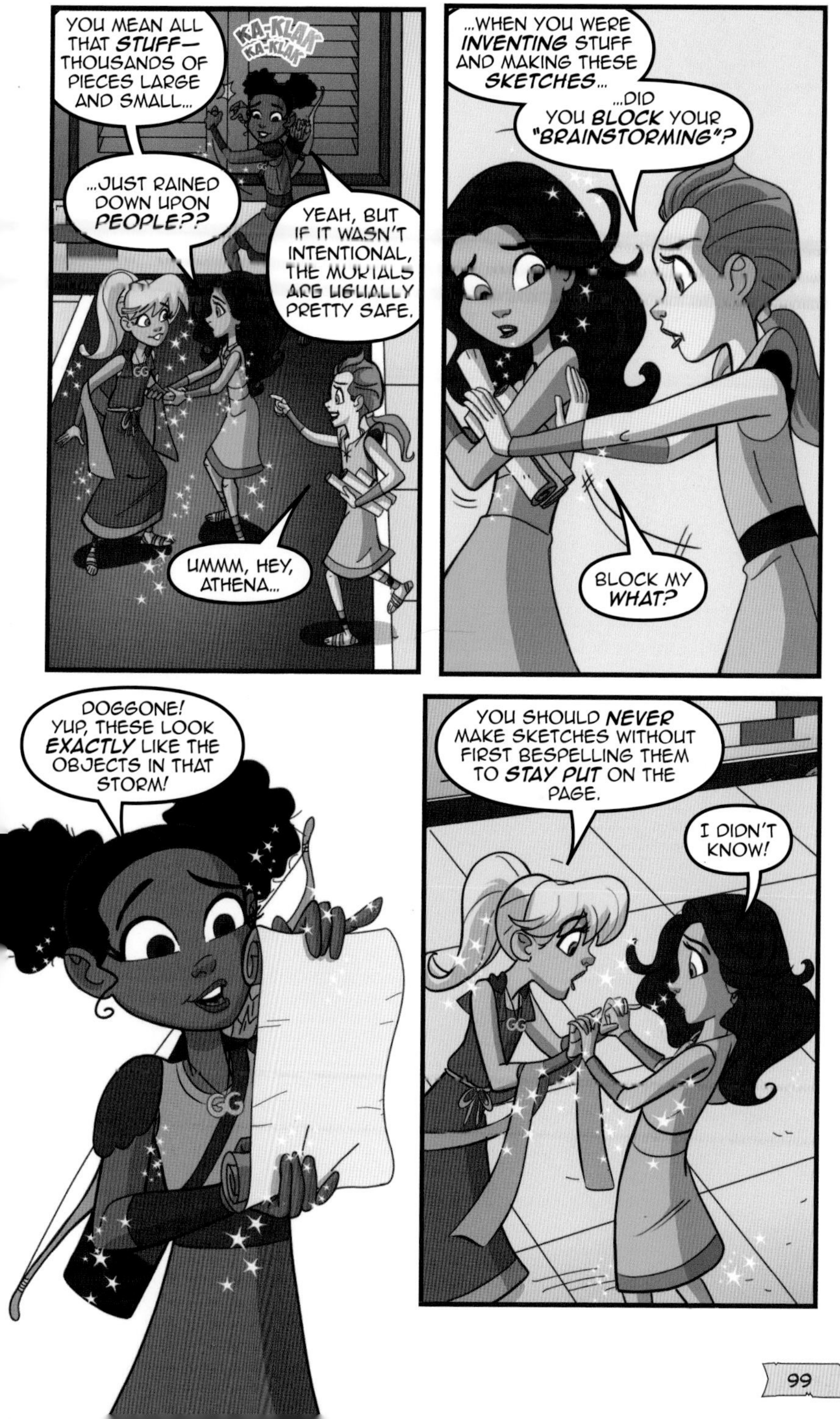

YOU MEAN ALL THAT STUFF— THOUSANDS OF PIECES LARGE AND SMALL...
KA-KLAK KA-KLAK
...JUST RAINED DOWN UPON PEOPLE??
YEAH, BUT IF IT WASN'T INTENTIONAL, THE MORTALS ARE USUALLY PRETTY SAFE.
UMMM, HEY, ATHENA...
...WHEN YOU WERE INVENTING STUFF AND MAKING THESE SKETCHES...
...DID YOU BLOCK YOUR "BRAINSTORMING"?
BLOCK MY WHAT?
DOGGONE! YUP, THESE LOOK EXACTLY LIKE THE OBJECTS IN THAT STORM!
YOU SHOULD NEVER MAKE SKETCHES WITHOUT FIRST BESPELLING THEM TO STAY PUT ON THE PAGE.
I DIDN'T KNOW!

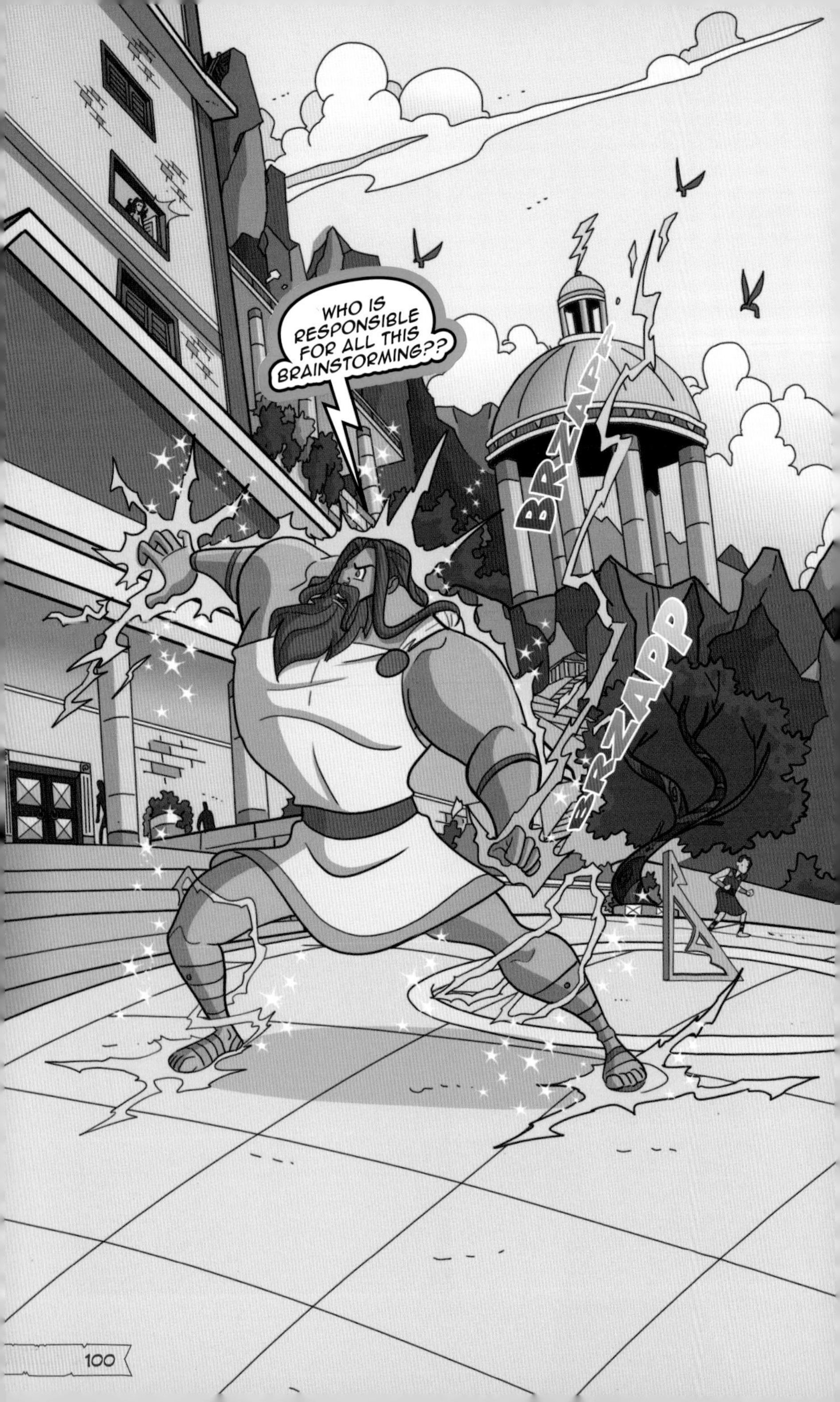
WHO IS RESPONSIBLE FOR ALL THIS BRAINSTORMING??
BRZAPP
BRZAPP

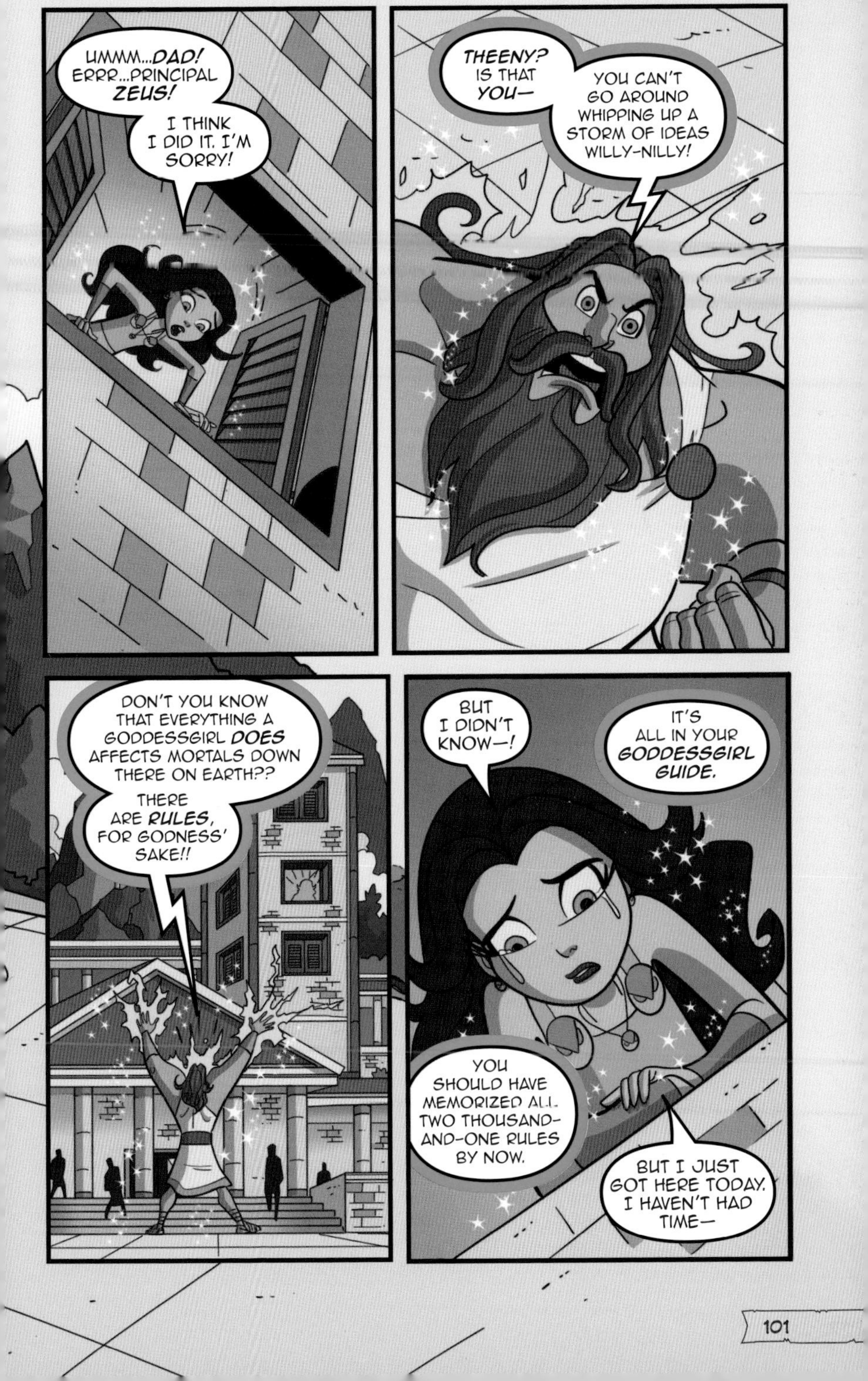
UMMM...DAD! ERRR...PRINCIPAL ZEUS!
I THINK I DID IT. I'M SORRY!
THEENY? IS THAT YOU—
YOU CAN'T GO AROUND WHIPPING UP A STORM OF IDEAS WILLY-NILLY!
DON'T YOU KNOW THAT EVERYTHING A GODDESSGIRL DOES AFFECTS MORTALS DOWN THERE ON EARTH??
THERE ARE RULES, FOR GODNESS' SAKE!!
BUT I DIDN'T KNOW—!
IT'S ALL IN YOUR GODDESSGIRL GUIDE.
YOU SHOULD HAVE MEMORIZED ALL TWO THOUSAND-AND-ONE RULES BY NOW.
BUT I JUST GOT HERE TODAY. I HAVEN'T HAD TIME—

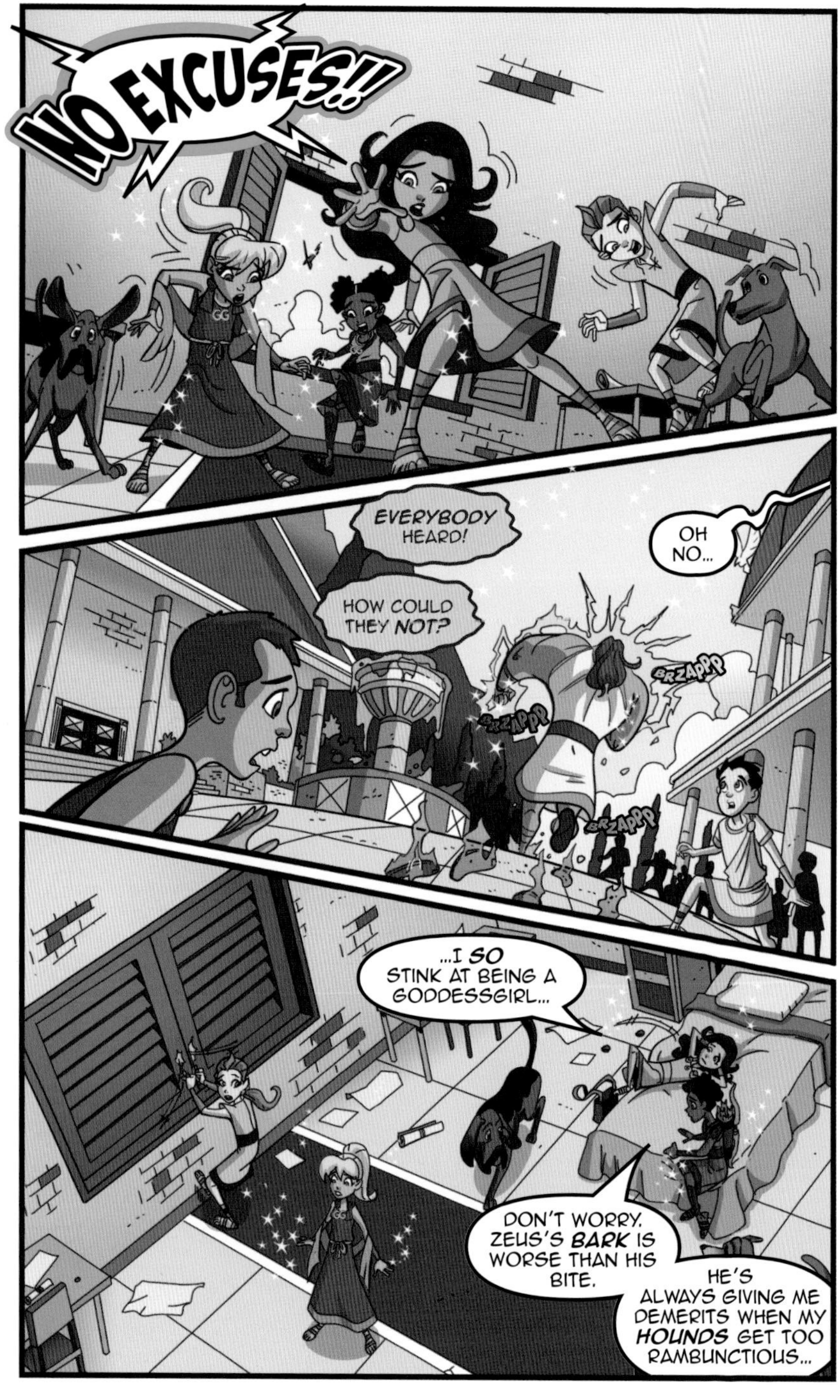
NO EXCUSES!!
EVERYBODY HEARD!
OH NO...
HOW COULD THEY NOT?
BRZAPPP
BRZAPPP
BRZAPPP
...I SO STINK AT BEING A GODDESSGIRL...
DON'T WORRY. ZEUS'S BARK IS WORSE THAN HIS BITE.
HE'S ALWAYS GIVING ME DEMERITS WHEN MY HOUNDS GET TOO RAMBUNCTIOUS...

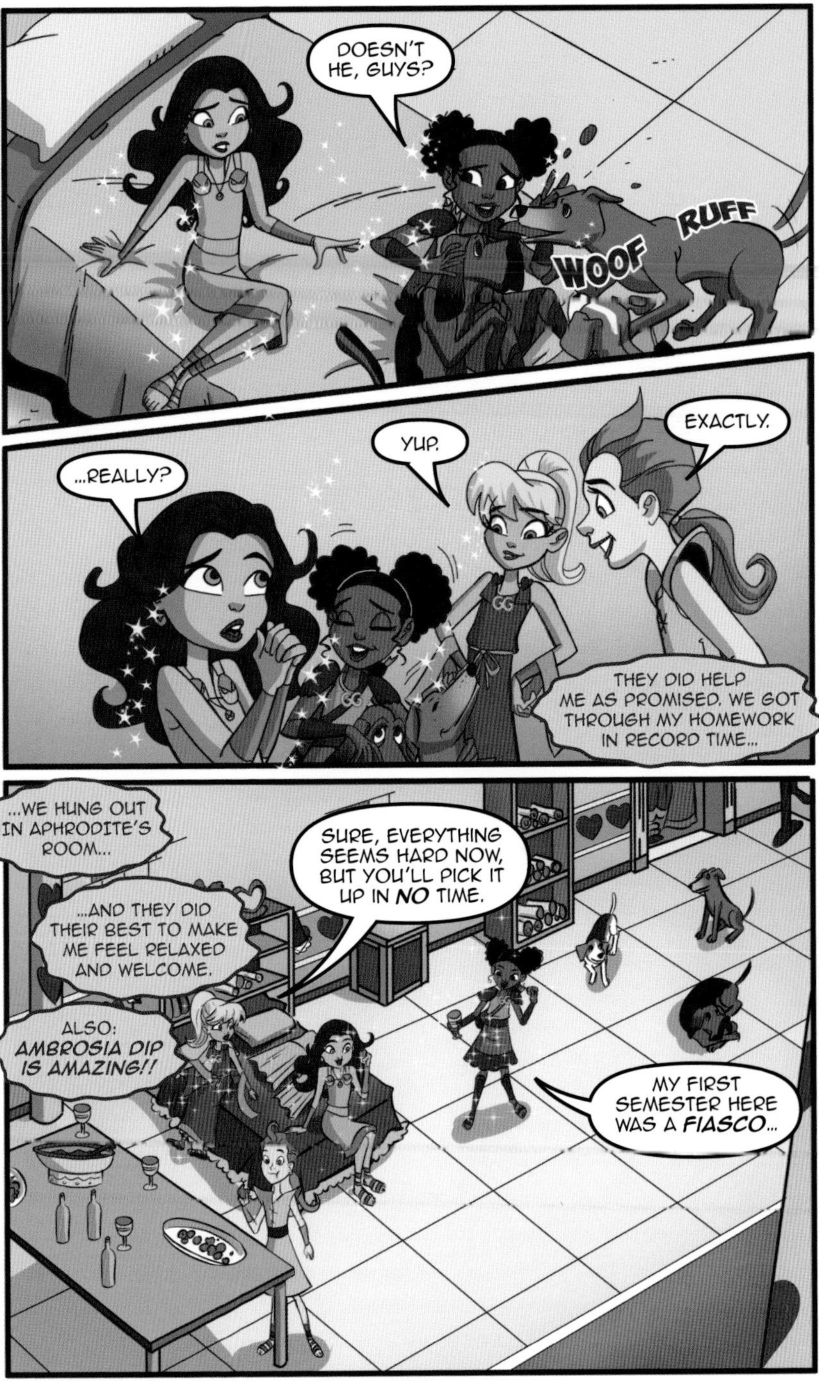
DOESN'T HE, GUYS?
RUFF
WOOF
...REALLY?
YUP.
EXACTLY.
THEY DID HELP ME AS PROMISED. WE GOT THROUGH MY HOMEWORK IN RECORD TIME...
...WE HUNG OUT IN APHRODITE'S ROOM...
SURE, EVERYTHING SEEMS HARD NOW, BUT YOU'LL PICK IT UP IN NO TIME.
...AND THEY DID THEIR BEST TO MAKE ME FEEL RELAXED AND WELCOME.
ALSO: AMBROSIA DIP IS AMAZING!!
MY FIRST SEMESTER HERE WAS A FIASCO...

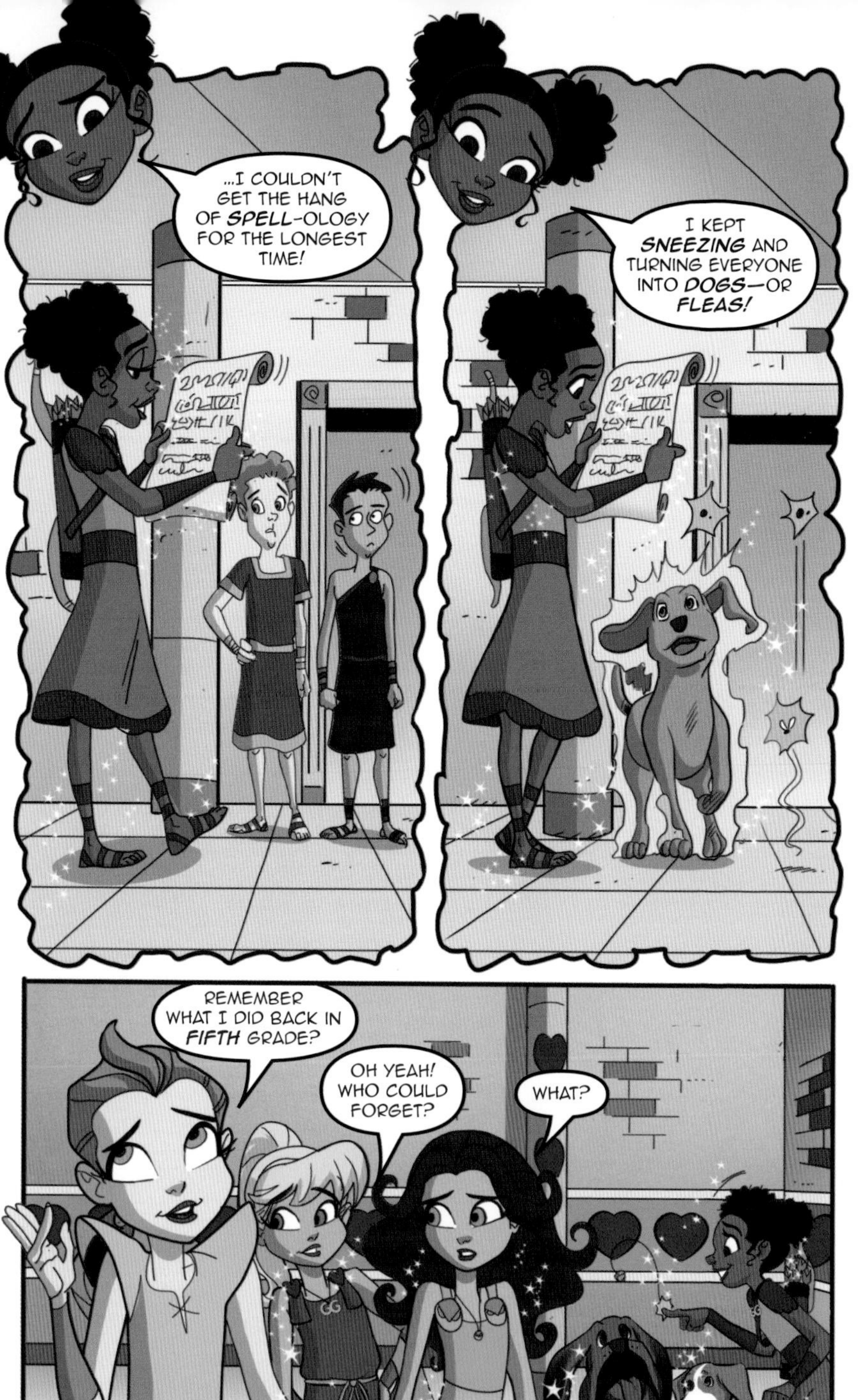

...I COULDN'T GET THE HANG OF SPELL-OLOGY FOR THE LONGEST TIME!
I KEPT SNEEZING AND TURNING EVERYONE INTO DOGS—OR FLEAS!
REMEMBER WHAT I DID BACK IN FIFTH GRADE?
OH YEAH! WHO COULD FORGET?
WHAT?

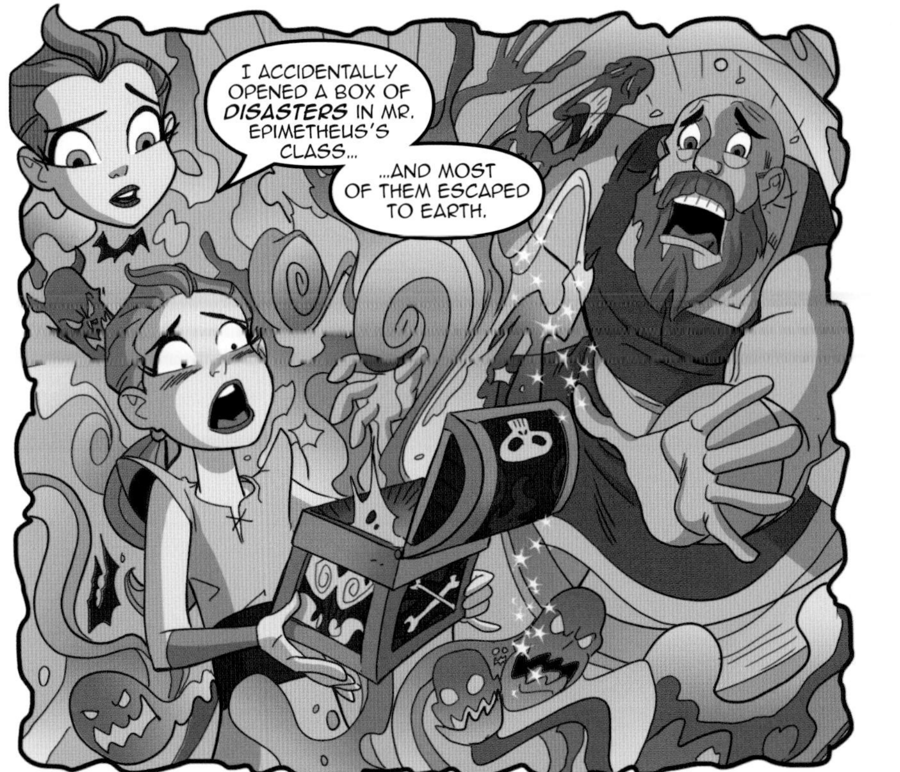
I ACCIDENTALLY OPENED A BOX OF ***DISASTERS*** IN MR. EPIMETHEUS'S CLASS...
...AND MOST OF THEM ESCAPED TO EARTH.

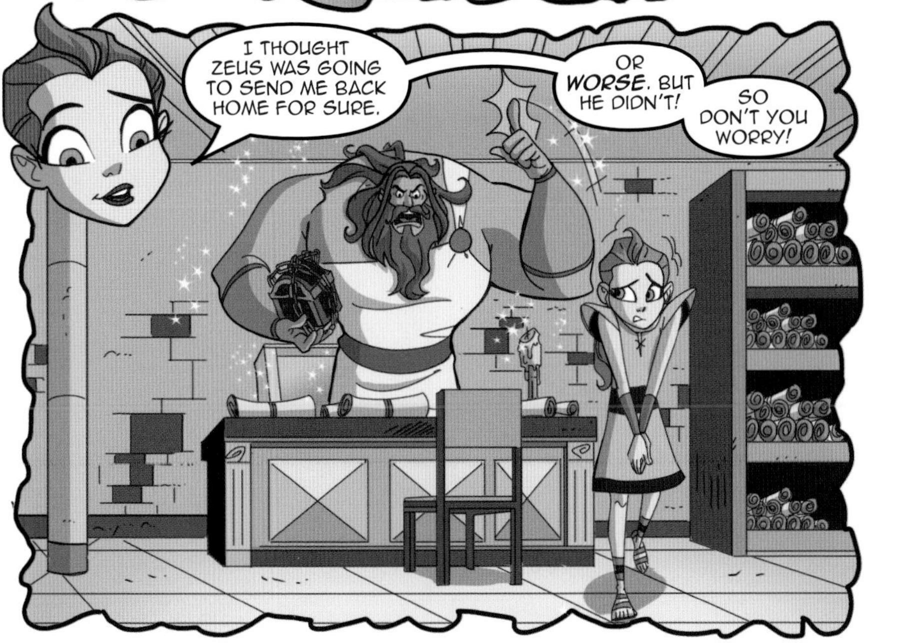
I THOUGHT ZEUS WAS GOING TO SEND ME BACK HOME FOR SURE.
OR ***WORSE***. BUT HE DIDN'T!
SO DON'T YOU WORRY!

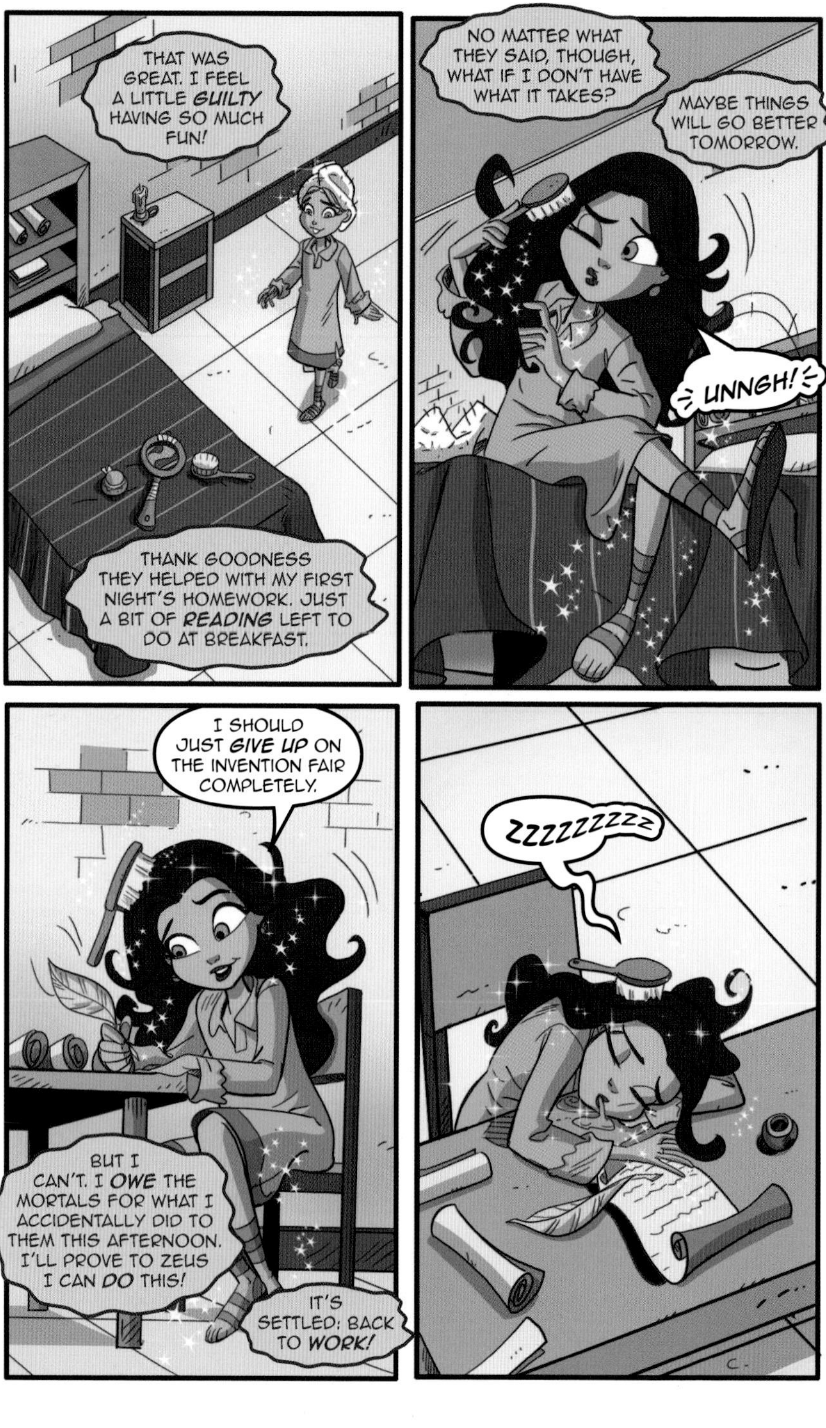

THAT WAS GREAT. I FEEL A LITTLE GUILTY HAVING SO MUCH FUN!
THANK GOODNESS THEY HELPED WITH MY FIRST NIGHT'S HOMEWORK. JUST A BIT OF READING LEFT TO DO AT BREAKFAST.
NO MATTER WHAT THEY SAID, THOUGH, WHAT IF I DON'T HAVE WHAT IT TAKES?
MAYBE THINGS WILL GO BETTER TOMORROW.
UNNGH!
I SHOULD JUST GIVE UP ON THE INVENTION FAIR COMPLETELY.
BUT I CAN'T. I OWE THE MORTALS FOR WHAT I ACCIDENTALLY DID TO THEM THIS AFTERNOON. I'LL PROVE TO ZEUS I CAN DO THIS!
IT'S SETTLED: BACK TO WORK!
ZZZZZZZZZ

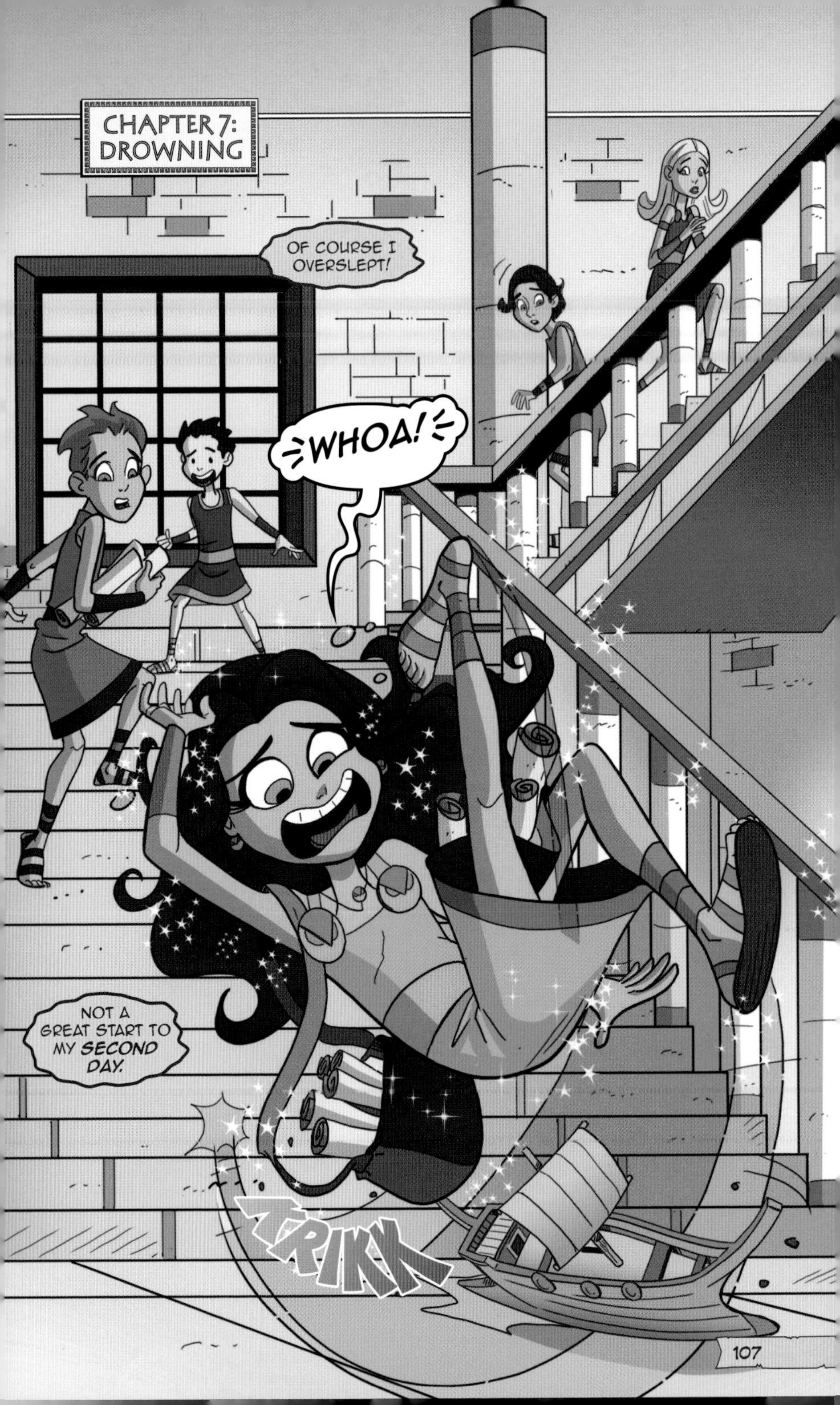
CHAPTER 7: DROWNING
OF COURSE I OVERSLEPT!
WHOA!
NOT A GREAT START TO MY SECOND DAY.
KRIKK

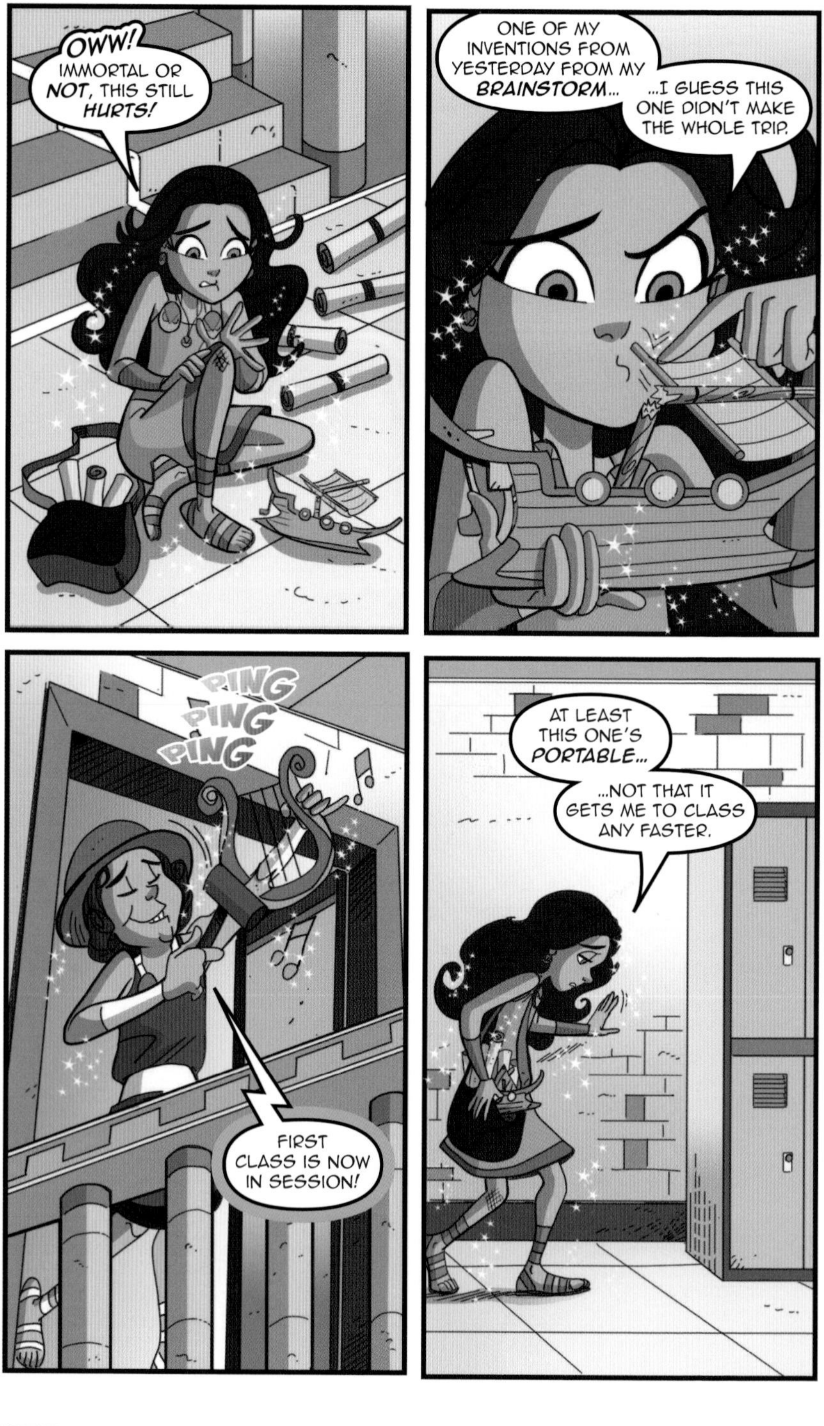
OWW!
IMMORTAL OR NOT, THIS STILL HURTS!
ONE OF MY INVENTIONS FROM YESTERDAY FROM MY BRAINSTORM...
...I GUESS THIS ONE DIDN'T MAKE THE WHOLE TRIP.
PING PING PING
FIRST CLASS IS NOW IN SESSION!
AT LEAST THIS ONE'S PORTABLE...
...NOT THAT IT GETS ME TO CLASS ANY FASTER.

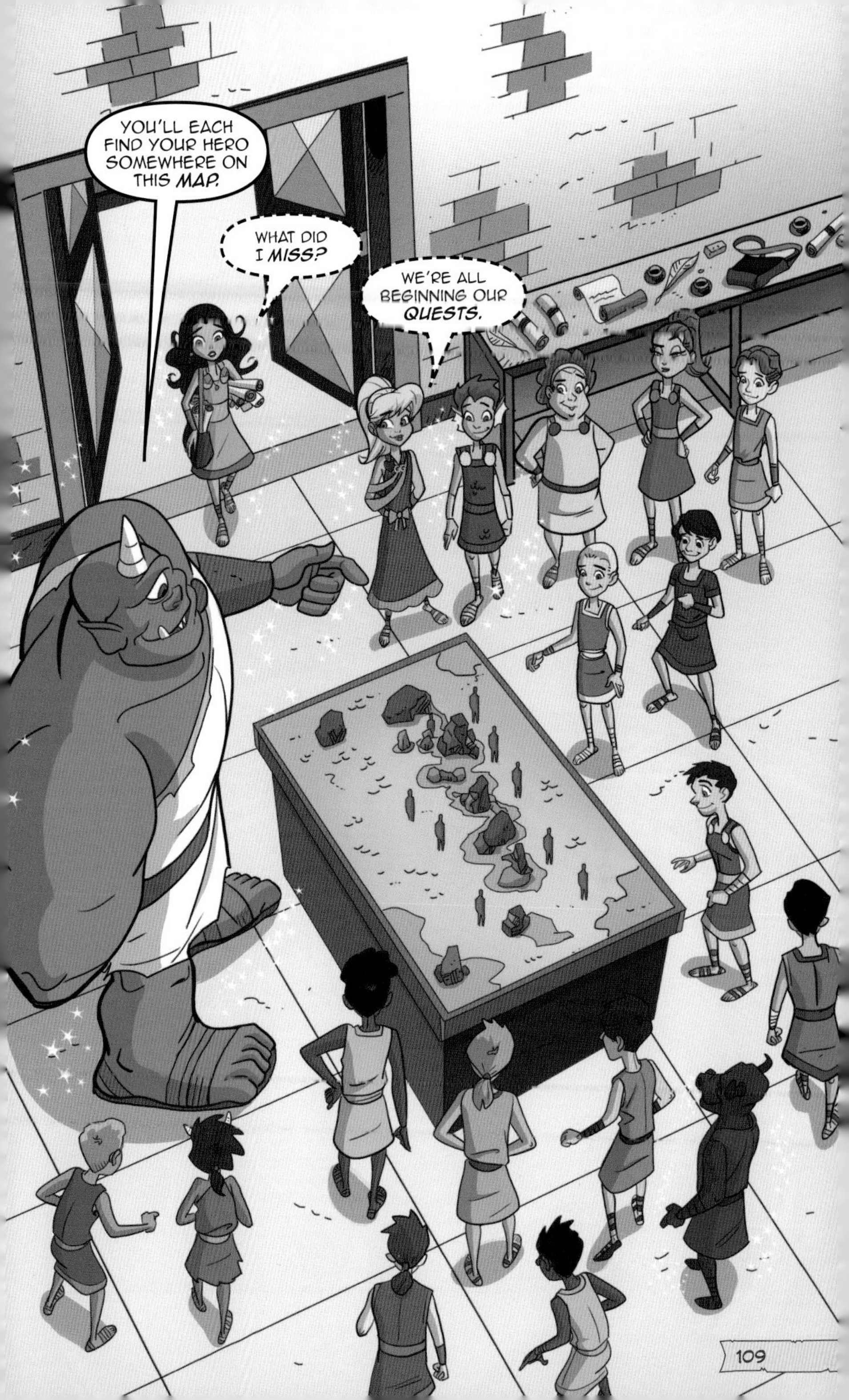
YOU'LL EACH FIND YOUR HERO SOMEWHERE ON THIS MAP.
WHAT DID I MISS?
WE'RE ALL BEGINNING OUR QUESTS.

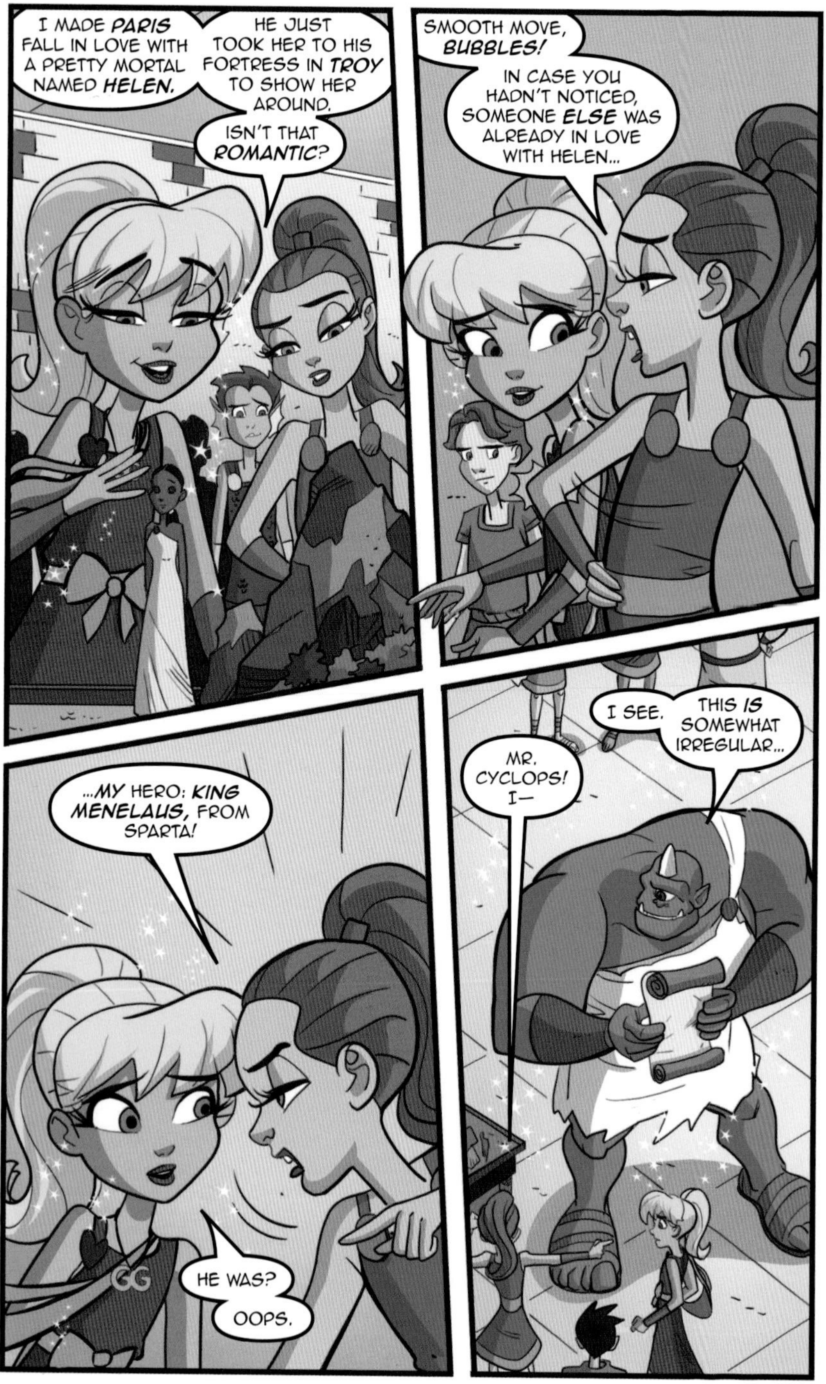
I MADE PARIS FALL IN LOVE WITH A PRETTY MORTAL NAMED HELEN.
HE JUST TOOK HER TO HIS FORTRESS IN TROY TO SHOW HER AROUND.
ISN'T THAT ROMANTIC?
SMOOTH MOVE, BUBBLES!
IN CASE YOU HADN'T NOTICED, SOMEONE ELSE WAS ALREADY IN LOVE WITH HELEN...
...MY HERO: KING MENELAUS, FROM SPARTA!
HE WAS?
OOPS.
MR. CYCLOPS! I—
I SEE.
THIS IS SOMEWHAT IRREGULAR...

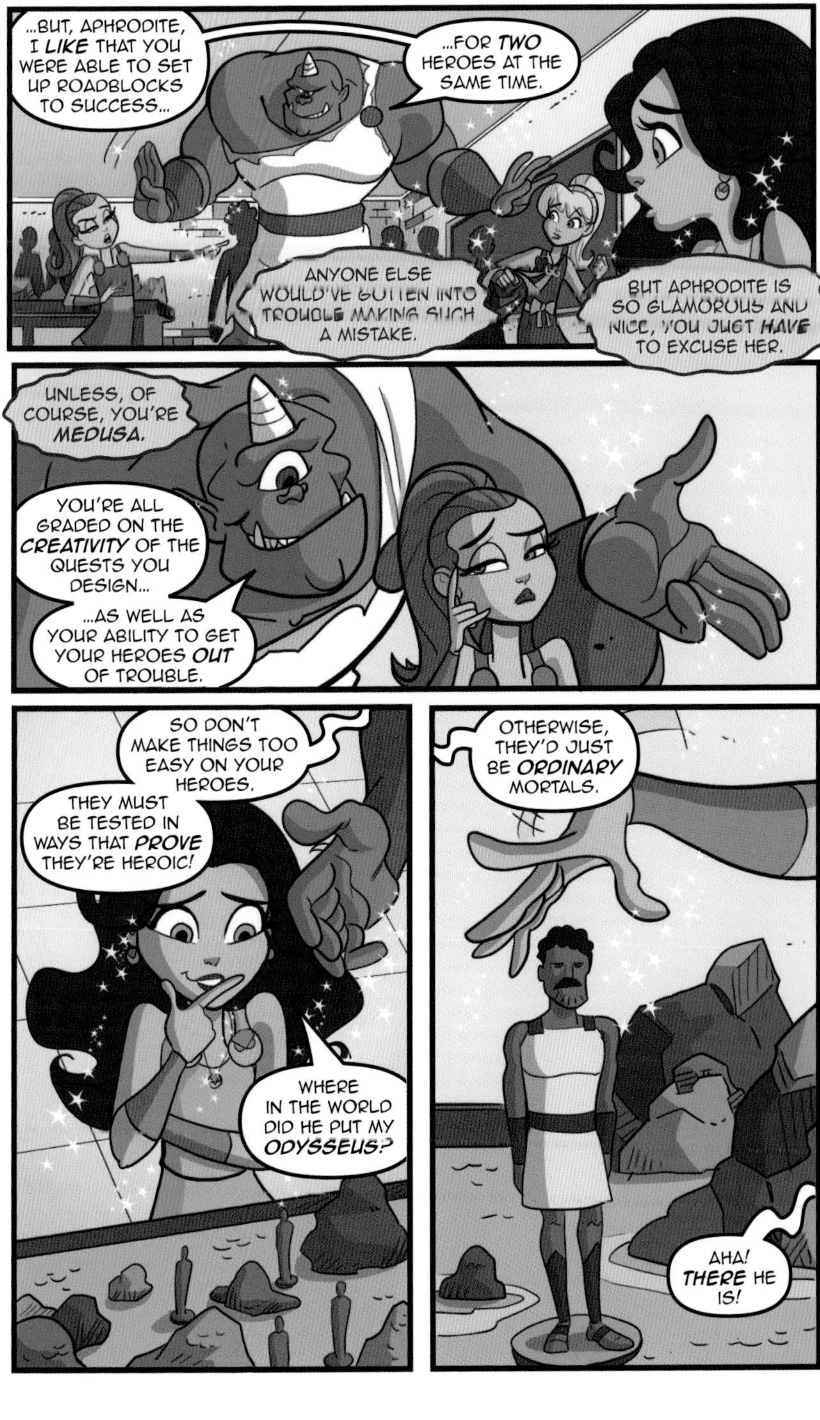
...BUT, APHRODITE, I LIKE THAT YOU WERE ABLE TO SET UP ROADBLOCKS TO SUCCESS...
...FOR TWO HEROES AT THE SAME TIME.
ANYONE ELSE WOULD'VE GOTTEN INTO TROUBLE MAKING SUCH A MISTAKE.
BUT APHRODITE IS SO GLAMOROUS AND NICE, YOU JUST HAVE TO EXCUSE HER.
UNLESS, OF COURSE, YOU'RE MEDUSA.
YOU'RE ALL GRADED ON THE CREATIVITY OF THE QUESTS YOU DESIGN...
...AS WELL AS YOUR ABILITY TO GET YOUR HEROES OUT OF TROUBLE.
SO DON'T MAKE THINGS TOO EASY ON YOUR HEROES.
THEY MUST BE TESTED IN WAYS THAT PROVE THEY'RE HEROIC!
WHERE IN THE WORLD DID HE PUT MY ODYSSEUS?
OTHERWISE, THEY'D JUST BE ORDINARY MORTALS.
AHA! THERE HE IS!

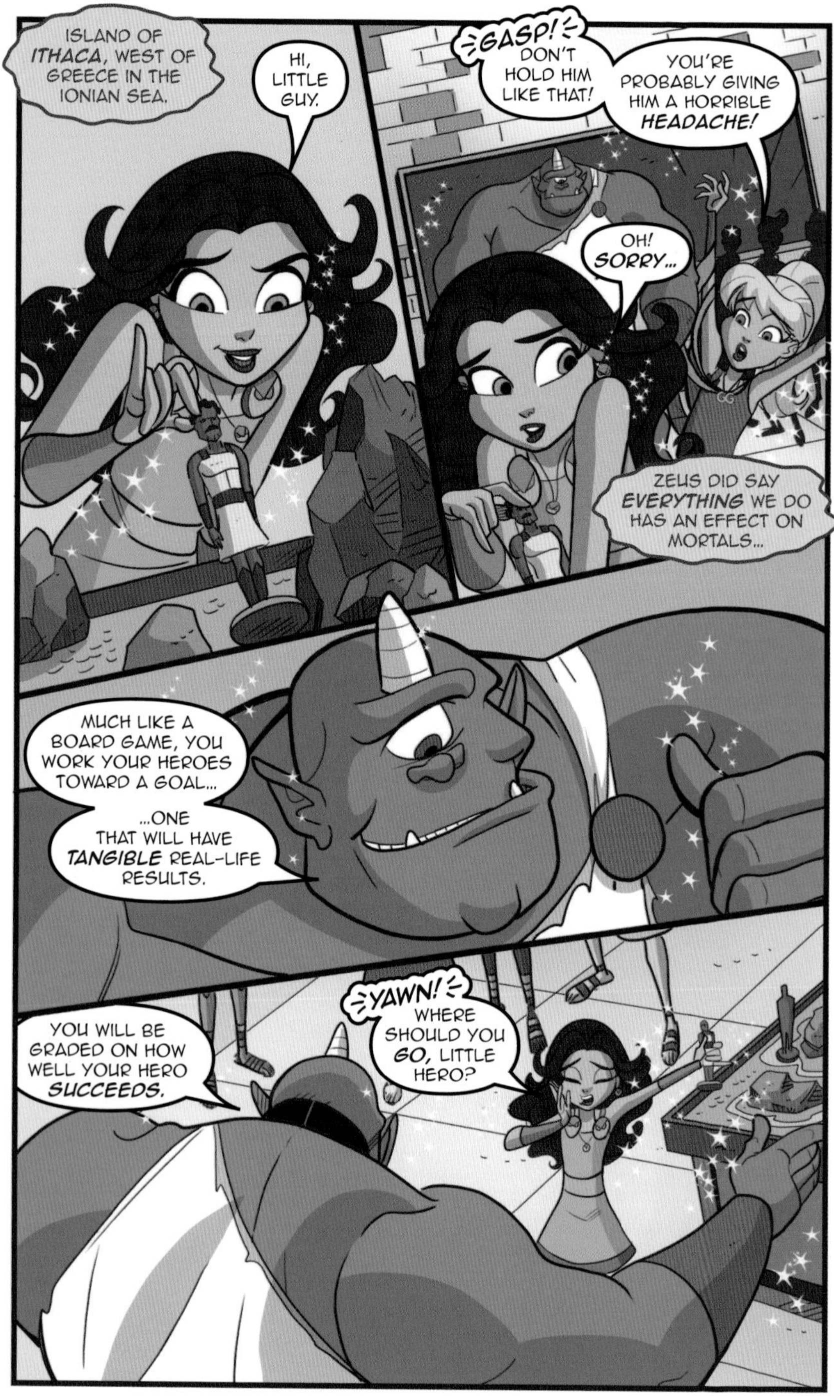
ISLAND OF ITHACA, WEST OF GREECE IN THE IONIAN SEA.
HI, LITTLE GUY.
GASP!
DON'T HOLD HIM LIKE THAT!
YOU'RE PROBABLY GIVING HIM A HORRIBLE HEADACHE!
OH! SORRY...
ZEUS DID SAY EVERYTHING WE DO HAS AN EFFECT ON MORTALS...
MUCH LIKE A BOARD GAME, YOU WORK YOUR HEROES TOWARD A GOAL...
...ONE THAT WILL HAVE TANGIBLE REAL-LIFE RESULTS.
YOU WILL BE GRADED ON HOW WELL YOUR HERO SUCCEEDS.
YAWN!
WHERE SHOULD YOU GO, LITTLE HERO?

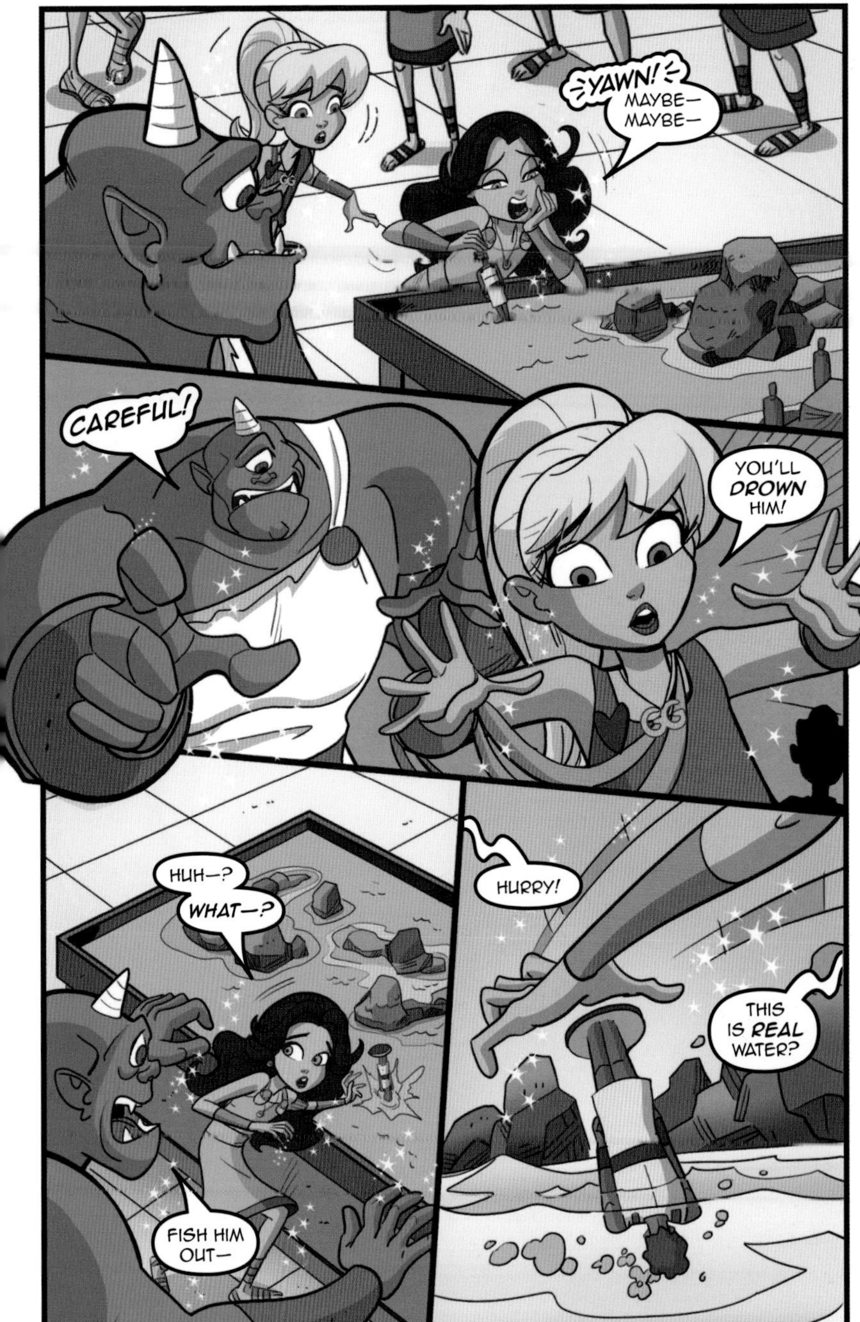
YAWN!
MAYBE—
MAYBE—
CAREFUL!
YOU'LL DROWN HIM!
HUH—?
WHAT—?
FISH HIM OUT—
HURRY!
THIS IS REAL WATER?

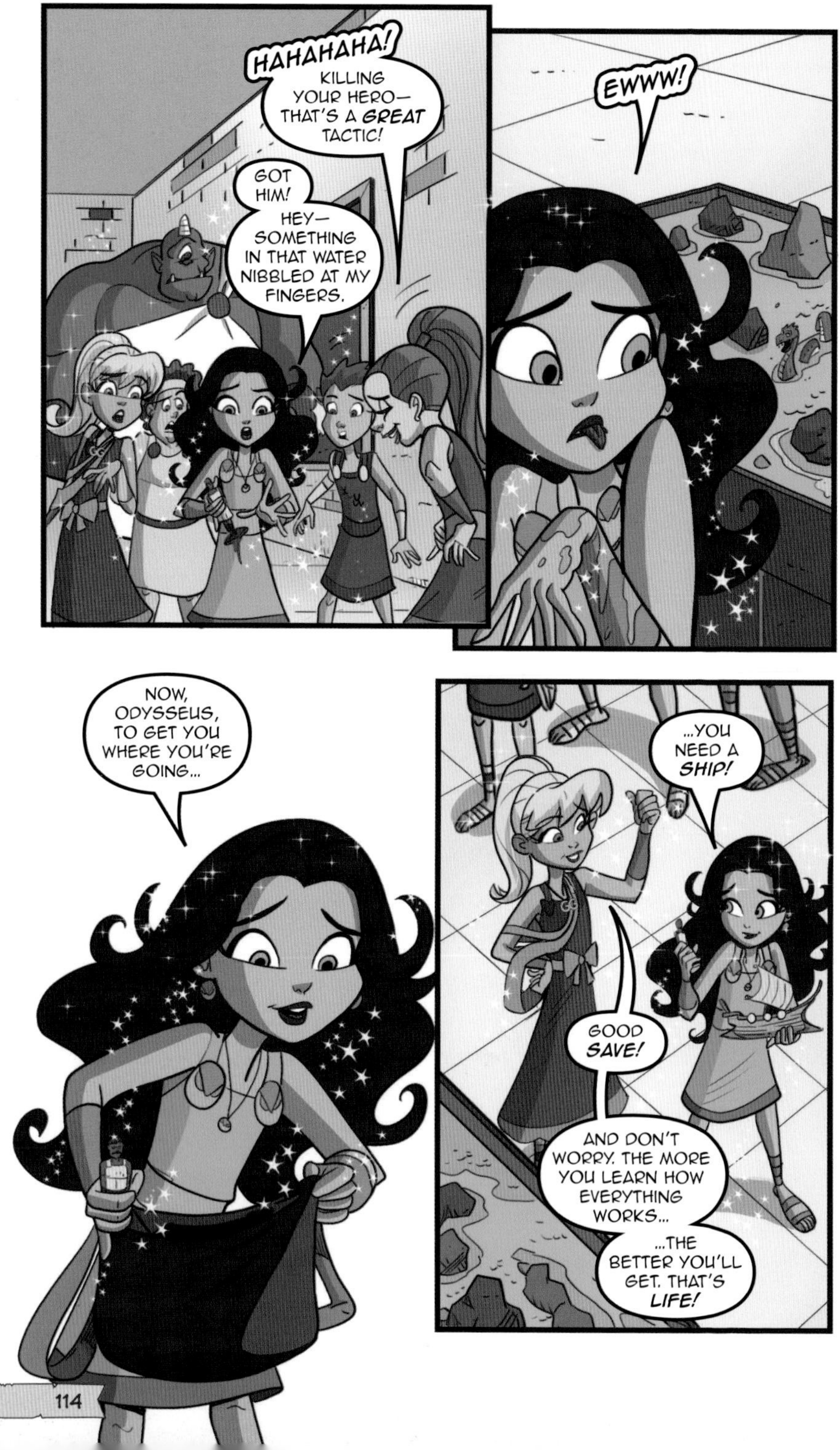
HAHAHAHA!
KILLING YOUR HERO— THAT'S A GREAT TACTIC!
GOT HIM!
HEY— SOMETHING IN THAT WATER NIBBLED AT MY FINGERS.
EWWW!
NOW, ODYSSEUS, TO GET YOU WHERE YOU'RE GOING...
...YOU NEED A SHIP!
GOOD SAVE!
AND DON'T WORRY. THE MORE YOU LEARN HOW EVERYTHING WORKS...
...THE BETTER YOU'LL GET. THAT'S LIFE!

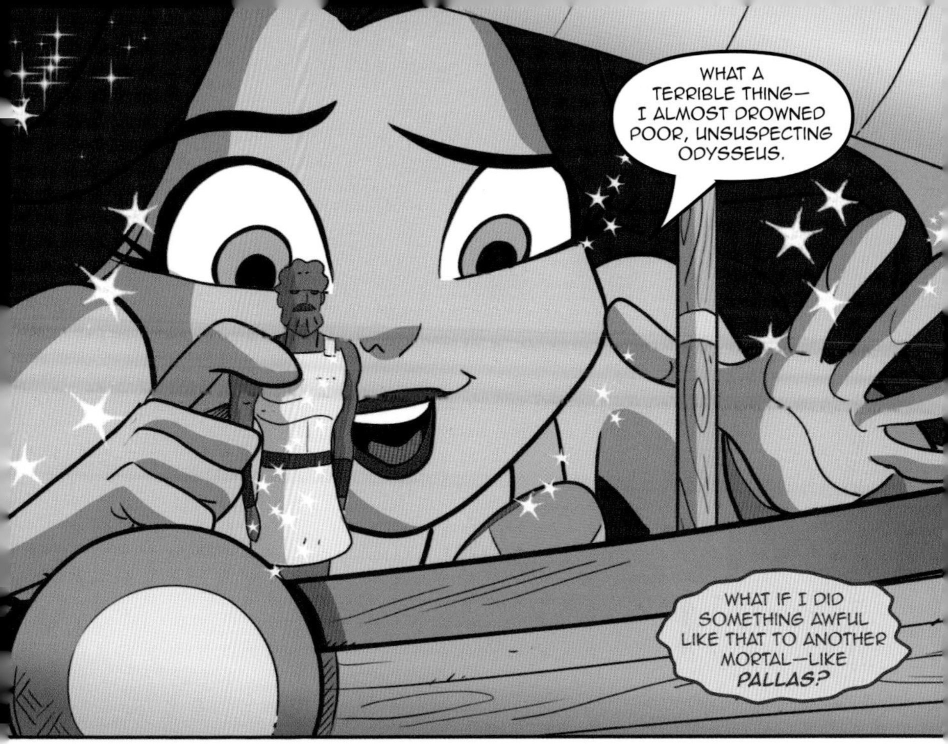
WHAT A TERRIBLE THING— I ALMOST DROWNED POOR, UNSUSPECTING ODYSSEUS.
WHAT IF I DID SOMETHING AWFUL LIKE THAT TO ANOTHER MORTAL—LIKE *PALLAS?*

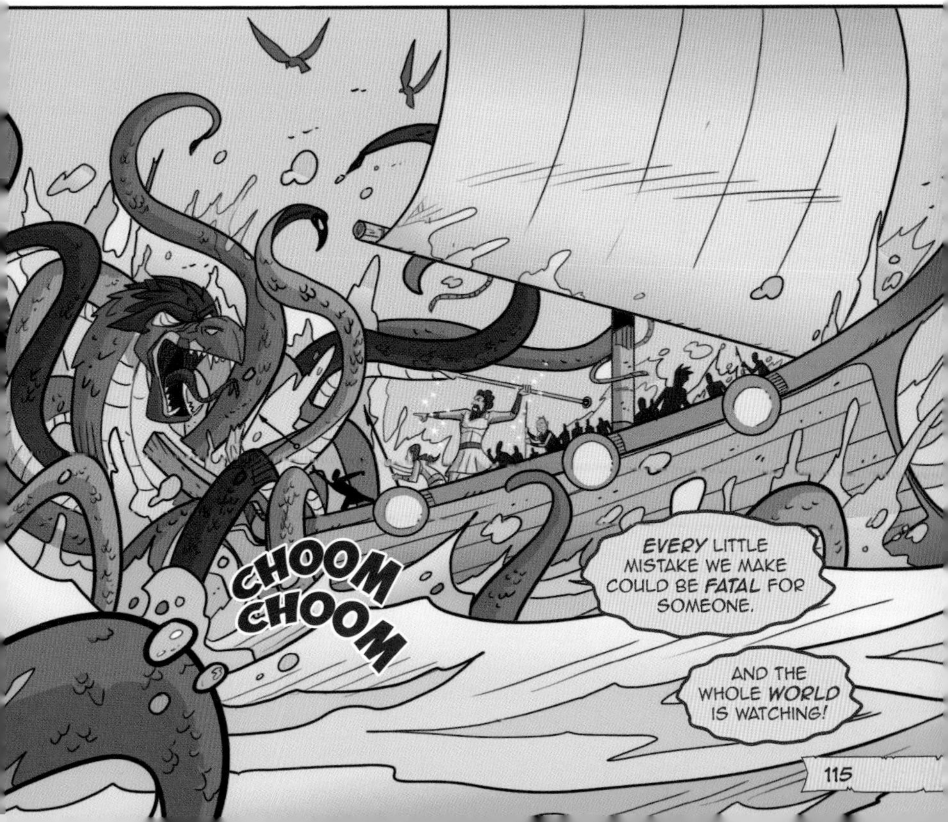
EVERY LITTLE MISTAKE WE MAKE COULD BE *FATAL* FOR SOMEONE.
CHOOM CHOOM
AND THE WHOLE *WORLD* IS WATCHING!

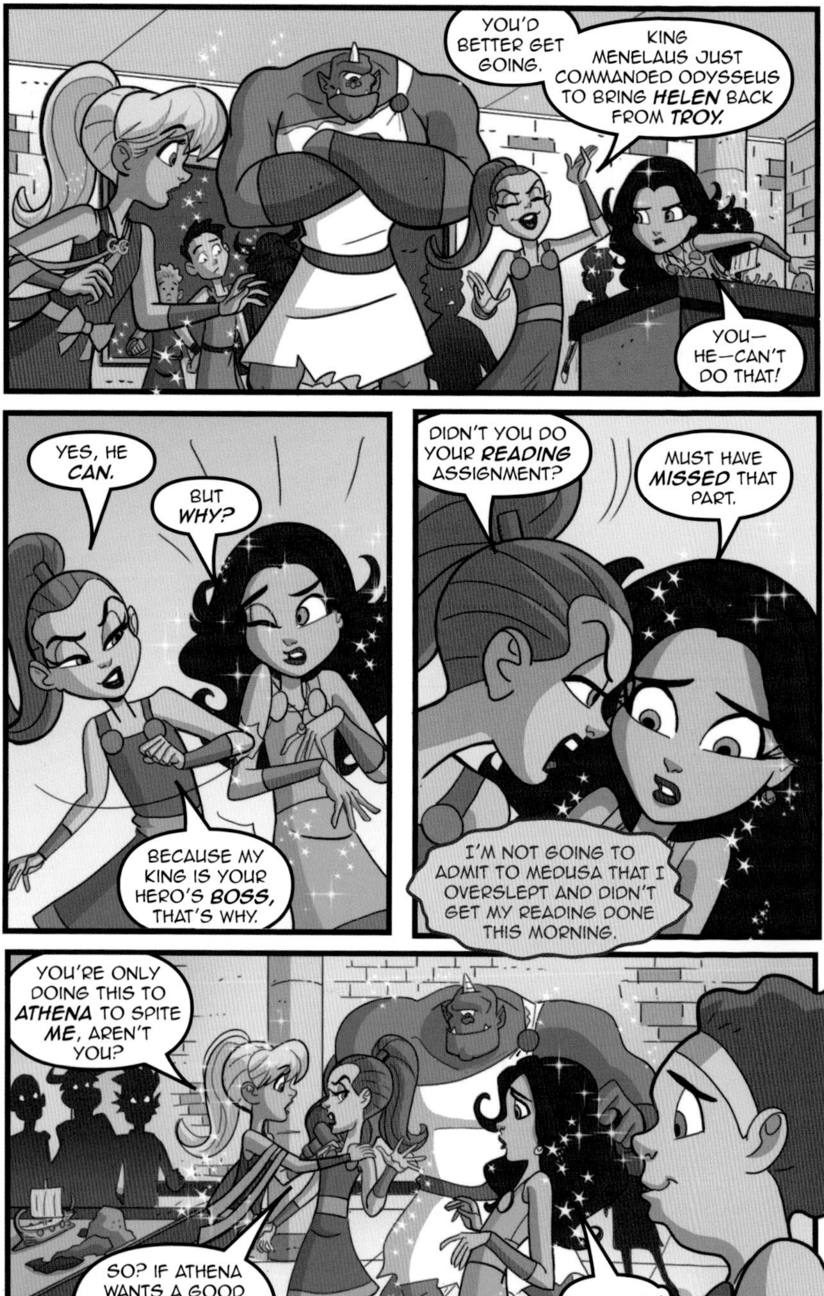

YOU'D BETTER GET GOING.
KING MENELAUS JUST COMMANDED ODYSSEUS TO BRING HELEN BACK FROM TROY.
YOU— HE—CAN'T DO THAT!
YES, HE CAN.
BUT WHY?
BECAUSE MY KING IS YOUR HERO'S BOSS, THAT'S WHY.
DIDN'T YOU DO YOUR READING ASSIGNMENT?
MUST HAVE MISSED THAT PART.
I'M NOT GOING TO ADMIT TO MEDUSA THAT I OVERSLEPT AND DIDN'T GET MY READING DONE THIS MORNING.
YOU'RE ONLY DOING THIS TO ATHENA TO SPITE ME, AREN'T YOU?
SO? IF ATHENA WANTS A GOOD GRADE, HER HERO HAS TO FOLLOW MY ORDERS!
SIGH!

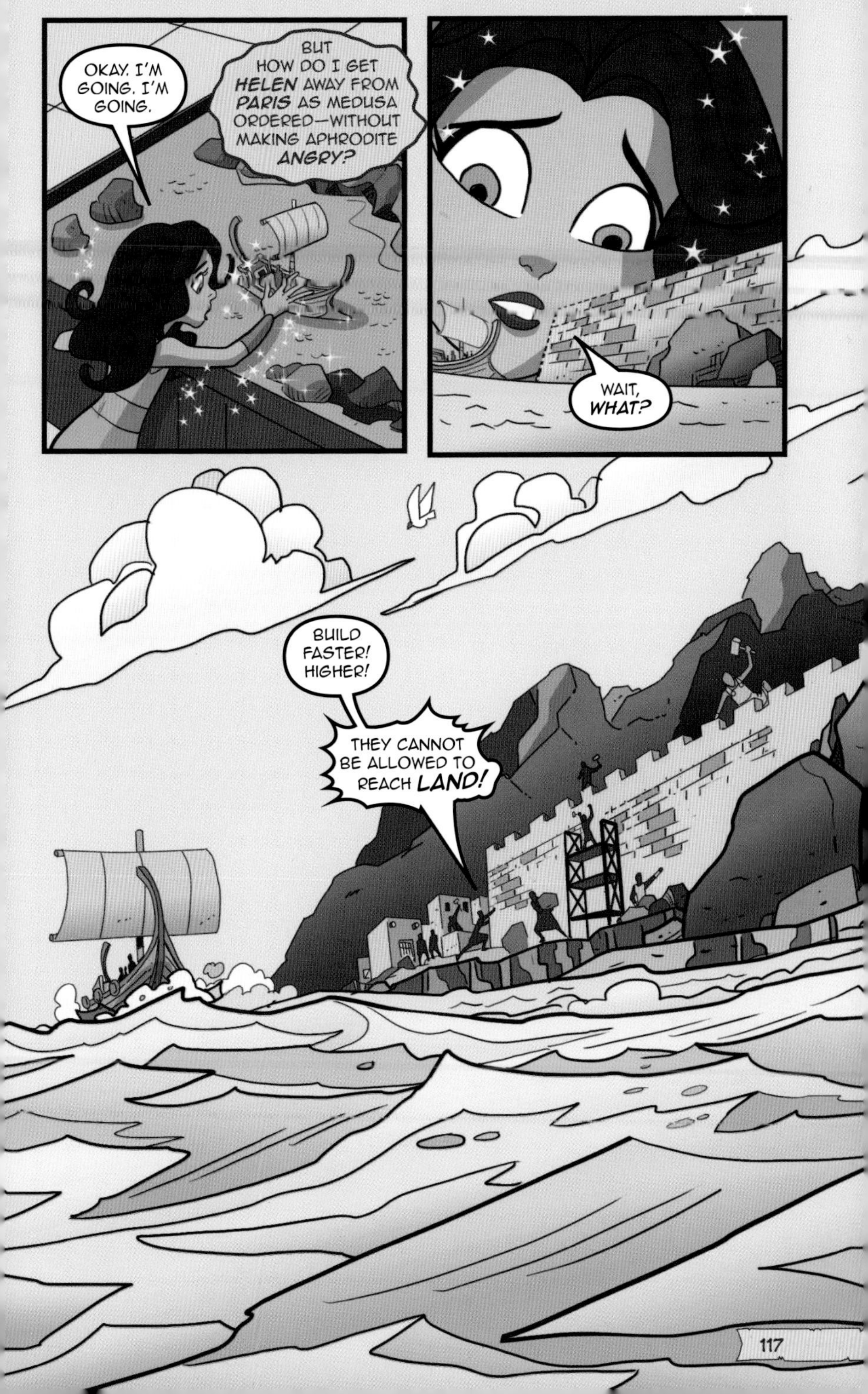
OKAY. I'M GOING. I'M GOING.
BUT HOW DO I GET HELEN AWAY FROM PARIS AS MEDUSA ORDERED—WITHOUT MAKING APHRODITE ANGRY?
WAIT, WHAT?
BUILD FASTER! HIGHER!
THEY CANNOT BE ALLOWED TO REACH LAND!

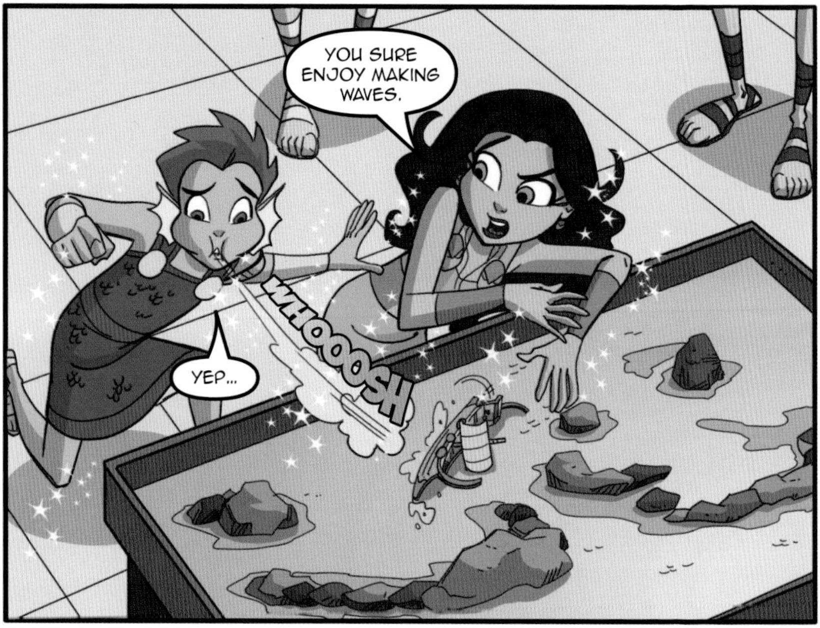
YOU SURE ENJOY MAKING WAVES.
YEP...
WHOOOSH

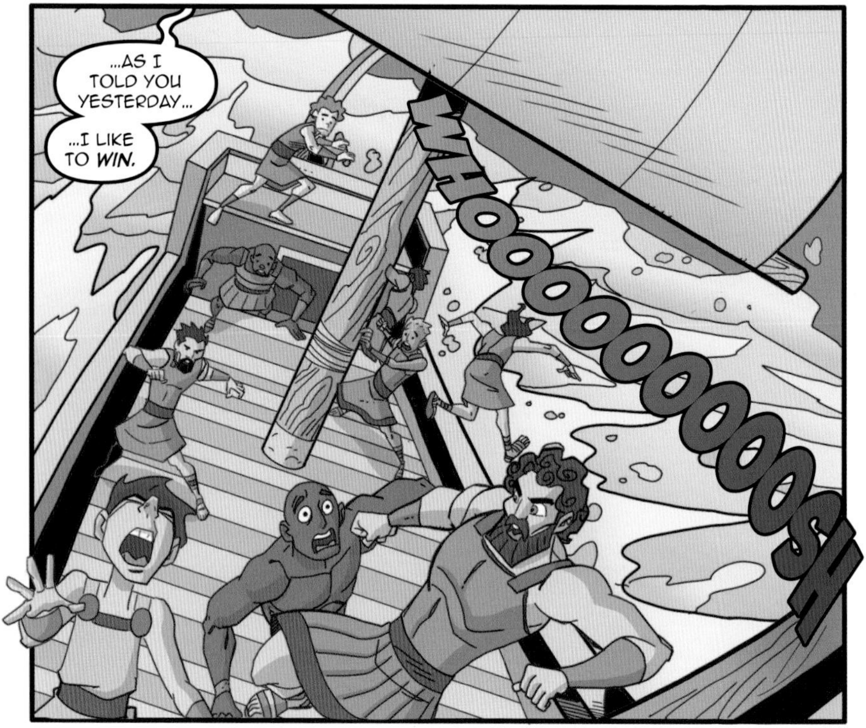
...AS I TOLD YOU YESTERDAY...
...I LIKE TO *WIN.*
WHOOOOOOOOOOOSH

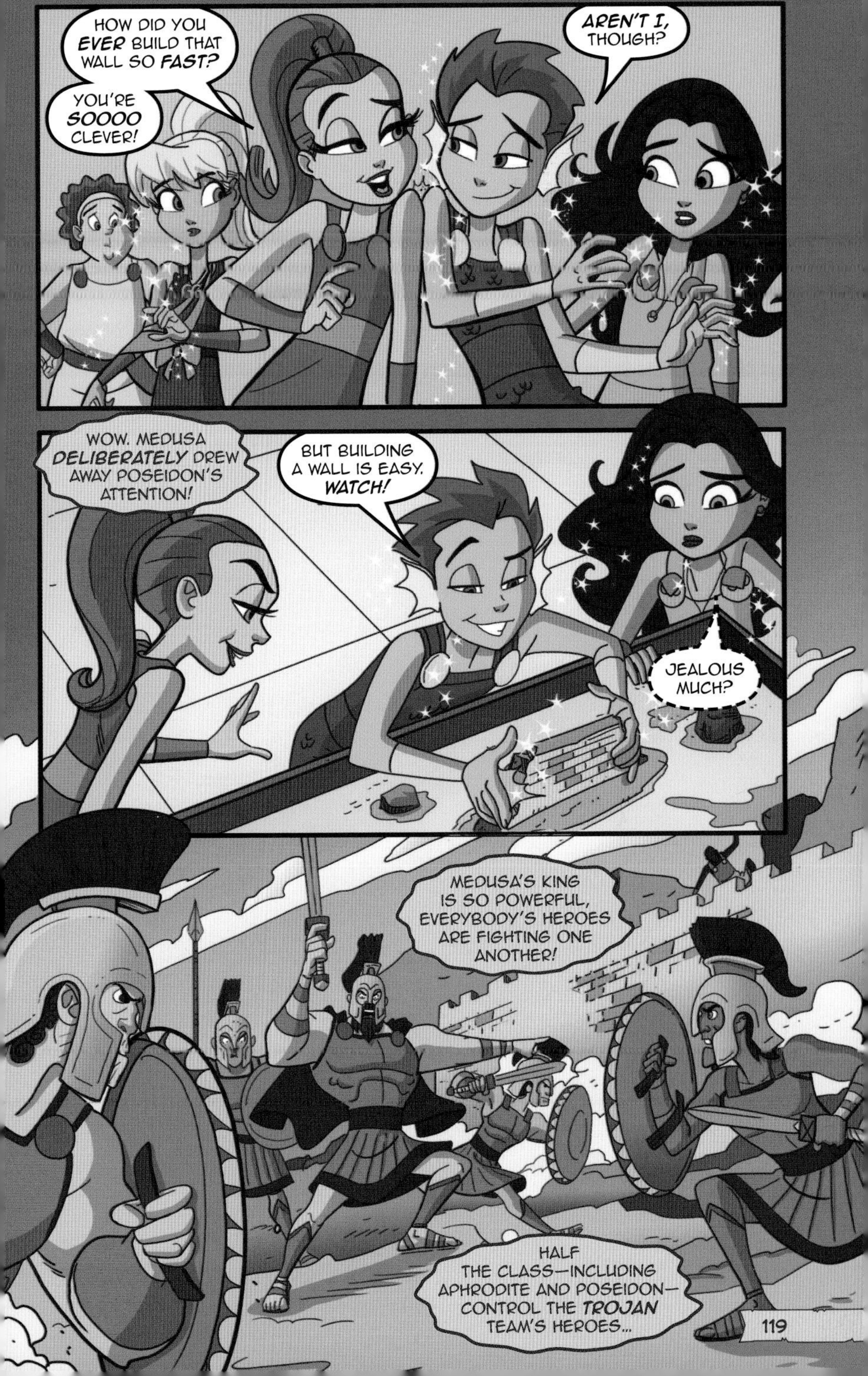
HOW DID YOU EVER BUILD THAT WALL SO FAST?
YOU'RE SOOOO CLEVER!
AREN'T I, THOUGH?
WOW. MEDUSA DELIBERATELY DREW AWAY POSEIDON'S ATTENTION!
BUT BUILDING A WALL IS EASY. WATCH!
JEALOUS MUCH?
MEDUSA'S KING IS SO POWERFUL, EVERYBODY'S HEROES ARE FIGHTING ONE ANOTHER!
HALF THE CLASS—INCLUDING APHRODITE AND POSEIDON—CONTROL THE TROJAN TEAM'S HEROES...

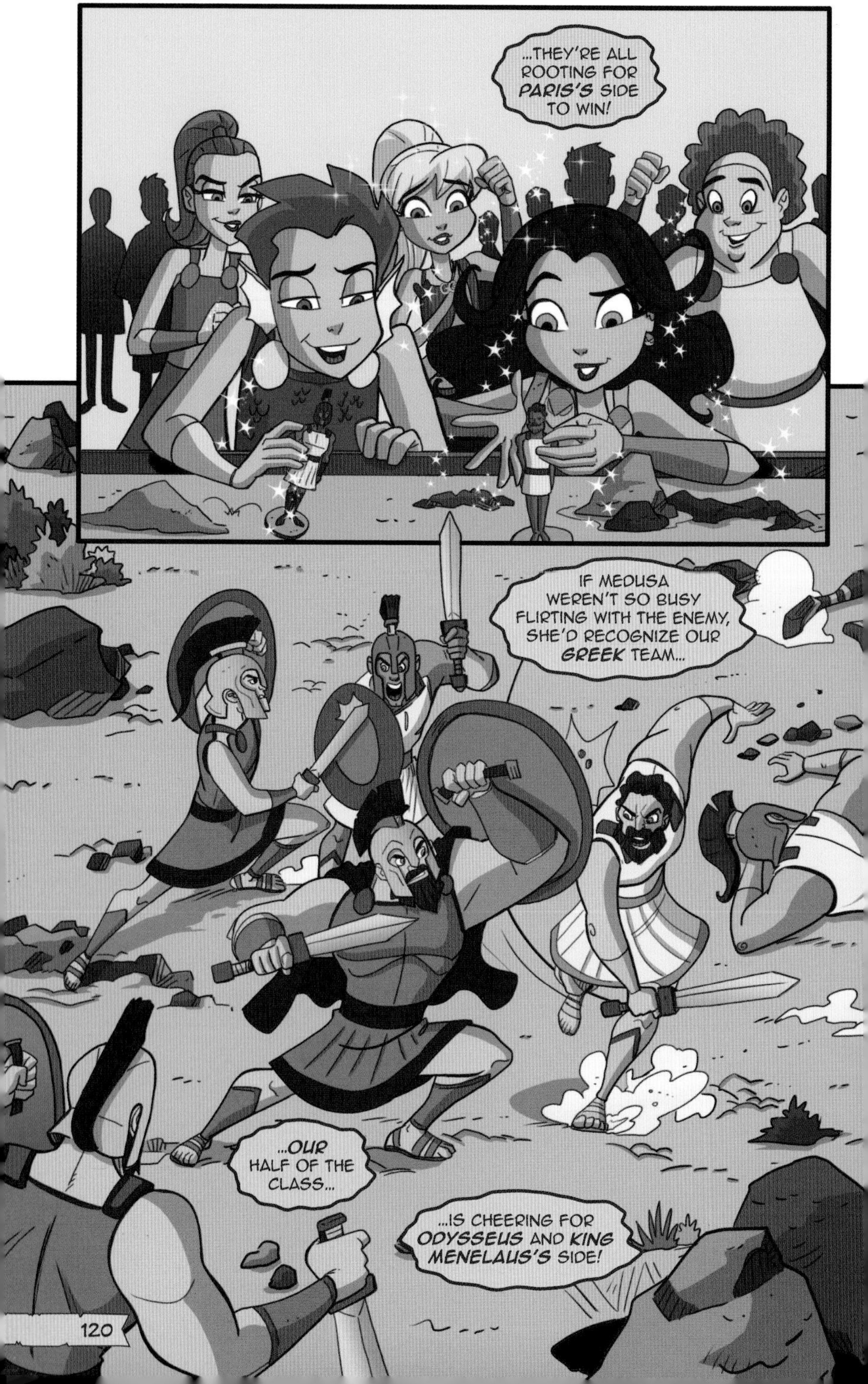
...THEY'RE ALL ROOTING FOR PARIS'S SIDE TO WIN!
IF MEDUSA WEREN'T SO BUSY FLIRTING WITH THE ENEMY, SHE'D RECOGNIZE OUR GREEK TEAM...
...OUR HALF OF THE CLASS...
...IS CHEERING FOR ODYSSEUS AND KING MENELAUS'S SIDE!

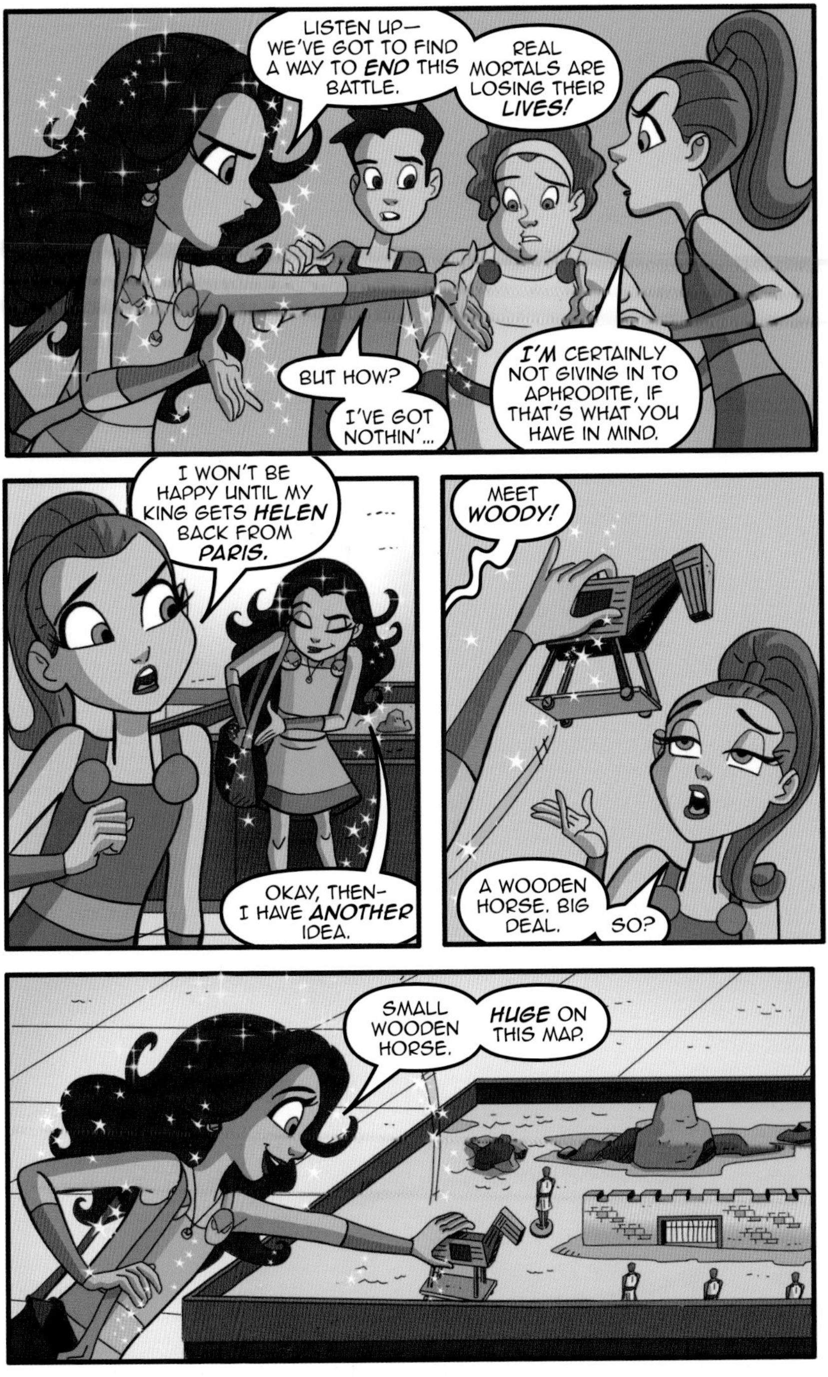
LISTEN UP—
WE'VE GOT TO FIND A WAY TO END THIS BATTLE.
REAL MORTALS ARE LOSING THEIR LIVES!
BUT HOW?
I'VE GOT NOTHIN'...
I'M CERTAINLY NOT GIVING IN TO APHRODITE, IF THAT'S WHAT YOU HAVE IN MIND.
I WON'T BE HAPPY UNTIL MY KING GETS HELEN BACK FROM PARIS.
OKAY, THEN-
I HAVE ANOTHER IDEA.
MEET WOODY!
A WOODEN HORSE. BIG DEAL.
SO?
SMALL WOODEN HORSE.
HUGE ON THIS MAP.

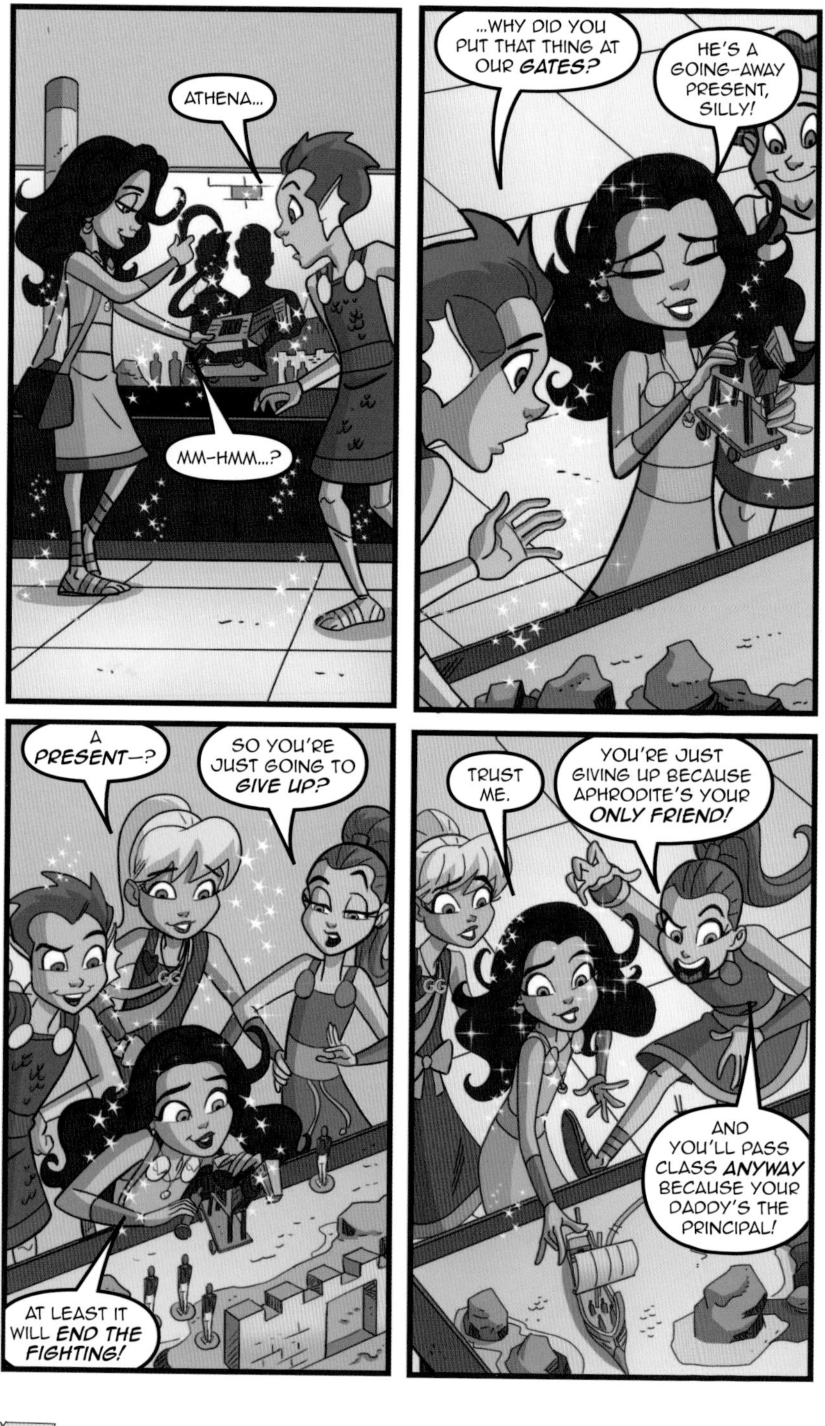
ATHENA...
MM-HMM...?
...WHY DID YOU PUT THAT THING AT OUR GATES?
HE'S A GOING-AWAY PRESENT, SILLY!
A PRESENT—?
SO YOU'RE JUST GOING TO GIVE UP?
AT LEAST IT WILL END THE FIGHTING!
TRUST ME.
YOU'RE JUST GIVING UP BECAUSE APHRODITE'S YOUR ONLY FRIEND!
AND YOU'LL PASS CLASS ANYWAY BECAUSE YOUR DADDY'S THE PRINCIPAL!

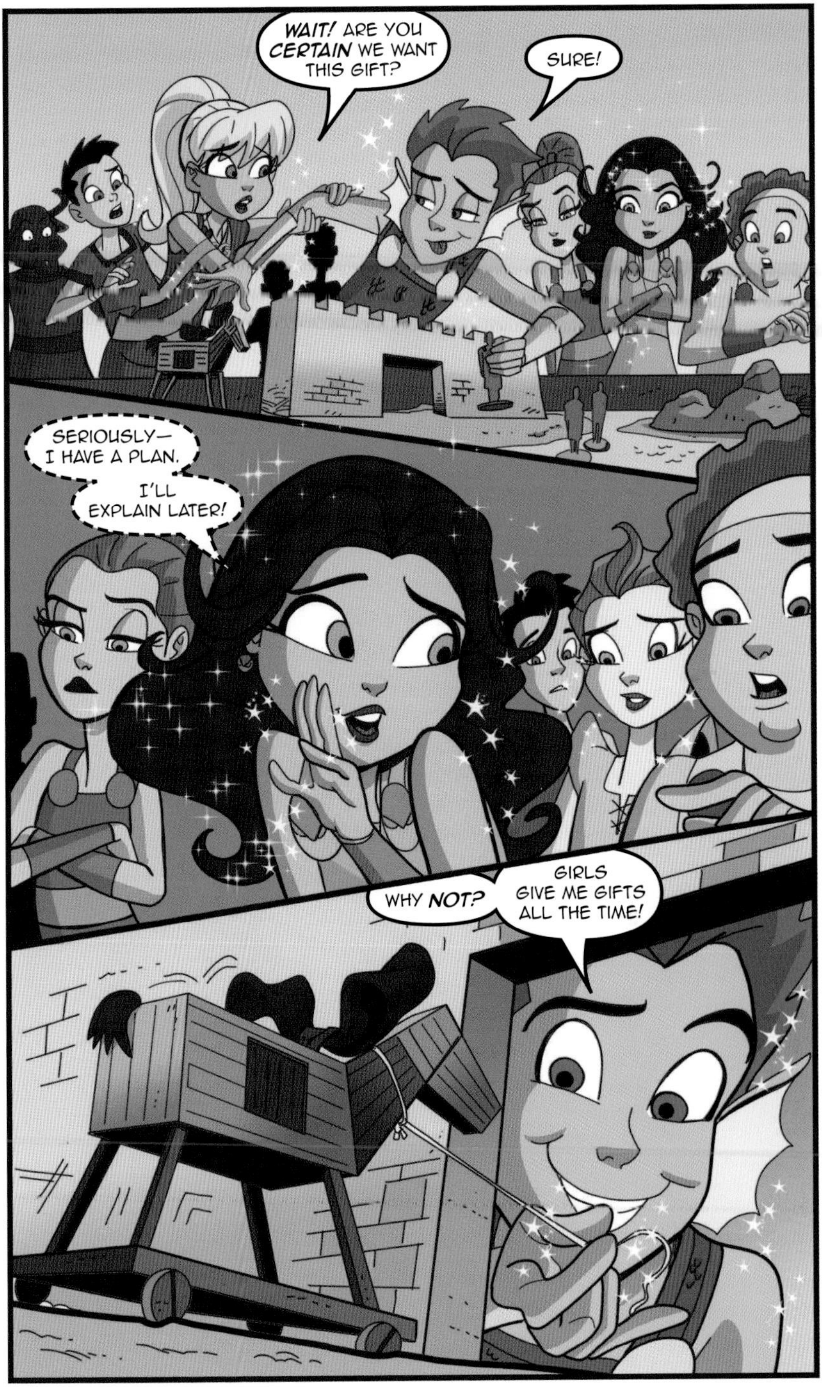

WAIT! ARE YOU *CERTAIN* WE WANT THIS GIFT?
SURE!
SERIOUSLY— I HAVE A PLAN.
I'LL EXPLAIN LATER!
WHY *NOT?*
GIRLS GIVE ME GIFTS ALL THE TIME!

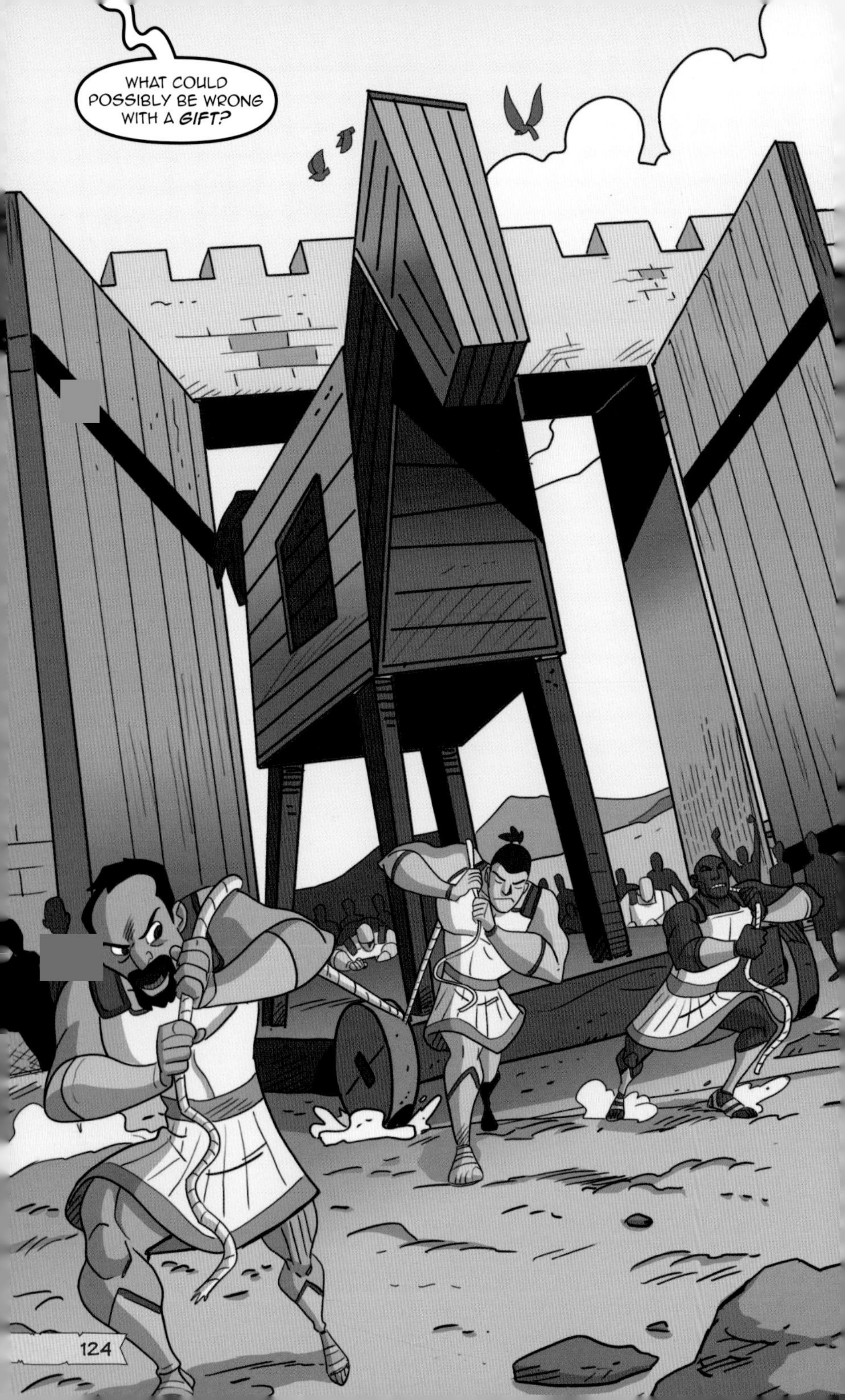
WHAT COULD POSSIBLY BE WRONG WITH A GIFT?

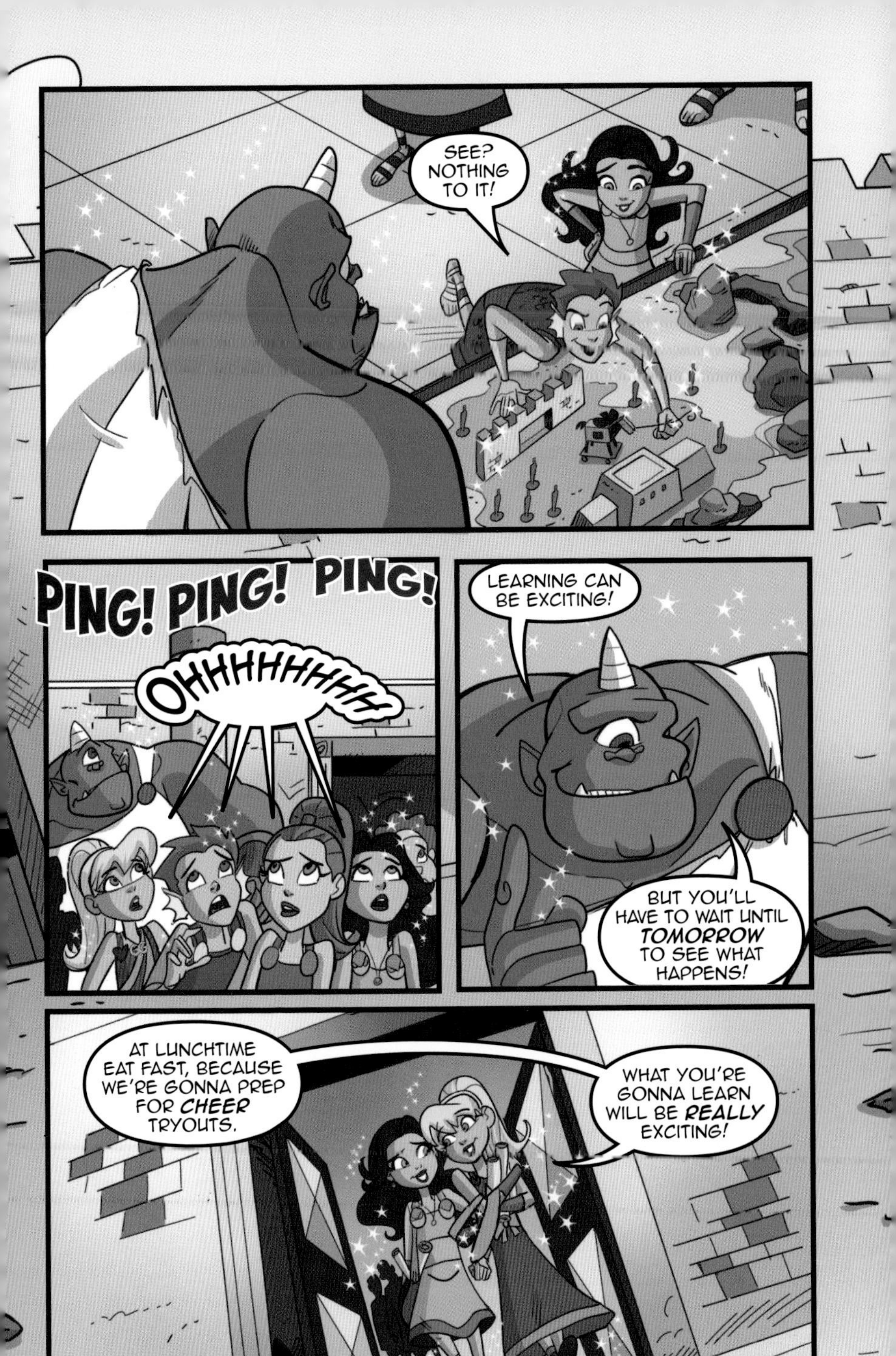
SEE? NOTHING TO IT!
PING! PING! PING!
OHHHHHHHH
LEARNING CAN BE EXCITING!
BUT YOU'LL HAVE TO WAIT UNTIL TOMORROW TO SEE WHAT HAPPENS!
AT LUNCHTIME EAT FAST, BECAUSE WE'RE GONNA PREP FOR CHEER TRYOUTS.
WHAT YOU'RE GONNA LEARN WILL BE REALLY EXCITING!

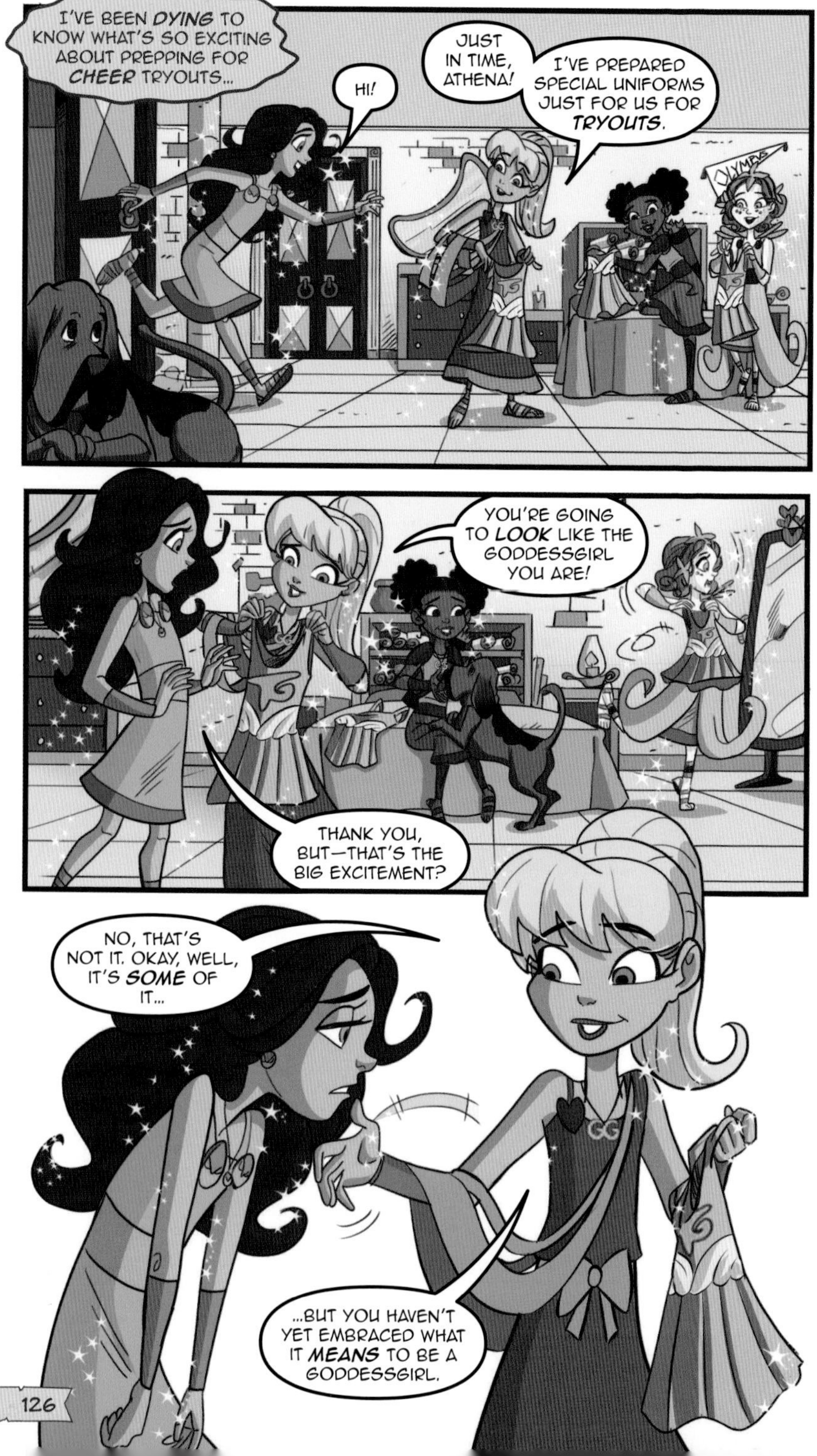
I'VE BEEN DYING TO KNOW WHAT'S SO EXCITING ABOUT PREPPING FOR CHEER TRYOUTS...
HI!
JUST IN TIME, ATHENA!
I'VE PREPARED SPECIAL UNIFORMS JUST FOR US FOR TRYOUTS.
YOU'RE GOING TO LOOK LIKE THE GODDESSGIRL YOU ARE!
THANK YOU, BUT—THAT'S THE BIG EXCITEMENT?
NO, THAT'S NOT IT. OKAY, WELL, IT'S SOME OF IT...
...BUT YOU HAVEN'T YET EMBRACED WHAT IT MEANS TO BE A GODDESSGIRL.

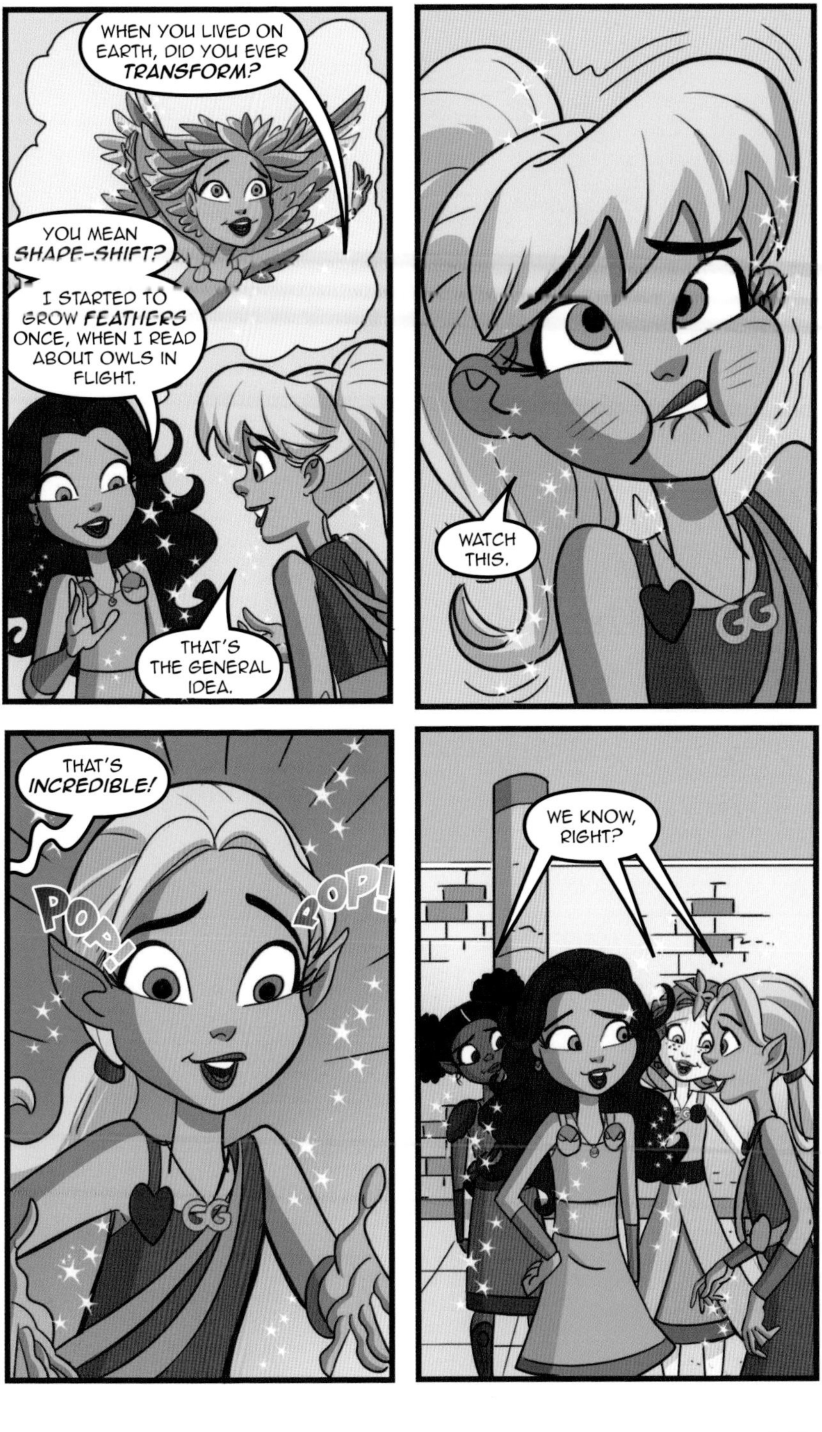
WHEN YOU LIVED ON EARTH, DID YOU EVER TRANSFORM?
YOU MEAN SHAPE-SHIFT?
I STARTED TO GROW FEATHERS ONCE, WHEN I READ ABOUT OWLS IN FLIGHT.
THAT'S THE GENERAL IDEA.
WATCH THIS.
THAT'S INCREDIBLE!
POP!
POP!
WE KNOW, RIGHT?

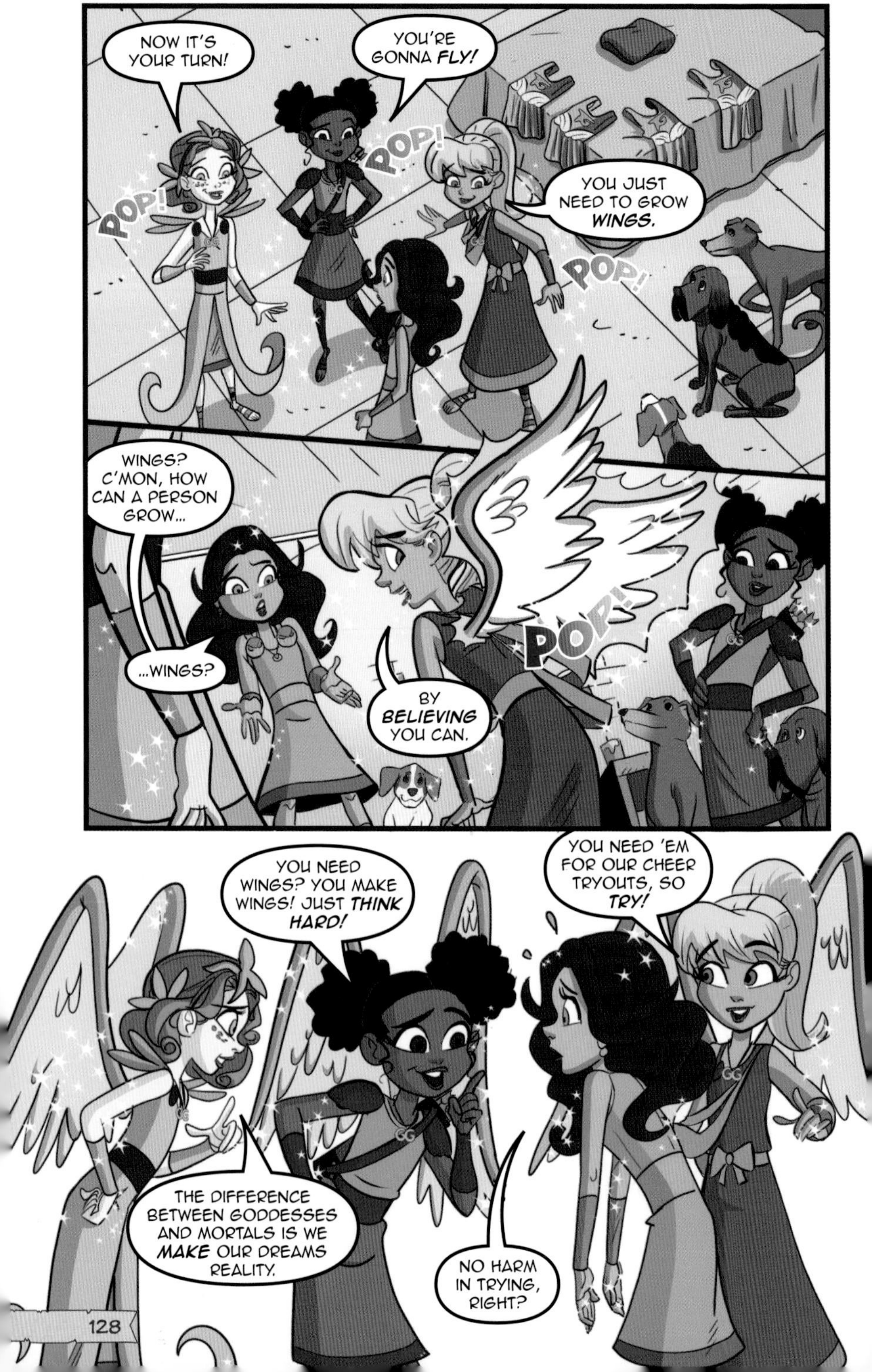
NOW IT'S YOUR TURN!
YOU'RE GONNA FLY!
POP!
POP!
YOU JUST NEED TO GROW WINGS.
POP!
WINGS? C'MON, HOW CAN A PERSON GROW...
...WINGS?
BY BELIEVING YOU CAN.
POP!
YOU NEED WINGS? YOU MAKE WINGS! JUST THINK HARD!
YOU NEED 'EM FOR OUR CHEER TRYOUTS, SO TRY!
THE DIFFERENCE BETWEEN GODDESSES AND MORTALS IS WE MAKE OUR DREAMS REALITY.
NO HARM IN TRYING, RIGHT?

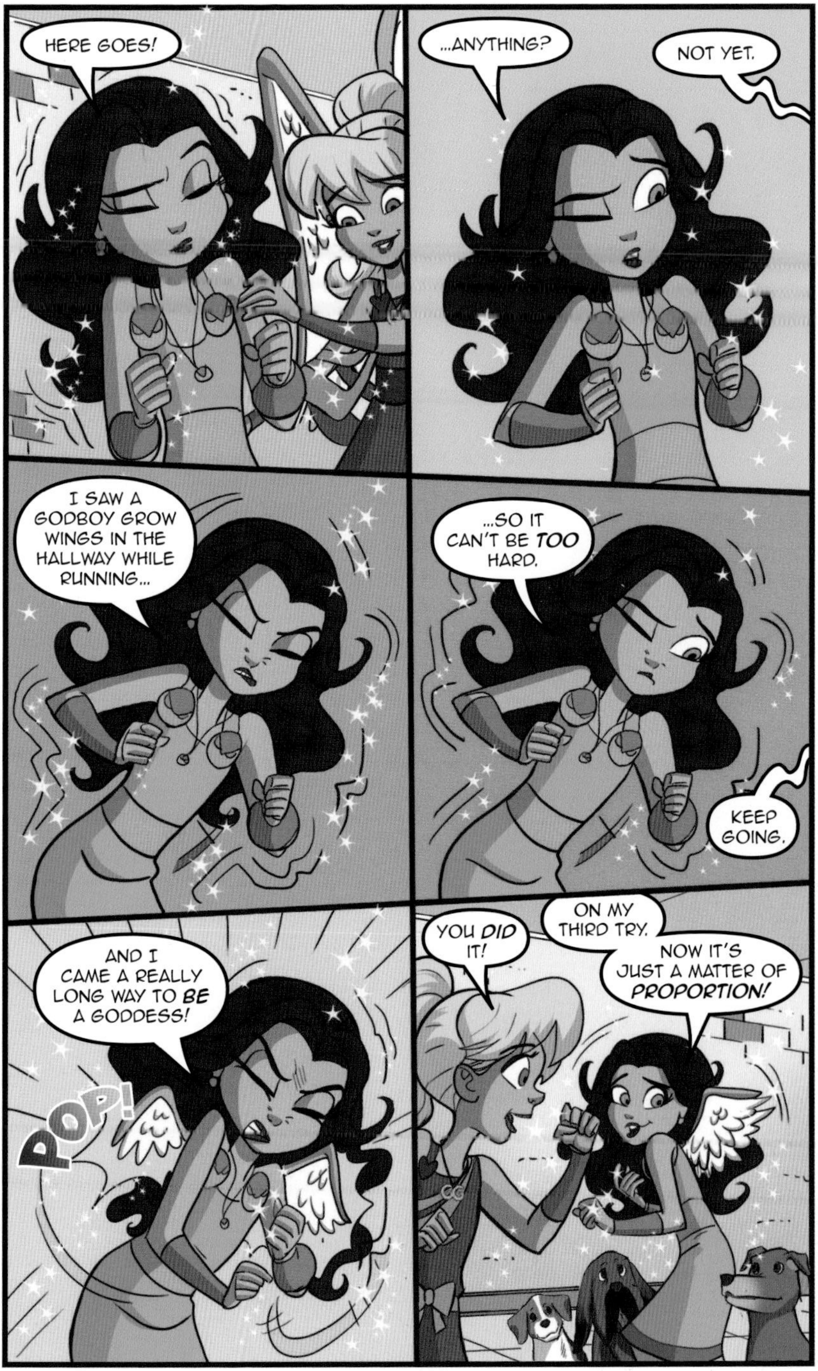
HERE GOES!
...ANYTHING?
NOT YET.
I SAW A GODBOY GROW WINGS IN THE HALLWAY WHILE RUNNING...
...SO IT CAN'T BE *TOO* HARD.
KEEP GOING.
AND I CAME A REALLY LONG WAY TO **BE** A GODDESS!
POP!
YOU *DID* IT!
ON MY THIRD TRY.
NOW IT'S JUST A MATTER OF ***PROPORTION!***

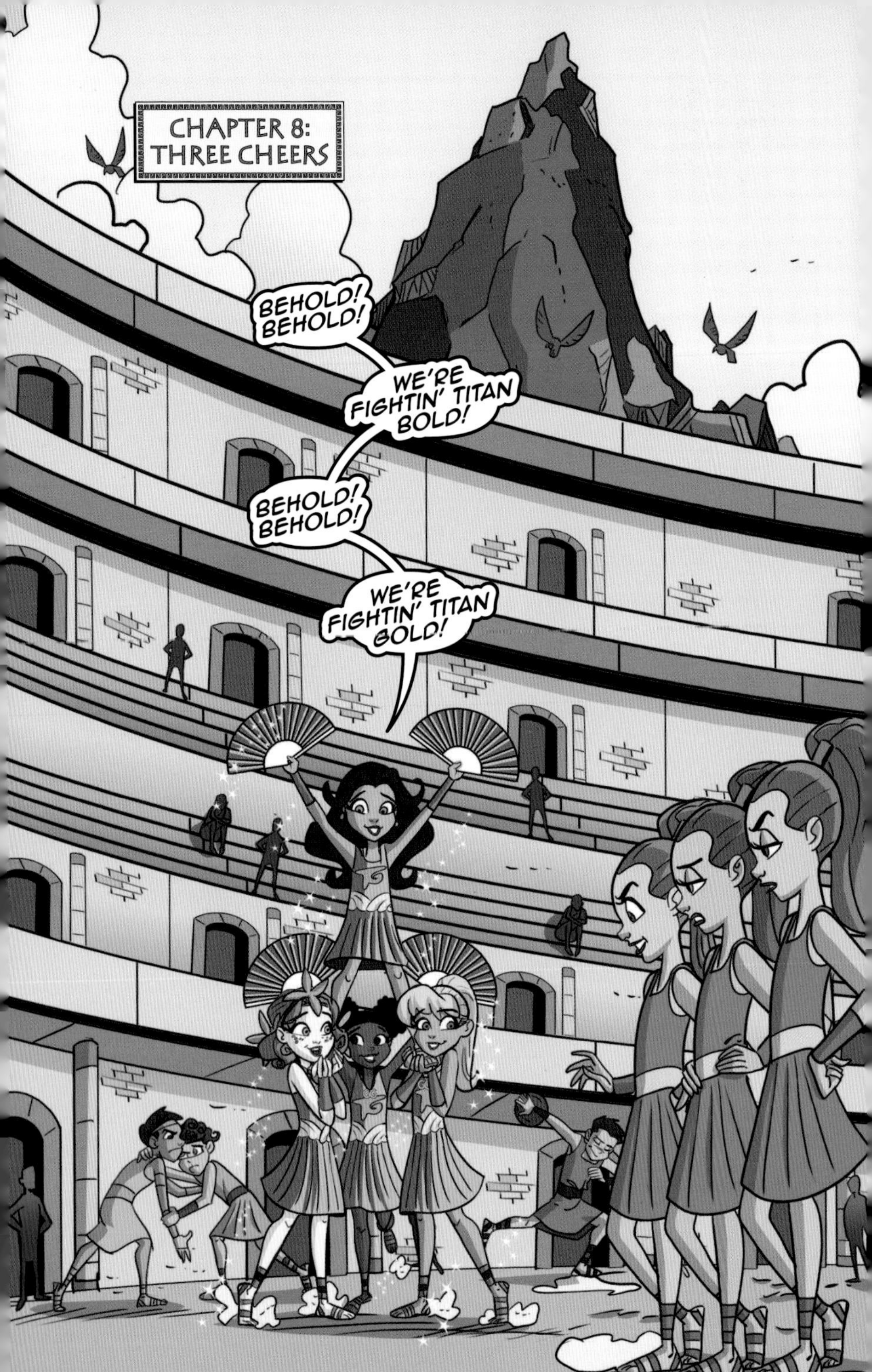
CHAPTER 8:
THREE CHEERS
BEHOLD! BEHOLD!
WE'RE FIGHTIN' TITAN BOLD!
BEHOLD! BEHOLD!
WE'RE FIGHTIN' TITAN GOLD!

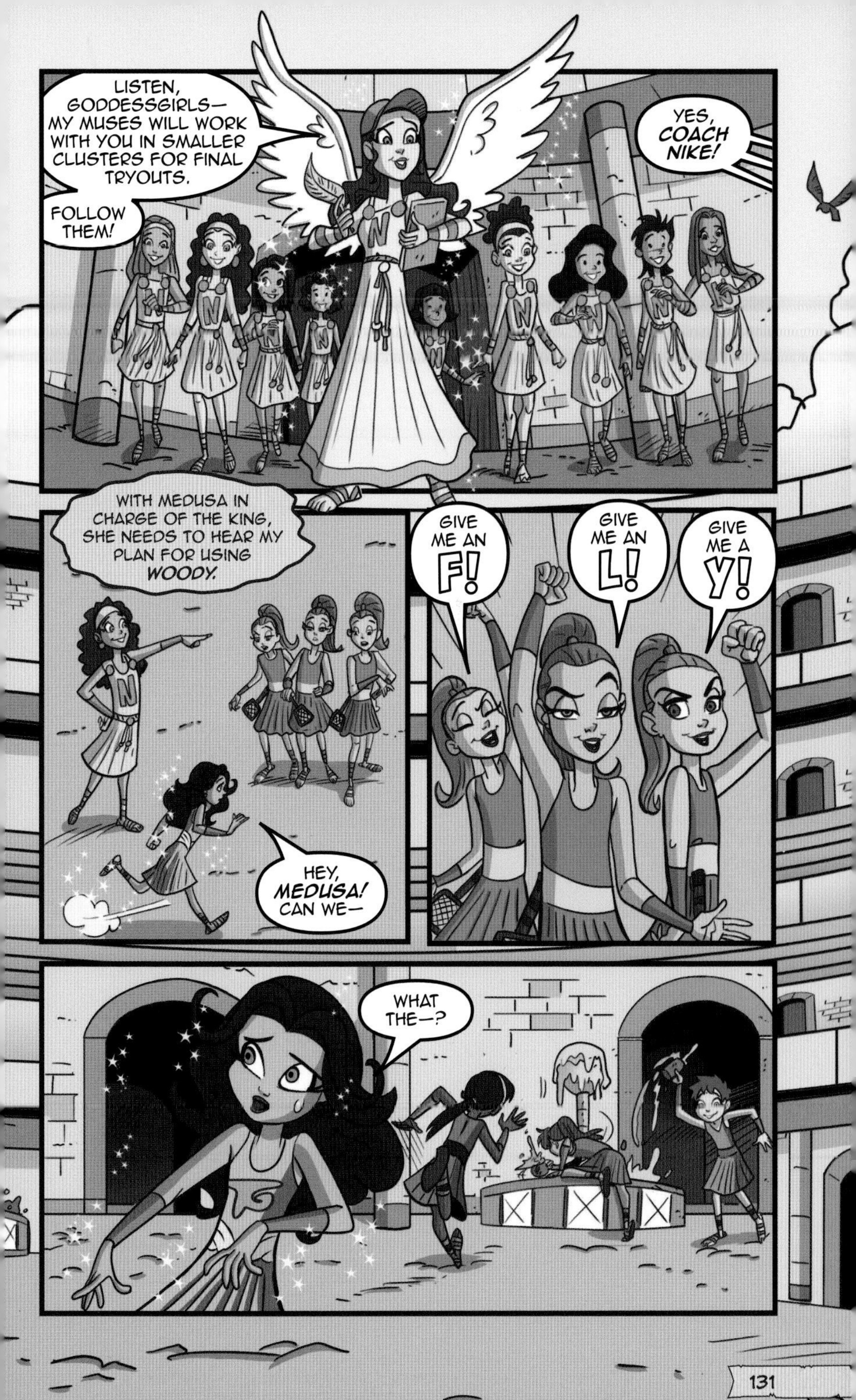

LISTEN, GODDESSGIRLS— MY MUSES WILL WORK WITH YOU IN SMALLER CLUSTERS FOR FINAL TRYOUTS.
FOLLOW THEM!
YES, COACH NIKE!
WITH MEDUSA IN CHARGE OF THE KING, SHE NEEDS TO HEAR MY PLAN FOR USING WOODY.
HEY, MEDUSA! CAN WE—
GIVE ME AN F!
GIVE ME AN L!
GIVE ME A Y!
WHAT THE—?

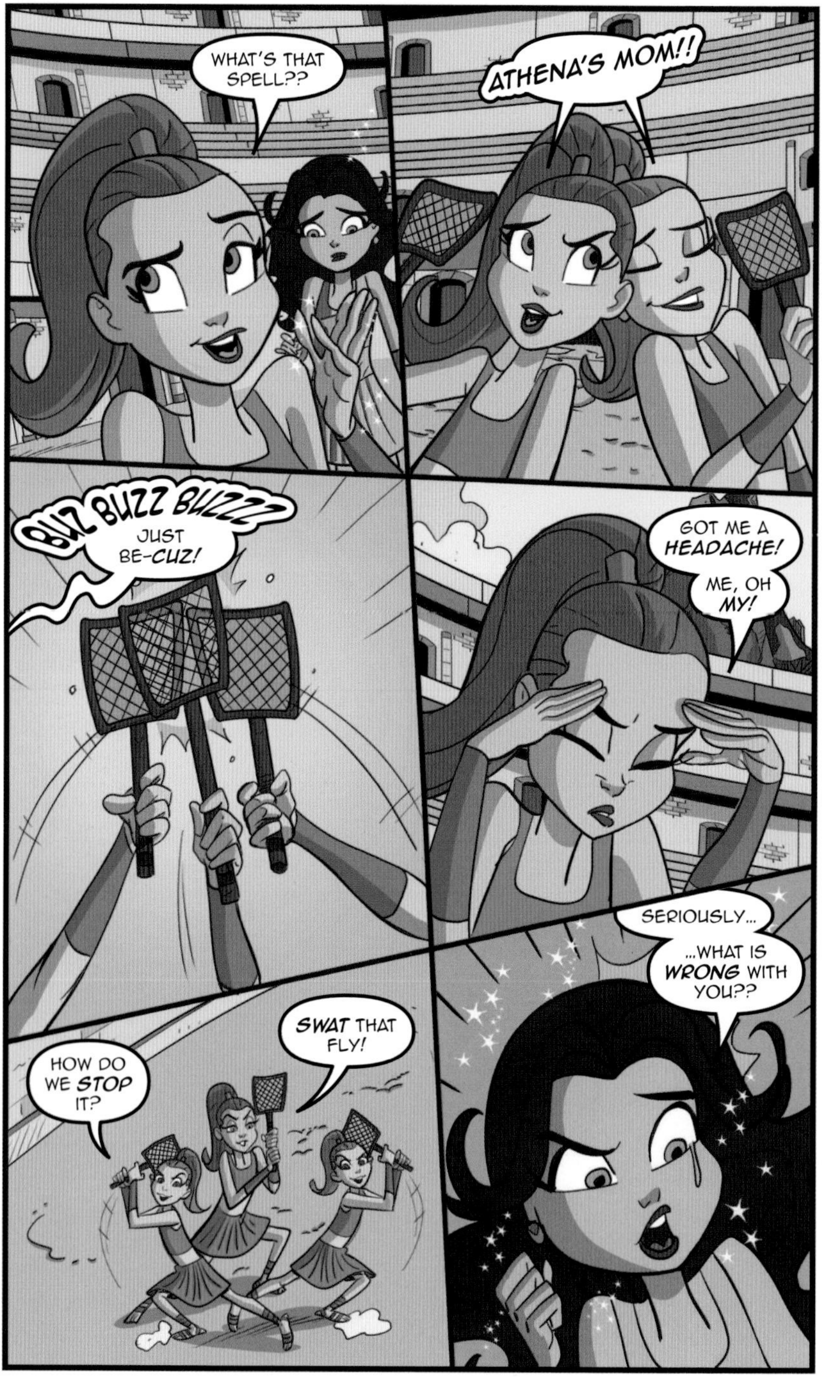
WHAT'S THAT SPELL??
ATHENA'S MOM!!
BUZ BUZZ BUZZZZ
JUST BE-CUZ!
GOT ME A HEADACHE!
ME, OH MY!
HOW DO WE STOP IT?
SWAT THAT FLY!
SERIOUSLY...
...WHAT IS WRONG WITH YOU??

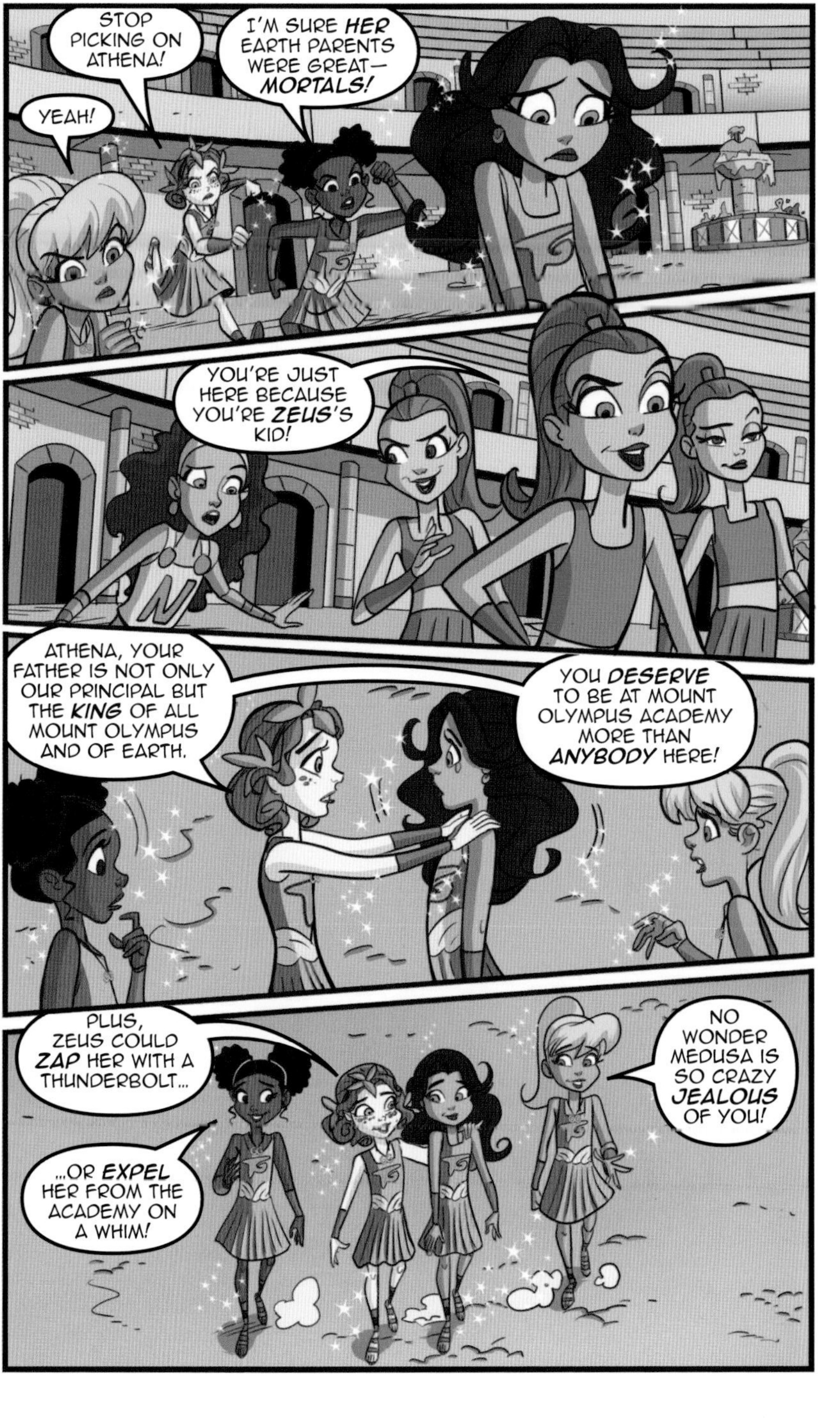
STOP PICKING ON ATHENA!
YEAH!
I'M SURE HER EARTH PARENTS WERE GREAT—MORTALS!
YOU'RE JUST HERE BECAUSE YOU'RE ZEUS'S KID!
ATHENA, YOUR FATHER IS NOT ONLY OUR PRINCIPAL BUT THE KING OF ALL MOUNT OLYMPUS AND OF EARTH.
YOU DESERVE TO BE AT MOUNT OLYMPUS ACADEMY MORE THAN ANYBODY HERE!
PLUS, ZEUS COULD ZAP HER WITH A THUNDERBOLT...
...OR EXPEL HER FROM THE ACADEMY ON A WHIM!
NO WONDER MEDUSA IS SO CRAZY JEALOUS OF YOU!

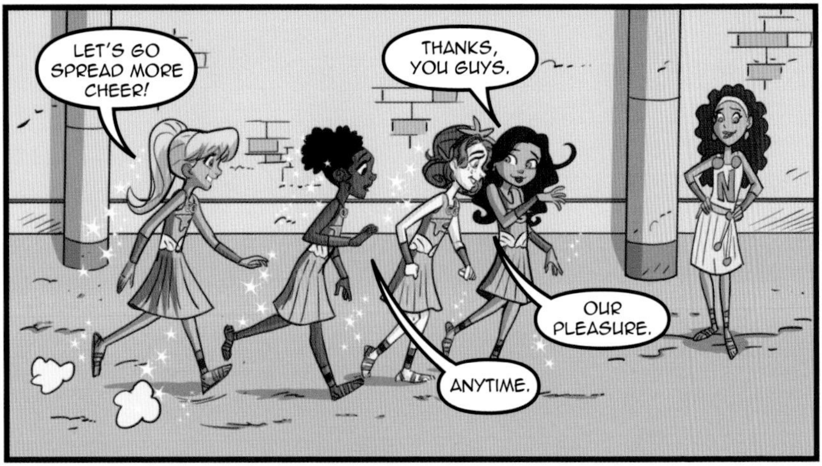
LET'S GO SPREAD MORE CHEER!
THANKS, YOU GUYS.
OUR PLEASURE.
ANYTIME.

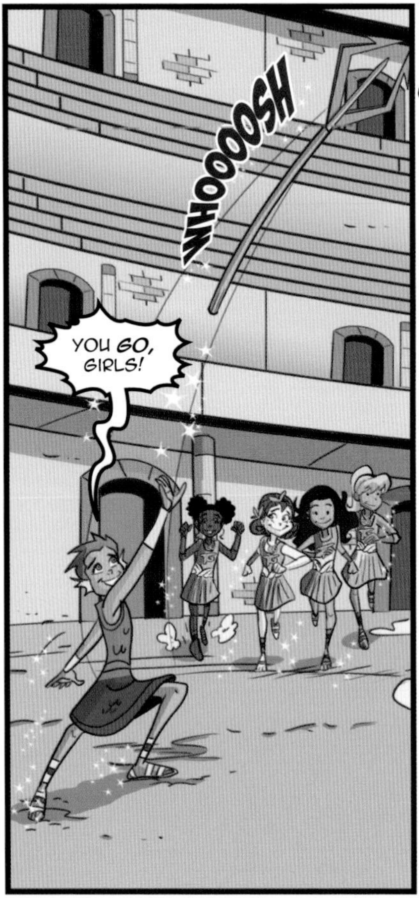
WHOOOOSH
YOU GO, GIRLS!

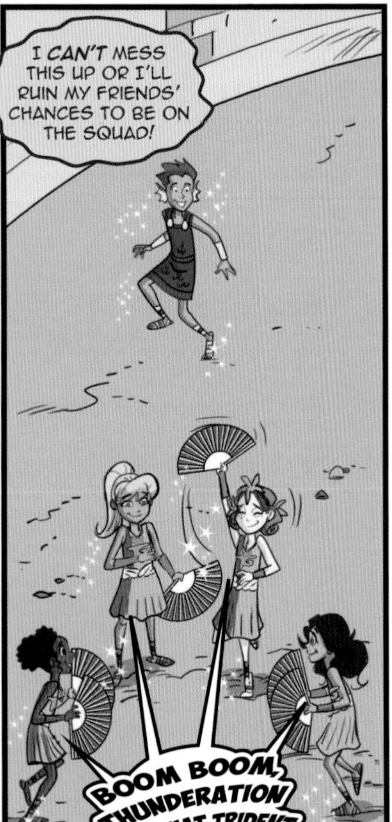
I CAN'T MESS THIS UP OR I'LL RUIN MY FRIENDS' CHANCES TO BE ON THE SQUAD!
BOOM BOOM, THUNDERATION SEND THAT TRIDENT ON VACATION!

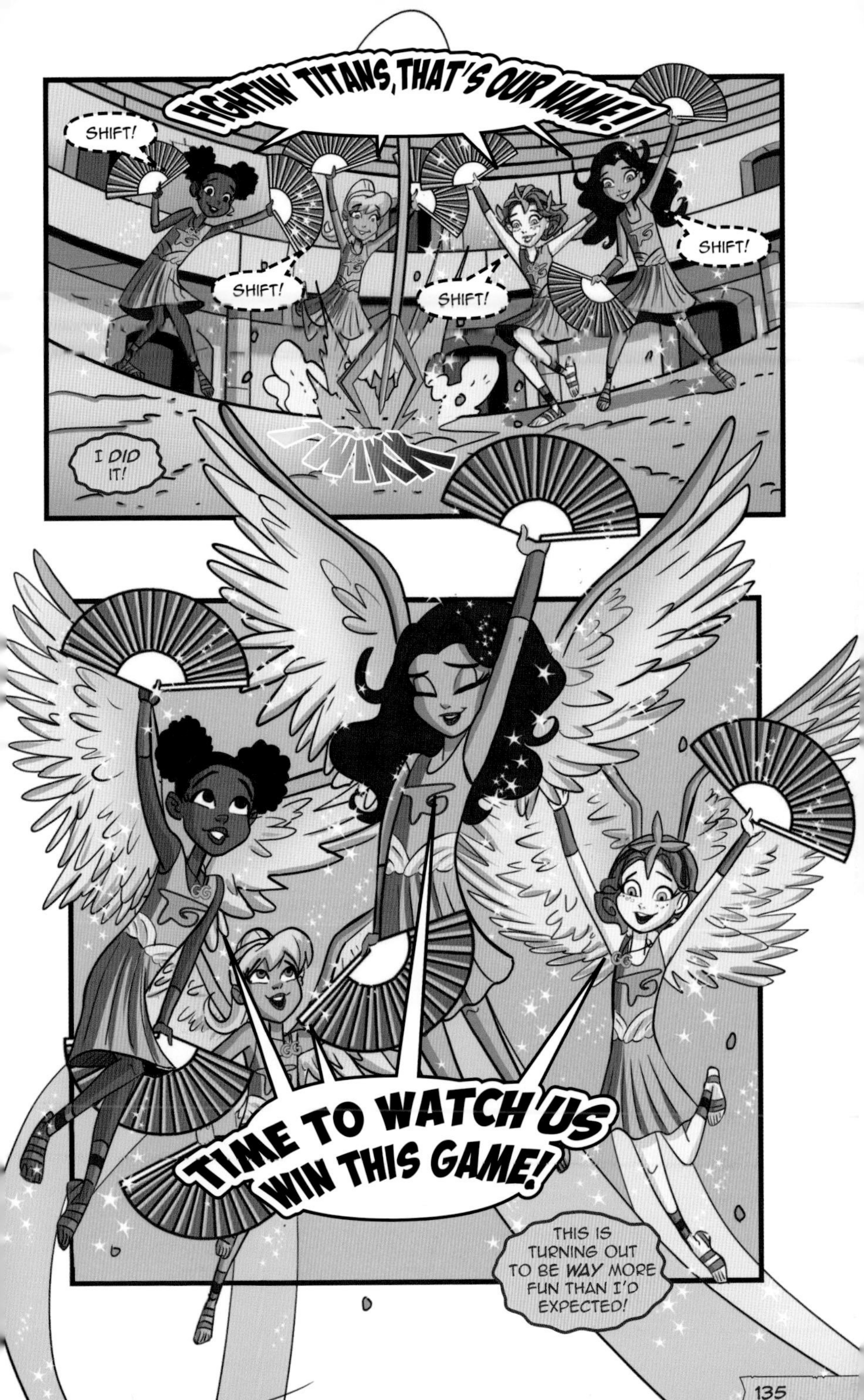
FIGHTIN' TITANS, THAT'S OUR NAME!
SHIFT!
SHIFT!
SHIFT!
SHIFT!
TWANG
I DID IT!
TIME TO WATCH US WIN THIS GAME!
THIS IS TURNING OUT TO BE WAY MORE FUN THAN I'D EXPECTED!

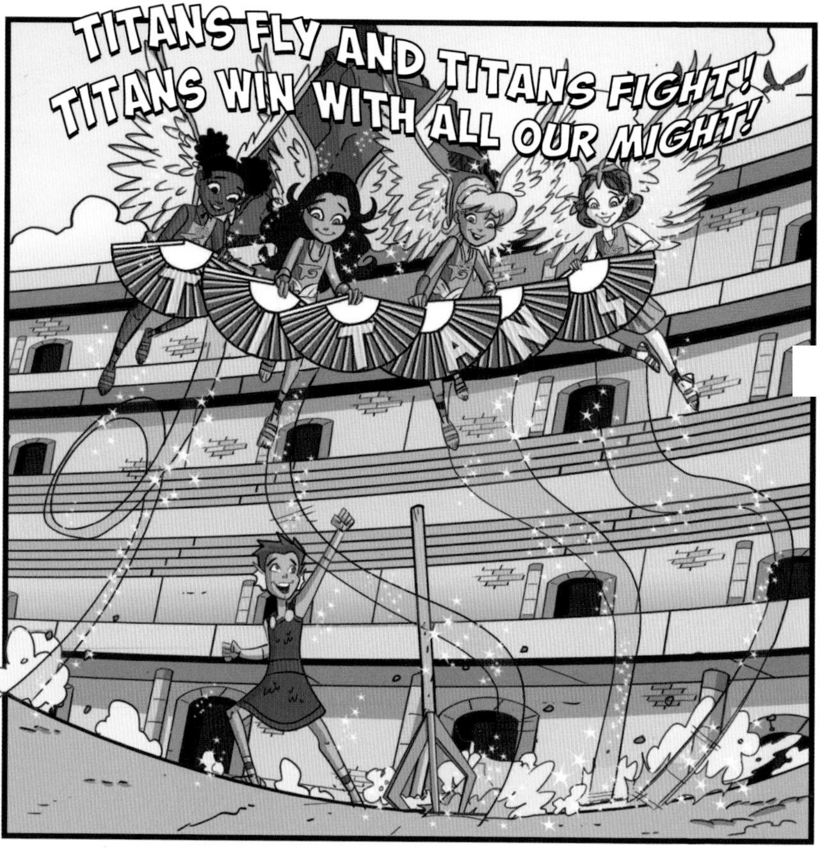
TITANS FLY AND TITANS FIGHT!
TITANS WIN WITH ALL OUR MIGHT!

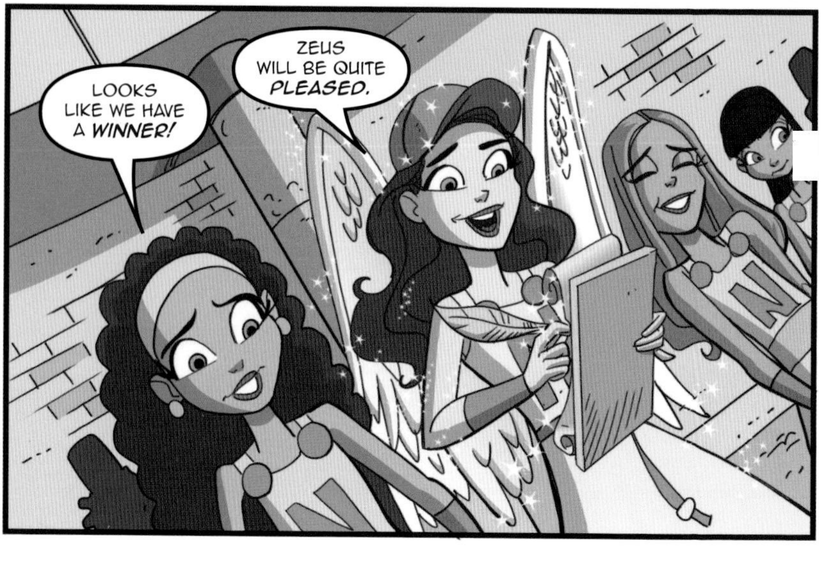
LOOKS LIKE WE HAVE A *WINNER!*
ZEUS WILL BE QUITE *PLEASED.*

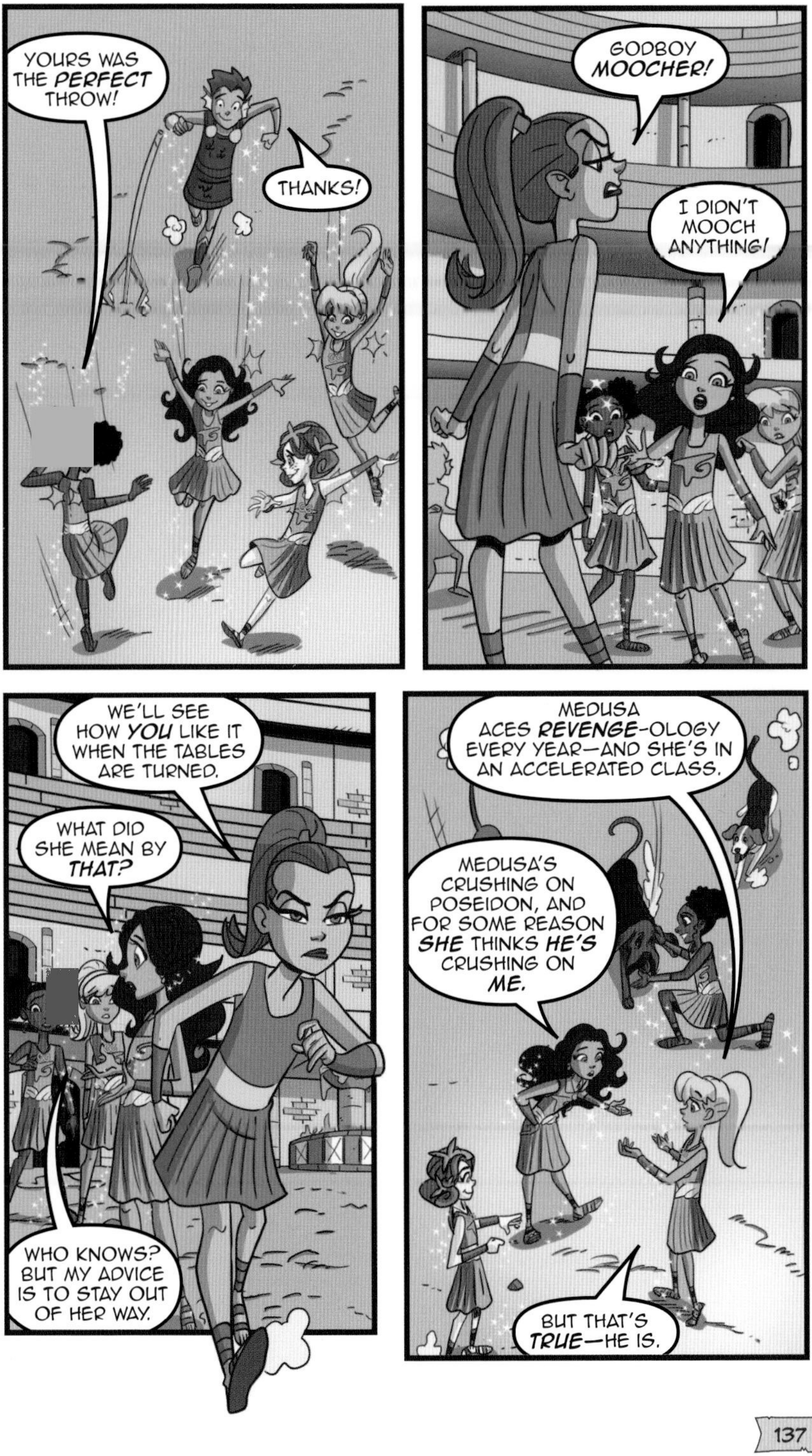
YOURS WAS THE PERFECT THROW!
THANKS!
GODBOY MOOCHER!
I DIDN'T MOOCH ANYTHING!
WE'LL SEE HOW YOU LIKE IT WHEN THE TABLES ARE TURNED.
WHAT DID SHE MEAN BY THAT?
WHO KNOWS? BUT MY ADVICE IS TO STAY OUT OF HER WAY.
MEDUSA ACES REVENGE-OLOGY EVERY YEAR—AND SHE'S IN AN ACCELERATED CLASS.
MEDUSA'S CRUSHING ON POSEIDON, AND FOR SOME REASON SHE THINKS HE'S CRUSHING ON ME.
BUT THAT'S TRUE—HE IS.

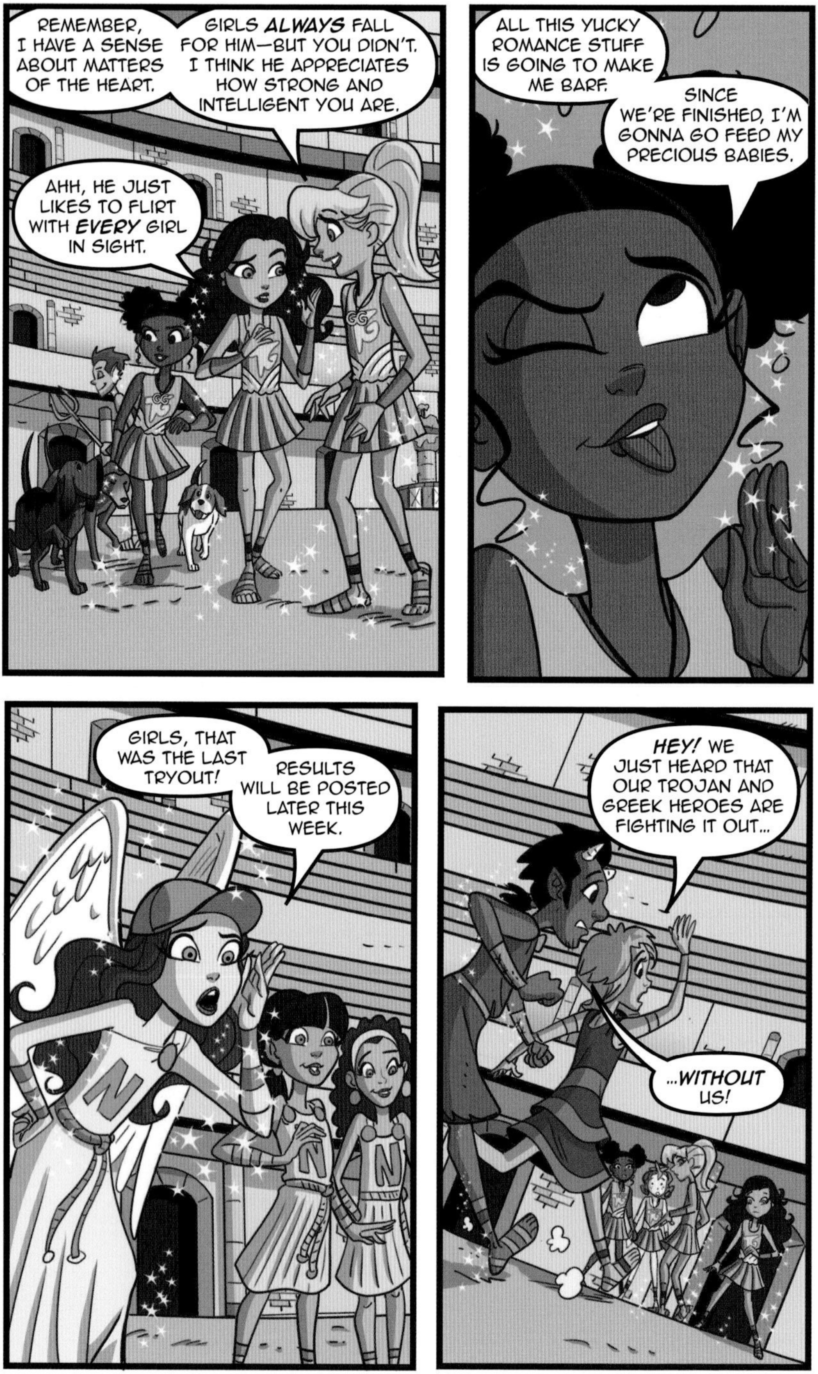
REMEMBER, I HAVE A SENSE ABOUT MATTERS OF THE HEART.
GIRLS ALWAYS FALL FOR HIM—BUT YOU DIDN'T. I THINK HE APPRECIATES HOW STRONG AND INTELLIGENT YOU ARE.
AHH, HE JUST LIKES TO FLIRT WITH EVERY GIRL IN SIGHT.
ALL THIS YUCKY ROMANCE STUFF IS GOING TO MAKE ME BARF.
SINCE WE'RE FINISHED, I'M GONNA GO FEED MY PRECIOUS BABIES.
GIRLS, THAT WAS THE LAST TRYOUT!
RESULTS WILL BE POSTED LATER THIS WEEK.
HEY! WE JUST HEARD THAT OUR TROJAN AND GREEK HEROES ARE FIGHTING IT OUT...
...WITHOUT US!

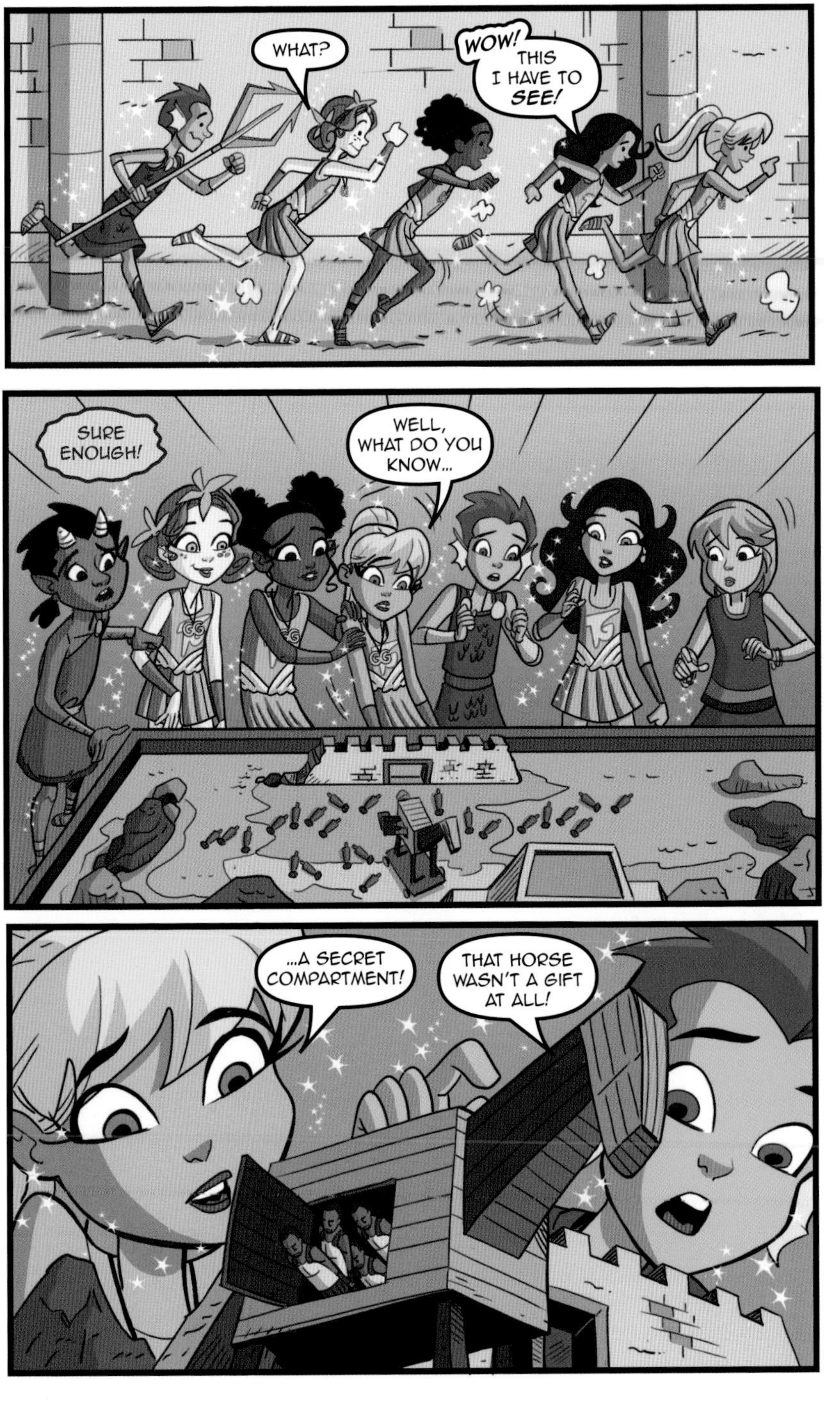
WHAT?
WOW! THIS I HAVE TO SEE!
SURE ENOUGH!
WELL, WHAT DO YOU KNOW...
...A SECRET COMPARTMENT!
THAT HORSE WASN'T A GIFT AT ALL!

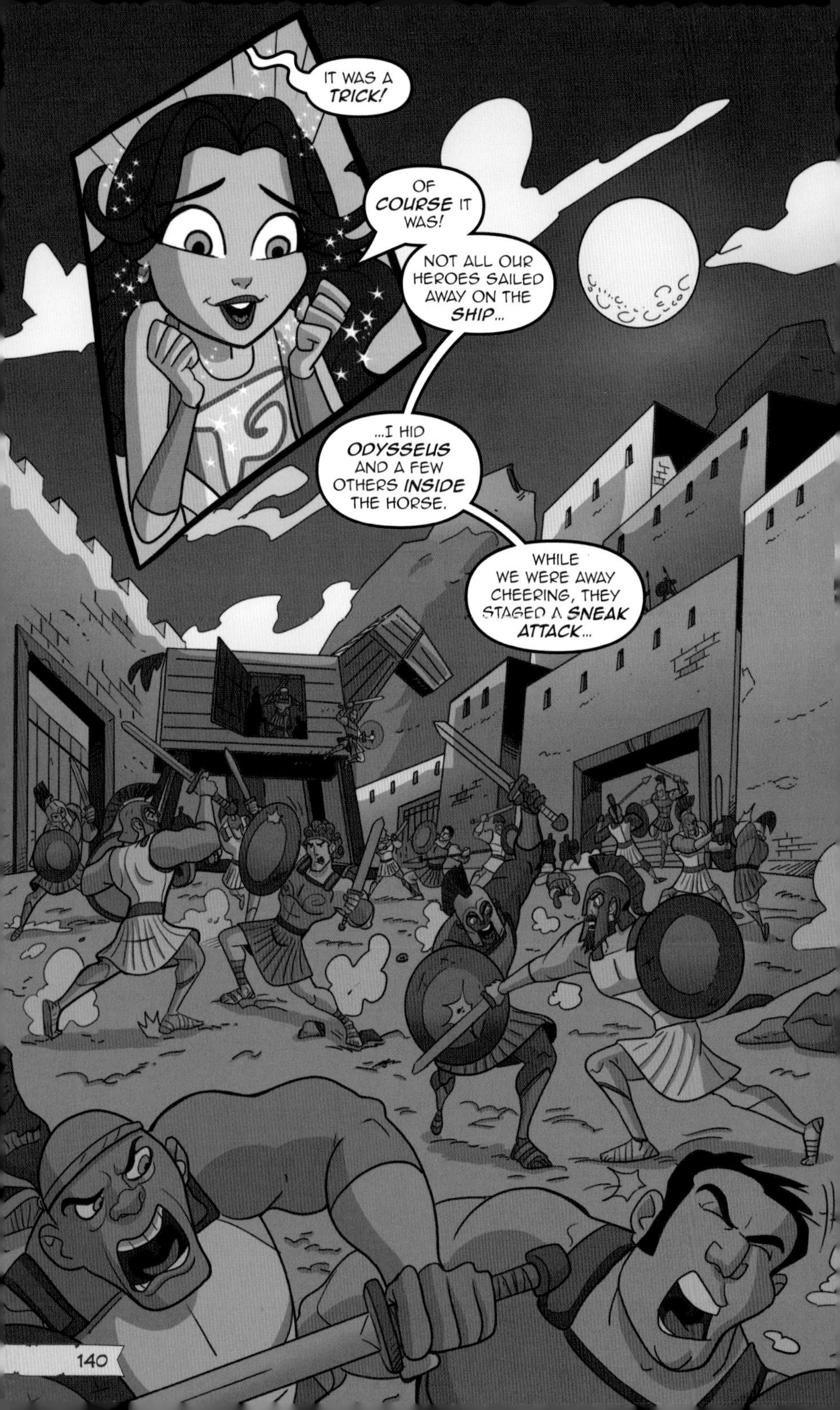
IT WAS A TRICK!
OF COURSE IT WAS!
NOT ALL OUR HEROES SAILED AWAY ON THE SHIP...
...I HID ODYSSEUS AND A FEW OTHERS INSIDE THE HORSE.
WHILE WE WERE AWAY CHEERING, THEY STAGED A SNEAK ATTACK...

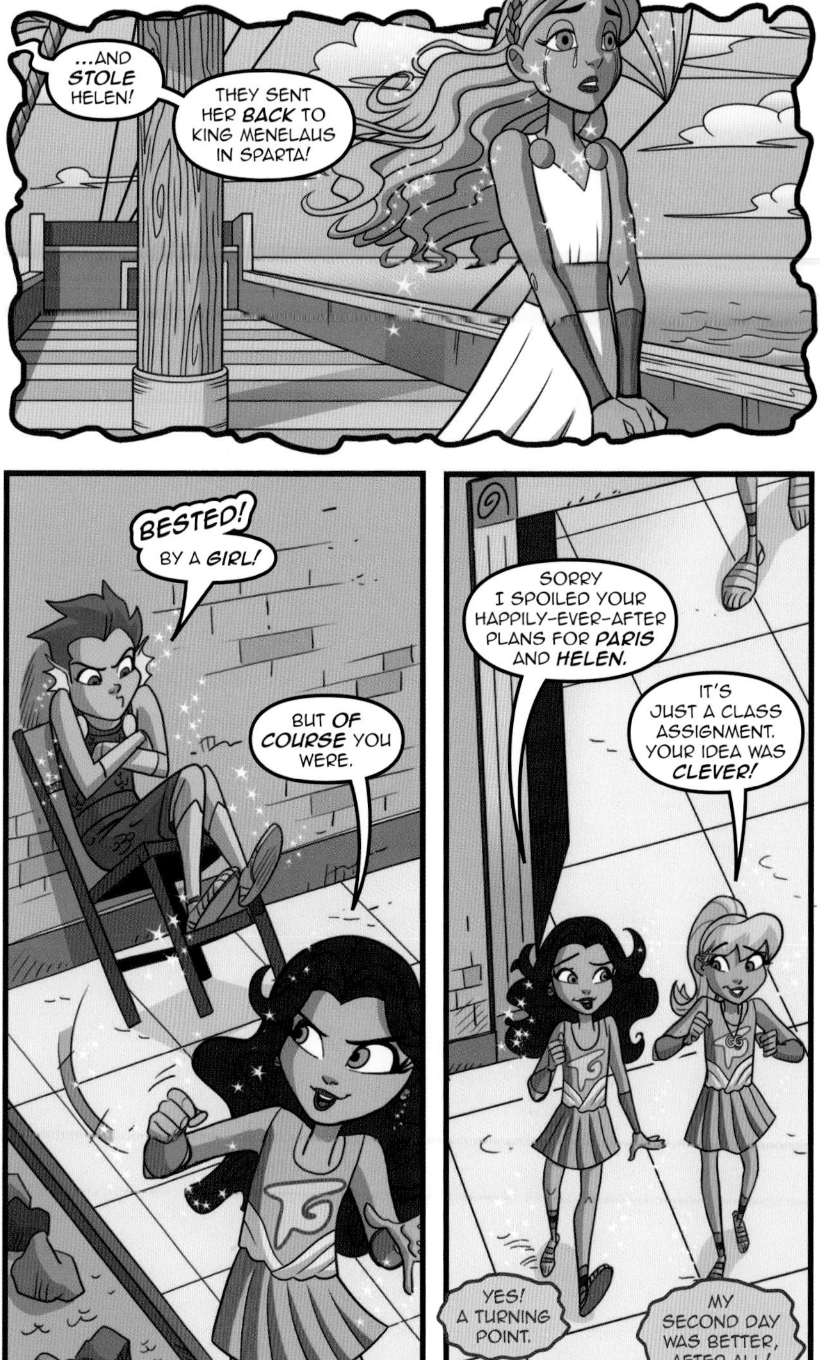
...AND STOLE HELEN!
THEY SENT HER BACK TO KING MENELAUS IN SPARTA!
BESTED! BY A GIRL!
BUT OF COURSE YOU WERE.
SORRY I SPOILED YOUR HAPPILY-EVER-AFTER PLANS FOR PARIS AND HELEN.
IT'S JUST A CLASS ASSIGNMENT. YOUR IDEA WAS CLEVER!
YES! A TURNING POINT.
MY SECOND DAY WAS BETTER, AFTER ALL!

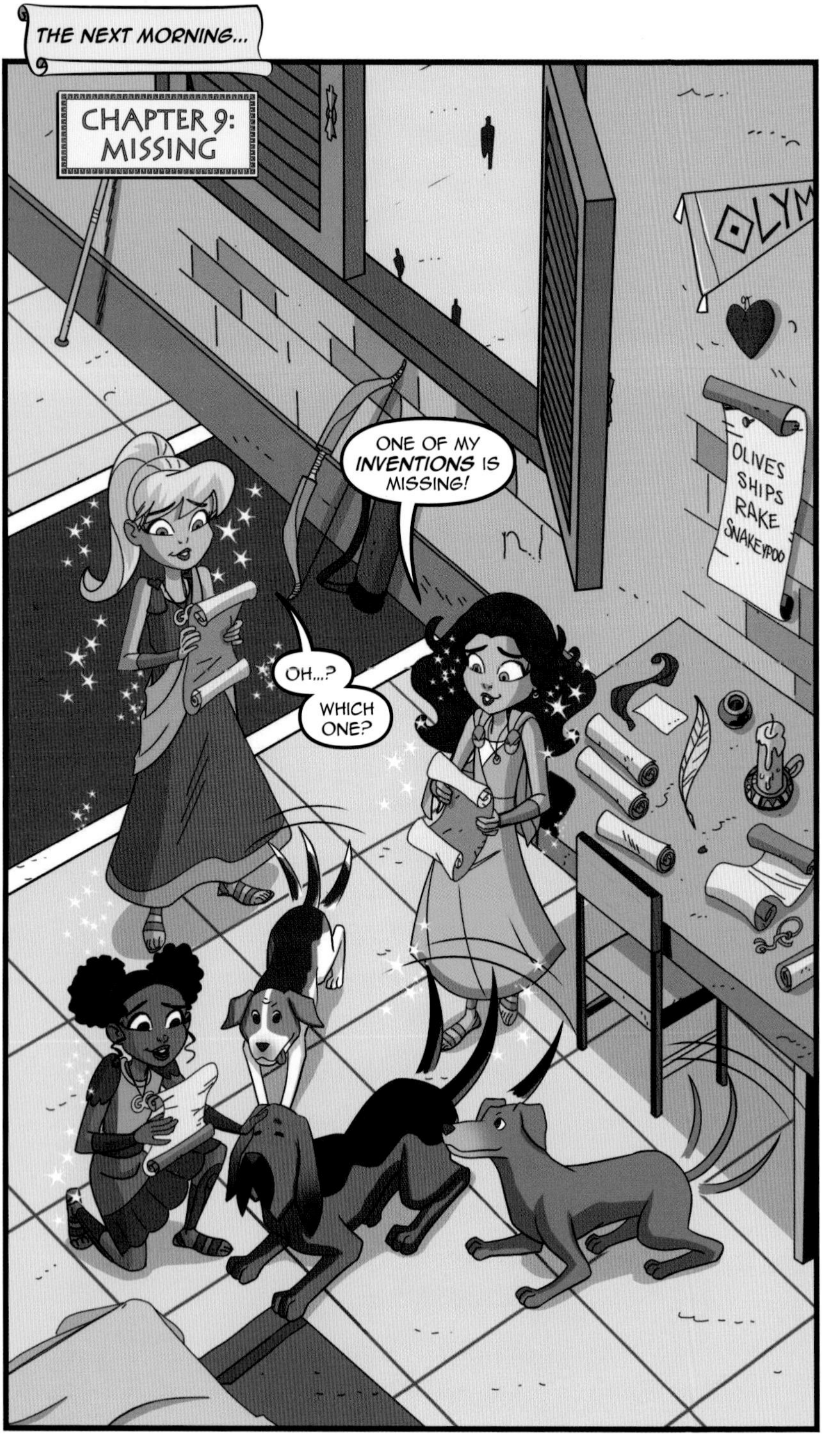
THE NEXT MORNING...
CHAPTER 9: MISSING
OLYM
OLIVES
SHIPS
RAKE
SNAKEYPOO
ONE OF MY *INVENTIONS* IS MISSING!
OH...?
WHICH ONE?

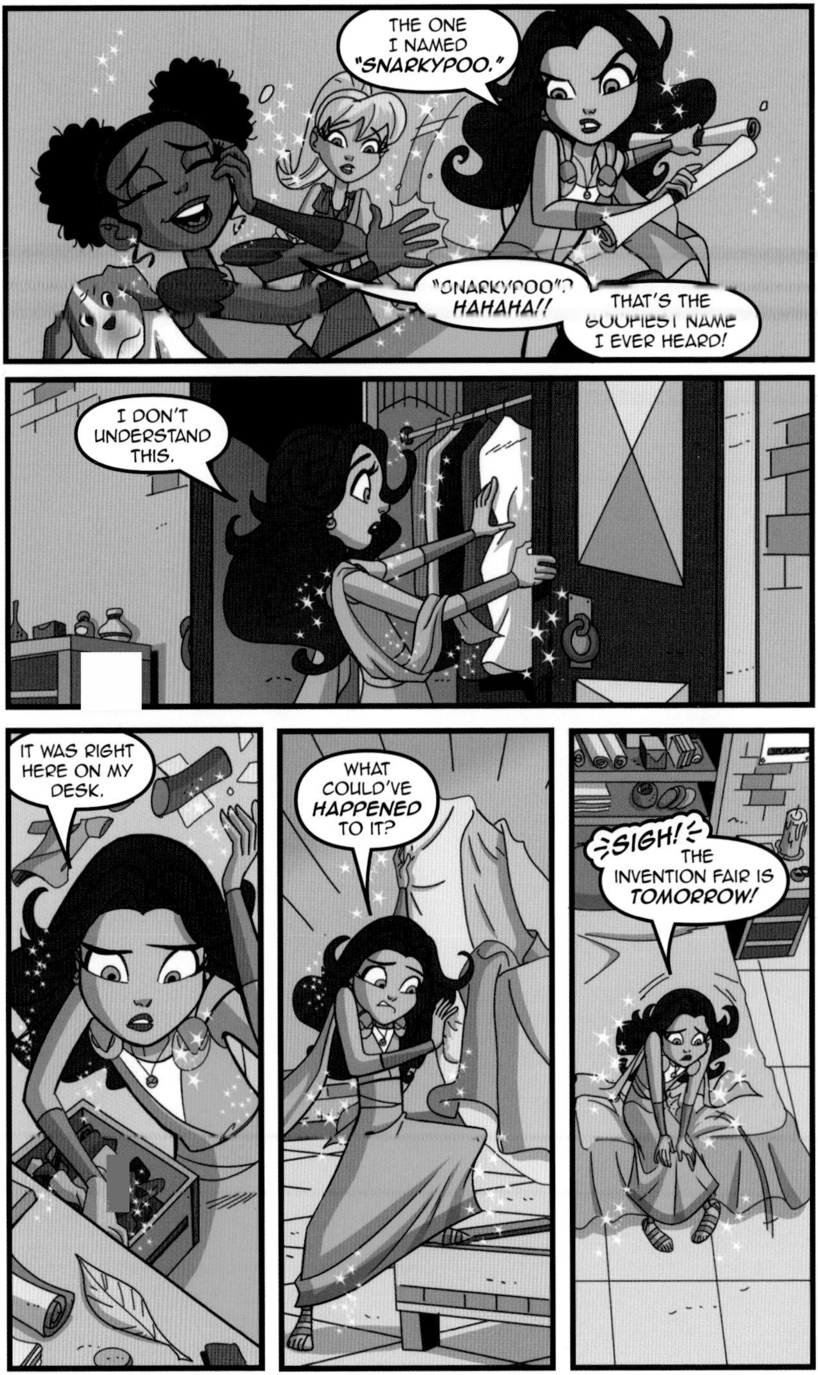
THE ONE I NAMED "SNARKYPOO."
"SNARKYPOO"? HAHAHA!!
THAT'S THE GOOFIEST NAME I EVER HEARD!
I DON'T UNDERSTAND THIS.
IT WAS RIGHT HERE ON MY DESK.
WHAT COULD'VE HAPPENED TO IT?
SIGH!
THE INVENTION FAIR IS TOMORROW!

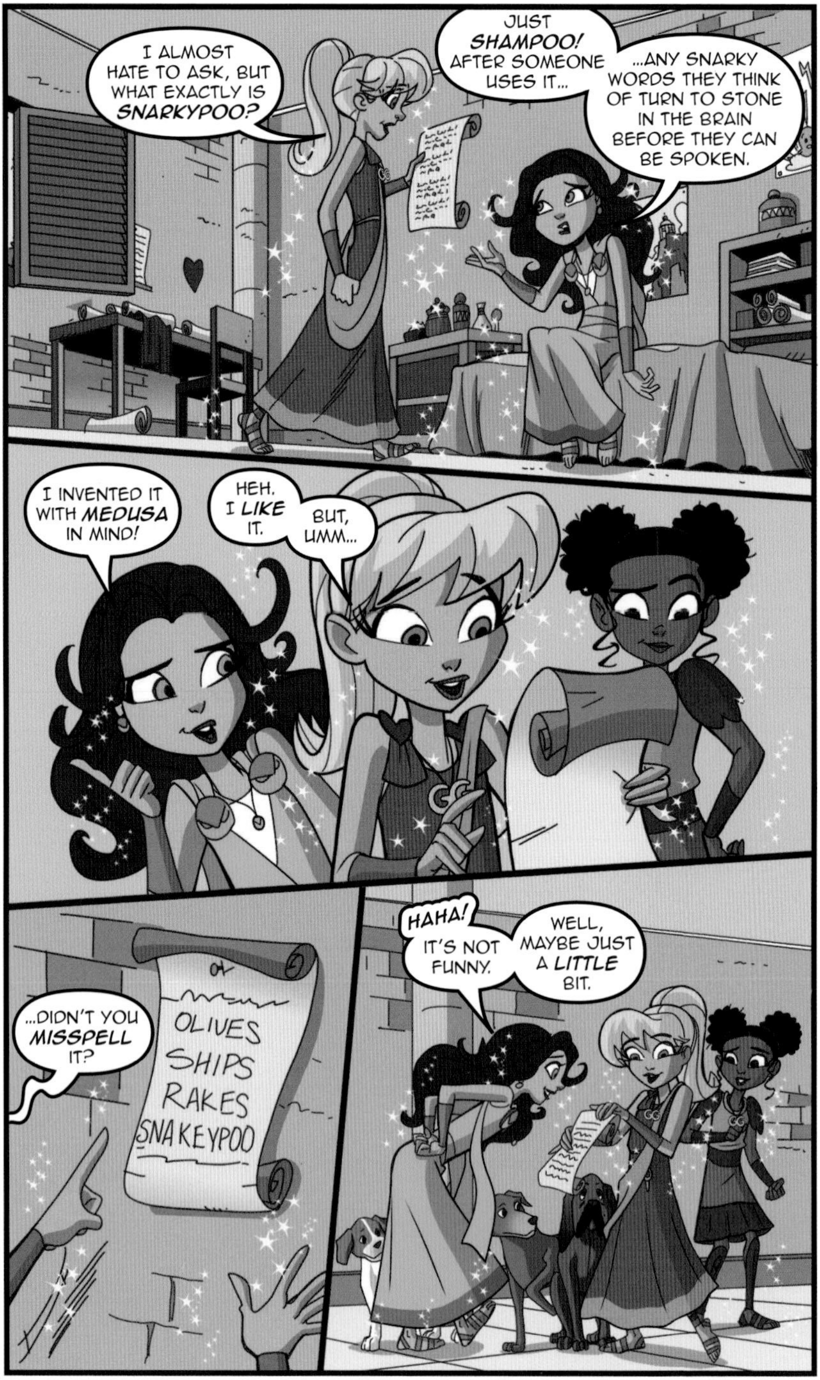
I ALMOST HATE TO ASK, BUT WHAT EXACTLY IS SNARKYPOO?
JUST SHAMPOO! AFTER SOMEONE USES IT...
...ANY SNARKY WORDS THEY THINK OF TURN TO STONE IN THE BRAIN BEFORE THEY CAN BE SPOKEN.
I INVENTED IT WITH MEDUSA IN MIND!
HEH. I LIKE IT.
BUT, UMM...
...DIDN'T YOU MISSPELL IT?
OLIVES
SHIPS
RAKES
SNAKEYPOO
HAHA!
IT'S NOT FUNNY.
WELL, MAYBE JUST A LITTLE BIT.

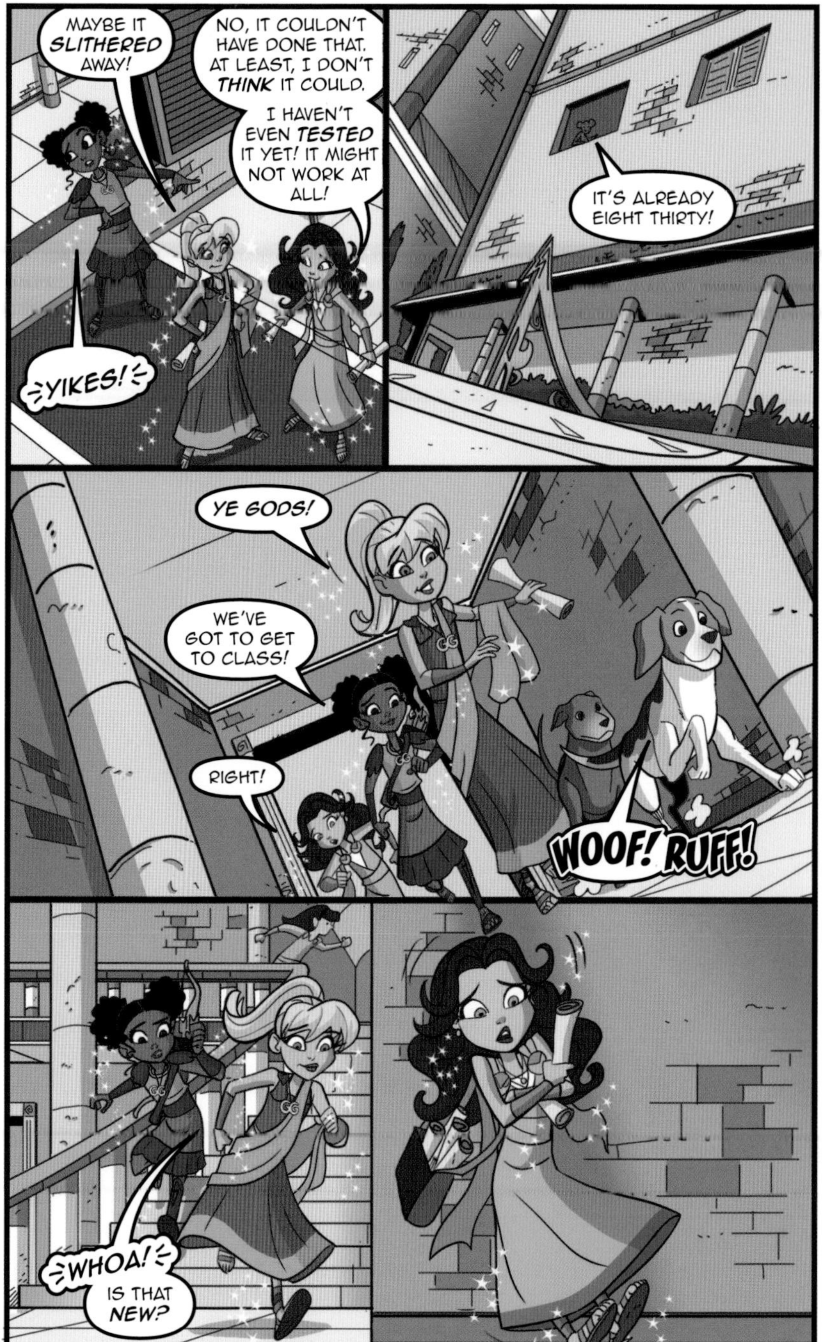
MAYBE IT SLITHERED AWAY!
NO, IT COULDN'T HAVE DONE THAT. AT LEAST, I DON'T THINK IT COULD.
I HAVEN'T EVEN TESTED IT YET! IT MIGHT NOT WORK AT ALL!
YIKES!
IT'S ALREADY EIGHT THIRTY!
YE GODS!
WE'VE GOT TO GET TO CLASS!
RIGHT!
WOOF! RUFF!
WHOA! IS THAT NEW?

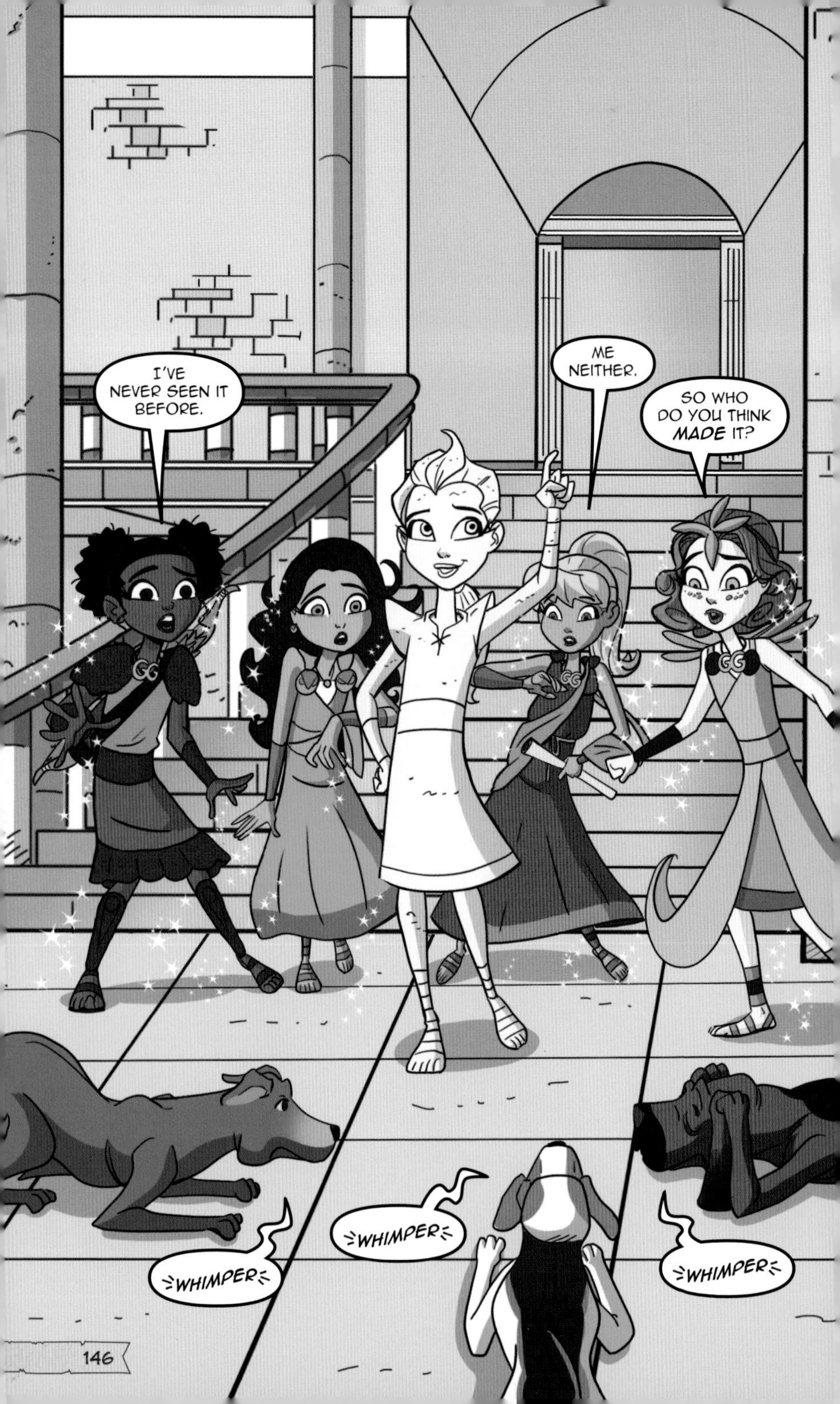

I'VE NEVER SEEN IT BEFORE.
ME NEITHER.
SO WHO DO YOU THINK *MADE* IT?
WHIMPER
WHIMPER
WHIMPER

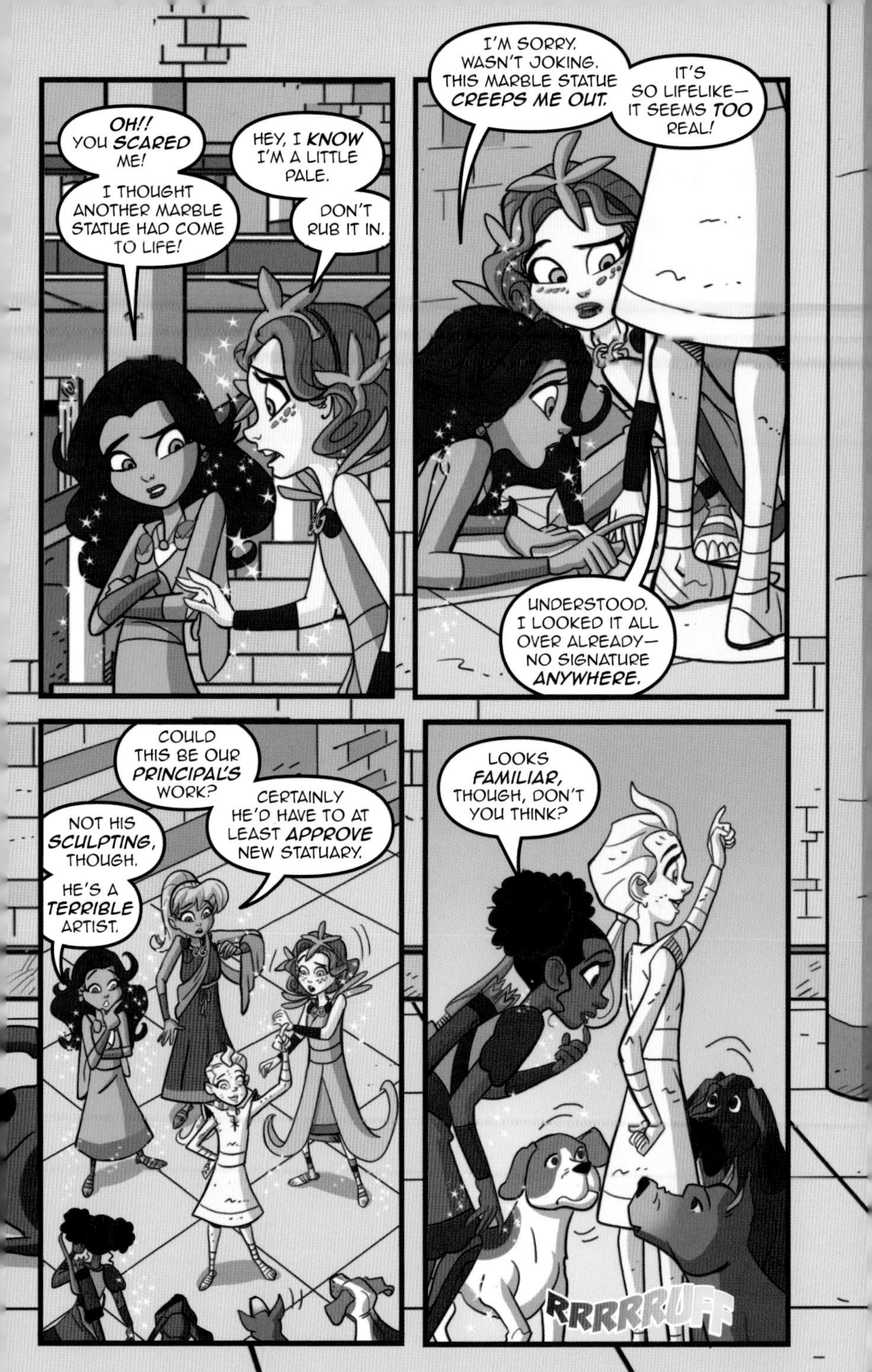
OH!! YOU SCARED ME!
I THOUGHT ANOTHER MARBLE STATUE HAD COME TO LIFE!
HEY, I KNOW I'M A LITTLE PALE.
DON'T RUB IT IN.
I'M SORRY. WASN'T JOKING. THIS MARBLE STATUE CREEPS ME OUT.
IT'S SO LIFELIKE— IT SEEMS TOO REAL!
UNDERSTOOD. I LOOKED IT ALL OVER ALREADY— NO SIGNATURE ANYWHERE.
COULD THIS BE OUR PRINCIPAL'S WORK?
CERTAINLY HE'D HAVE TO AT LEAST APPROVE NEW STATUARY.
NOT HIS SCULPTING, THOUGH.
HE'S A TERRIBLE ARTIST.
LOOKS FAMILIAR, THOUGH, DON'T YOU THINK?
RRRRRUFF

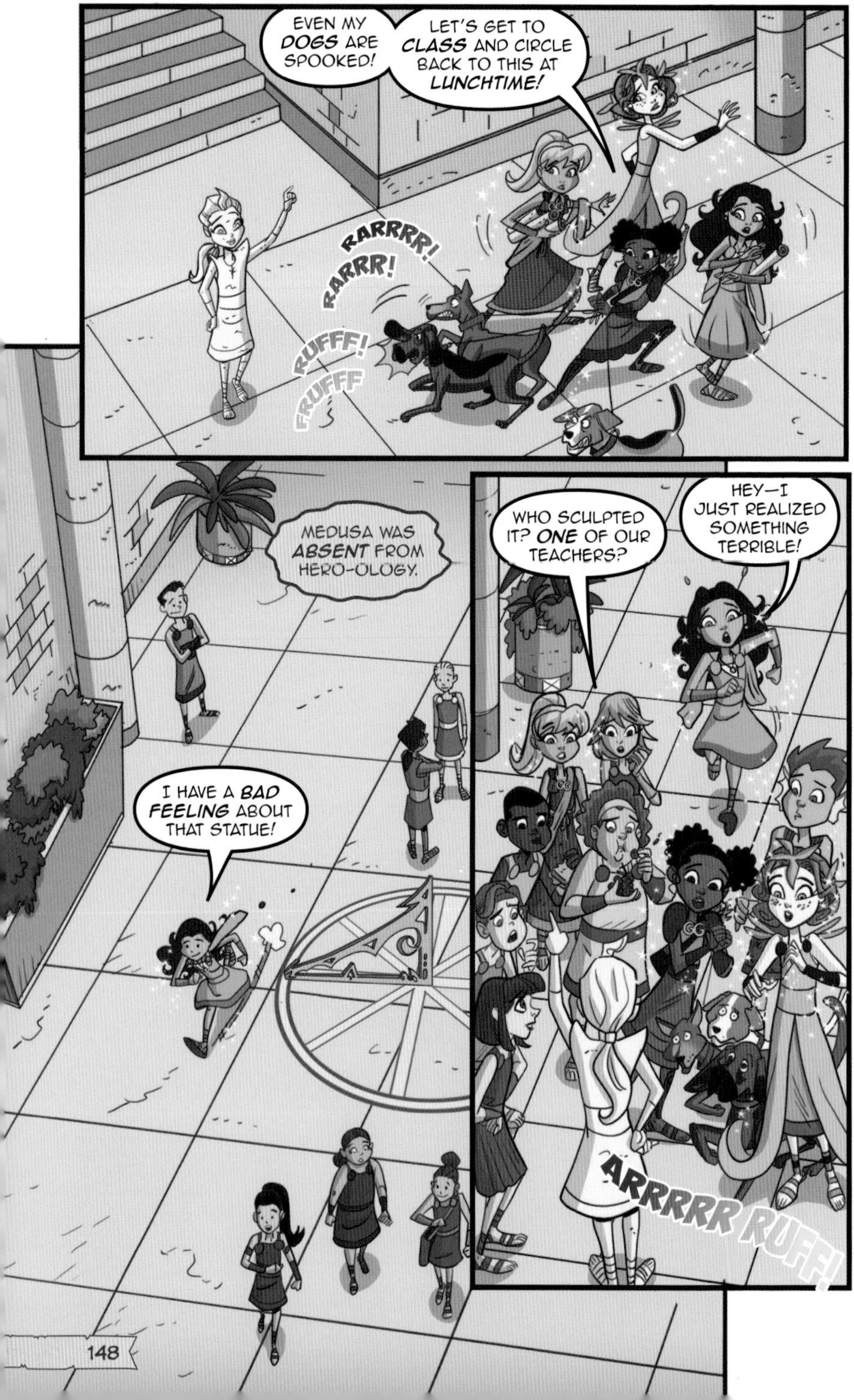

EVEN MY DOGS ARE SPOOKED!
LET'S GET TO CLASS AND CIRCLE BACK TO THIS AT LUNCHTIME!
RARRRR!
RARRR!
RUFFF!
FRUFFF
MEDUSA WAS ABSENT FROM HERO-OLOGY.
I HAVE A BAD FEELING ABOUT THAT STATUE!
WHO SCULPTED IT? ONE OF OUR TEACHERS?
HEY—I JUST REALIZED SOMETHING TERRIBLE!
ARRRRRR RUFF!

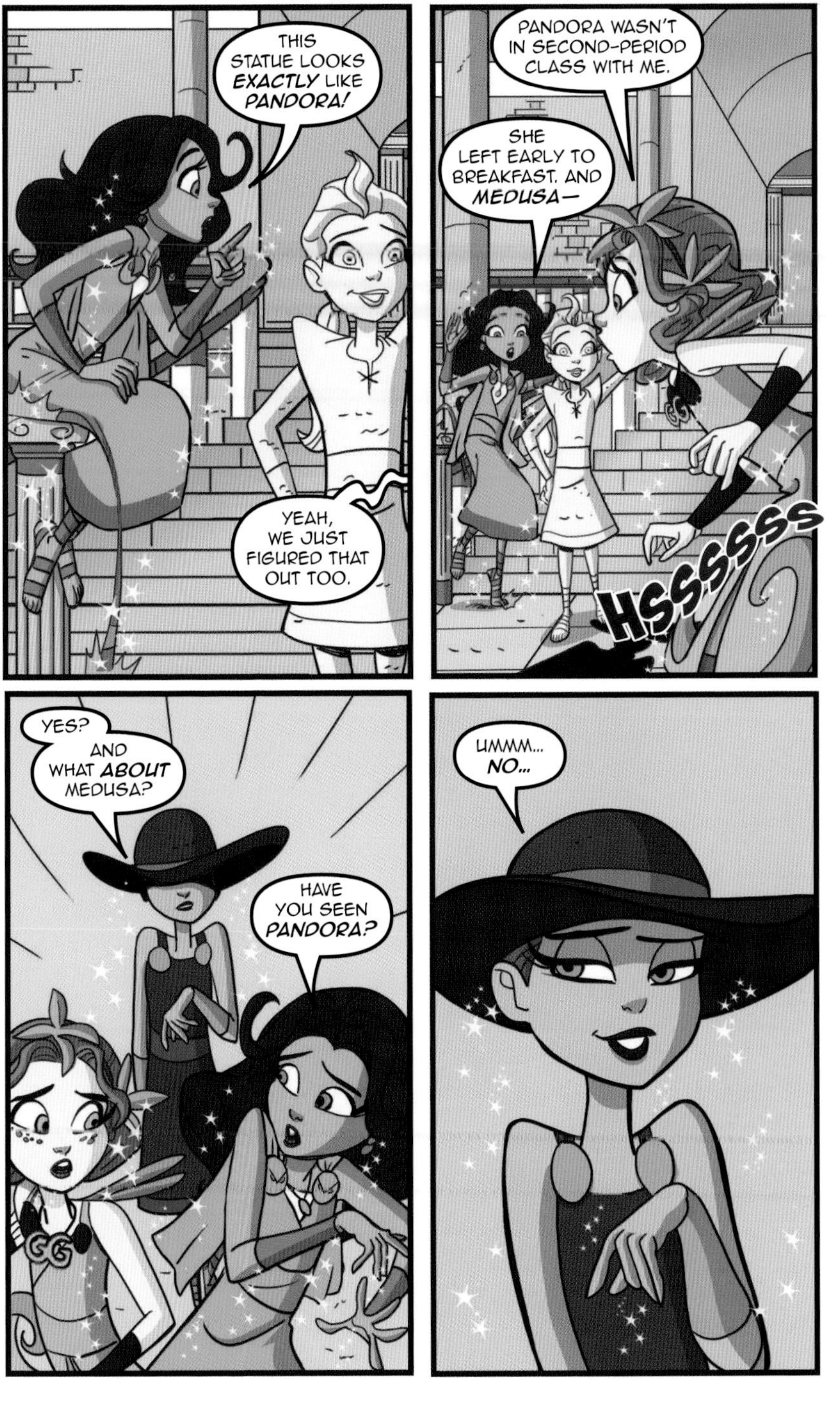
THIS STATUE LOOKS EXACTLY LIKE PANDORA!
YEAH, WE JUST FIGURED THAT OUT TOO.
PANDORA WASN'T IN SECOND-PERIOD CLASS WITH ME.
SHE LEFT EARLY TO BREAKFAST. AND MEDUSA—
HSSSSSS
YES? AND WHAT ABOUT MEDUSA?
HAVE YOU SEEN PANDORA?
UMMM... NO...

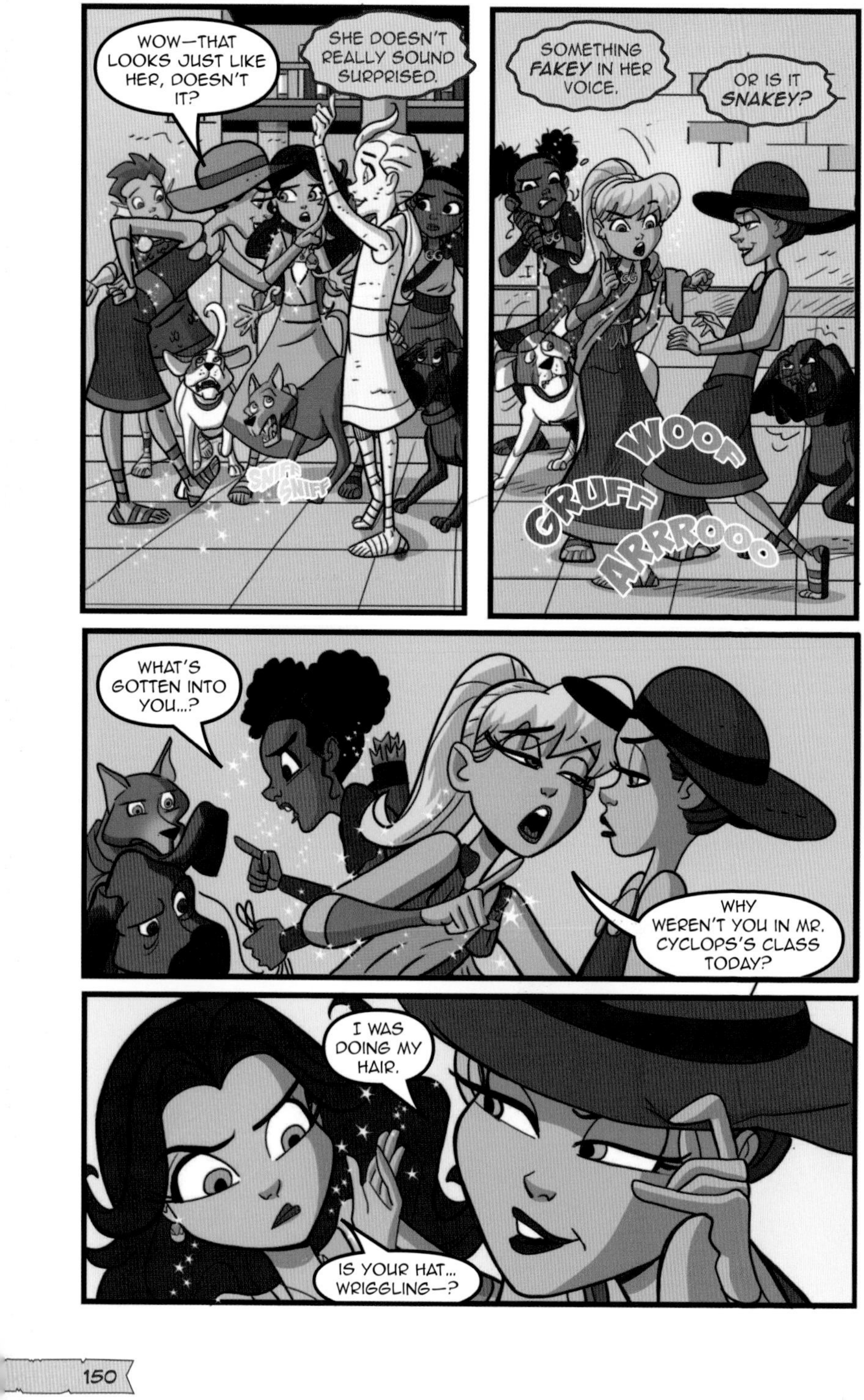
WOW—THAT LOOKS JUST LIKE HER, DOESN'T IT?
SHE DOESN'T REALLY SOUND SURPRISED.
SNIFF SNIFF
SOMETHING FAKEY IN HER VOICE.
OR IS IT SNAKEY?
WOOF
GRUFF
ARRROOOO
WHAT'S GOTTEN INTO YOU...?
WHY WEREN'T YOU IN MR. CYCLOPS'S CLASS TODAY?
I WAS DOING MY HAIR.
IS YOUR HAT... WRIGGLING—?

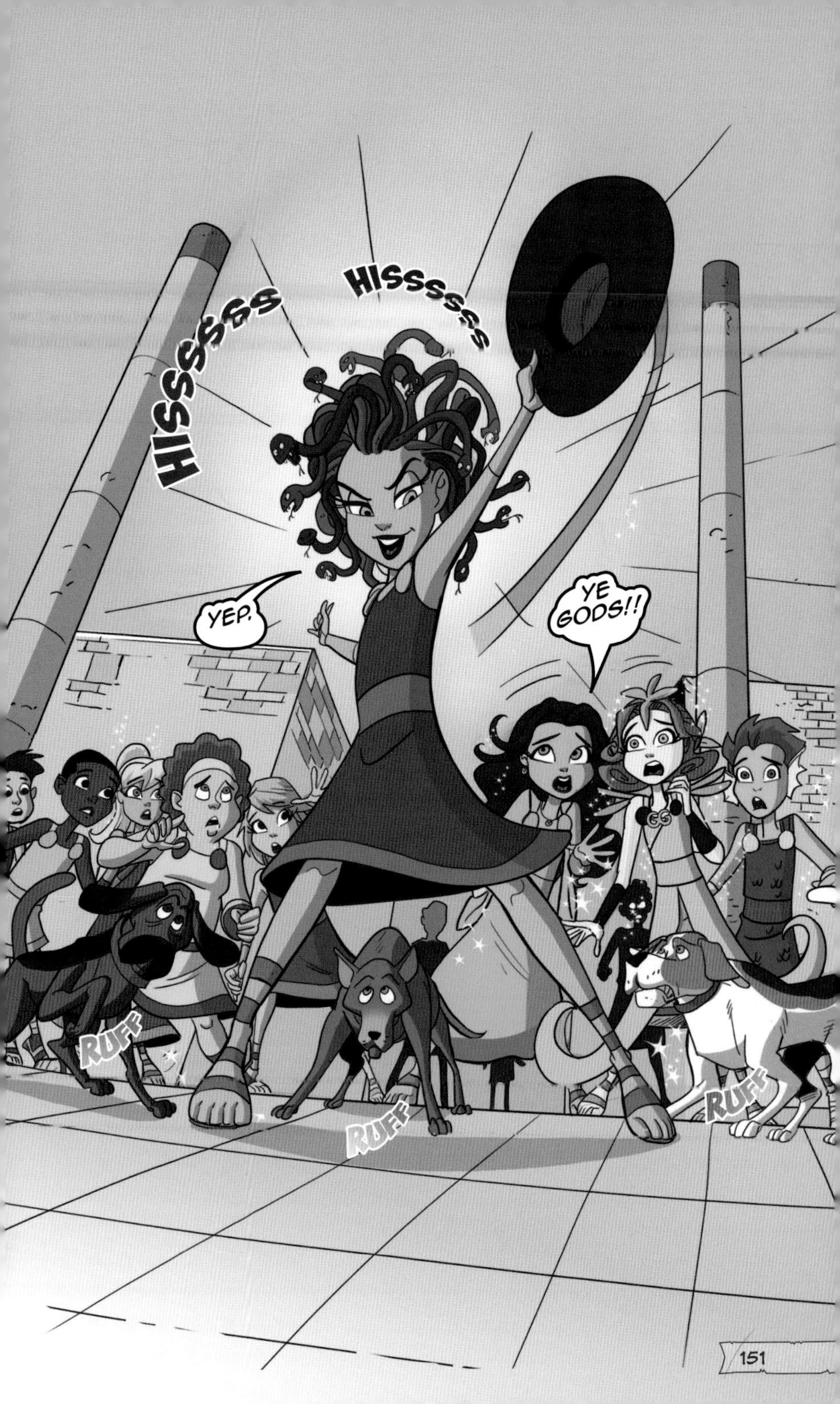
HISSSSSS
HISSSSSS
YEP.
YE GODS!!
RUFF
RUFF
RUFF

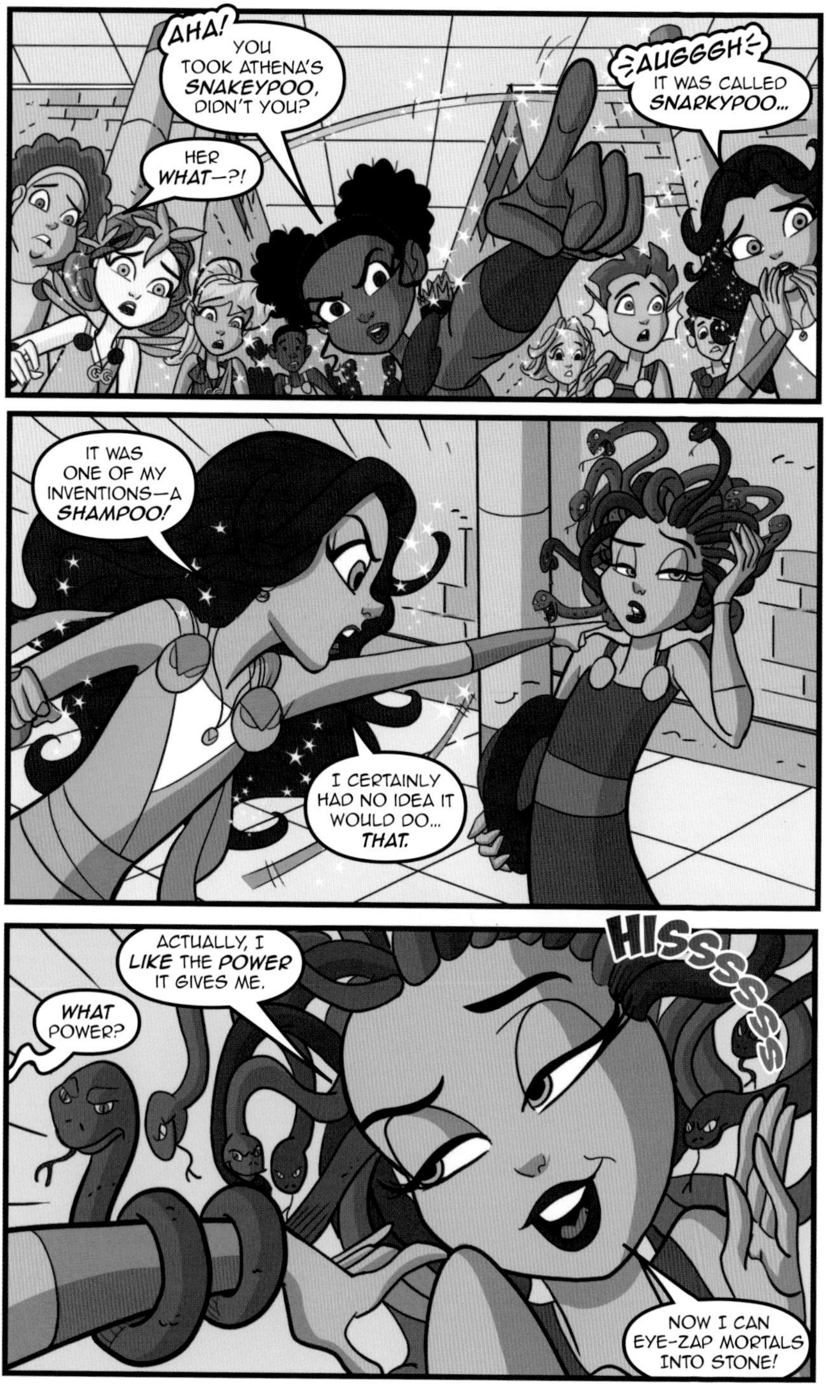
AHA! YOU TOOK ATHENA'S SNAKEYPOO, DIDN'T YOU?
HER WHAT—?!
AUGGGH IT WAS CALLED SNARKYPOO...
IT WAS ONE OF MY INVENTIONS—A SHAMPOO!
I CERTAINLY HAD NO IDEA IT WOULD DO... THAT.
ACTUALLY, I LIKE THE POWER IT GIVES ME.
WHAT POWER?
HISSSSSS
NOW I CAN EYE-ZAP MORTALS INTO STONE!

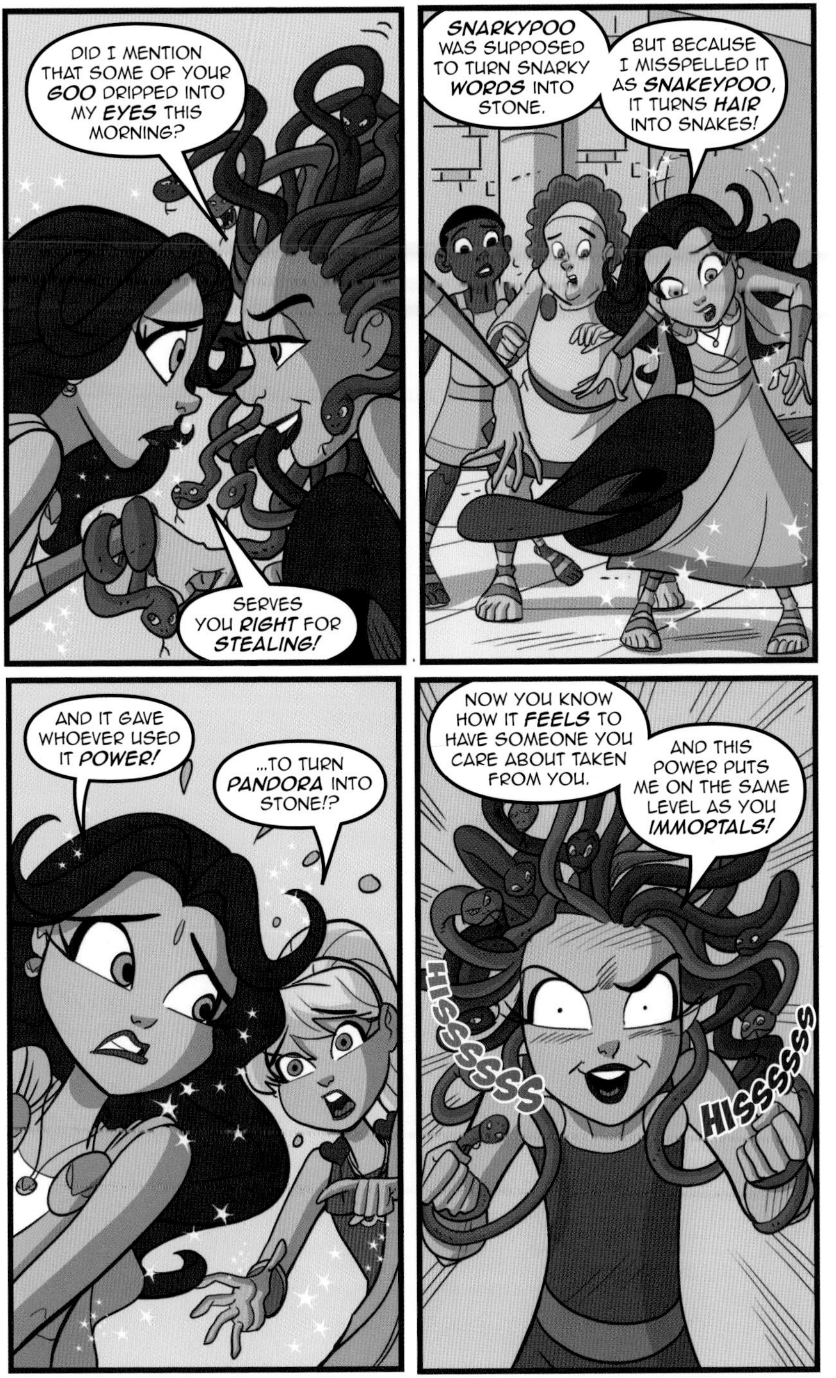
DID I MENTION THAT SOME OF YOUR GOO DRIPPED INTO MY EYES THIS MORNING?
SERVES YOU RIGHT FOR STEALING!
SNARKYPOO WAS SUPPOSED TO TURN SNARKY WORDS INTO STONE.
BUT BECAUSE I MISSPELLED IT AS SNAKEYPOO, IT TURNS HAIR INTO SNAKES!
AND IT GAVE WHOEVER USED IT POWER!
...TO TURN PANDORA INTO STONE!?
NOW YOU KNOW HOW IT FEELS TO HAVE SOMEONE YOU CARE ABOUT TAKEN FROM YOU.
AND THIS POWER PUTS ME ON THE SAME LEVEL AS YOU IMMORTALS!
HISSSSSS
HISSSSSS

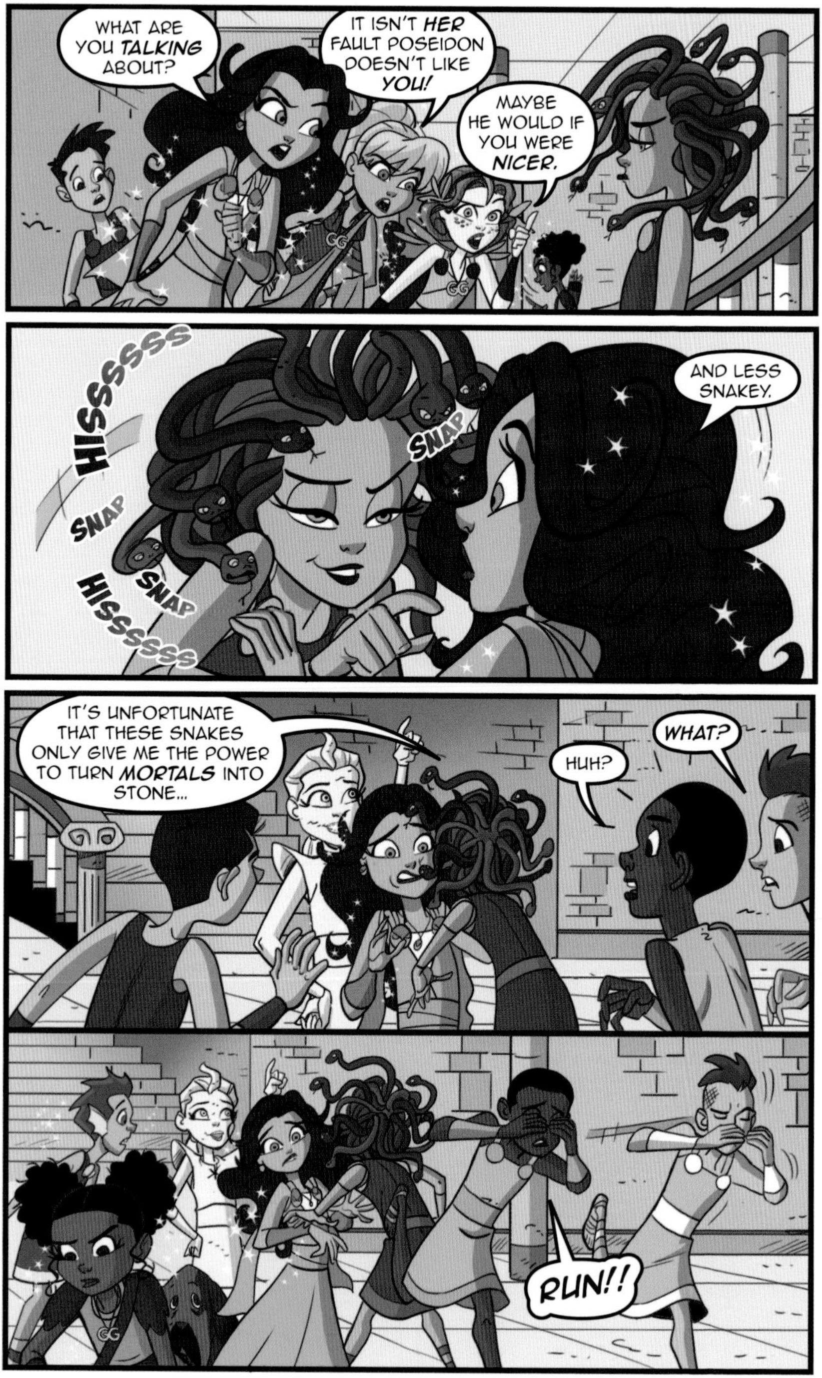
WHAT ARE YOU TALKING ABOUT?
IT ISN'T HER FAULT POSEIDON DOESN'T LIKE YOU!
MAYBE HE WOULD IF YOU WERE NICER.
HISSSSSS
SNAP
SNAP
SNAP
HISSSSSS
AND LESS SNAKEY.
IT'S UNFORTUNATE THAT THESE SNAKES ONLY GIVE ME THE POWER TO TURN MORTALS INTO STONE...
HUH?
WHAT?
RUN!!

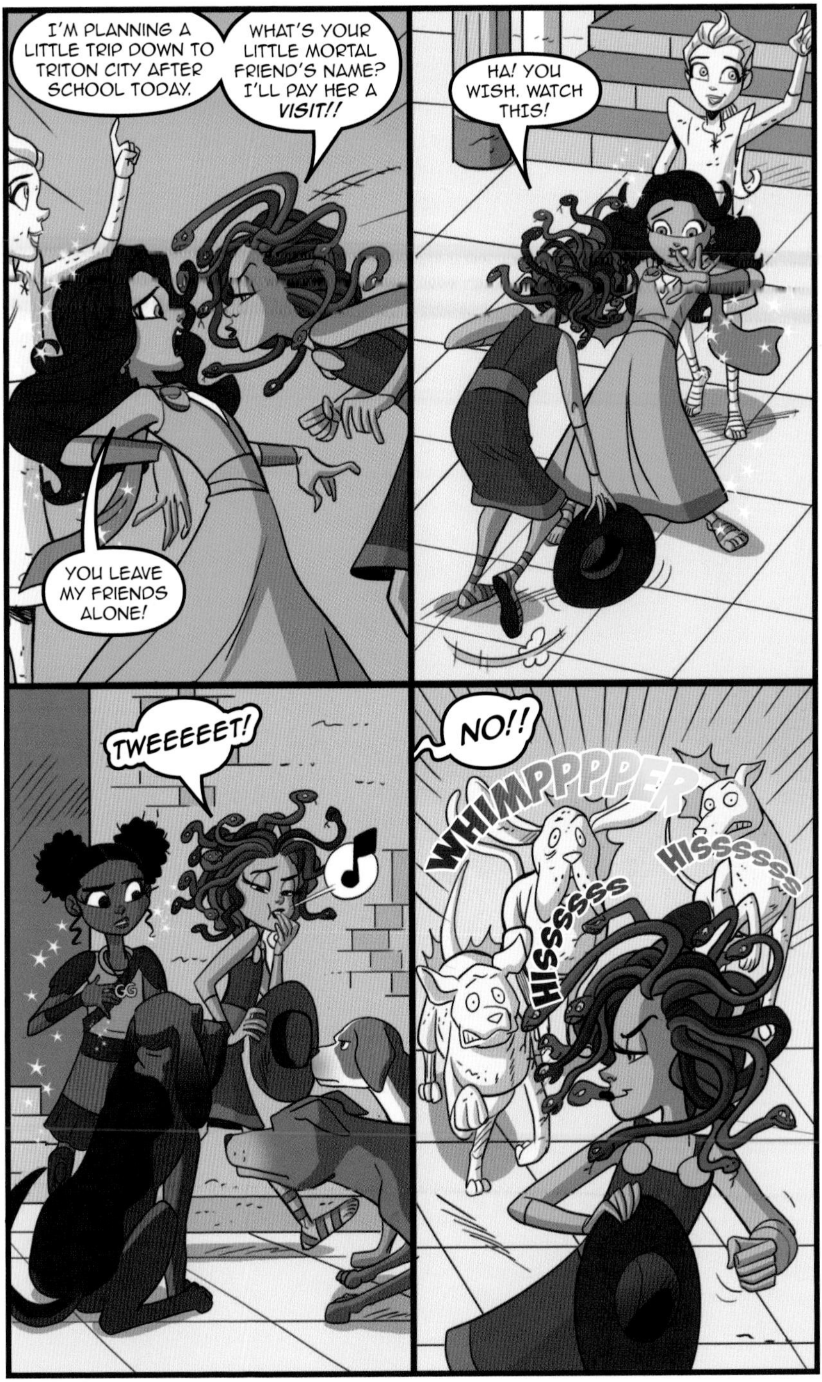
I'M PLANNING A LITTLE TRIP DOWN TO TRITON CITY AFTER SCHOOL TODAY.
WHAT'S YOUR LITTLE MORTAL FRIEND'S NAME? I'LL PAY HER A VISIT!!
YOU LEAVE MY FRIENDS ALONE!
HA! YOU WISH. WATCH THIS!
TWEEEEET!
NO!!
WHIMPPPPER
HISSSSSS
HISSSSSS
HISSSSS

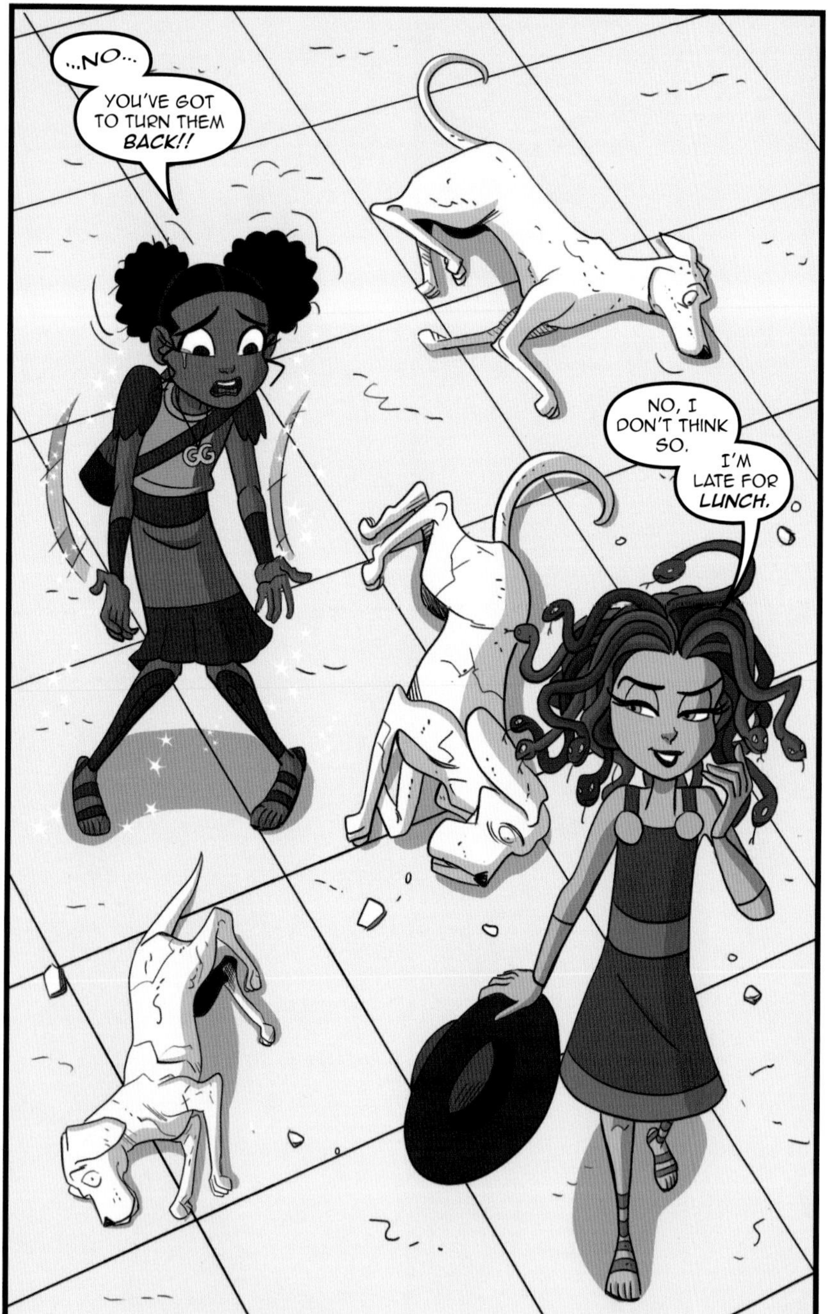
...NO...
YOU'VE GOT TO TURN THEM BACK!!
NO, I DON'T THINK SO.
I'M LATE FOR LUNCH.

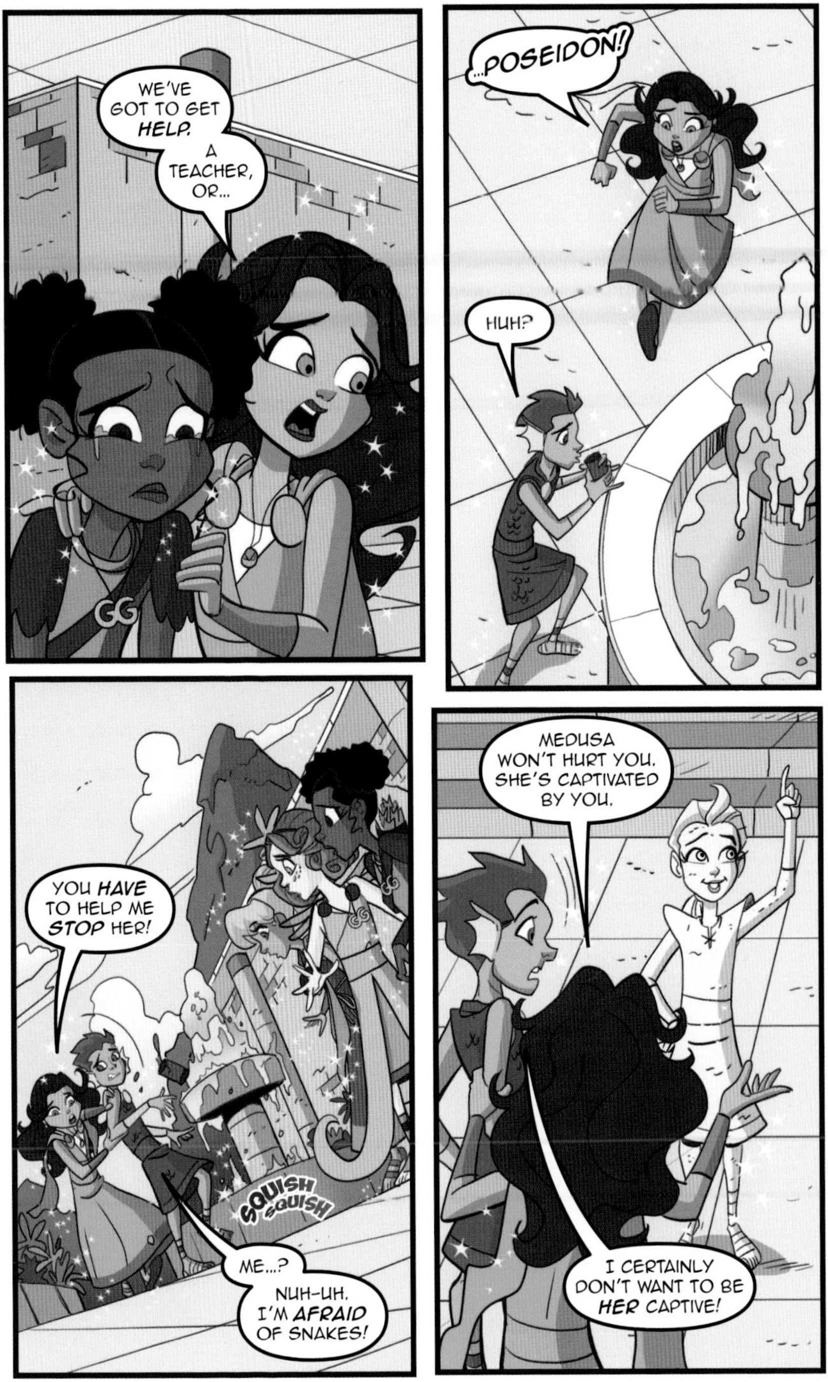
WE'VE GOT TO GET HELP.
A TEACHER, OR...
...POSEIDON!
HUH?
YOU HAVE TO HELP ME STOP HER!
SQUISH SQUISH
ME...?
NUH-UH. I'M AFRAID OF SNAKES!
MEDUSA WON'T HURT YOU. SHE'S CAPTIVATED BY YOU.
I CERTAINLY DON'T WANT TO BE HER CAPTIVE!

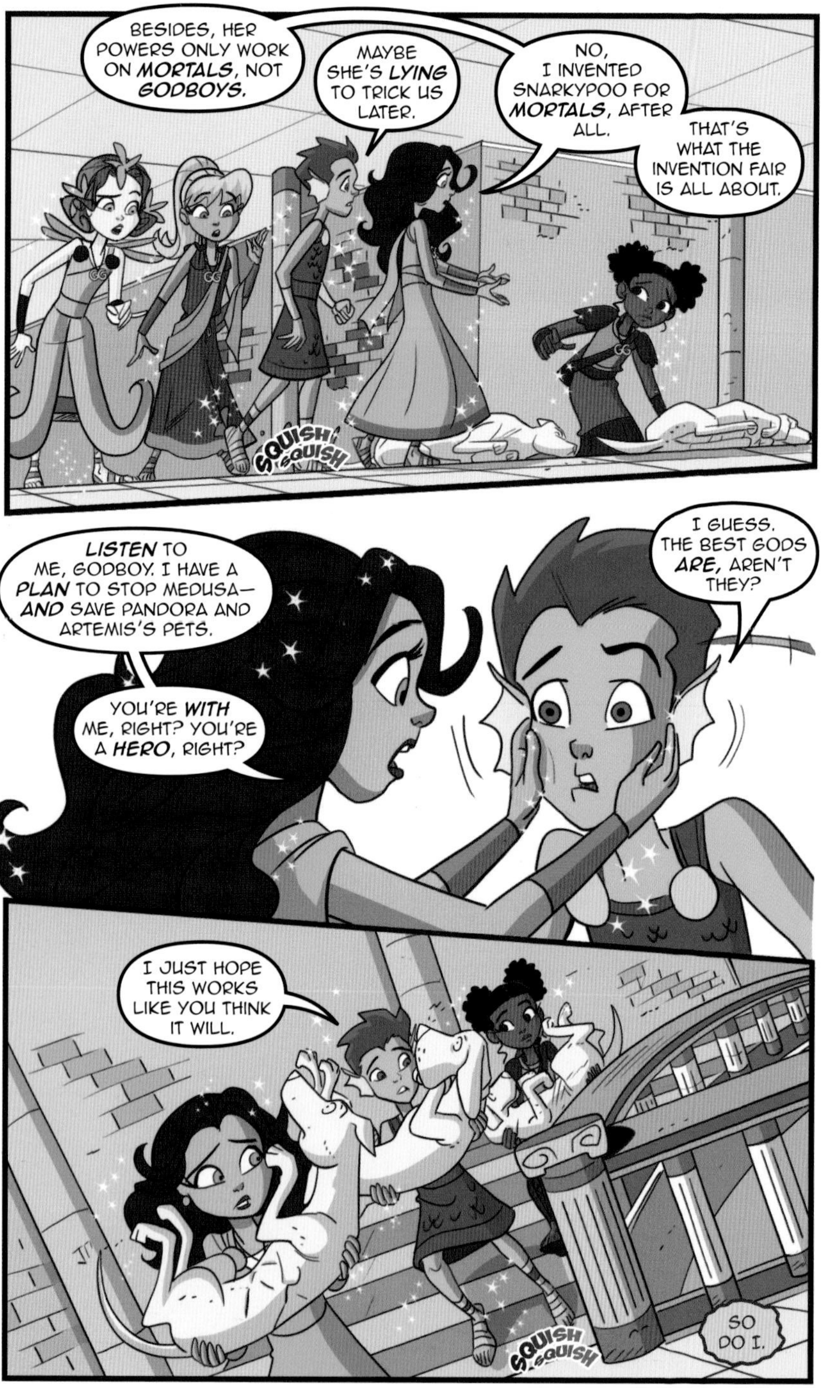

BESIDES, HER POWERS ONLY WORK ON ***MORTALS***, NOT ***GODBOYS.***
MAYBE SHE'S ***LYING*** TO TRICK US LATER.
NO, I INVENTED SNARKYPOO FOR ***MORTALS***, AFTER ALL.
THAT'S WHAT THE INVENTION FAIR IS ALL ABOUT.
SQUISH! SQUISH
LISTEN TO ME, GODBOY. I HAVE A ***PLAN*** TO STOP MEDUSA—***AND*** SAVE PANDORA AND ARTEMIS'S PETS.
YOU'RE ***WITH*** ME, RIGHT? YOU'RE A ***HERO***, RIGHT?
I GUESS. THE BEST GODS ***ARE,*** AREN'T THEY?
I JUST HOPE THIS WORKS LIKE YOU THINK IT WILL.
SO DO I.
SQUISH SQUISH

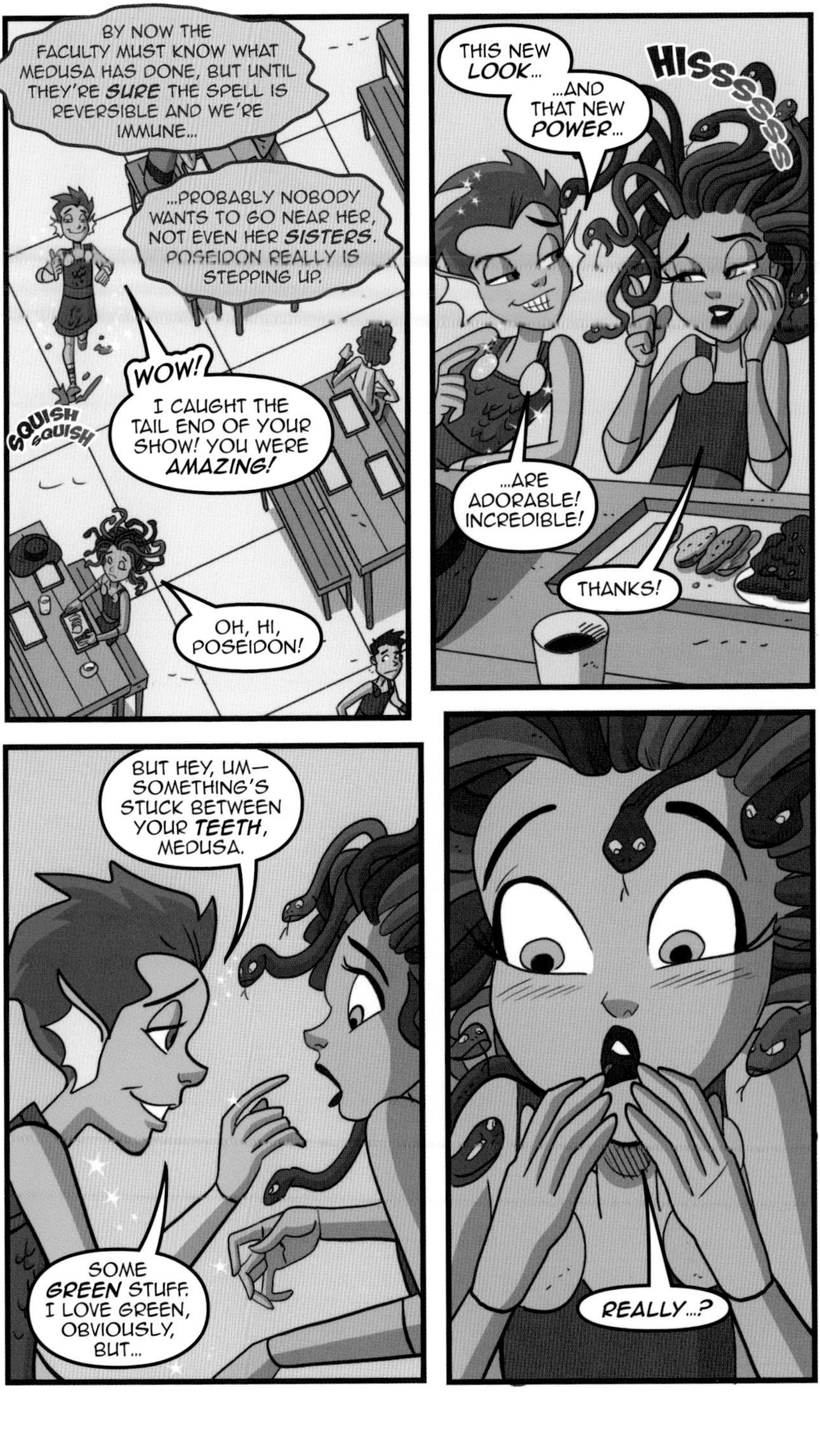
BY NOW THE FACULTY MUST KNOW WHAT MEDUSA HAS DONE, BUT UNTIL THEY'RE *SURE* THE SPELL IS REVERSIBLE AND WE'RE IMMUNE...
...PROBABLY NOBODY WANTS TO GO NEAR HER, NOT EVEN HER *SISTERS*. POSEIDON REALLY IS STEPPING UP.
WOW!
I CAUGHT THE TAIL END OF YOUR SHOW! YOU WERE *AMAZING!*
SQUISH SQUISH
OH, HI, POSEIDON!
THIS NEW *LOOK*...
...AND THAT NEW *POWER*...
HISSSSSSS
...ARE ADORABLE! INCREDIBLE!
THANKS!
BUT HEY, UM— SOMETHING'S STUCK BETWEEN YOUR *TEETH*, MEDUSA.
SOME *GREEN* STUFF. I LOVE GREEN, OBVIOUSLY, BUT...
REALLY...?

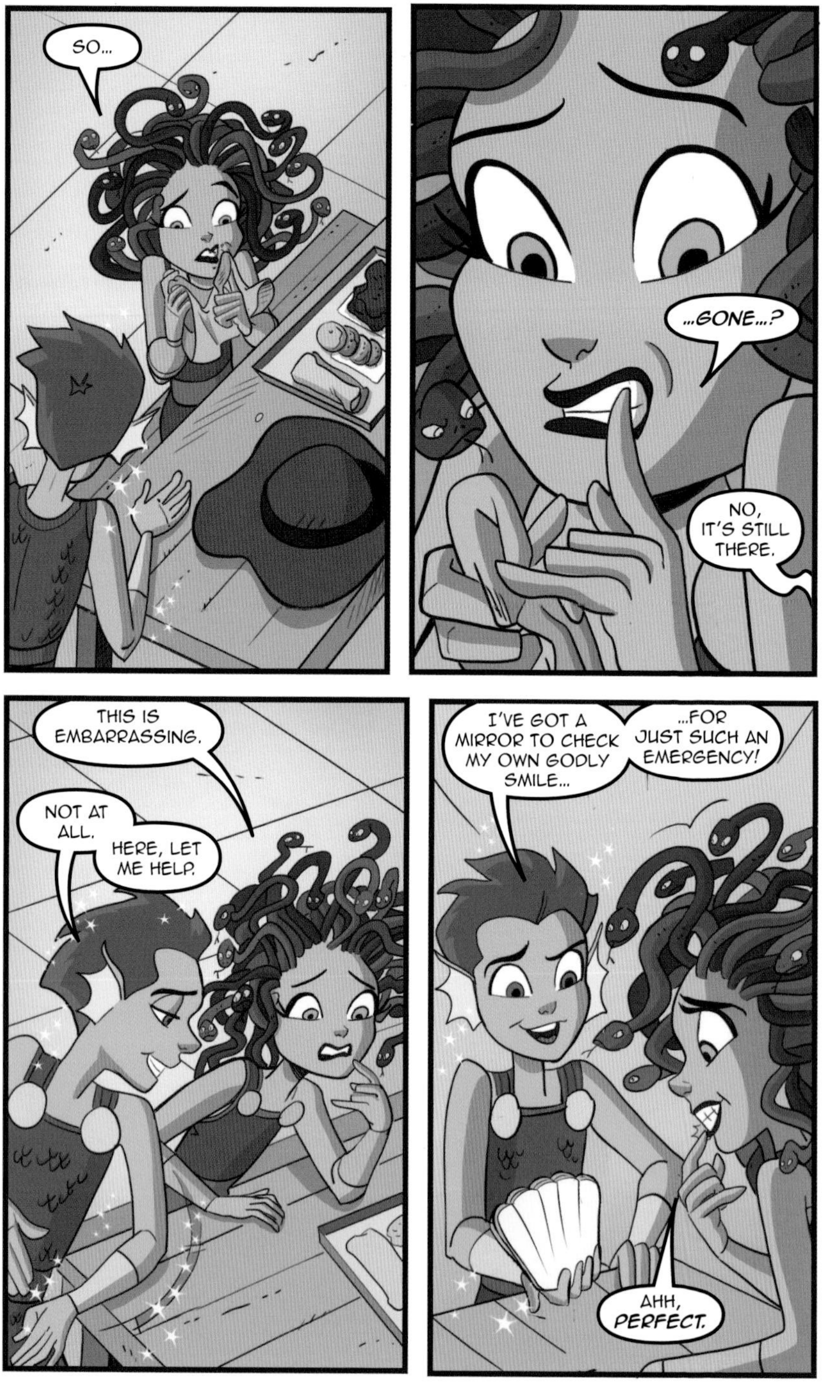
SO...
...GONE...?
NO, IT'S STILL THERE.
THIS IS EMBARRASSING.
NOT AT ALL.
HERE, LET ME HELP.
I'VE GOT A MIRROR TO CHECK MY OWN GODLY SMILE...
...FOR JUST SUCH AN EMERGENCY!
AHH, PERFECT.

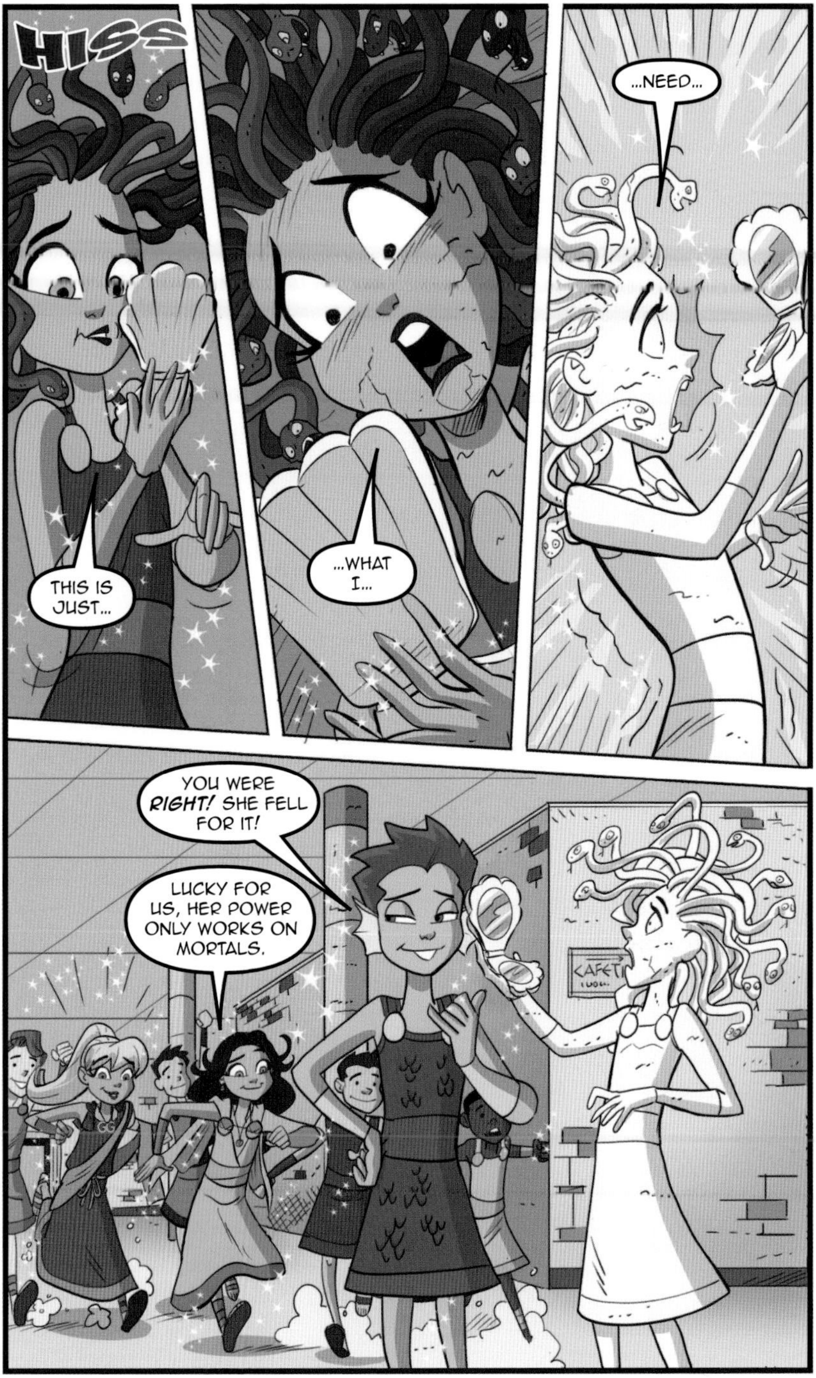

HISS
THIS IS JUST...
...WHAT I...
...NEED...
YOU WERE RIGHT! SHE FELL FOR IT!
LUCKY FOR US, HER POWER ONLY WORKS ON MORTALS.

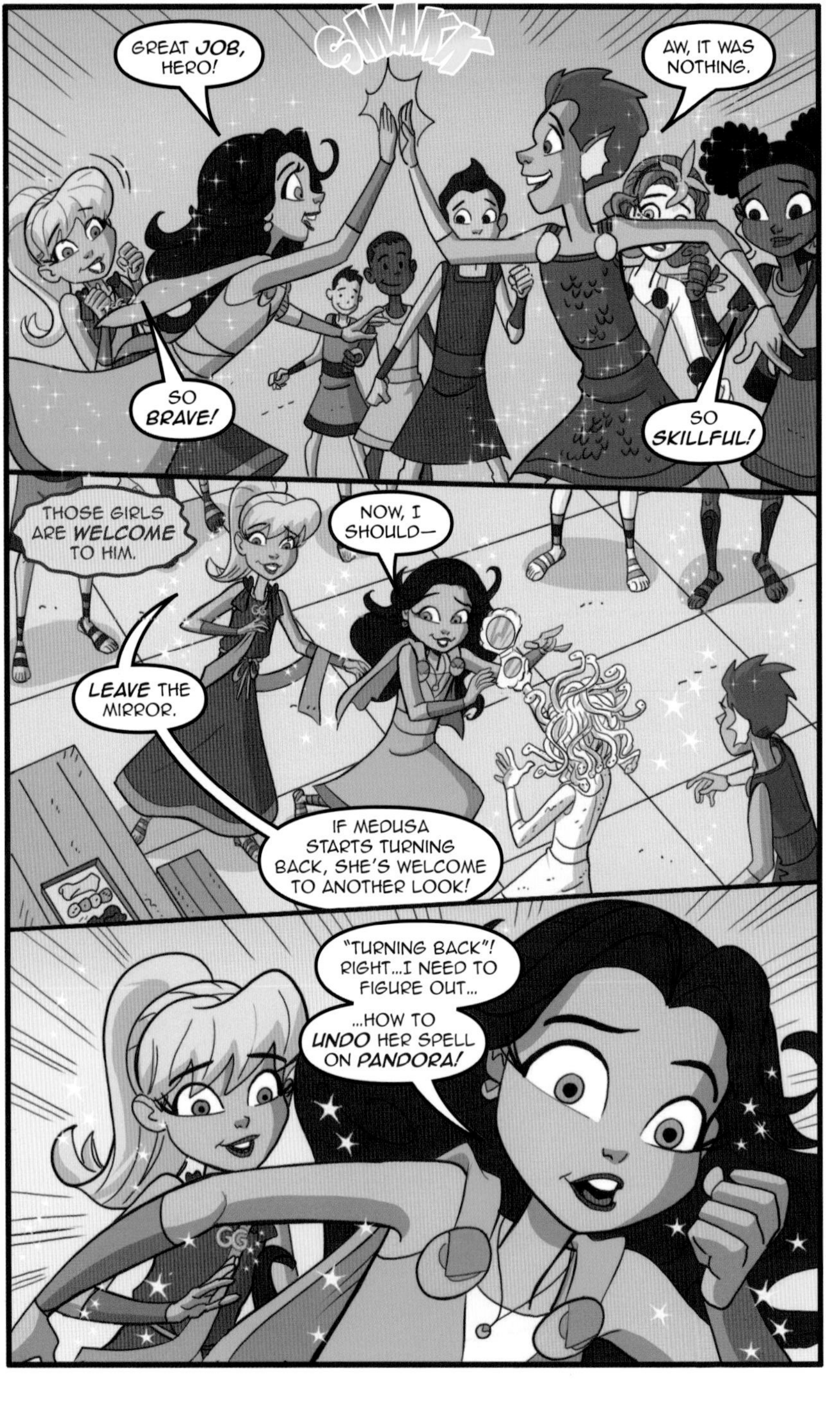
GREAT JOB, HERO!
SMACK
AW, IT WAS NOTHING.
SO BRAVE!
SO SKILLFUL!
THOSE GIRLS ARE WELCOME TO HIM.
NOW, I SHOULD—
LEAVE THE MIRROR.
IF MEDUSA STARTS TURNING BACK, SHE'S WELCOME TO ANOTHER LOOK!
"TURNING BACK"! RIGHT...I NEED TO FIGURE OUT...
...HOW TO UNDO HER SPELL ON PANDORA!

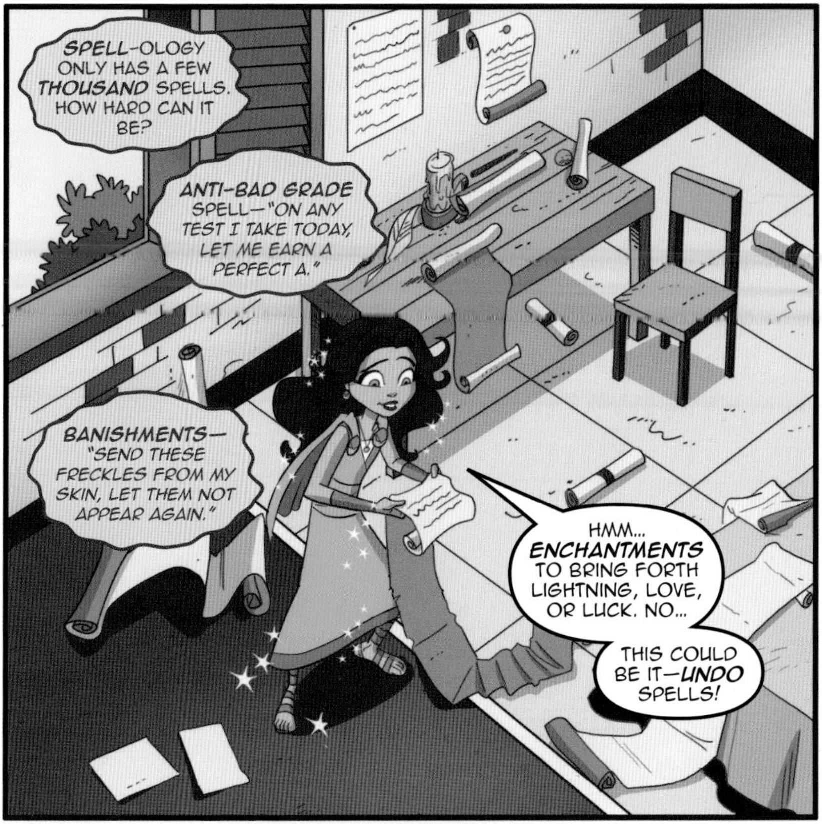
SPELL-OLOGY ONLY HAS A FEW THOUSAND SPELLS. HOW HARD CAN IT BE?
ANTI-BAD GRADE SPELL—"ON ANY TEST I TAKE TODAY, LET ME EARN A PERFECT A."
BANISHMENTS—"SEND THESE FRECKLES FROM MY SKIN, LET THEM NOT APPEAR AGAIN."
HMM... ENCHANTMENTS TO BRING FORTH LIGHTNING, LOVE, OR LUCK. NO...
THIS COULD BE IT—UNDO SPELLS!

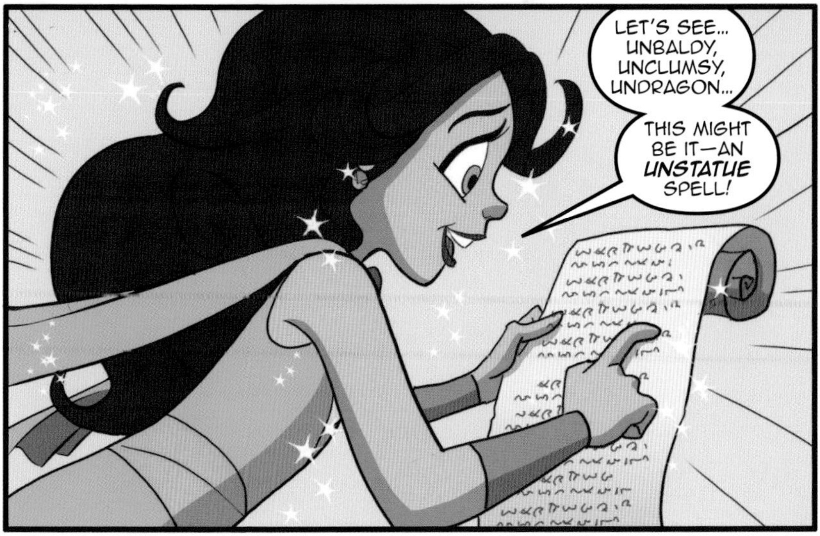
LET'S SEE... UNBALDY, UNCLUMSY, UNDRAGON...
THIS MIGHT BE IT—AN UNSTATUE SPELL!

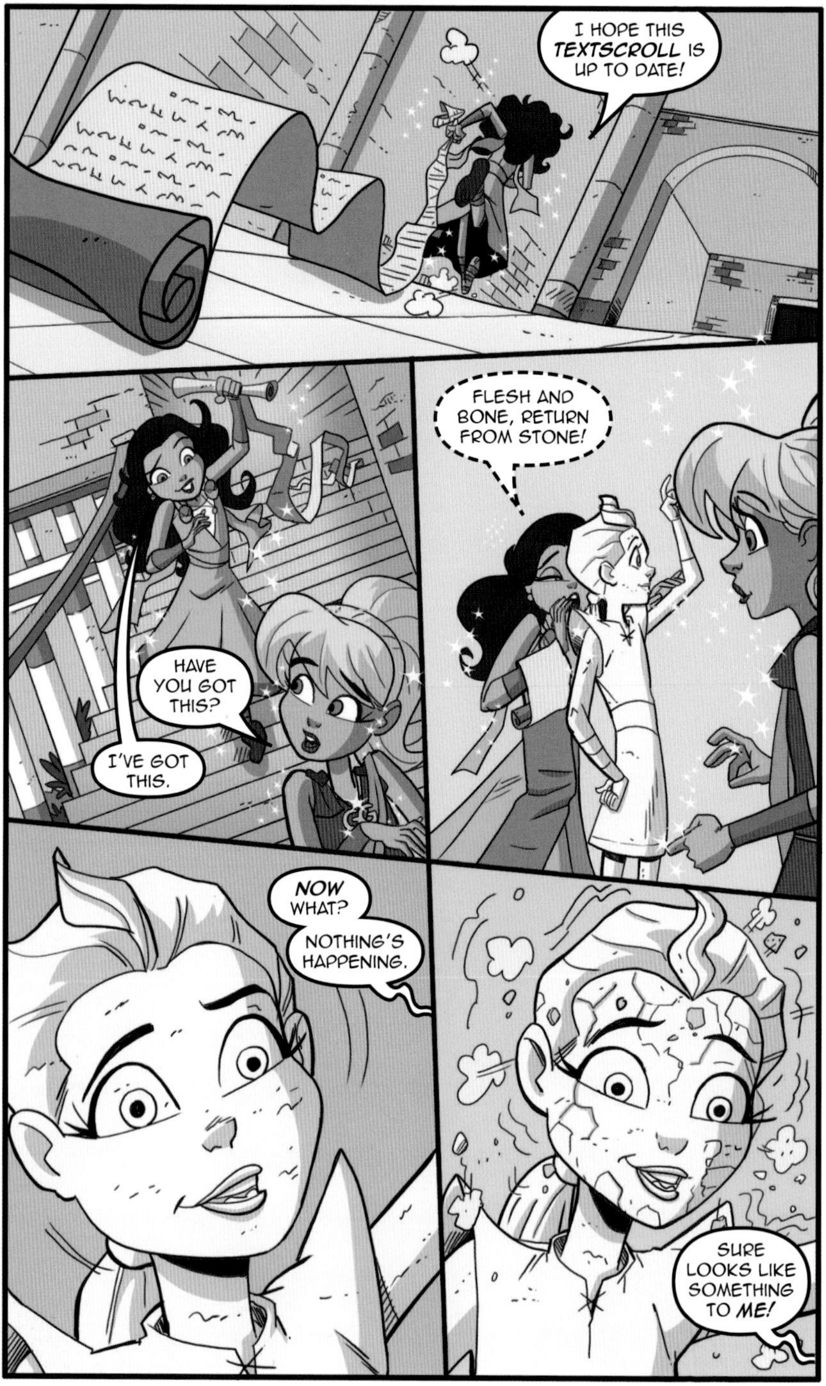
I HOPE THIS TEXTSCROLL IS UP TO DATE!
HAVE YOU GOT THIS?
I'VE GOT THIS.
FLESH AND BONE, RETURN FROM STONE!
NOW WHAT?
NOTHING'S HAPPENING.
SURE LOOKS LIKE SOMETHING TO ME!

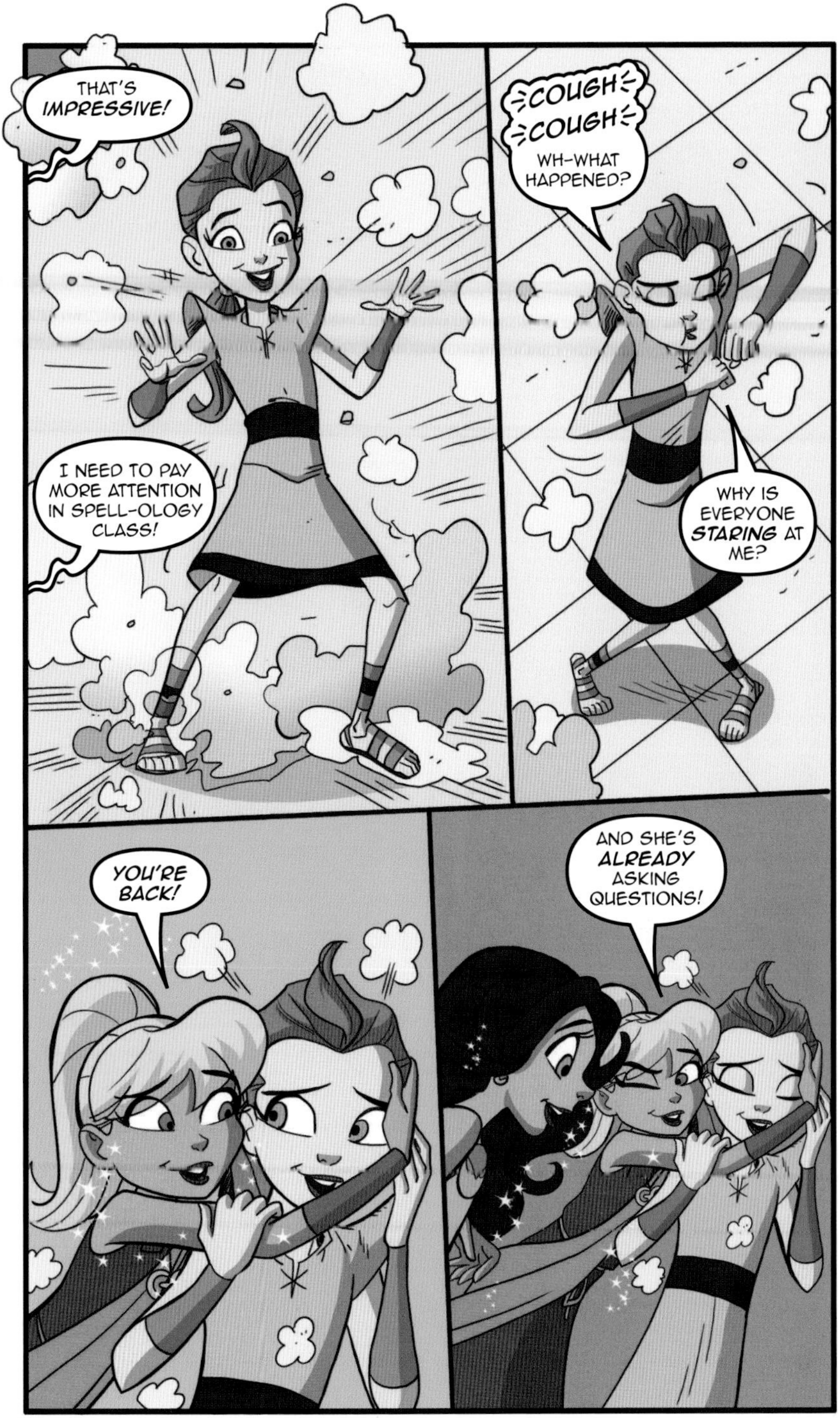
THAT'S IMPRESSIVE!
I NEED TO PAY MORE ATTENTION IN SPELL-OLOGY CLASS!
COUGH COUGH
WH-WHAT HAPPENED?
WHY IS EVERYONE STARING AT ME?
YOU'RE BACK!
AND SHE'S ALREADY ASKING QUESTIONS!

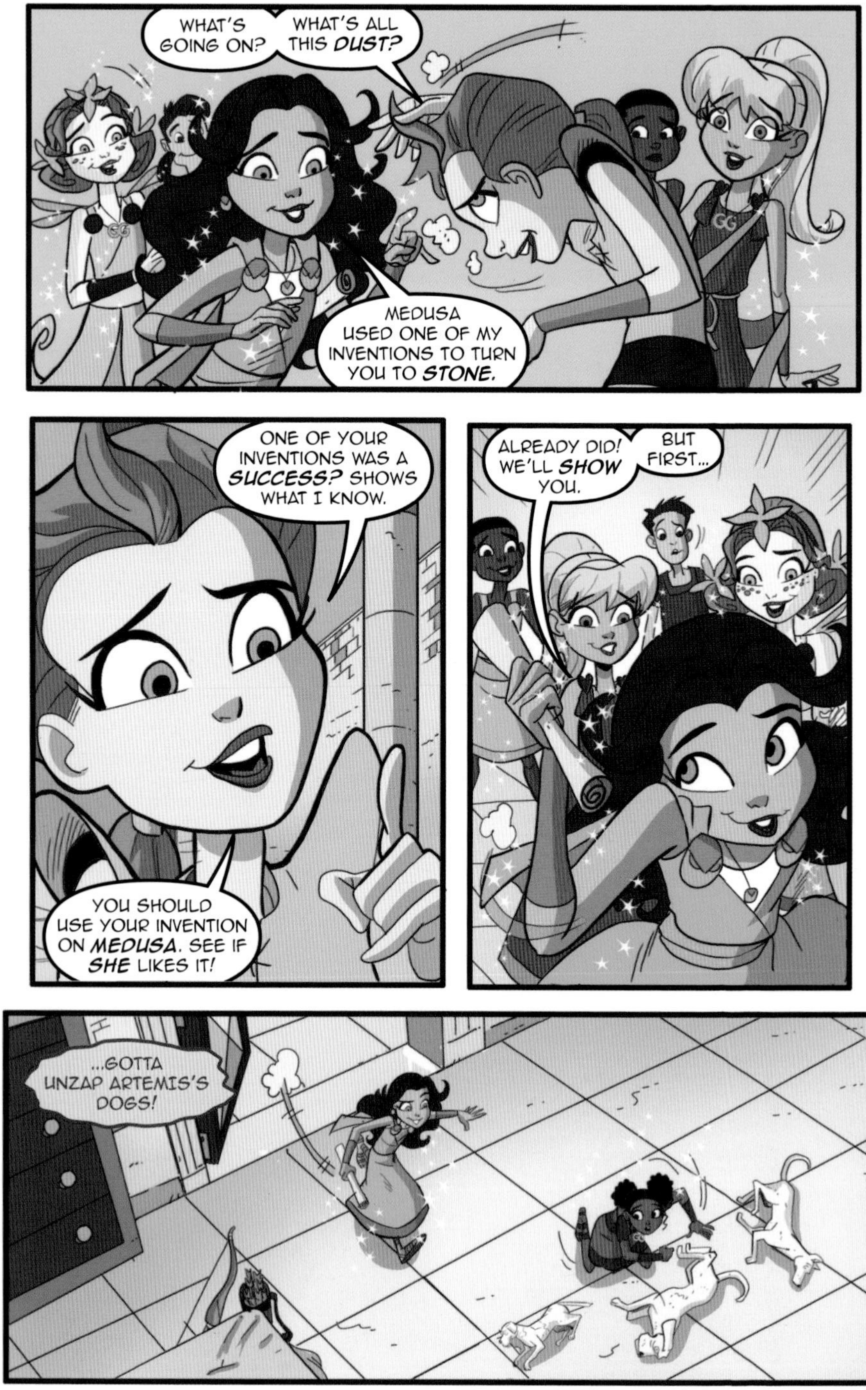
WHAT'S GOING ON?
WHAT'S ALL THIS DUST?
MEDUSA USED ONE OF MY INVENTIONS TO TURN YOU TO STONE.
ONE OF YOUR INVENTIONS WAS A SUCCESS? SHOWS WHAT I KNOW.
YOU SHOULD USE YOUR INVENTION ON MEDUSA. SEE IF SHE LIKES IT!
ALREADY DID! WE'LL SHOW YOU.
BUT FIRST...
...GOTTA UNZAP ARTEMIS'S DOGS!

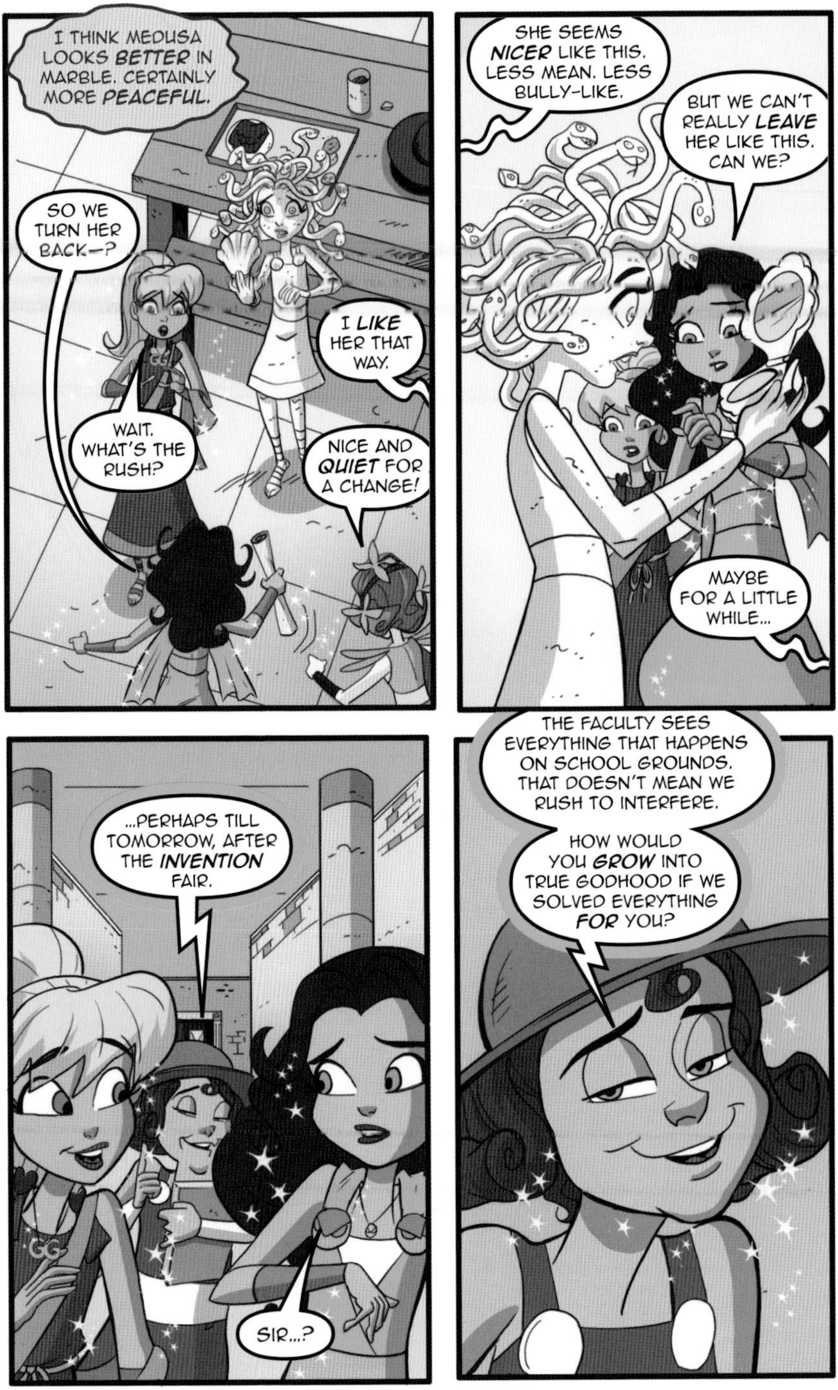
I THINK MEDUSA LOOKS BETTER IN MARBLE. CERTAINLY MORE PEACEFUL.
SO WE TURN HER BACK—?
WAIT. WHAT'S THE RUSH?
I LIKE HER THAT WAY.
NICE AND QUIET FOR A CHANGE!
SHE SEEMS NICER LIKE THIS. LESS MEAN. LESS BULLY-LIKE.
BUT WE CAN'T REALLY LEAVE HER LIKE THIS. CAN WE?
MAYBE FOR A LITTLE WHILE...
...PERHAPS TILL TOMORROW, AFTER THE INVENTION FAIR.
SIR...?
THE FACULTY SEES EVERYTHING THAT HAPPENS ON SCHOOL GROUNDS. THAT DOESN'T MEAN WE RUSH TO INTERFERE.
HOW WOULD YOU GROW INTO TRUE GODHOOD IF WE SOLVED EVERYTHING FOR YOU?

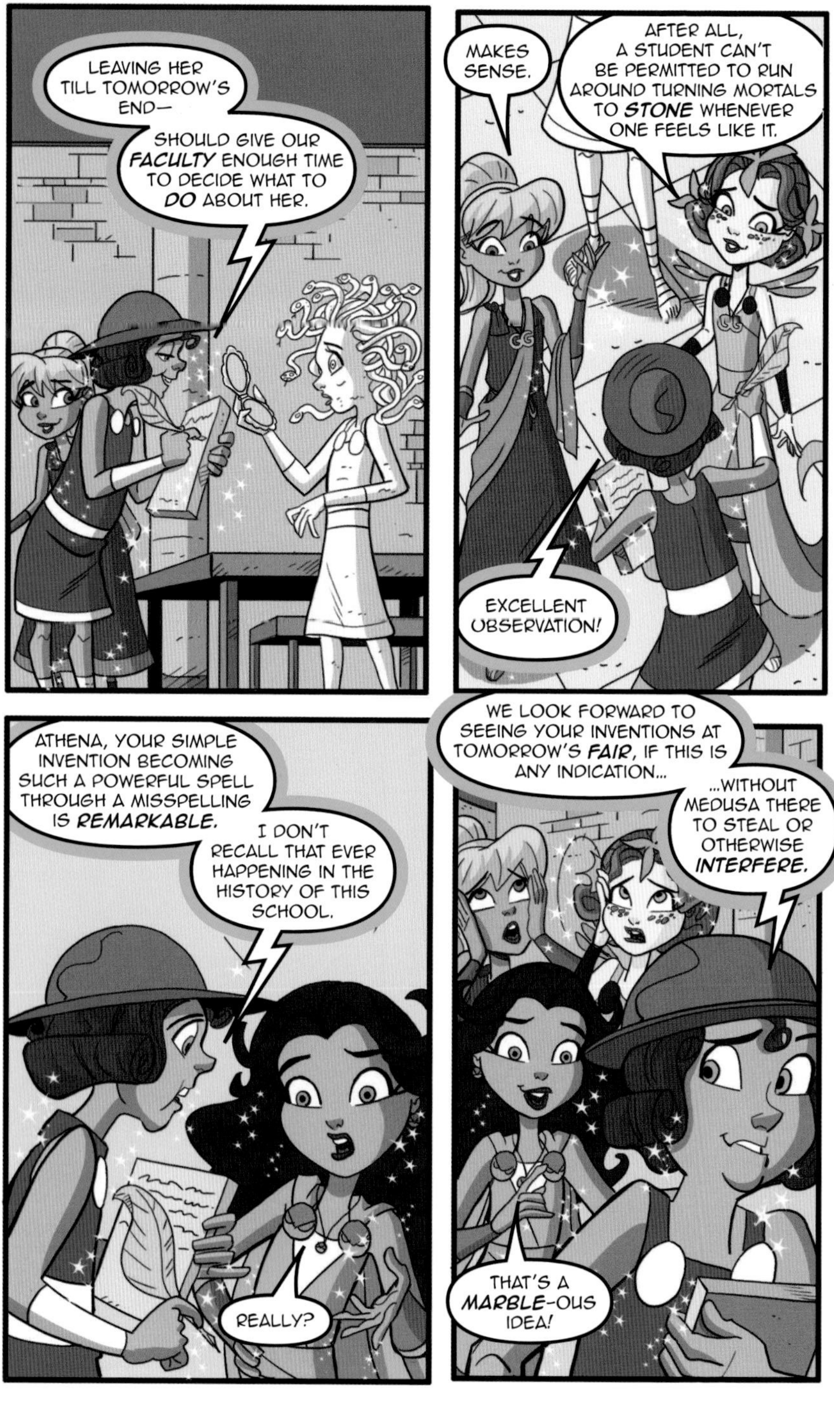
LEAVING HER TILL TOMORROW'S END—
SHOULD GIVE OUR FACULTY ENOUGH TIME TO DECIDE WHAT TO DO ABOUT HER.
MAKES SENSE.
AFTER ALL, A STUDENT CAN'T BE PERMITTED TO RUN AROUND TURNING MORTALS TO STONE WHENEVER ONE FEELS LIKE IT.
EXCELLENT OBSERVATION!
ATHENA, YOUR SIMPLE INVENTION BECOMING SUCH A POWERFUL SPELL THROUGH A MISSPELLING IS REMARKABLE.
I DON'T RECALL THAT EVER HAPPENING IN THE HISTORY OF THIS SCHOOL.
REALLY?
WE LOOK FORWARD TO SEEING YOUR INVENTIONS AT TOMORROW'S FAIR, IF THIS IS ANY INDICATION...
...WITHOUT MEDUSA THERE TO STEAL OR OTHERWISE INTERFERE.
THAT'S A MARBLE-OUS IDEA!

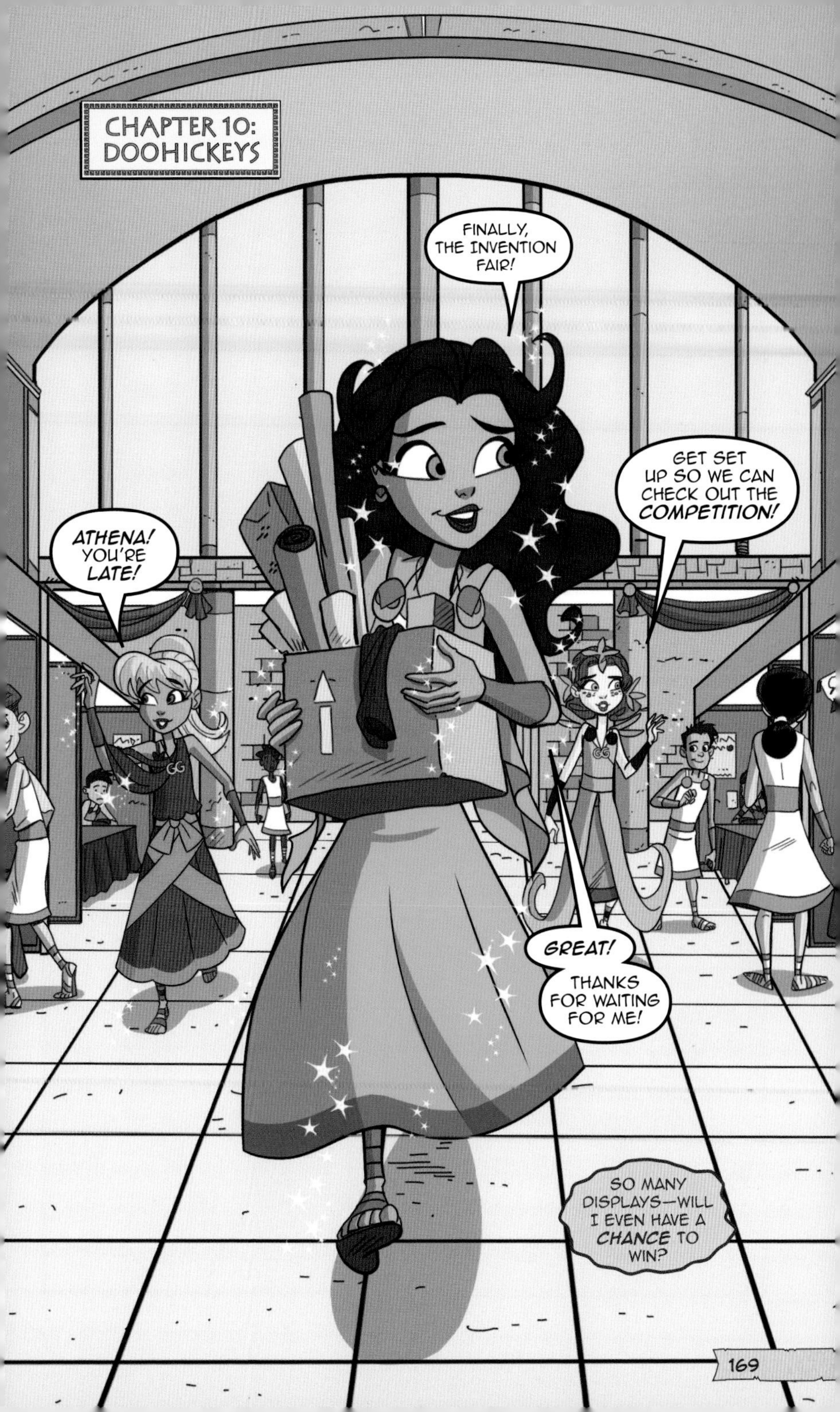
CHAPTER 10: DOOHICKEYS
FINALLY, THE INVENTION FAIR!
ATHENA! YOU'RE LATE!
GET SET UP SO WE CAN CHECK OUT THE COMPETITION!
GREAT!
THANKS FOR WAITING FOR ME!
SO MANY DISPLAYS—WILL I EVEN HAVE A CHANCE TO WIN?

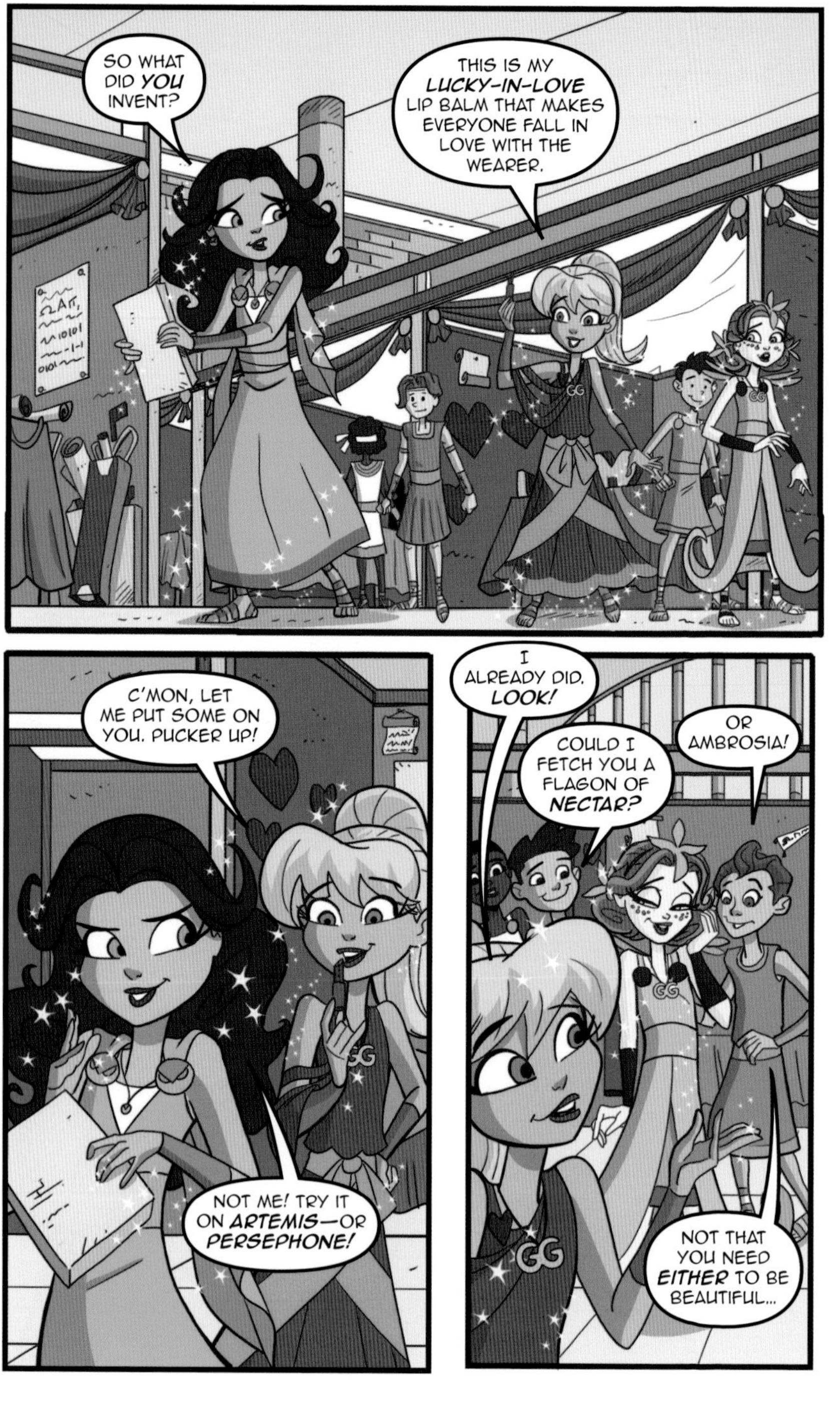
SO WHAT DID *YOU* INVENT?
THIS IS MY ***LUCKY-IN-LOVE*** LIP BALM THAT MAKES EVERYONE FALL IN LOVE WITH THE WEARER.
C'MON, LET ME PUT SOME ON YOU. PUCKER UP!
NOT ME! TRY IT ON ***ARTEMIS***—OR ***PERSEPHONE!***
I ALREADY DID. ***LOOK!***
COULD I FETCH YOU A FLAGON OF ***NECTAR?***
OR AMBROSIA!
NOT THAT YOU NEED ***EITHER*** TO BE BEAUTIFUL...

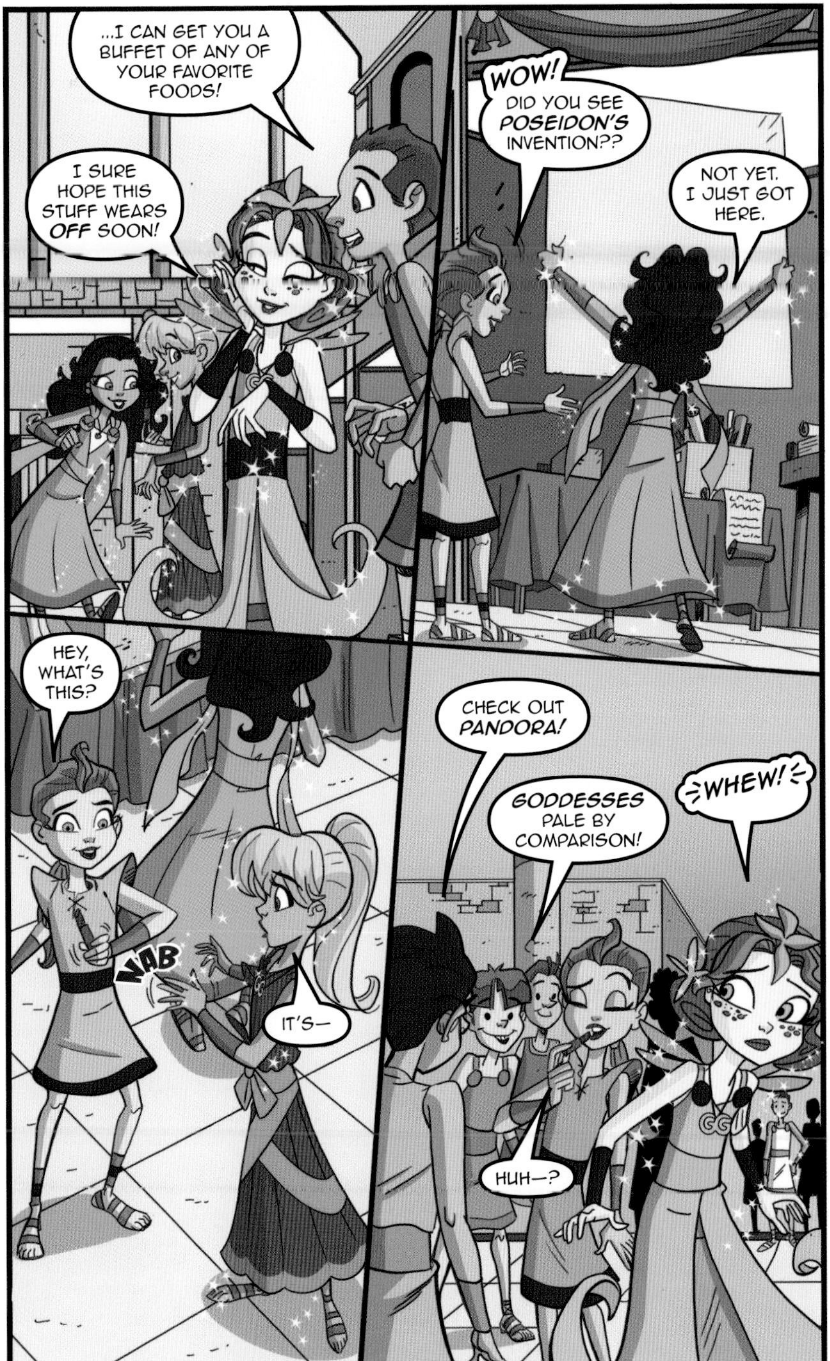

...I CAN GET YOU A BUFFET OF ANY OF YOUR FAVORITE FOODS!
I SURE HOPE THIS STUFF WEARS OFF SOON!
WOW! DID YOU SEE POSEIDON'S INVENTION??
NOT YET. I JUST GOT HERE.
HEY, WHAT'S THIS?
NAB
IT'S—
CHECK OUT PANDORA!
GODDESSES PALE BY COMPARISON!
WHEW!
HUH—?

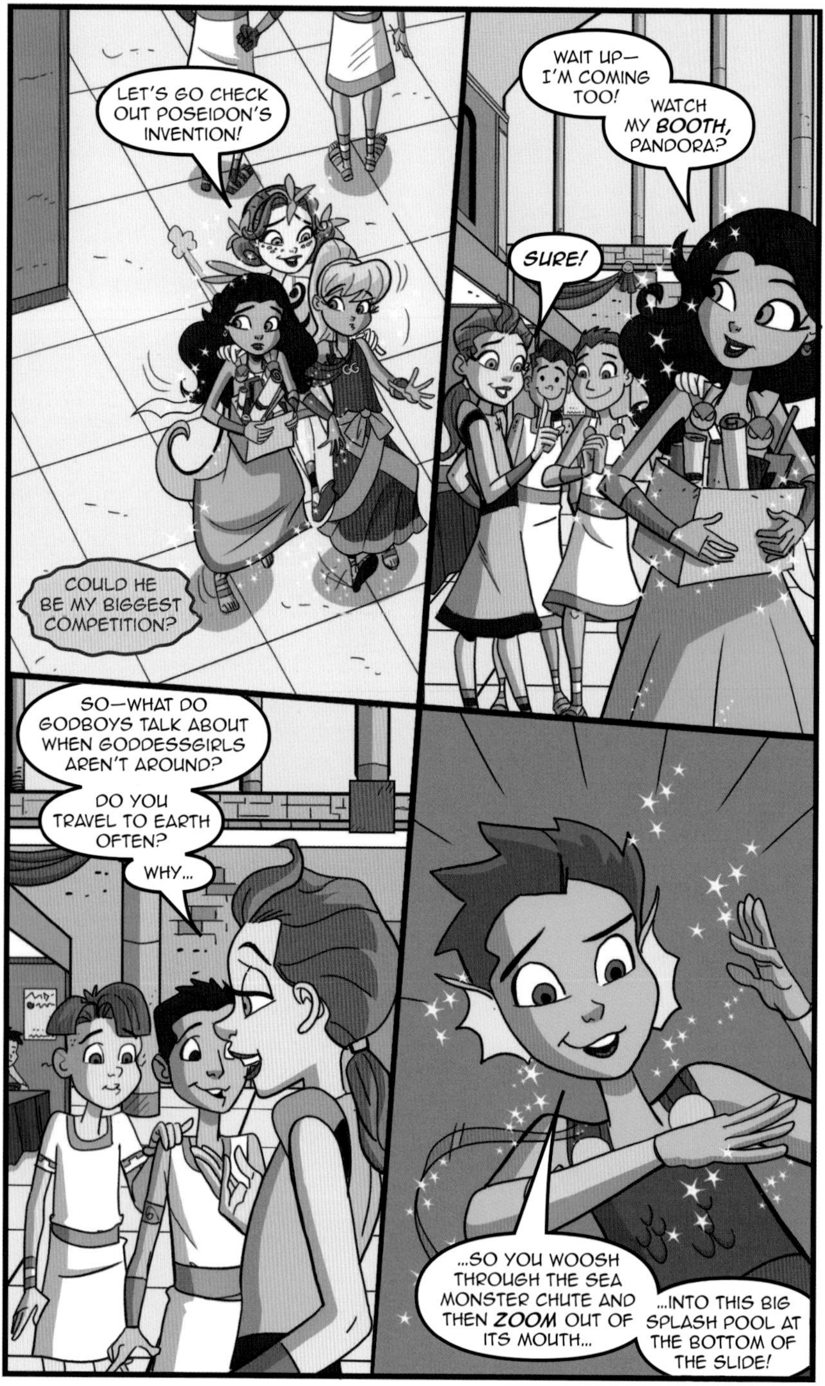

LET'S GO CHECK OUT POSEIDON'S INVENTION!
COULD HE BE MY BIGGEST COMPETITION?
WAIT UP— I'M COMING TOO!
WATCH MY **BOOTH,** PANDORA?
SURE!
SO—WHAT DO GODBOYS TALK ABOUT WHEN GODDESSGIRLS AREN'T AROUND?
DO YOU TRAVEL TO EARTH OFTEN?
WHY...
...SO YOU WOOSH THROUGH THE SEA MONSTER CHUTE AND THEN **ZOOM** OUT OF ITS MOUTH...
...INTO THIS BIG SPLASH POOL AT THE BOTTOM OF THE SLIDE!

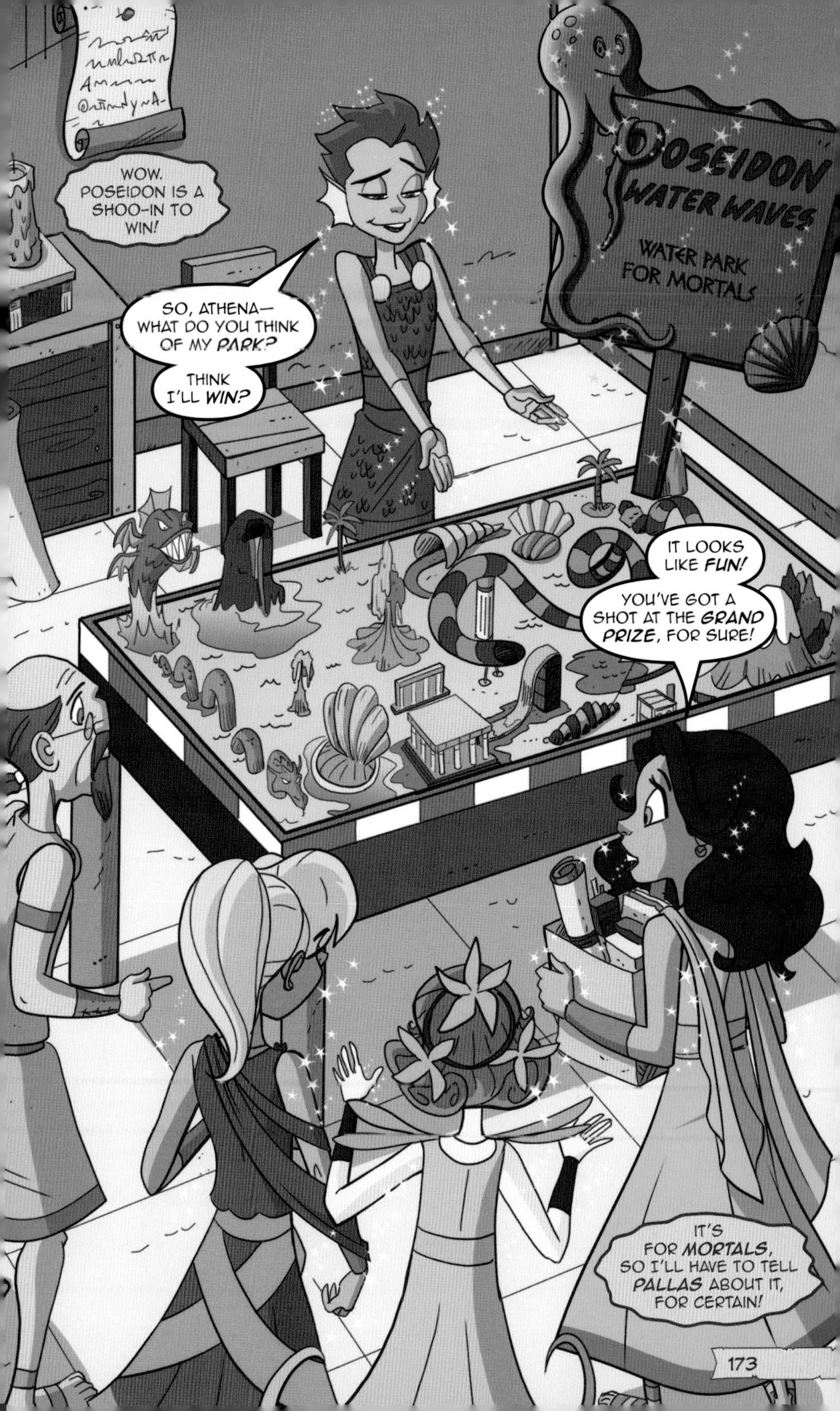

WOW. POSEIDON IS A SHOO-IN TO WIN!
SO, ATHENA— WHAT DO YOU THINK OF MY PARK?
THINK I'LL WIN?
POSEIDON WATER WAVES
WATER PARK FOR MORTALS
IT LOOKS LIKE FUN!
YOU'VE GOT A SHOT AT THE GRAND PRIZE, FOR SURE!
IT'S FOR MORTALS, SO I'LL HAVE TO TELL PALLAS ABOUT IT, FOR CERTAIN!

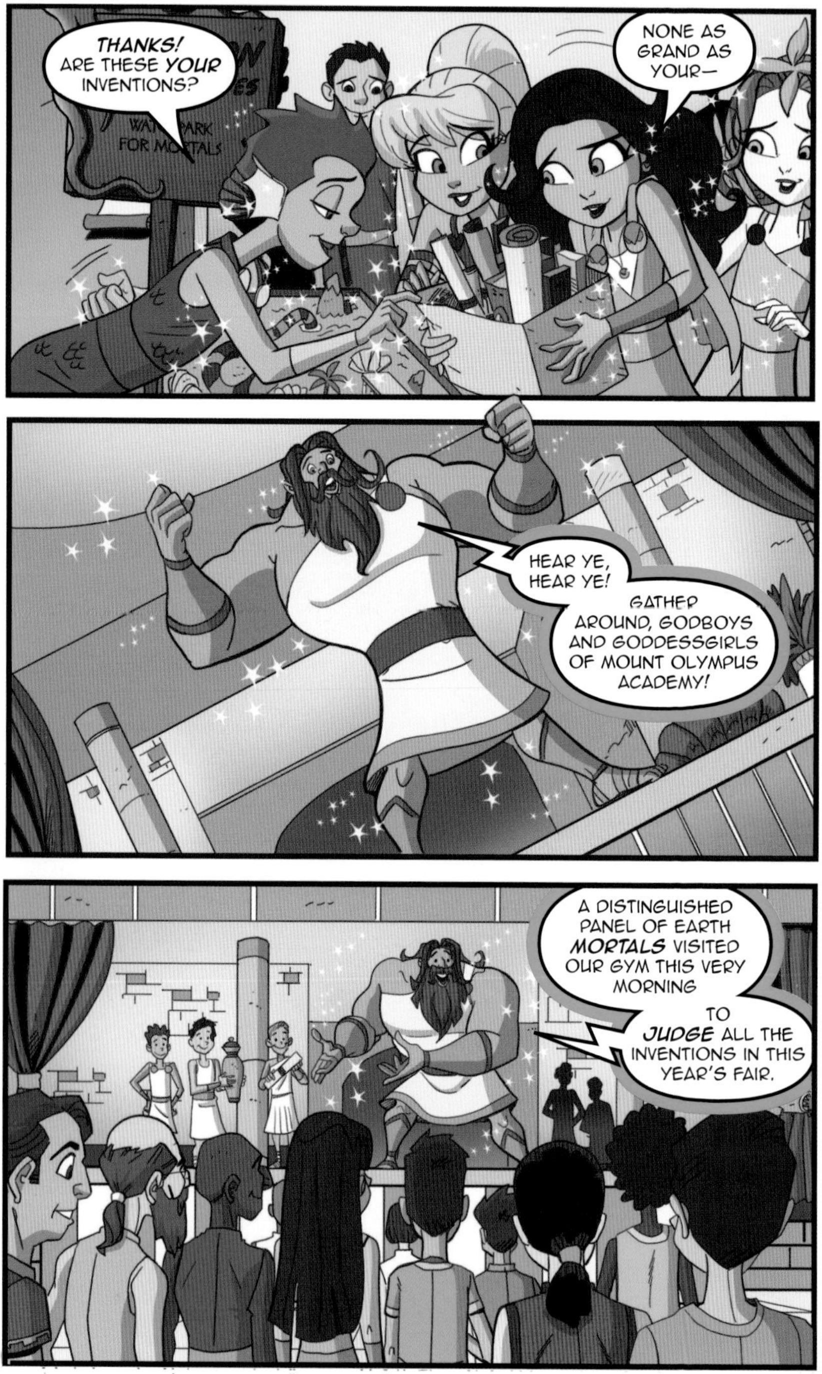
THANKS! ARE THESE YOUR INVENTIONS?
NONE AS GRAND AS YOUR—
HEAR YE, HEAR YE!
GATHER AROUND, GODBOYS AND GODDESSGIRLS OF MOUNT OLYMPUS ACADEMY!
A DISTINGUISHED PANEL OF EARTH MORTALS VISITED OUR GYM THIS VERY MORNING
TO JUDGE ALL THE INVENTIONS IN THIS YEAR'S FAIR.

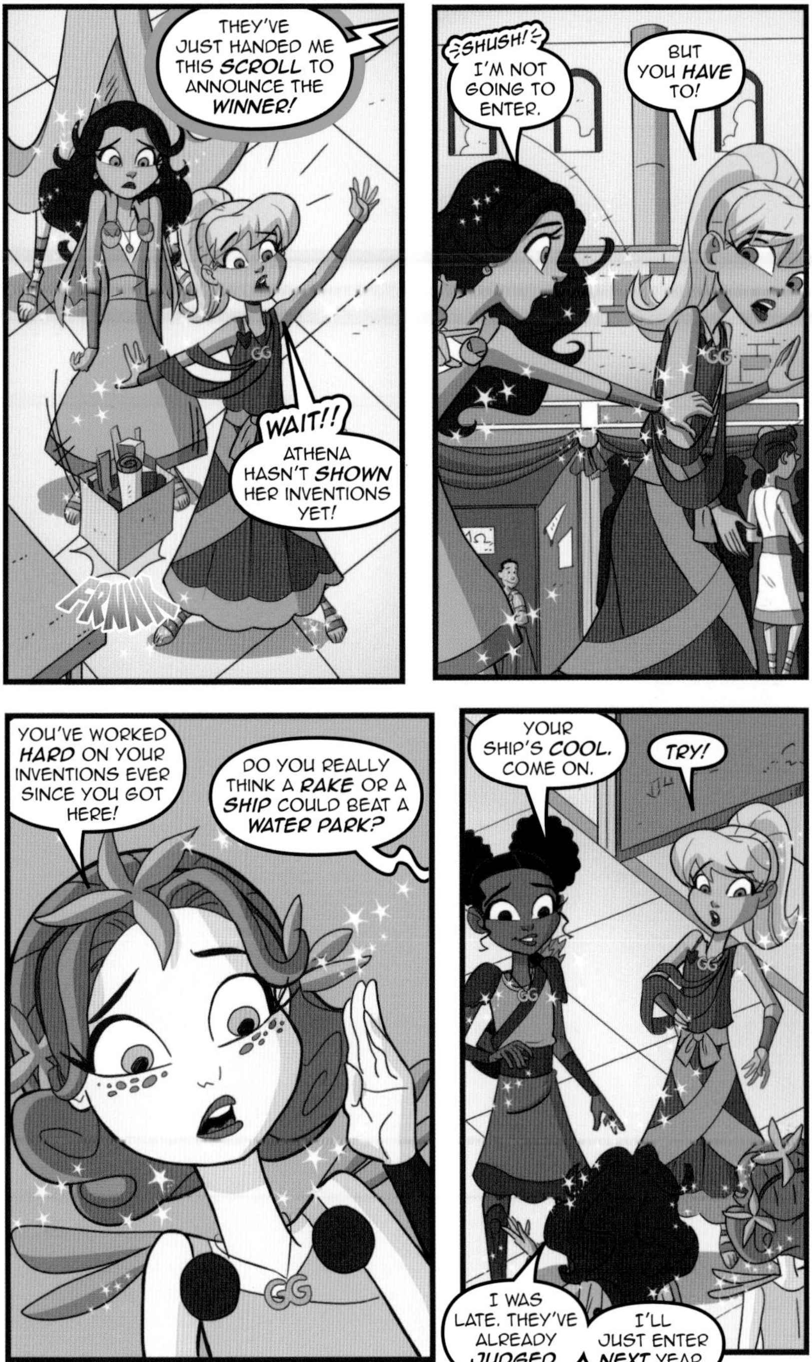

THEY'VE JUST HANDED ME THIS SCROLL TO ANNOUNCE THE WINNER!
WAIT!! ATHENA HASN'T SHOWN HER INVENTIONS YET!
SHUSH! I'M NOT GOING TO ENTER.
BUT YOU HAVE TO!
YOU'VE WORKED HARD ON YOUR INVENTIONS EVER SINCE YOU GOT HERE!
DO YOU REALLY THINK A RAKE OR A SHIP COULD BEAT A WATER PARK?
YOUR SHIP'S COOL. COME ON.
TRY!
I WAS LATE. THEY'VE ALREADY JUDGED.
I'LL JUST ENTER NEXT YEAR.

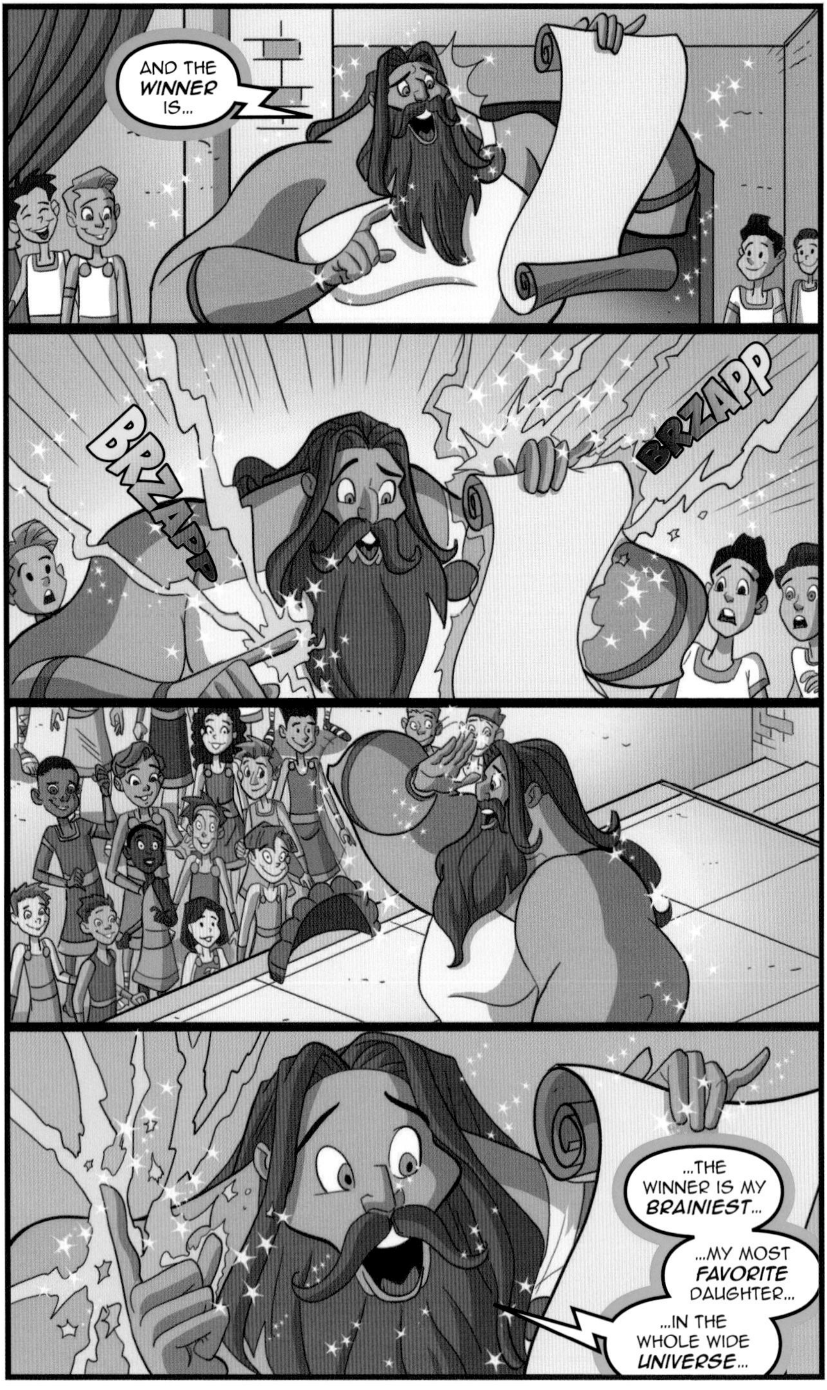
AND THE WINNER IS...
BRZAPP
BRZAPP
...THE WINNER IS MY BRAINIEST...
...MY MOST FAVORITE DAUGHTER...
...IN THE WHOLE WIDE UNIVERSE...

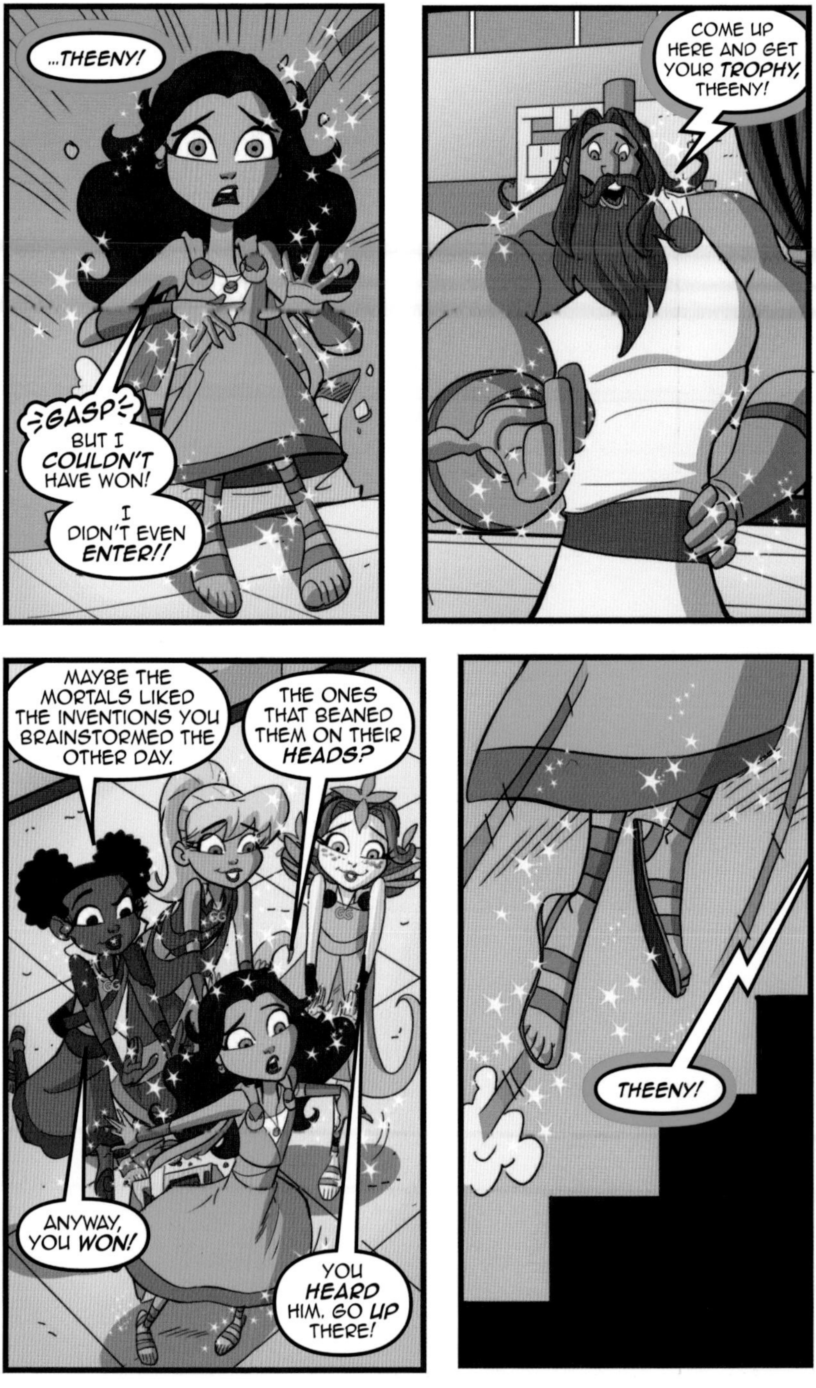
...THEENY!
GASP BUT I COULDN'T HAVE WON!
I DIDN'T EVEN ENTER!!
COME UP HERE AND GET YOUR TROPHY, THEENY!
MAYBE THE MORTALS LIKED THE INVENTIONS YOU BRAINSTORMED THE OTHER DAY.
THE ONES THAT BEANED THEM ON THEIR HEADS?
ANYWAY, YOU WON!
YOU HEARD HIM. GO UP THERE!
THEENY!

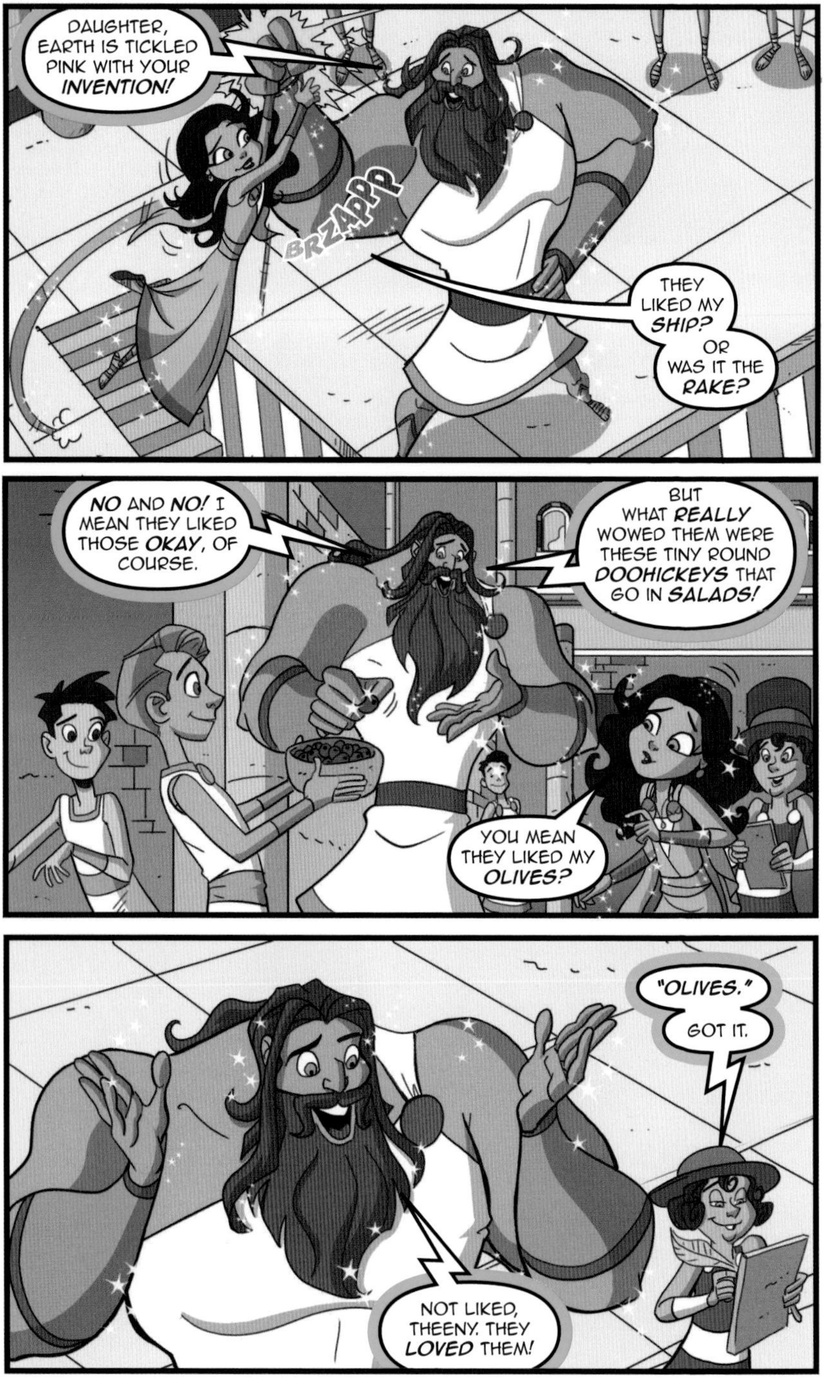
DAUGHTER, EARTH IS TICKLED PINK WITH YOUR INVENTION!
BRZAPP
THEY LIKED MY SHIP?
OR WAS IT THE RAKE?
NO AND NO! I MEAN THEY LIKED THOSE OKAY, OF COURSE.
BUT WHAT REALLY WOWED THEM WERE THESE TINY ROUND DOOHICKEYS THAT GO IN SALADS!
YOU MEAN THEY LIKED MY OLIVES?
"OLIVES."
GOT IT.
NOT LIKED, THEENY. THEY LOVED THEM!

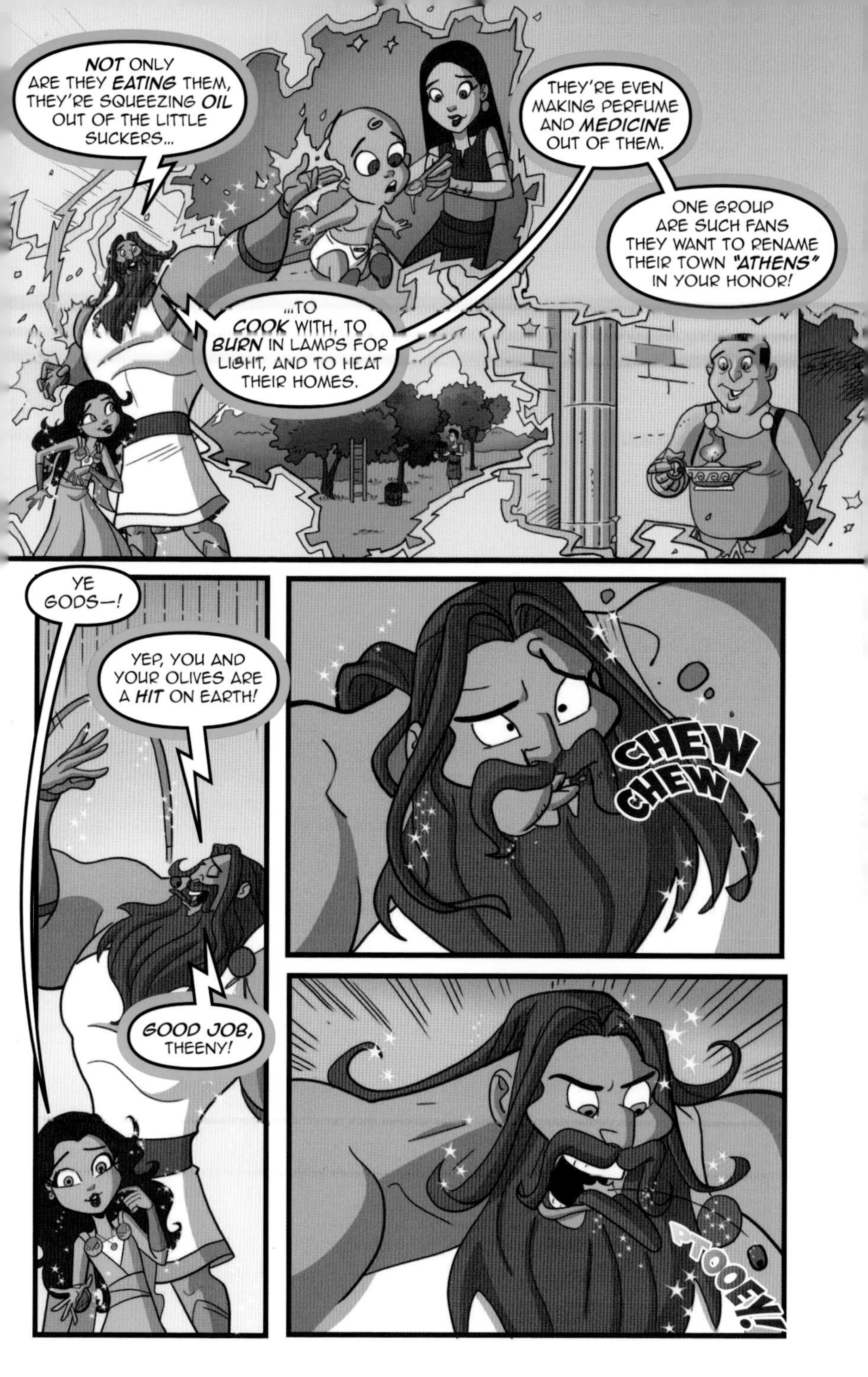

NOT ONLY ARE THEY EATING THEM, THEY'RE SQUEEZING OIL OUT OF THE LITTLE SUCKERS...
...TO COOK WITH, TO BURN IN LAMPS FOR LIGHT, AND TO HEAT THEIR HOMES.
THEY'RE EVEN MAKING PERFUME AND MEDICINE OUT OF THEM.
ONE GROUP ARE SUCH FANS THEY WANT TO RENAME THEIR TOWN "ATHENS" IN YOUR HONOR!
YE GODS—!
YEP, YOU AND YOUR OLIVES ARE A HIT ON EARTH!
GOOD JOB, THEENY!
CHEW CHEW
PTOOEY!!

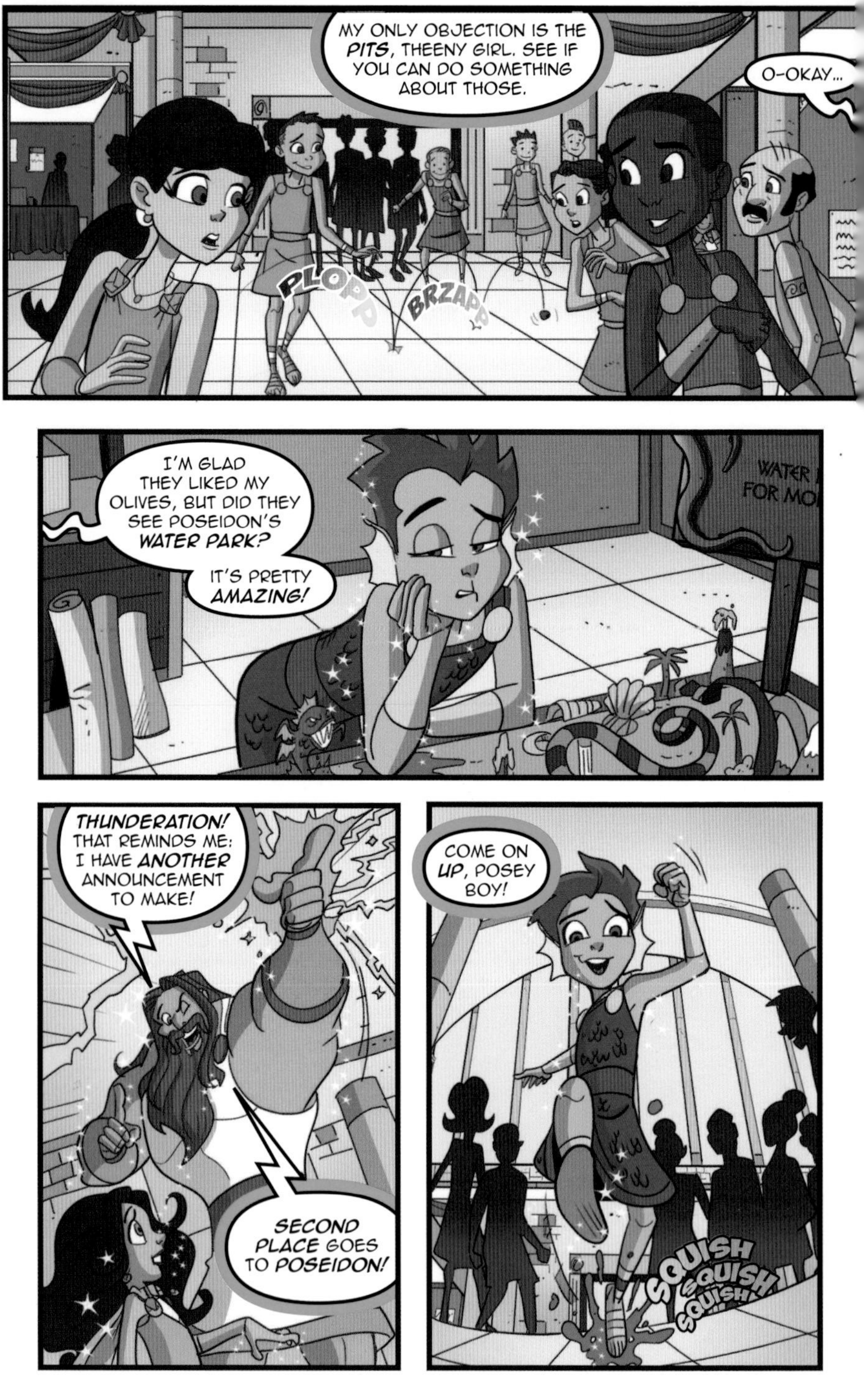

MY ONLY OBJECTION IS THE PITS, THEENY GIRL. SEE IF YOU CAN DO SOMETHING ABOUT THOSE.
O-OKAY...
PLOPP
BRZAPP
I'M GLAD THEY LIKED MY OLIVES, BUT DID THEY SEE POSEIDON'S WATER PARK?
IT'S PRETTY AMAZING!
THUNDERATION! THAT REMINDS ME: I HAVE ANOTHER ANNOUNCEMENT TO MAKE!
SECOND PLACE GOES TO POSEIDON!
COME ON UP, POSEY BOY!
SQUISH SQUISH SQUISH

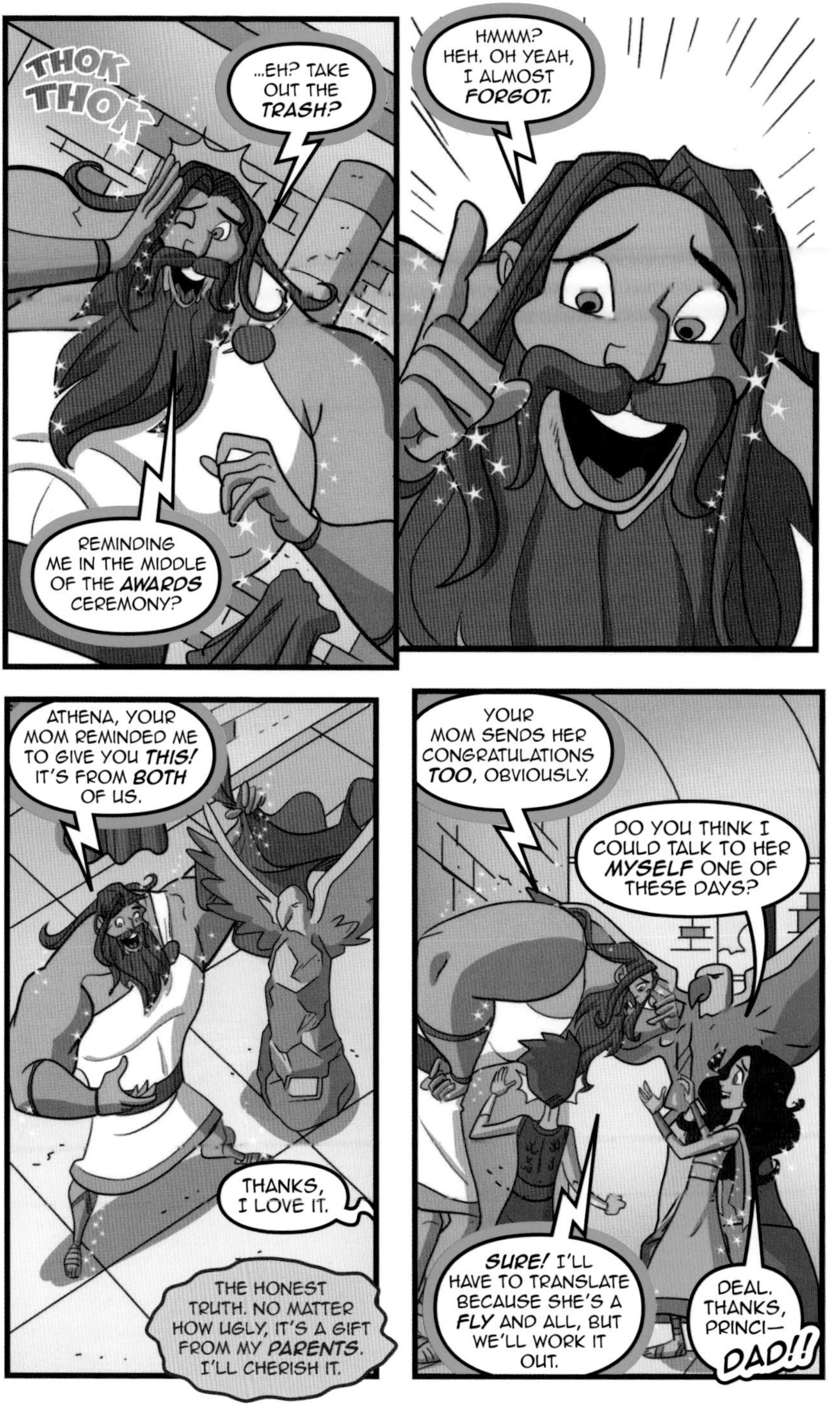
THOK THOK
...EH? TAKE OUT THE TRASH?
REMINDING ME IN THE MIDDLE OF THE AWARDS CEREMONY?
HMMM? HEH. OH YEAH, I ALMOST FORGOT.
ATHENA, YOUR MOM REMINDED ME TO GIVE YOU THIS! IT'S FROM BOTH OF US.
THANKS, I LOVE IT.
THE HONEST TRUTH. NO MATTER HOW UGLY, IT'S A GIFT FROM MY PARENTS. I'LL CHERISH IT.
YOUR MOM SENDS HER CONGRATULATIONS TOO, OBVIOUSLY.
DO YOU THINK I COULD TALK TO HER MYSELF ONE OF THESE DAYS?
SURE! I'LL HAVE TO TRANSLATE BECAUSE SHE'S A FLY AND ALL, BUT WE'LL WORK IT OUT.
DEAL. THANKS, PRINCI—
DAD!!

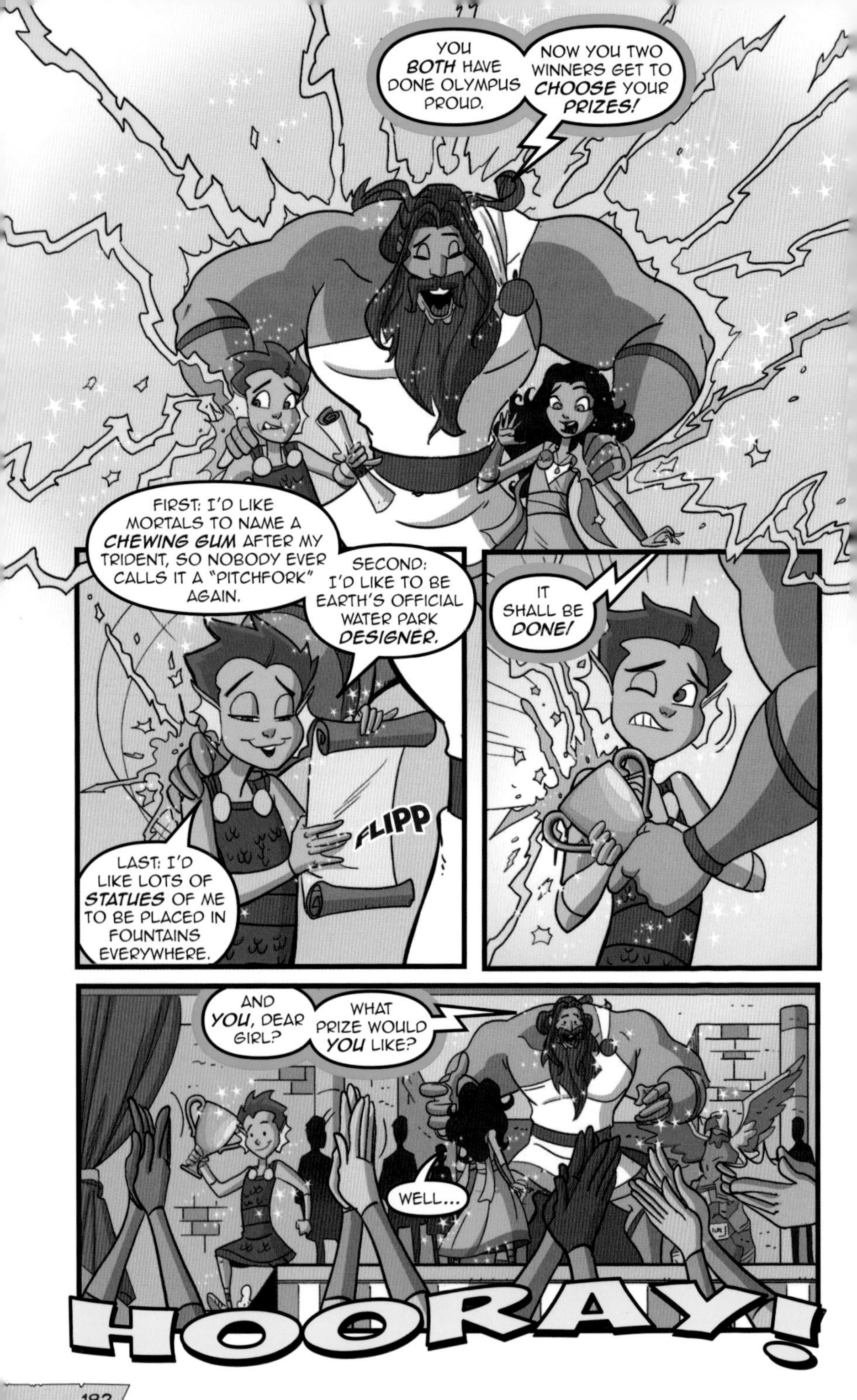
YOU BOTH HAVE DONE OLYMPUS PROUD.
NOW YOU TWO WINNERS GET TO CHOOSE YOUR PRIZES!
FIRST: I'D LIKE MORTALS TO NAME A CHEWING GUM AFTER MY TRIDENT, SO NOBODY EVER CALLS IT A "PITCHFORK" AGAIN.
SECOND: I'D LIKE TO BE EARTH'S OFFICIAL WATER PARK DESIGNER.
LAST: I'D LIKE LOTS OF STATUES OF ME TO BE PLACED IN FOUNTAINS EVERYWHERE.
FLIPP
IT SHALL BE DONE!
AND YOU, DEAR GIRL?
WHAT PRIZE WOULD YOU LIKE?
WELL...
HOORAY!

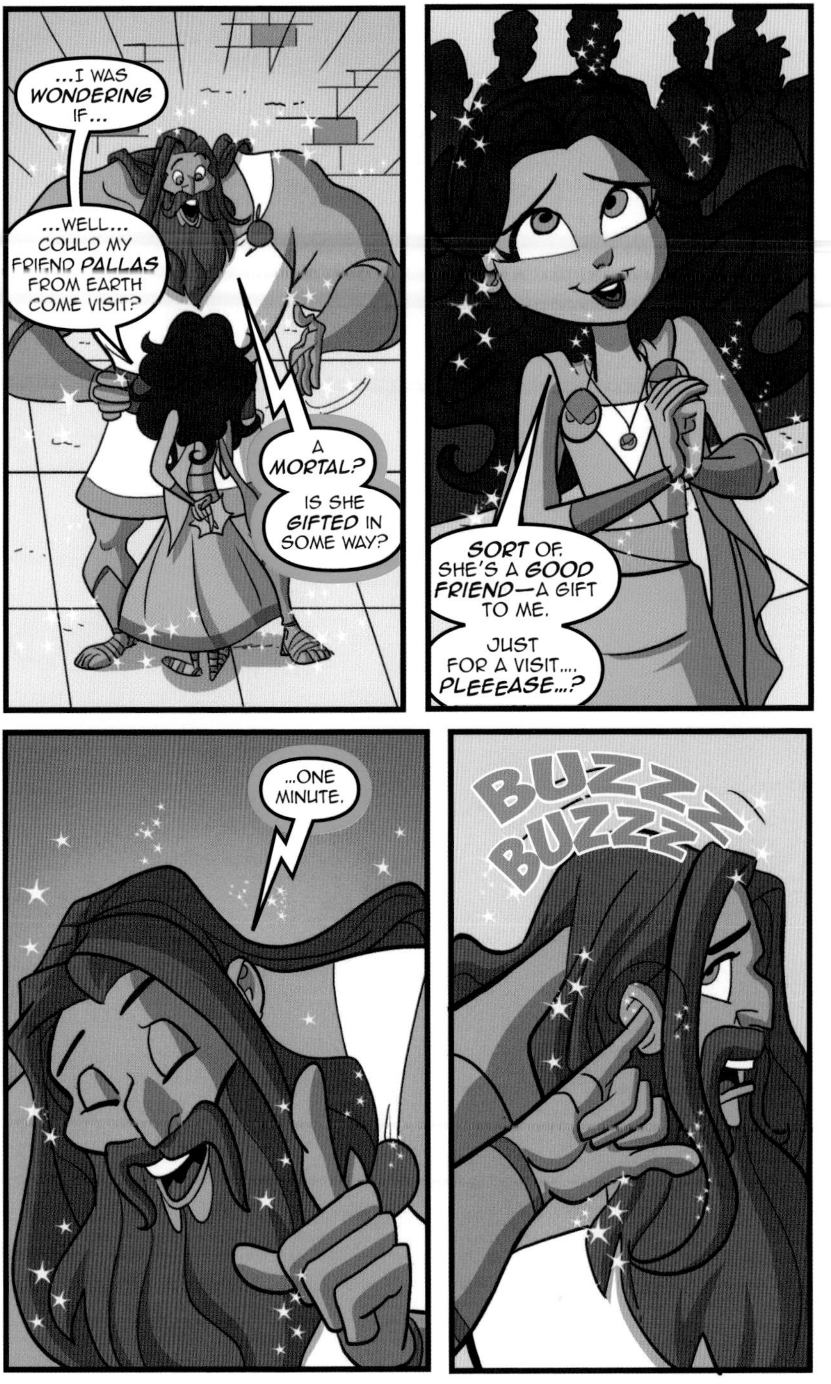
...I WAS WONDERING IF...
...WELL... COULD MY FRIEND PALLAS FROM EARTH COME VISIT?
A MORTAL?
IS SHE GIFTED IN SOME WAY?
SORT OF. SHE'S A GOOD FRIEND—A GIFT TO ME.
JUST FOR A VISIT.... PLEEEASE...?
...ONE MINUTE.
BUZZZ BUZZZ

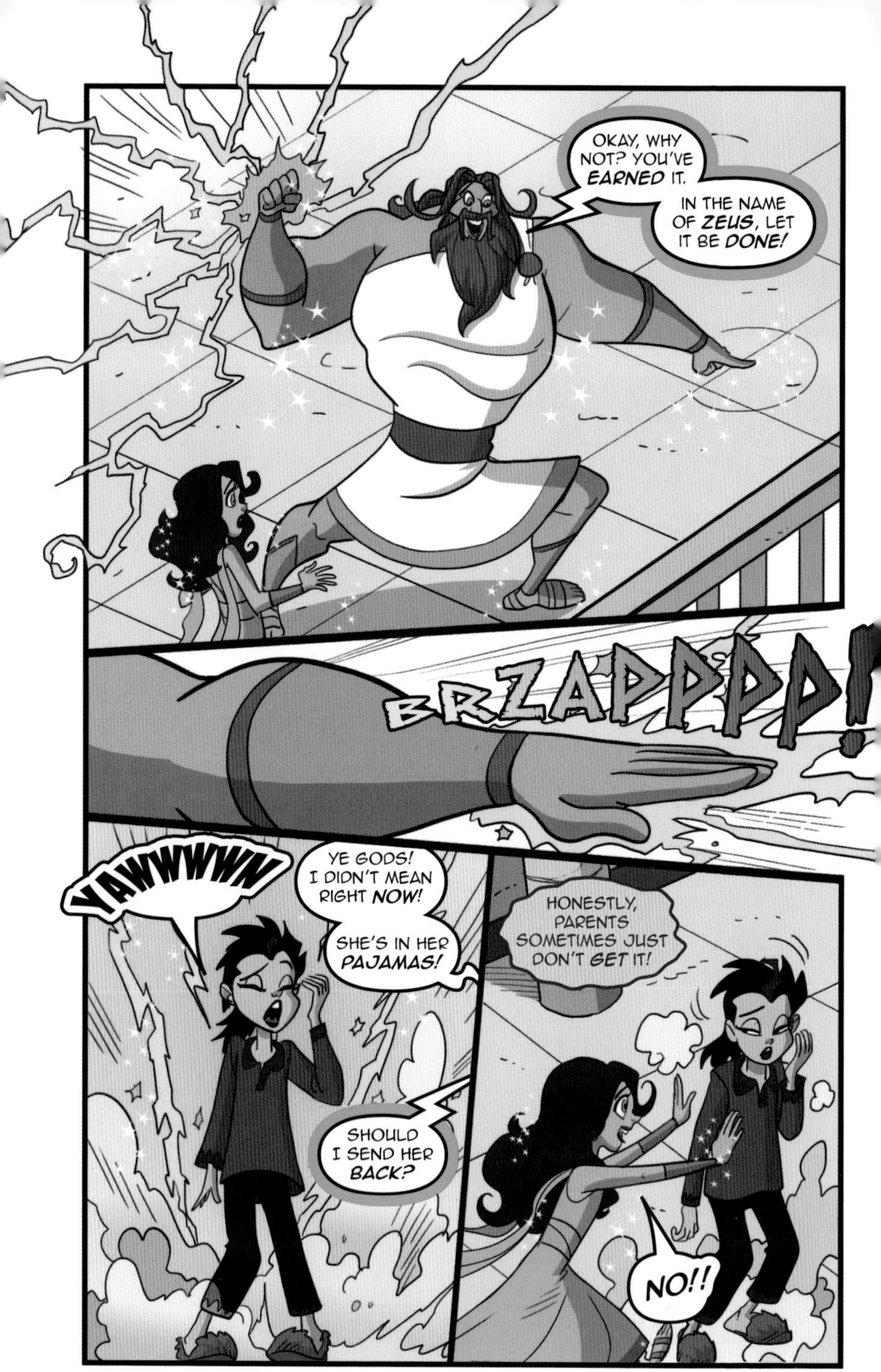
OKAY, WHY NOT? YOU'VE EARNED IT.
IN THE NAME OF ZEUS, LET IT BE DONE!
BRZAPPPP!
YAWWWWN
YE GODS! I DIDN'T MEAN RIGHT NOW!
SHE'S IN HER PAJAMAS!
SHOULD I SEND HER BACK?
HONESTLY, PARENTS SOMETIMES JUST DON'T GET IT!
NO!!

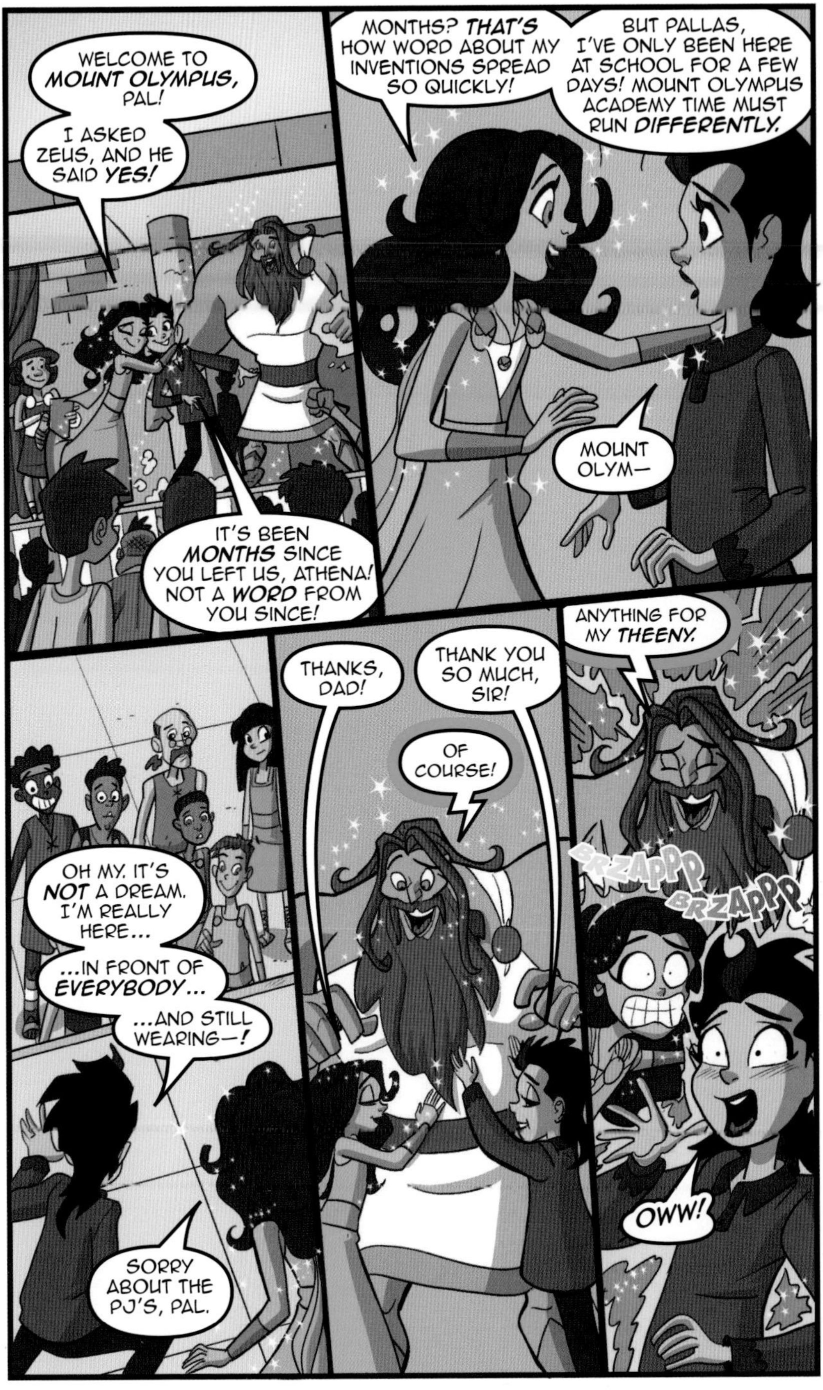
WELCOME TO MOUNT OLYMPUS, PAL!
I ASKED ZEUS, AND HE SAID YES!
IT'S BEEN MONTHS SINCE YOU LEFT US, ATHENA! NOT A WORD FROM YOU SINCE!
MONTHS? THAT'S HOW WORD ABOUT MY INVENTIONS SPREAD SO QUICKLY!
BUT PALLAS, I'VE ONLY BEEN HERE AT SCHOOL FOR A FEW DAYS! MOUNT OLYMPUS ACADEMY TIME MUST RUN DIFFERENTLY.
MOUNT OLYM—
OH MY. IT'S NOT A DREAM. I'M REALLY HERE...
...IN FRONT OF EVERYBODY...
...AND STILL WEARING—!
SORRY ABOUT THE PJ'S, PAL.
THANKS, DAD!
THANK YOU SO MUCH, SIR!
OF COURSE!
ANYTHING FOR MY THEENY.
BRZAPPP
BRZAPPP
OWW!

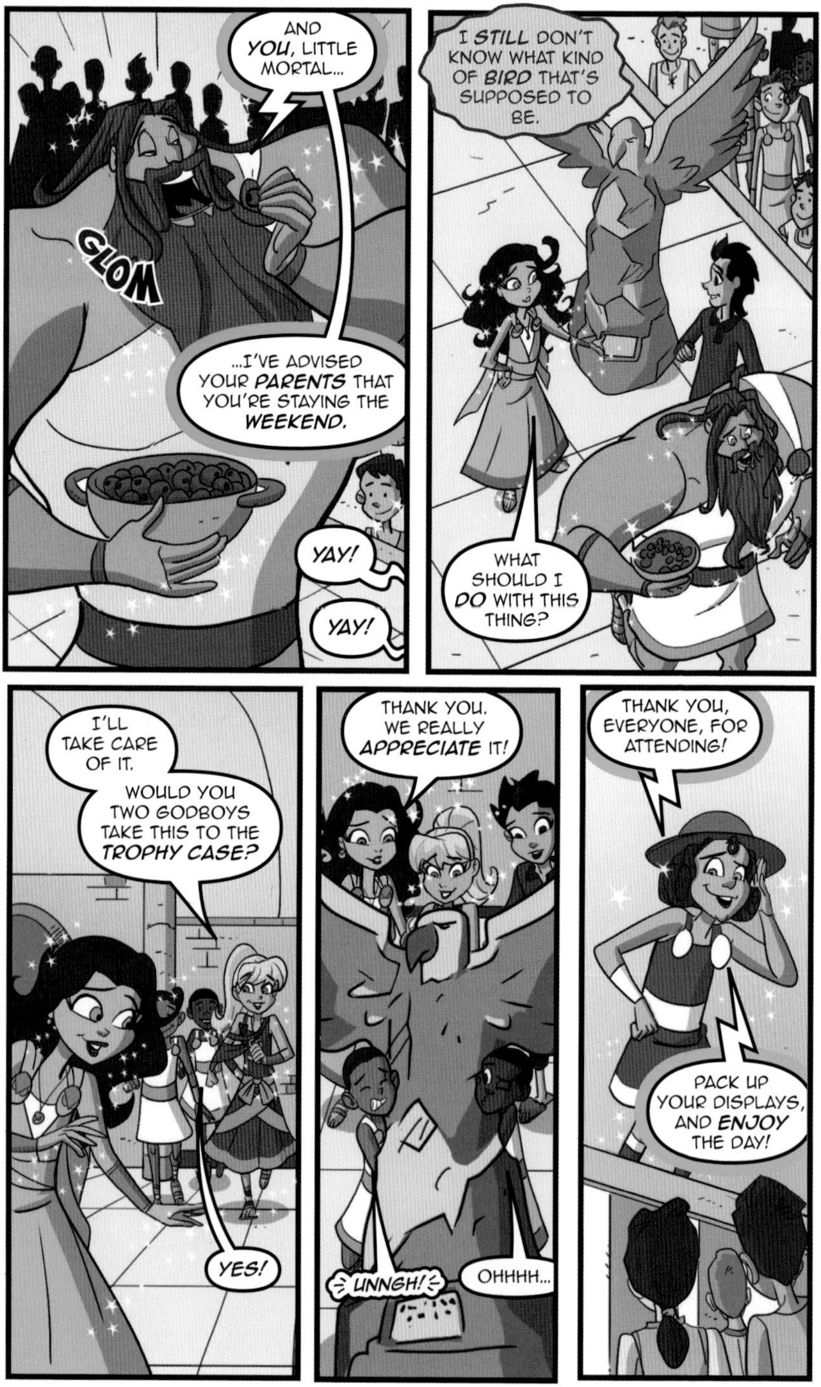
AND YOU, LITTLE MORTAL...
GLOM
...I'VE ADVISED YOUR PARENTS THAT YOU'RE STAYING THE WEEKEND.
YAY!
YAY!
I STILL DON'T KNOW WHAT KIND OF BIRD THAT'S SUPPOSED TO BE.
WHAT SHOULD I DO WITH THIS THING?
I'LL TAKE CARE OF IT.
WOULD YOU TWO GODBOYS TAKE THIS TO THE TROPHY CASE?
YES!
THANK YOU. WE REALLY APPRECIATE IT!
UNNGH!
OHHHH...
THANK YOU, EVERYONE, FOR ATTENDING!
PACK UP YOUR DISPLAYS, AND ENJOY THE DAY!

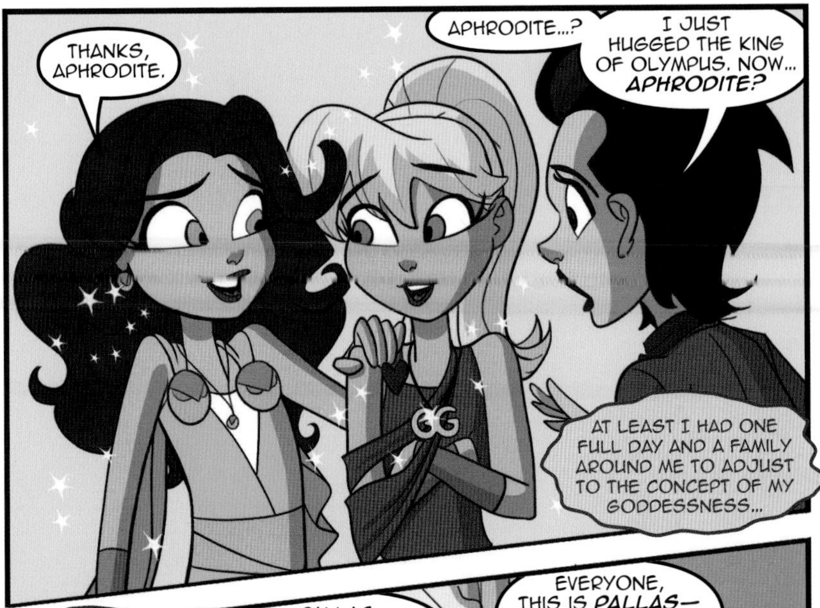
THANKS, APHRODITE.
APHRODITE...?
I JUST HUGGED THE KING OF OLYMPUS. NOW... *APHRODITE?*
AT LEAST I HAD ONE FULL DAY AND A FAMILY AROUND ME TO ADJUST TO THE CONCEPT OF MY GODDESSNESS...

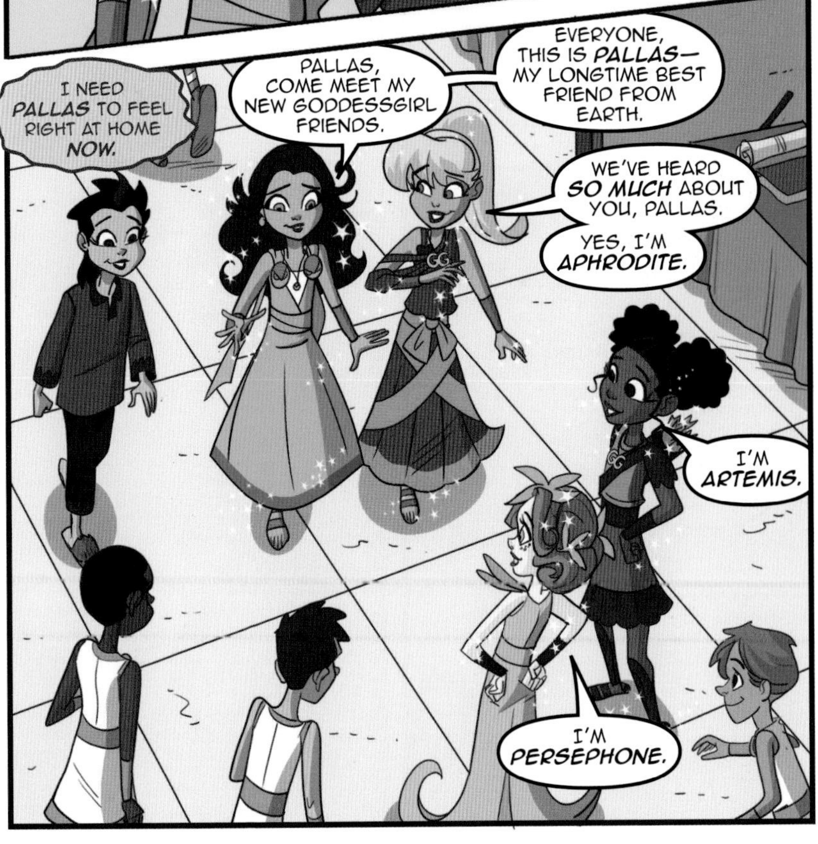
I NEED *PALLAS* TO FEEL RIGHT AT HOME *NOW.*
PALLAS, COME MEET MY NEW GODDESSGIRL FRIENDS.
EVERYONE, THIS IS *PALLAS*— MY LONGTIME BEST FRIEND FROM EARTH.
WE'VE HEARD *SO MUCH* ABOUT YOU, PALLAS.
YES, I'M *APHRODITE.*
I'M *ARTEMIS.*
I'M *PERSEPHONE.*

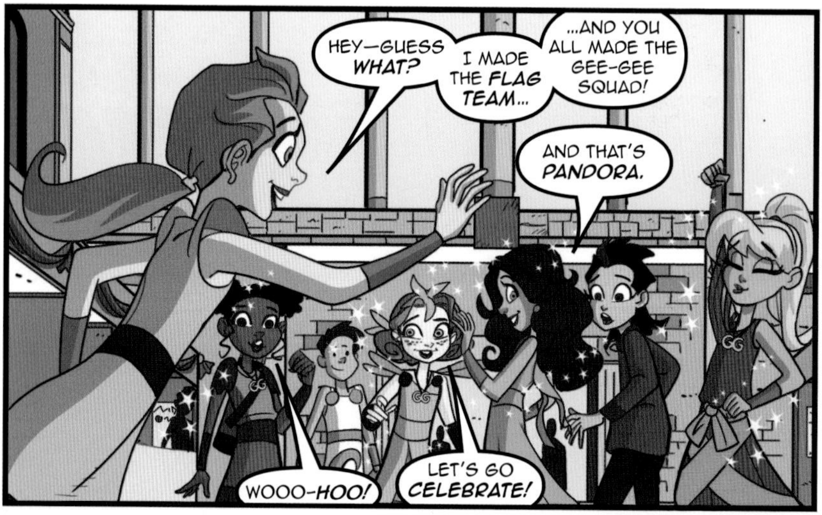
HEY—GUESS *WHAT?*
I MADE THE *FLAG TEAM*...
...AND YOU ALL MADE THE GEE-GEE SQUAD!
AND THAT'S *PANDORA.*
WOOO-*HOO!*
LET'S GO *CELEBRATE!*

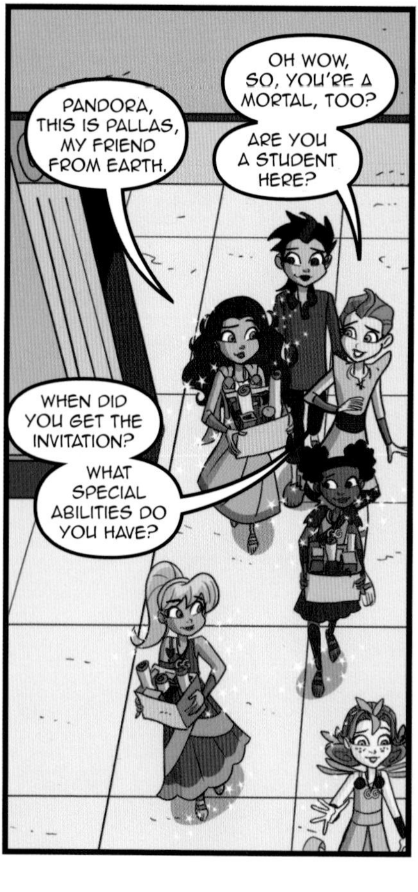
PANDORA, THIS IS PALLAS, MY FRIEND FROM EARTH.
OH WOW, SO, YOU'RE A MORTAL, TOO?
ARE YOU A STUDENT HERE?
WHEN DID YOU GET THE INVITATION?
WHAT SPECIAL ABILITIES DO YOU HAVE?

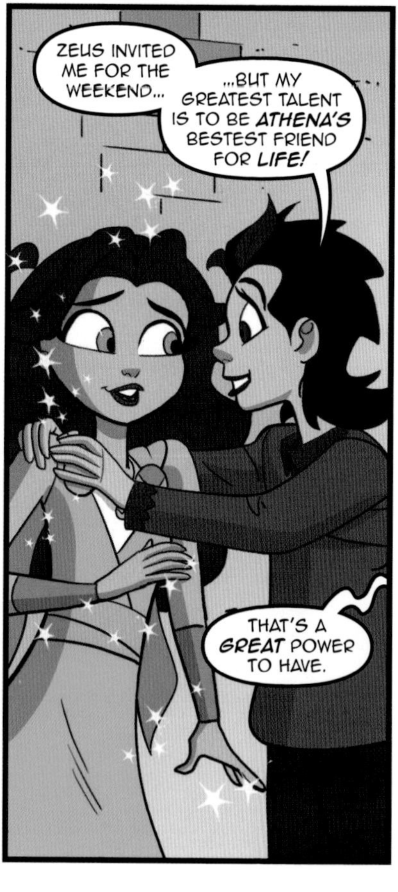
ZEUS INVITED ME FOR THE WEEKEND...
...BUT MY GREATEST TALENT IS TO BE *ATHENA'S* BESTEST FRIEND FOR *LIFE!*
THAT'S A *GREAT* POWER TO HAVE.

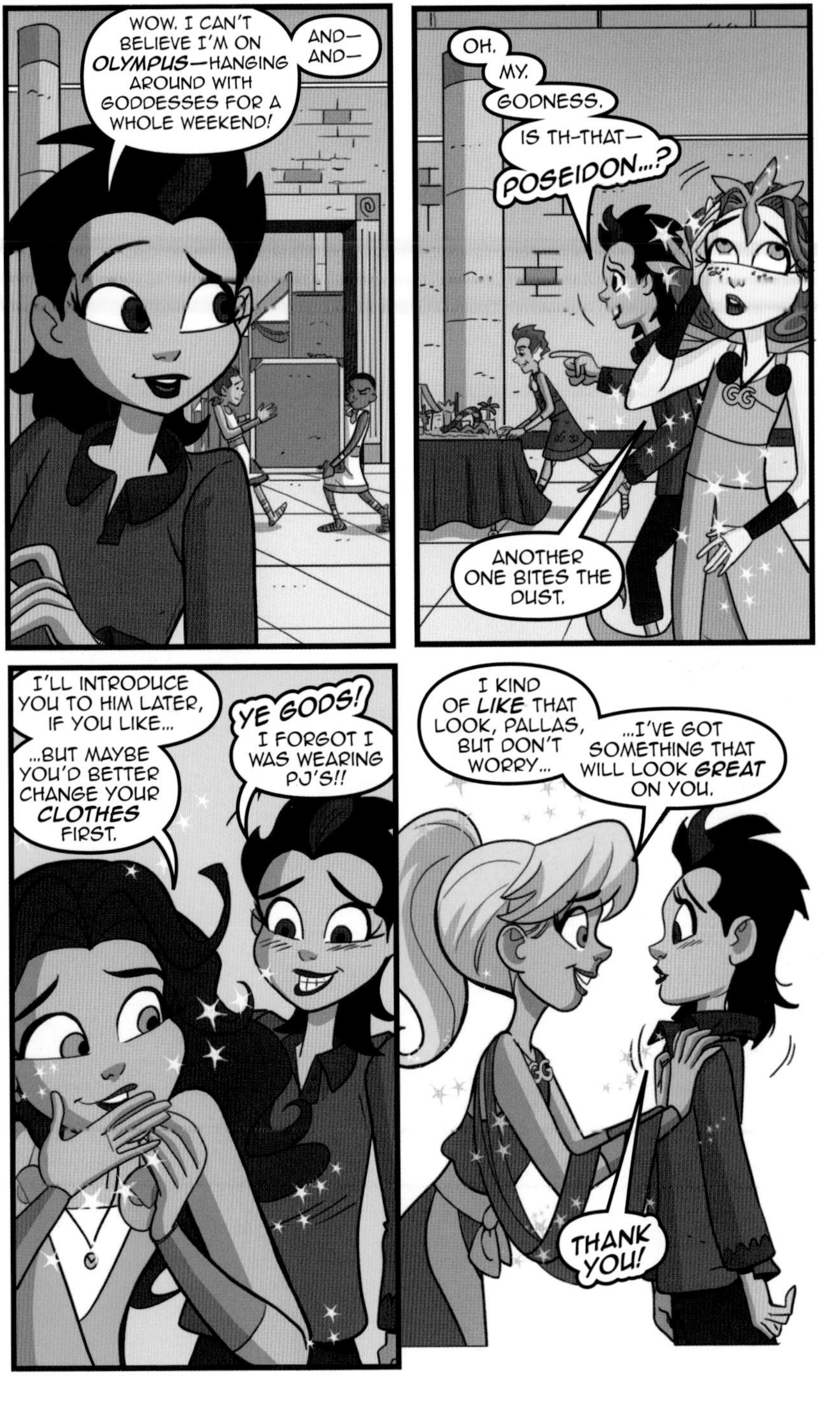
WOW. I CAN'T BELIEVE I'M ON OLYMPUS—HANGING AROUND WITH GODDESSES FOR A WHOLE WEEKEND!
AND— AND—
OH.
MY.
GODNESS.
IS TH-THAT—
POSEIDON...?
ANOTHER ONE BITES THE DUST.
I'LL INTRODUCE YOU TO HIM LATER, IF YOU LIKE...
...BUT MAYBE YOU'D BETTER CHANGE YOUR CLOTHES FIRST.
YE GODS!
I FORGOT I WAS WEARING PJ'S!!
I KIND OF LIKE THAT LOOK, PALLAS, BUT DON'T WORRY...
...I'VE GOT SOMETHING THAT WILL LOOK GREAT ON YOU.
THANK YOU!

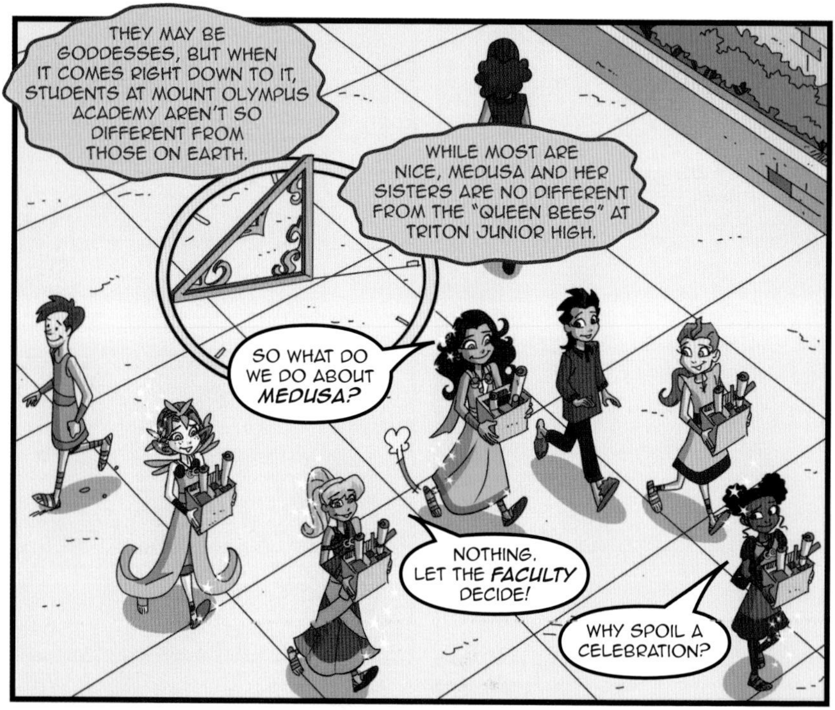
THEY MAY BE GODDESSES, BUT WHEN IT COMES RIGHT DOWN TO IT, STUDENTS AT MOUNT OLYMPUS ACADEMY AREN'T SO DIFFERENT FROM THOSE ON EARTH.
WHILE MOST ARE NICE, MEDUSA AND HER SISTERS ARE NO DIFFERENT FROM THE "QUEEN BEES" AT TRITON JUNIOR HIGH.
SO WHAT DO WE DO ABOUT *MEDUSA?*
NOTHING. LET THE *FACULTY* DECIDE!
WHY SPOIL A CELEBRATION?

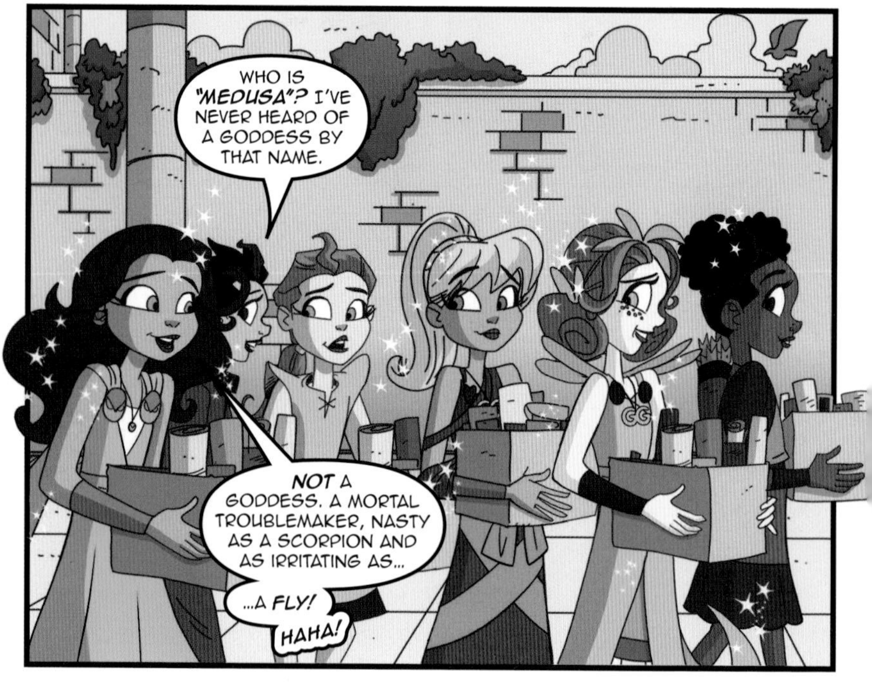
WHO IS *"MEDUSA"?* I'VE NEVER HEARD OF A GODDESS BY THAT NAME.
NOT A GODDESS. A MORTAL TROUBLEMAKER, NASTY AS A SCORPION AND AS IRRITATING AS...
...A *FLY!*
HAHA!

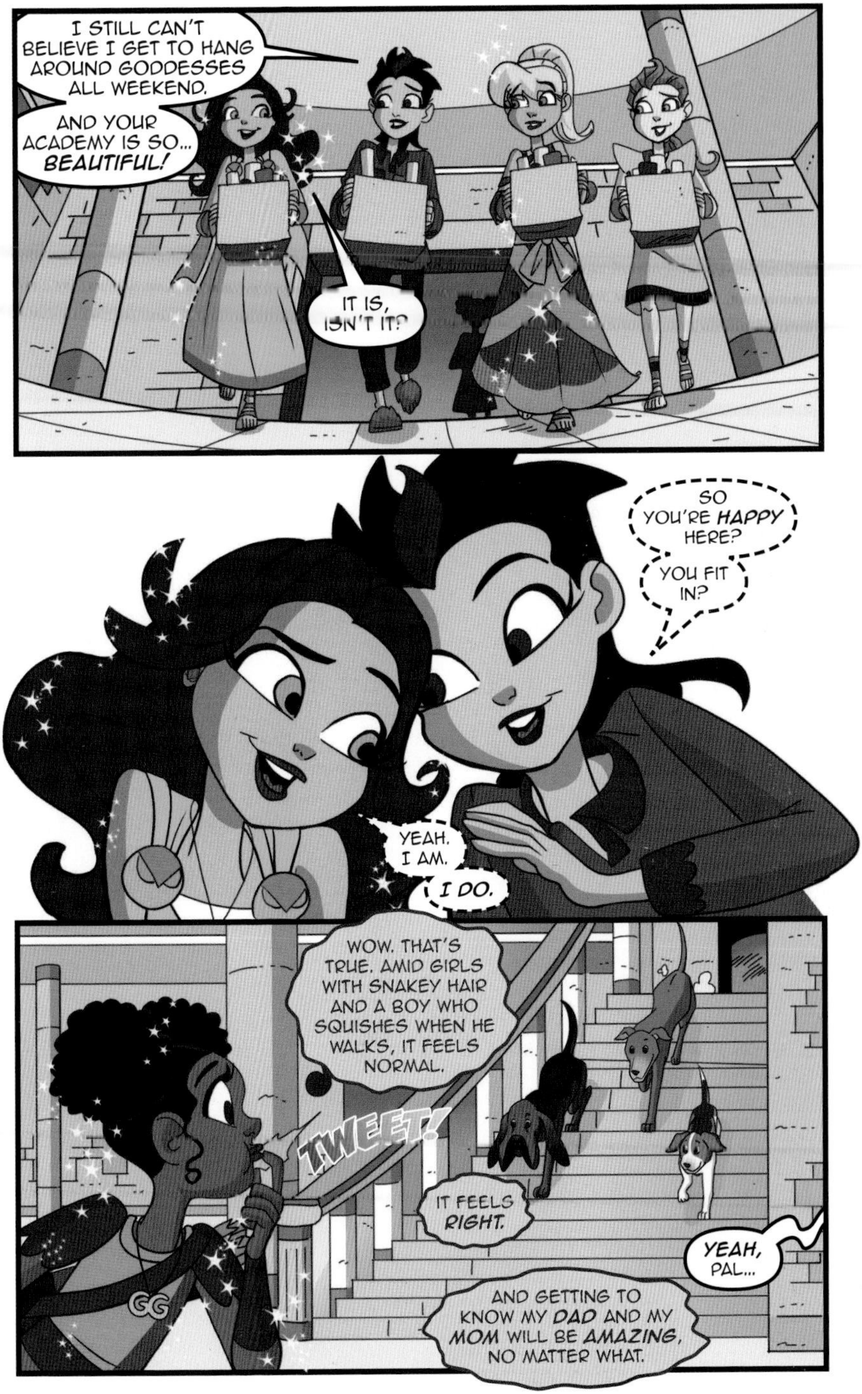
I STILL CAN'T BELIEVE I GET TO HANG AROUND GODDESSES ALL WEEKEND.
AND YOUR ACADEMY IS SO... *BEAUTIFUL!*
IT IS, ISN'T IT?
SO YOU'RE *HAPPY* HERE?
YOU FIT IN?
YEAH. I AM.
I DO.
WOW. THAT'S TRUE. AMID GIRLS WITH SNAKEY HAIR AND A BOY WHO SQUISHES WHEN HE WALKS, IT FEELS NORMAL.
TWEET!
IT FEELS *RIGHT.*
YEAH, PAL...
AND GETTING TO KNOW MY *DAD* AND MY *MOM* WILL BE *AMAZING,* NO MATTER WHAT.

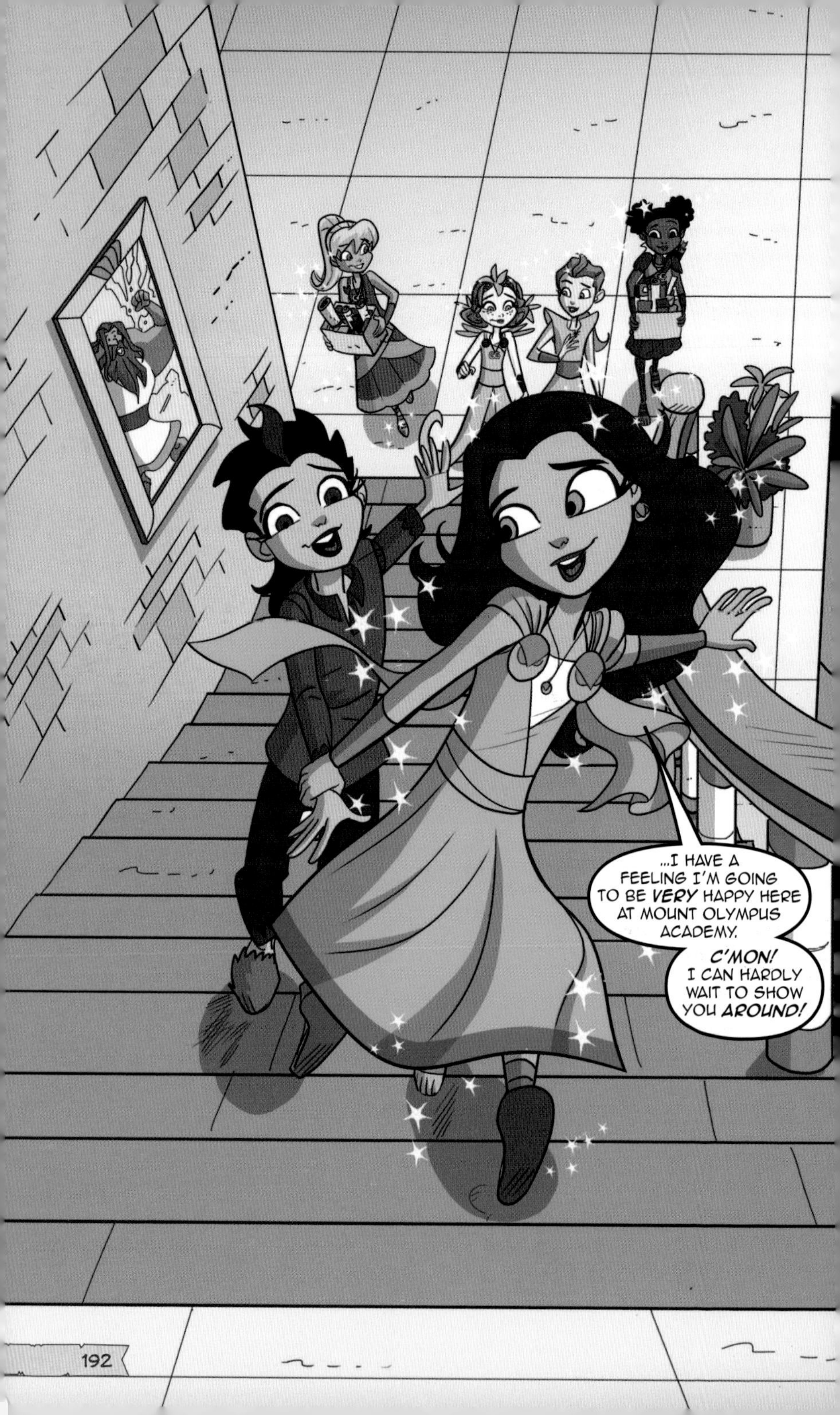
...I HAVE A FEELING I'M GOING TO BE VERY HAPPY HERE AT MOUNT OLYMPUS ACADEMY.
C'MON! I CAN HARDLY WAIT TO SHOW YOU AROUND!